After the Dance

A NOVEL BY

APRIL CHRISTOFFERSON

204 Second Avenue West
Seattle, Washington 98119

Published by
Peanut Butter Publishing
226 Second Avenue West
Seattle, WA 98109
(206) 281-5965

To my beloved husband, Steve,
and my parents, Isabel and Chris.

For everything.

Acknowledgments

As a first time novel, this would not have been possible without the support and encouragement of a good many people. To the friends and family members who read along as I wrote and offered nothing but kind words, thank you from the bottom of my heart. You kept me going.

To my dear sister, Lisa Christofferson, for the many hours she spent typing; Robert Dietz, Kristen Nelson and Martha McDonough for the benefit of their considerable talent and good taste; and Elliott Wolf, my publisher, for his unshakable belief in me, goes my everlasting gratitude.

Finally, I want to acknowledge two of my greatest inspirations. To my children, Mike and Ashley, thank you for the goodness, energy, and abundant love and affection you bring to my life. Thank you for making my every day an adventure.

1

Paul hardly knew what hit him. He'd started the morning off uptight. Nothing seemed to be going right. The financing he'd been counting on to get started on the new movie had fallen through. There were major conflicts within the company and, as president and head cheerleader, he was inevitably drawn into them to play the role of peacemaker. And after interviewing five attorneys for the legal position the company recently decided to create, he couldn't muster even the slightest bit of enthusiasm for any of them.

Now, with a stack of messages sitting in front of him and a desk cluttered with unanswered correspondence and half-completed projects, his secretary was buzzing to tell him that another interviewee for the legal position was there for her appointment.

"God, no!" he muttered. "Why the hell didn't you tell me I was interviewing another person today? That's the last thing I need to start my day off."

In the most contained tone she could manage Candy responded, "Paul, before you left last night, I told you to expect Ms. Kennedy this morning."

"You did?"

"And did you notice anything on the light switch when you turned the lights on this morning?" Candy went on, a touch of bitchiness creeping into her voice. Recently she'd resorted to this tactic—especially when, like last night, she'd known by the vacant look in his eyes (his beautiful, green eyes, she couldn't help but observe), that he hadn't heard a word of the conversation they'd just had.

Paul looked up to see a little yellow Post-it note stuck firmly to the light switch. "Appointment at 9 A.M. with Laura Kennedy."

Now his voice sounded almost sheepish. "Give me five minutes to try to mellow out, then send her in."

*   *   *

Laura's day hadn't exactly started off with a bang either. It was the first morning in almost two years that she had to get up and get herself dressed, made up and looking professional at the same time she was getting the kids ready for school. She'd forgotten how rough that could be. As she put the last touch of mascara on her lashes (as the kids' soft-boiled eggs were cooking), she wondered how on Earth she had accomplished this juggling act for all those years before Michael died. In those days, it hadn't even seemed like that big a deal to her. She had always been amazed, and a little turned off, by those articles in women's magazines detailing the agony of the working mother, when she found her work as an attorney a wonderful complement to raising two children. But somehow she knew things had changed. The ominous feeling she had this morning signaled to her that things might not be so easy this time around.

Her thoughts were cut short by the scream of her five-year-old daughter, Hailey. "Mommy, Christopher left the back gate open, and I just saw Jake go running down the street!"

As Laura dashed to get her trench coat (a must on this rainy Seattle morning) and headed out the back door after Jake, their rambunctious yellow lab, she thought again, "No indeed, things won't be so easy this time around."

Jake was in an especially good mood this morning. There were some days when he responded to even the most softly spoken command. On those days, little Hailey took great pride in bossing Jake around, taking him for a walk, making him heel. (Hailey actually pronounced it with a 'k' so it came out "keel," but Jake didn't seem to know the difference.) Then there were the other days, when the dog had a mind of his own. No, actually, thought Laura as she raced down the street in her high heels after the happy canine, with her carefully blown dry hair becoming frizzier by the moment, there were times when Jake had *no* mind. None whatsoever. And no sense of hearing. Today was one of those days.

Now, as she sat waiting to be ushered into the office of the President of Brooks Productions, Laura brushed her hand over her frizzy hair, took a deep breath to calm herself and wondered how on Earth she would pull all of this off.

* * *

So far, Paul had interviewed four men, all of whom left him cold, and one woman, who'd left him in a deep freeze. He couldn't quite figure it out. To a person, the interviewees had either been dull, stuffy and seemingly very impressed with themselves, or, in

3

the case of two of the men, they'd gone to the other extreme in an attempt to appear laid back and hip. Maybe they thought that was a prerequisite for the entertainment industry. At any rate, he was beginning to question his recent conclusion that it would be more cost-effective to hire a full-time attorney than to continue shelling out exorbitant payments to Winnifred and Barry, the prestigious legal firm that had handled Brooks' legal affairs since the company's inception.

Just as he was wishing to himself that he'd never placed the ad for an entertainment attorney in the local business journal, in walked Candy with Laura Kennedy.

"Paul, this is Laura Kennedy. She's here to interview for the legal position."

Paul was completely taken off guard when he looked up to see Laura enter the room behind Candy. She was tall and slender, with long, wavy golden-brown hair. Her face was absolutely exquisite—delicate yet vibrant, with high cheekbones, perfect rosebud lips, and a chiseled nose. But it was the eyes that Paul found most arresting, almost haunting. He had never before seen such eyes—huge, blue-grey almonds that one moment twinkled and the next seemed full of pain.

A man rarely at a loss for words, Paul was momentarily speechless. Laura seemed to recognize this and graciously extended her hand. "I'm pleased to meet you, Mr. Brooks."

"Paul, please!" responded Paul, rising to clasp Laura's fine boned hand in his own. "You'll soon discover that none of us are big on formalities around here, Laura."

Moments later, when he was once again seated behind his imposing mahogany desk, Paul could feel his old confident self return. Still, he found himself wondering what the hell had just happened. He was, after all, a man accustomed to and comfortable with being thrown into any situation, a man who in any given day might be found lunching with the most high-powered bankers, politicians and lawyers in the cities of Seattle or Los Angeles; joining a pick-up game of basketball after work with his regular group of jocks, many of whom were ex-professional athletes; and still later joining the company's film crew and other professional colleagues at one of several night spots frequented by the entertainment industry. Long used to the attention of lovely women, Paul was certainly not a man easily discomfited by the presence of a beautiful woman. Yet there was no denying that something about this lady now seated in front of him had unnerved him.

Totally oblivious to the effect she'd just had on him, Laura was feeling rattled herself. Ever since scheduling this interview, in an effort to boost her confidence, she had made a point of reminding herself of the successful career she enjoyed before Michael's death. In the few short years she worked as an attorney at Emery, Johnson, a mid-sized, well-established Seattle law firm, she had earned a respected name for herself. But when Michael died, Laura took a leave of absence from the firm. She'd planned on returning to work within a month or so, but as time wore on, she kept putting off her return. She'd received enough money from Michael's life insurance that finances were not a major concern. And, she rationalized, her kids needed her to be there for them on a 24-hour basis, which, at first, was true; but as time passed, she suspected that it was *her* need for the kids that was the real force keeping her home. Christopher, Hailey, and her home, so full of memories, were her only solace—they were what kept her going when little else seemed to matter.

But now the money that had once seemed more than adequate was dwindling. And, more importantly, even if her heart was not in it, Laura knew that she had to stop grieving and get on with life—her life. And so, at her friends' and family's urging, she put the word out that she was available again. And when her close friend and former legal associate, Corinne, called to tell her of the opening at Brooks Productions, she knew it was time to venture out from the security of her home and family. Still, she was plagued with worries, foremost of which was the fact that she was so totally out of touch with the legal world. How was she going to walk into an office and impress anyone with her legal knowledge and expertise when, for two years now, all that her mind had been filled with were details of her and the children's lives— basketball schedules, gymnastic classes, homework, sleep-overs? In an effort to block out as much of the outside world as possible, she hadn't even watched the news or picked up a newspaper. And now, on top of her already shaky confidence, she found herself face to face with Paul Brooks.

*　　*　　*

Paul Brooks. It had never even occurred to Laura that he might be attractive. Years ago, that fact would have made a challenge like this all the more exciting to Laura. She'd always enjoyed that added dimension that inevitably entered the picture when she dealt with an attractive man on a professional level. Though she was deeply in love with Michael, Laura enjoyed the attention she received from men. She used to think that Michael appreciated it himself. He often told her that she got more attention from men than any woman he'd ever known. And now, at the age of 39, Laura was turning more heads than ever. But since Michael's death, none of that mattered anymore. In fact, she now felt distinct displeasure and unease at finding herself opposite Paul Brooks. She was also feeling quite annoyed with Corinne and was beginning to understand why her meddlesome friend had been so insistent about Laura applying for this job.

The first thing that anyone—male or female—noticed about Paul Brooks was his size. Six-foot four, with the body and grace of an athlete ten years his junior, Paul was a head-turner himself. Dark curly hair, closely cropped on the sides, enhanced the initial impression. Usually that was about as far as a woman needed to look before being totally taken with Paul. Upon closer examination, Paul could not be said to be classically handsome. His features were somewhat irregular—his was a face with character, one capable of conveying both strength and sensitivity. His eyes, however, were truly beautiful. Oftentimes, as now with Laura seated opposite him, they had a mysteriously mischievous quality to them. And when he smiled, any doubts one might have about Paul Brooks' appeal quickly vanished into thin air.

Snapping out of the trancelike state she'd lapsed into, Laura suddenly realized that Paul Brooks was staring at her, a big smile on his face.

God help me, thought Laura Kennedy.

*   *   *

When Paul offered Laura the job after less than an hour, she was incredulous. Something did not sit right with her. Maybe she had been fooling herself in thinking she was really ready to go back to work. At

7

any rate, instead of being thrilled, Laura suddenly found herself tongue-tied and elusive.

She did have enough composure to thank Paul for the opportunity, but when he asked her how soon she could start, Laura muttered something about checking her schedule and getting back to him, realizing even as the words left her mouth just how absurd an answer this was—for two years now, she'd *had* no schedule. But somehow she was not about to commit to anything right there on the spot.

*   *   *

Things had always come easily to Laura Kennedy. And that fact always embarrassed her. Whether it was an award she was up for during her school days, a job she applied for, a scholarship or even someone she wanted to date, inevitably Laura met with success. It wasn't that she didn't deserve good fortune. Laura had always been a very conscientious, hard worker. And she'd never let her successes go to her head—in fact, the more successful she became, the more concerned about those less fortunate than her she grew. But Laura was more than a little uneasy with situations where things were just too easy for her. And this was one of those situations.

Two days had passed since her interview. Tired of trying to understand her curious reaction to being offered the job, Laura picked up the phone, dialed Brooks Productions, and asked to speak to Paul.

"Mr. Brooks, this is Laura Kennedy," she started when she heard his rich, distinctive voice on the other end.

"Hello, Ms. Kennedy," responded Paul. Why did she instinctively know that he said this with a smile?

"I've called to thank you for the opportunity

8

you've offered me with your company. But I'm afraid I can't accept the job."

Paul was silent for a moment. "Perhaps we should reconsider the starting salary I referred to?"

Embarrassed, Laura blurted out, "No, no. Please, your offer was a very generous one. Money is not an issue at all. It's just that, after giving it a lot of thought, I've decided my children aren't ready for me to go back to work yet."

Her words were greeted by another silence. He was not about to make this easy for her.

"Again, I just want to thank you for considering me. It was very nice to meet you." Laura desperately wanted this conversation to come to an end.

"Very well, Laura," Paul finally answered coolly. "Best of luck to you."

* * *

Candy had about had it with Paul. One more day like yesterday and she'd let him have it. It was rare for her to feel this way. Although she found his unpredictability exasperating at times, she adored Paul and looked forward to working with him every day. Life was never dull with Paul around. She marveled at how he could be so crazy, hot-tempered and impetuous at times, and yet so smooth and in control when the situation called for it. She loved his sense of humor, bizarre as it could often be. Most of all, she loved those rare times when he let down his guard and allowed her to see the tender, compassionate side of Paul Brooks that very few others were privileged to see. But just now, this side of Paul Brooks was the furthest thing from her mind.

For almost a week now, Paul had been acting distant and distracted. Yesterday afternoon when her attempts to discuss the growing list of things needing his attention were met with another faraway look in his eyes, she'd felt like grabbing hold of him and shaking him. It certainly wasn't that she'd never seen him in a bad mood before, but Paul had never been one to let anything bother him too much or for too long. Even his ugly divorce hardly seemed to faze him. Candy couldn't imagine what it was that had gotten to him now, but whatever it was, she knew he had to snap out of it. The whole company seemed to rest on Paul's shoulders. He still hadn't worked out the financing for *After the Dance.* His messages went unanswered. And when was he going to get around to hiring the new attorney? It was embarrassing to keep telling the persistent two or three who'd interviewed for the job and who called regularly to inquire about it, that a decision had still not been made.

Candy decided it was time to take matters into her own hands. Shortly after he arrived for work, she walked into his office and announced, "Paul, I've scheduled a second interview for you with Bob Schwartz and Betsy Reed. Bob will be in today at 10 A.M."

"You WHAT?" came Paul's response.

Here goes, thought Candy. "Well, *someone* around here needs to have their mind on the company. We need to hire an attorney and we need to do it now. Silver Moon's attorney has been calling asking when to expect that recording agreement. We're scheduled to begin production on *After the Dance* in less than two months, and not only do we not have any financing in place, as you well know, we don't have a single agreement in writing yet. Rumor has it that Shawn Long has heard the movie's in jeopardy and is thinking of walking. If you don't snap out of it, we're all in big trouble. So, yes, I scheduled second interviews for you, and you had damn well better hire one of these people. Today!"

Candy closed her eyes dramatically and held her breath while she waited for the eruption. She had never before talked like this to her boss, and she knew what was in store for her now. She'd witnessed enough meetings where Paul had lost his temper—he was actually quite famous for it, in fact. She waited. And waited.

When she finally opened her eyes, slowly, and looked at him, he was grinning ear to ear. They looked at each other for a moment then simultaneously burst into laughter. By the time Paul finished his imitation of her speech ("SOMEONE has to take care of business...") with his hand on his hip and a peculiar tilt to his head, like he always teased her about, Candy was in tears.

"Point well taken, Candy," said Paul. "I *will* interview Mr. Schwartz and Ms. Reed again, but even at the risk of angering you, my dear, I may not have our new attorney hired this very day. I do promise you, though, that I will give this matter my full attention. Does that make you feel any better?"

"Lots," answered Candy sheepishly, as she walked, still grinning, out the door.

As he sat there reflecting on Candy's little lecture, Paul felt his spirits rise. What had gotten into him? Ever since meeting Laura Kennedy, he'd done little else but think of her. When she called and informed him of her decision not to take the job, he'd felt totally dejected. For days now, he'd been moping about, feeling as though he'd lost his best friend, when he'd spent, at best, one hour with this woman. This was absurd. He could at any time pick up the phone and get a date with any number of beautiful, and certainly younger, less complicated, ladies. Why then had he developed such a thing for this one? It didn't make sense.

But Paul knew himself well enough to realize that whether it made sense or not, it was not going to just go away. And moping around like an adolescent was not going to accomplish a damn thing. As he resolved to deal with this bothersome situation, a smile slowly crept into his eyes. "Laura Kennedy," he thought with that mischievous look of his, "you haven't seen the last of me."

2

After what must have been the tenth or eleventh ring, Corinne hung up the phone, buzzed her secretary and told her she'd be leaving the office for a short while.

Climbing into her new white BMW, she told herself she was probably overreacting. Still, she'd been trying to reach Laura for days. For two years now, ever since the plane crash, Laura rarely left the house. Despite Corinne's efforts to get her back in circulation, Laura stubbornly resisted and basically went out only for her daily walk, to do errands or to chauffeur the kids around. So though she'd tried, Corinne just couldn't come up with an explanation for her inability to reach Laura on the phone this week. Flipping on her fuzz buster, she gunned the car onto the freeway. Vacillating between annoyance and worry, she cursed Laura for interfering with her full schedule that day. Why on Earth she and Michael had chosen to live way the hell out in the sticks she'd never understood. Of course, there were many things about this friend of hers that she'd never understand. Like why this gorgeous woman, blessed with one of the

the best minds in their law firm, was living the life of a recluse. Corinne truly understood how devastating losing Michael was. Michael was incredible. If Laura hadn't been such a close friend, Corinne would have gone after him in a big way. She, too, would have been devastated to lose a man like that, especially one who was so totally in love with her, as was Michael with Laura. But enough was enough. Really. Life goes on.

But as she pulled into the long drive of the Kennedy home, any exasperation she'd been feeling with Laura vanished. Just let her be okay, she thought.

Corinne's knock went unanswered. Even more significantly, it was not greeted by barking dogs. God, how Corinne hated all of Laura's animals! Her place was a regular zoo. But this time, the absence of the dogs gave her hope. They must be on a walk, thought Corinne. Laura loved to walk with her two dogs. More and more, if Corinne wanted to spend time with her friend, she had to be willing to go along on one of these walks. Actually, though she protested vigorously every time, Corinne had come to enjoy these times with her friend. She and Laura poured their hearts out to each other as they strode purposefully along the country roads. And somehow, despite her own pain, in the time they spent together Laura always managed to instill some warmth and optimism in Corinne's jaded heart. It was with this thought in mind that Corinne raced along the path they traveled with the dogs.

She caught up with Laura at the railroad tracks. Her back was turned to Corinne, as she stood watching Jake and his furry companion, Cheyenne, scramble for the tennis ball she'd just thrown. The sound of Corinne's voice made her jump.

"What the hell is going on with you?" demanded Corinne.

"Corinne, what are you doing here? And what do you mean, what's going on with me?" Laura had turned at the sound of Corinne's voice. Her eyes had the look of a startled deer—one whose contented grazing has just been interrupted by the crackling of heavy footsteps on a dry forest floor. She was surprised not only by Corinne's presence, but by her brusque greeting as well.

"I've been calling you for four or five days now. Why on Earth aren't you answering your phone?" Now that Corinne knew Laura was okay, her anger surfaced.

It took just seconds for Laura to realize that she had worried her friend terribly. "I am so sorry, Corinne. Honestly, I had no idea you were trying to reach me. I've just been in a real funk and haven't been answering the phone. I know that's a rotten thing to do, but it's just how I felt. What did you think happened to me?"

"How was I supposed to know? I just couldn't figure out where you could be. The kids are in school, so I knew you weren't visiting your folks. I didn't know *what* to think," responded Corinne.

"Well, the kids always answer when they're home. I'm surprised you haven't reached them. At any rate, I'm truly sorry. You know I wouldn't worry you intentionally. I do appreciate your concern. And knowing your schedule, I'm sure you've left an office full of clients to come out here looking for me."

Laura was clearly sorry, even embarrassed. It was hard for Corinne to stay angry with her. In fact, her anger was slowly turning to concern. She could see that something was troubling her friend.

Before she had the chance to ask what it was, Laura offered, "You'd be proud of me, Corinne. I applied for that job you told me about."

"At Brooks Productions?" Corinne exclaimed.

When Laura nodded her head, Corinne eagerly grabbed her arm and demanded, "Laura, tell me. TELL me!! Did you meet Paul Brooks?"

"Yes. He interviewed me," Laura answered.

"And...??"

"He offered me the job."

"He what?!! That's incredible!" cried Corinne.

"I turned it down," said Laura, her voice barely audible.

"Shit, oh dear, Laura!" exclaimed Corinne in disbelief. That was a favorite expression of hers. "What is your problem?"

"Do you always have to be so crass?" asked Laura. "What exactly does, "Shit, oh dear" mean? That is the dumbest expression."

"Quit changing the subject. Do you mean to tell me you actually met Paul Brooks, *the* Paul Brooks, were offered a job, and turned the man down?"

Laura braced herself for the chastisement she was about to receive. But instead of launching into a tirade, all Corinne muttered was, "You're hopeless." Then she turned and started walking back toward the house.

Laura had been prepared for the tirade, but she didn't quite know how to respond to *this* reaction. She ran along behind Corinne, trying to get her attention, but Corinne refused to respond. Finally, Laura reached out and grabbed her friend's shoulders. "Corinne, *please*, help me with this. I need you now. You have to at least try to understand."

Corinne stopped. She turned and faced Laura, the

frustration and hopelessness she felt giving her face a pained look. "Laura, I will never understand you. I know that you've been through hell losing Michael so suddenly. My heart went out to you then and it still does. But how long do you plan to let life pass you by? And why? For Michael? Do you think he would have wanted you to drop out and spend the rest of your days in solitude? I want to understand, Laura, I really do. But I just don't."

"I'm so scared, Corinne," uttered Laura in response, fighting to hold back tears.

Corinne couldn't take this. Any anger she'd been feeling was totally erased now with just one look at the anguish on Laura's face. With a gentleness totally uncharacteristic of her, Corinne wrapped her arms around her friend, then stroked her hair as Laura, sobbing, buried her head in Corinne's shoulder.

"I know you are, Laura. But you *have* to do it. You're not a quitter. Before Michael died, you lived life with a passion and joy that I used to pray I could experience for just one day. You radiated it. And it's still there inside you. Maybe you don't think it is, but I know it's there."

"All I do is just go through the motions," Laura started, "except with the kids. The rest of my life is so... so mechanical. So meaningless. But sitting there, when I was being interviewed for that job, I got this, this... feeling," she continued, struggling to find the right words. "Something I hadn't felt for so long. I've analyzed it and analyzed it and still don't know what to make of it. All I know is that it scared me. I'd almost rather be mechanical and..."

"Safe," finished Corinne.

"Yes, safe," admitted Laura. "I just don't know if I'm ready yet, Corinne. And the kids need me here for them..."

"Bullshit," came Corinne's split-second response. "Don't use those two kids of yours as an excuse, Laura. They're doing great. They've adjusted. Now it's your turn. Nothing in the world would be better for those kids than for you to be your old self again."

Laura was silent for a moment. "Do you honestly believe that?" she finally asked.

"Yes. And deep down, I think you know I'm right about this."

"Well, if you are right, and I suspect that you are, then I've screwed up royally over this job at Brooks Productions. Haven't I?"

Corinne didn't even attempt to hide the "I told you so" tone of her response: "Royally!"

* * *

This would prove to be Laura's day for surprise visits.

As usual, the kids had come home from school ravenous. Laura looked forward to this time of day immensely. It was the closest she came to feeling happy. Most afternoons she walked down to meet them as they got off the bus, usually with both dogs in tow and a ball in hand so that Christopher, whose bus arrived ten minutes before Hailey's, could play with Jake as they waited for his little sister to arrive. Jake was a big hit with Christopher and his friends. Laura often kidded Chris, telling him that he and Jake had a lot in common—both of them never stopped moving and they were both obsessed with balls. Maybe that explained why they got along so well.

Once Hailey's bus arrived, the group would head home, usually with an extra child or two from the neighborhood tagging along. The Kennedy home was a favorite of the neighborhood kids. Laura had always encouraged that. One of the reasons she'd fallen in love with the big old farm house was that it looked like one of those houses that should belong to a big family. Like there should be bikes propped against the porch railing, baseball bats lying on the front walk, radios blasting from upstairs windows. Nowadays, usually there were.

Once home, she always put out an after-school snack. Then, as they all sat around the old-fashioned kitchen, talking about their day, Laura would sit back and happily take in the scene. At times like this, she could almost forget, at least momentarily, the void she usually felt so acutely—the hollow feeling that for two years now inhabited her body, somewhere in the region of her chest. Almost.

Later, as the kids scattered in various directions, she headed out to the barn, to tend to Spencer.

Spencer was a gift from Michael. The first time the realtor had taken them to see the house, Laura was thrilled to discover it had a small, two-stall barn on the property. It was somewhat run down, but it had electricity and running water. Laura thought it was perfect. Before the ink had dried on the closing papers, she announced her intention to get a horse. But Michael was dead set against it. They already had their hands full, he argued. An older house in need of upkeep. Two kids. Two dogs. A cat and four rabbits. No, he wasn't about to tackle the responsibilities of a horse, too. And then there was the barn. Just think of how much work that would entail. And the fence was old and in need of repair.

When both Laura and Michael refused to back down from their respective positions, what followed was the biggest fight of their twelve-year relationship,

APRIL CHRISTOFFERSON

then three days of silence between them, followed by a week of Michael watching Laura haul ten-foot lengths of fencing rails around the perimeter of their property, hearing her pound nails into them, and watching her struggle to hold the cumbersome boards in place with one hand while taking aim with a hammer with other. For several evenings, the summer breeze carried the smell of fresh paint from the barn through their bedroom window.

As soon as he realized he'd lost the battle, Michael did what any sensible man in love would do. He bought his wife a beautiful, thoroughbred gelding. She named him Spencer. And she thanked Michael profusely and tenderly that night. And the next. And the one after that. Michael kicked himself for holding out so long. And shortly thereafter, he, too, fell in love with the majestic animal. In fact, Michael grew so enamored of Spencer that just the week before his death, he'd taken Laura to look at a Palomino mare he wanted to buy for the kids.

*   *   *

Laura's time with Spencer had a comforting effect on her. Once, jokingly, Michael accused Laura of feeling more comfortable with animals than with people. In reality, Laura's love of children and animals only served to endear her more to Michael. But his comment stayed with her. She knew there was a grain of truth to it—certainly not when it came to her family or close friends, but the truth was, outside of Michael and a handful of others, Laura did prefer to spend her time surrounded by either kids or animals. She found their presence soothing and uplifting. There was something so pure and sweet, so unquestioning in their devotion and their desire to please.

After the emotional scene with Corinne earlier in the day, she felt more anxious than usual to get out to the barn and spend some time with her beloved horse. As she entered the barn to Spencer's soft greeting, she could hear the radio she kept on for him playing her favorite country song, "Do Ya" by K.T. Oslin. As usual, Spencer was waiting for her, his beautiful, sculpted head hanging over the half door. She walked up to him, wrapped her arms around his massive neck, and laid her face against his.

"Oh, Spencer," she sighed.

Seeming to sense her despair, he leaned into her and softly nickered again.

"Thank you." Laura smiled, moved as always, by the rapport that the two shared. "Now, big guy, let's get to work."

Brandishing a pitchfork, she set to work cleaning his stall. Instead of removing Spencer from his stall during this process, Laura preferred to leave him there and work around him. She enjoyed sharing this time with him and sensed he enjoyed it, too. As she worked, she talked to him, confiding her innermost thoughts and feelings. She sang along with country songs. Then, the new bed of cedar shavings under their feet giving both her and Spencer a sense of satisfaction, she ended the process by brushing him down.

As she was asking him why he insisted on rolling in the mud, a deep voice startled her:

"I didn't hear her answer!"

She knew, even before turning to look, that the voice belonged to Paul Brooks.

"His," she corrected, turning to face her unexpected visitor. "*His* answer. What on earth are you doing here?" She looked and sounded more than a little annoyed.

Her annoyance, however, was soon vastly over-shadowed by a growing embarrassment, as she realized that, for all she knew, Paul might have been standing there for some time, listening to her pour her heart out to a horse. And, of course, she hadn't bothered to put any make-up on this morning. Her hair was pulled back in a ponytail. And, to top it off, she thought, I've been crying, so my face is probably puffy and blotchy.

Paul, on the other hand, looked to be enjoying himself immensely.

"I didn't realize you lived on a farm," he said.

"It's not exactly a farm. I only have one acre. I've just managed to fill it up with as many animals as one acre will hold," answered Laura. What on Earth are you doing here, she thought irritably. And, I wish to hell you'd wipe that grin off your face.

"I'm afraid I'm the original city boy," Paul went on. "I..."

Interrupting him in mid-sentence, Laura blurted out, "I don't mean to be rude, Mr. Brooks, but would you mind telling me what you've come all the way out here for?"

"That's a fair request, I guess," Paul responded, rather hesitantly. For a brief moment, Laura thought Paul actually seemed somewhat self-conscious. It took him a few seconds to continue.

"I'd like you to reconsider the job I offered you." There, he'd said it.

Laura could hardly believe her ears. She was silent for a long time, trying to sort out her incredible confusion.

"I don't understand why you feel so strongly about hiring me. I've heard through the legal grape-

vine that you had a number of well-qualified appli-
cants. To be perfectly honest, Mr. Brooks, my background is not in entertainment law. It's in contract
law. I would have explained that to you during my
interview, but basically, you didn't even ask me about
my background. And I have to say that fact troubled
me a great deal." Laura was obviously just getting
started when it was Paul's turn to interrupt.

"So that's it!" he cried.

"What do you mean?" asked Laura crossly.

"You didn't accept the job because you suspected
my motives. What, did you think I was only offering
you the job because you're attractive?" Paul asked.

Laura recognized the glint that she'd seen in his
eyes that first day. A sense of amusement. It angered
her. But worse yet, she felt embarrassed. Self-
conscious.

"I didn't know *what* to think," answered Laura,
her face turning a light crimson. "I certainly didn't
feel I'd had an opportunity to impress you with my
legal expertise, since we never even discussed the
subject. So, yes, I guess I'd have to admit that the
thought occurred to me."

"Laura," answered Paul patiently, "I want you to
listen to me and listen good. You are an attractive
woman. I'd be the first to admit that. And yes, that
did play into my decision to offer you the job. But
before you go jumping to conclusions, let me explain
why. We are in the entertainment business. Image is
everything in this business. And all other things being
equal, appearances often times are the deciding factor.

"In this situation I'd already done my homework." Always able to exaggerate the truth for a
worthy cause, Paul wasn't fazed in the least by this
inaccuracy. And he somehow sensed that his response

to this accusation was critical. "And I'd determined that you were as well-qualified as any of my top candidates for the position. True, your experience wasn't a perfect match, but I'm more concerned with hiring someone who's proven to be a dedicated, competent attorney—one with a reputation for her integrity—and someone whom I feel I can work well with, rather than someone who already knows the business. You're an exceptionally bright woman," he went on. This he *had* been able to verify through a call to an old friend who happened to be a University of Washington law professor. "You'd be able to learn this business in no time. I've no doubts about that."

Laura did not respond. She was experiencing the same disquieting feelings she was unable to describe earlier to Corinne. Yet, what had she just concluded? That she'd made a big mistake in not accepting the job Paul had offered her. And now here he was, offering her a second chance. Laura had always believed somewhat in fate; that if things were meant to be, they'd be. To turn down the job again would surely fly in the face of that belief.

She looked up into Paul's eyes. The laughter that she'd already grown accustomed to seeing in them was gone. He looks truly anxious, thought Laura. Trembling imperceptibly, with the weakest of voices, she finally answered. "I'll take the job "

*   *   *

The sun was just breaking through the clouds as Paul left Laura's house and headed back to the office. By the time he reached the bridge spanning Lake Washington, a huge body of water that separates the Eastside suburbs from the city of Seattle, the sky had turned an aquamarine blue. As he crossed the bridge,

Paul slowed to give himself a chance to take in the incredible spectacle to which he and his fellow commuters were suddenly being treated. His snail-like pace went unnoticed, as virtually every driver on the bridge, almost in concert, slowed down. Though they may deny it vehemently (right up to the day they pack up their Jeep Cherokees and roll out of town), Seattlites do indeed tire of the dreary weather they subject themselves to in choosing to live in the damp, dark reaches of the Northwest. But Mother Nature can be devious. Just as many feel they've reached the limit of their tolerance for pale skin, rotting porch decks and mossy roof shingles, She senses their despair and tricks them into staying just a little longer by bestowing upon them a sight such as the one now greeting Paul and his fellow travelers—a sight so powerful, so humbling and so awe-inspiring that even a man who professes not to be religious, a man like Paul Brooks, can find himself overwhelmed with a spirituality that he somehow suspects closely resembles the oneness with God and the Universe that he has heard born-again Christians speak of.

His car seemingly suspended in midair as it approached the apex of the bridge, that section which magically opens wide its jaws to allow for the passage of tall ships, Paul's eyes greedily flitted from one visual feast to another, almost frantically trying to record and store for future inspiration the scene that encircled him. From this vantage point, one could scan an entire 360 degrees and be hard pressed to declare one view superior to the others. Straight ahead lay more water, lapping to a shoreline crowded with a congregation of funky, colorful houseboats. Breaking the expanse of blue above, the skyline of Seattle, its Space Needle hovering like a UFO resting on a toothpick. And farther still lay the majestic, snow-capped peaks of the Olympics. Scanning the horizon counterclockwise—more of the lake, its shoreline now populated by the estate-sized homes of the affluent, and, rising mystically above, to heights that made one wonder if this were actually some sublime optical illusion, Mount Rainier. How many times, Paul was thinking, had he described that sight to visitors to the area only to later be chided when, upon their departure, never having caught so much as a glimpse of it through the clouds, they accused him (and presumably the rest of Seattle) of fabricating the existence of this slumbering volcano? A volcano which, according to local folk lore, towered majestically and protectively (despite its mind-blowing capacity for destruction) over the city. Directly behind him, looking due East, the rolling, densely forested hills gave way to more jagged, snow-capped peaks of the Cascade Mountains. And scanning full circle, the lake stretched farther still, forever in the shadow of white-frosted peaks, still more of the Cascades, with Mount Baker now visible to the North.

This, thought Paul (along with many other bridge travelers at that moment), is why I came and why I will stay. He was reminded of the only other times he'd experienced anything even remotely like what he now felt. They were just a handful of times, times he'd shared with Kim, his ex-wife. Usually it had been after they'd made love. Sometimes he wondered if he'd spend the rest of his life hoping to recapture that feeling. But that was in those first few months, when they were still mad about each other. How ironic, he now thought sadly, that this beauty, in its purity and goodness, should remind me of *her*. But then his thoughts turned to Laura, and the euphoria he'd been feeling before he'd been reminded of Kim returned.

Laura. Just the thought of her brought a smile to his face. He'd seen an entirely different side of her today. The woman in his office had seemed so composed and sure of herself as to seem, at first, almost unapproachable. But there was something about her today that contradicted that initial impression. He couldn't quite put his finger on it, but as the interview wore on, he had a clear sense that Laura Kennedy was infinitely more interesting, more complicated, than one might at first assume. She'd dressed subtly and professionally, in an elegantly tailored suit, but its peach color and the short slim skirt set hers apart from other business women's attire. And the way she carried herself, the way she sat with those delicate, perfectly-shaped legs gracefully crossed at the ankle, positively exuded sensuality. That this effect seemed so uncontrived, that she conveyed such sensuality so naturally, made it all the more powerful. And, aside from enjoying just looking at her, Paul had also found that he *liked* this woman. After years of dealing with attorneys, and the five he'd recently interviewed, he'd found her to be a breath of fresh air. She was understated and relaxed, able to converse with ease, but also comfortable with the occasional silence. This was the Laura Kennedy who'd haunted his thoughts for days now.

The Laura Kennedy he discovered today was a far cry from this. She'd seemed almost childlike to him. He knew he should be ashamed of himself for sneaking up on her as he did, but as he stood there, watching her, listening to her, he was spellbound. Her long sun-streaked hair, so carefully styled when he last saw her, was pulled back into a rather disheveled ponytail, long wisps of which framed her unmade up

27

face. Her attire of a faded work shirt, blue jeans and boots showcased her lean, fit physique. She moved with the carriage and grace of a dancer. Paul had never seen anyone quite so lovely. She seemed fragile and sad, yet as she stroked the horse, all the while speaking softly, lovingly to him, in a voice as soothing as a shot of sweet Irish cream, it was clear that she also felt a sense of serenity.

Paul hated breaking the spell, but finally had felt compelled to disclose his presence. Her reaction, the strength of her anger at him for intruding upon her that way, in such stark contrast to the serenity she'd just conveyed, had surprised him. It was not evident so much in her words as in her eyes. For a moment they were filled with a fire that, under other circumstances, might have excited Paul. Fortunately, the fire seemed to fade almost as quickly as it arose, and, in those awkward moments after he'd offered her the job, the agony visible in those enormous eyes had made him wish with all his heart that he could just reach out and comfort her.

But, finally, she'd accepted. He could hardly believe it. He wanted to ask her to repeat her almost whispered acceptance, but dared not. Instead, in order to avoid giving her the chance to retract it, he'd made a hasty exit. It wasn't until he reached the car that he began to grin. By the time he pulled out of the driveway, he felt safe in letting out a whoop. And once he was on the freeway, he was flying high! Then, to top it all off, Mother Nature had smiled upon Paul and all of Seattle!

Paul Brooks would remember this day, in vivid detail, for a long time to come.

* * *

"Hey, Mom," shouted Christopher, in the midst of a free throw, as Laura stepped out of the barn on her way back to the house. "Who was that guy?"

"That was Paul Brooks," Laura responded, taken aback that her son had been aware of her visitor. She settled on the front step to watch him as he jumped and weaved adeptly, working his way into the basketball hoop in the face of an imaginary opponent. "Remember that job I interviewed for last week?"

"The one you turned down?" Christopher never missed a beat, as he drove to the basket and succeeded in banking the ball into the net with a graceful left-handed layup. Laura loved to watch her son on a basketball court, real or imaginary. Only ten years old when Michael died, he'd already shown remarkable talent and promise for the sport. Before Michael's death, almost every night after school and for hours at a time on weekends, Michael and Christopher would play game after game of hoop. Michael had been convinced Christopher would one day be a star. Laura knew that it was in large part Christopher's passion for basketball that had enabled him to get through the past two years. Christopher's every spare minute was devoted to the game. Though he never discussed it with her, Laura knew that in most games now, it was his dad out there on the court with him, his imaginary teammate—one day the two of them would be up against Charles Barkley and the Phoenix Suns, the next they were taking on Shaquille O'Neal and the Orlando Magic. Laura was very grateful that he derived so much comfort from this game, a game that she, too, found exciting.

As both kids often did, Christopher was on to another question before Laura even had a chance to answer the first one. "Did you see the car he was driving? It was sweet!"

"What kind was it?"

"An awesome Porsche Targa—white convertible with a black rag top." Christopher also loved hot cars. "We played a game of one on one. He's really good, Mom. Did you know he played for the Huskies?"

"No, Chris," she answered somewhat distractedly. Laura was wondering why it was she was disturbed by the thought of the two of them playing basketball together.

"I like him, Mom," Christopher continued. "Can we see him again?"

"Oh, I imagine we'll be seeing him again all right," Laura answered, without much enthusiasm. "Next week I'm going to start working for him."

As the ball followed a perfect arch, dropping effortlessly, cleanly through the rim, Christopher's response left little doubt of his sentiments about his mother's news:

"Sweet!"

3

Mackenzie Montana hung up the phone, turned to her agent with a sugary-sweet smile on her lovely face, and demanded, "Get me that part."

Neil Roberts cringed, an automatic response to her tone, and that smile. It was the same tone and same smile he encountered every time the lovely Ms. Montana set that ferociously determined heart of hers on something, all too often something that was not rightfully hers. Something that she would undoubtedly expect Neil to deliver, he was now thinking. But as usual, the pleasant smile on his face belied his thoughts. Here we go again, thought Neil with dread.

Neil Roberts knew better than to take Mackenzie Montana's whims lightly. For the past two years he'd served as her agent. Oftentimes, he felt more like her servant or Boy Friday. Or, at times like this, he thought wryly, maybe hit man was an appropriate description. But Neil Roberts was no dummy, and no ingrate either. No one knew better than Neil what representing a star of Mackenzie Montana's magnitude meant to his career. He'd been nothing before Mackenzie. So on this sunny morning in Beverly Hills, not a trace of Neil Roberts' true feelings for his pampered client was discernible.

"But I've heard they've already got Amy Griffin for that role," responded Neil.

"According to Shawn, they have." It was Shawn Long, the hot young director, to whom Mackenzie had just been speaking on the telephone. "But *I'm* going to play Ashley in *After the Dance*. Not that washed up, neurotic, has-been Griffin," answered Mackenzie with her usual diplomacy. "That film is going to need all the help it can get. I can give it box office appeal. With Griffin, it's history before it's even released."

"But Brooks is so small time. You're a major star now. Not only can they not afford you, why would you want to digress to a company of their stature? Besides, they're too political—too artsy. They're up in Seattle, Washington, for God's sake. I don't like the sounds of this, Mackenzie." Neil was becoming more alarmed the longer he considered this idea.

"You're the one who's been telling me I need to do something with more substance. Something to prove I can act, and not just look good. Not just turn on those horndogs who turn out for my films in droves. This is perfect. If I want to be taken seriously, what better vehicle? For Christ's sake, Neil, they're even dealing with AIDS in this movie!" Neil's hopes of dissuading Mackenzie were fading fast. "Besides, Shawn's directing, so the movie will automatically get some attention, some credibility, though I can't for the life of me figure out why he'd agree to direct this one. I think he and Paul Brooks are old friends or something. But that's all beside the point, Neil. The point is, I want this part!"

"Putting aside my reservations—and that's putting

it mildly—about you being in this movie, just how do you propose going about getting a part that another major star has already signed to do? Have you given that minor obstacle any thought?" queried a slightly discomposed Neil.

"That's what I pay you for. You get it for me. Or start looking for another meal ticket."

As usual, Neil was amazed, even slightly impressed, with Mackenzie's ability to deliver a line as cold and heartless as this, all the while with a smile so angelic, so innocent on that face, a face that looked to be custom-made in Heaven. No wonder they love her, thought this man who, ironically, hated her every fiber.

"You can start by talking to Shawn. He owes me a favor. A big one."

With that, Mackenzie Montana turned and walked out of the room.

*   *   *

Ever since the furor over her last film subsided, Mackenzie Montana had been discontented, bored. And horny. It wasn't, however, for lack of excitement or opportunity in her life. *Busting Out* had been a tremendous commercial success. After she'd starred in a string of respectable money makers, this film had catapulted Mackenzie into that category of actresses who practically guaranteed big dollars to the studio. Mackenzie had been inundated with scripts and offers. And every self-imagined stud in the business, young or old, was more than attentive when Ms. Montana walked into a room. No, Mackenzie did not want for opportunity, be it a script or willing male.

But some months ago, actually in the wake of all the media attention she received after *Busting Out's* success, her six-month marriage to rock star Ricky Mo ended abruptly. Though Mackenzie would be the first to admit that the marriage had been founded not on love but on wild, uninhibited passion, the breakup left her depressed. While the press attributed the breakup to Mackenzie's tremendous success and proclaimed that the star had devastated Ricky in leaving him, the little-known truth was that Mo, despite his reputation as a shallow and decadent musician, had left Mackenzie for a sweet young nurse he'd met while hospitalized for a concussion sustained in a motorcycle accident after one of his concerts. In reality, being a man of some integrity and great tolerance, Ricky stoically endured the tabloids' exploitation of his and Mackenzie's situation, never attempting to correct their inaccuracies. He knew how humiliated Mackenzie would be if the truth were made public and, being a believer in karma, he figured that, in the long run, Mackenzie would need all the help she could get in this world. Besides, he felt some sense of gratitude to her, as prior to being linked with the rising star, his popularity had been rapidly diminishing; but ever since Mackenzie and he became tabloid fodder, his concert bookings and album sales skyrocketed. He'd been, as they say in the industry, "rediscovered."

Adding to Mackenzie's distress at being mateless, even if by choice, was a matter over which she, to date anyway, had little control. She had almost become obsessed with the film critics' continued refusal to take her seriously as an actress. Box office takes meant little to the critics; in fact, Mackenzie suspected that her reviews would be kinder had she not been so successful in a commercial sense. What a bunch of hypocrites, she thought as she recalled for the thousandth time Kevin Jensen's review of *Busting Out*. At the screening, she'd carefully orchestrated events to ensure that she ended up seated next to the esteemed critic. As they sat talking before the lights dimmed and the film began to roll, Kevin had lavished his attention on her, practically devouring her with those sleazeball eyes of his. The guy made her skin crawl. Still, Mackenzie turned on the charm, in the hopes of befriending this man on whose every word Tinsel Town seemed to hang. During her favorite scene, which, not surprisingly, was also the most erotic scene of the movie, even the shelter of the dark theater could not hide the man's arousal. It filled the air between them. The scuzz bucket even had the nerve to run his hand up her thigh. And, instead of spitting in his face, which she had an acute urge to do, what did she do? She turned to him and smiled seductively. That, thought Mackenzie now, may have been my finest acting yet. But that evening she felt the act had been worth it, and she left the party that followed the screening with great anticipation for the next morning's reviews. Just thinking of Jensen's words now, these many months later, had the same effect on Mackenzie as they did the morning she eagerly opened the entertainment section of the *L.A. Times* and read:

Mackenzie Montana fans will not be disappointed with her performance in this movie. To many, watching this young seductress in action—this time without so much as a G-string to hide her abundant charms—will alone be worth the price of admission. But though blessed with a physical beauty that practically takes one's breath away, Ms. Montana was painfully shortchanged when

APRIL CHRISTOFFERSON

talent was being meted out. And this film
critic, for one, continues to be amazed that
an actress of this caliber can repeatedly find
her way into otherwise worthwhile movies,
instead of being relegated to the skin-flick
productions for which Ms. Montana was
surely destined.

Oddly enough, many insiders felt this review did
nothing but contribute to the success of this movie. So
far, the public couldn't get enough of Mackenzie
Montana. Though she'd invariably been cast in sexy
roles, the jury (in this case, the American public) was
still out on whether her performances constituted art
or mere trash. After all, nowadays even the most
respected and successful of actors disrobed on screen
for steamy love scenes. And while of little comfort to
her following the stinging review of Kevin Jensen,
other critics had been far more generous regarding her
performance.

Still, those piercing words replayed themselves
over and over again in Mackenzie's head. She went to
bed with them ringing in her ears and woke up
reciting them. If ever Mackenzie Montana had been
determined about something, it was to avenge Kevin
Jensen's review.

That's why Mackenzie knew the moment inspiration struck that her call this morning to Shawn Long
had been nothing short of fate. For, while discussing
Shawn's upcoming project, a movie entitled *After the
Dance* by Brooks Productions, Mackenzie Montana
was struck with an idea that was, in her opinion at
least, positively brilliant. In one split second, she
knew. She knew that she had concocted a plan that
could solve both sources of her unhappiness—her love
life *and* her public image.

36

4

He calls her "girl." And the crazy thing about it, Laura thought on her drive home from work, she lets him. In fact, she halfway believed she liked it. Just this morning he'd sauntered into her office, dropped his large, powerful frame gracefully, casually into the chair opposite her desk, and asked, with that mischievous glint in his eyes, "What's up, Girl?"

If anyone else had used that name for her, the first time would also have been the last. But when Paul said it, it sounded so natural and endearing—even comforting.

That was just one of many curious reactions she'd experienced since starting work three weeks ago. She'd been so full of dread, so full of regret for accepting this job, that when the day finally came for her to start, she felt physically ill. The kids actually comforted *her*, reassuring her and telling her that they *wanted* her to go back to work. Walking into the Brooks Productions' offices that Monday, just three short weeks ago, had been more traumatic than any adolescent experience she remembered. In fact, that's exactly how it felt—like she was an adolescent all over again, nervous about the first day of high school or a first date.

But within a few relatively painless days, Laura felt at home there. In fact, though she had not yet admitted it to herself, Laura Kennedy was coming back to life. Her kids already sensed it. They missed her waiting for them at the bus stop each day, and she didn't have as much time in the evening to help with homework or to just talk, but those things didn't matter to them nearly as much as seeing the life come back into their mother's eyes, hearing her laughter again.

Until today, most of Laura's apprehensions—and she'd had plenty—had evaporated. She'd been so anxious about her two years away and her lack of experience in entertainment law, but it had taken no time at all for her to recover her confidence.

She'd never wanted to be a litigator. That aspect of the legal profession didn't appeal to her at all. Though not lacking in self-confidence, Laura was in some ways a shy person, one who did not like the limelight that often goes hand in hand with trial work. And she'd gone to great lengths to avoid divorce and child custody cases, knowing that emotionally, a practice in family law would devastate her. And so it was through a process of default that Laura found herself in the field of contract and business law. Over the years, however, Laura grew to feel challenged by it and was more than competent at it. Business law. Her specialty. By default, yes, but still, she liked the challenge of negotiations, and the power of dealing with the heavy hitters and vasts amount of monies. She was somewhat of a novelty in this field, and she realized it. Many assumed that her looks and gentle nature would work against her, but Laura had quickly learned to use them to her advantage.

At Emery, Johnson, the firm Laura had been with before Michael's death, she succeeded in negotiating a major acquisition for the firm's premier client, Robert Poor—a deal that, if it hadn't gone through, would have resulted in the firm's loss of Mr. Poor's business. CEO of Poor Enterprises, Inc., Seattle's largest shipping conglomerate, this client alone accounted for hundreds of thousands of dollars in revenue at Emery, Johnson annually. At the request of the disgruntled client, Laura stepped in at the eleventh hour, after two senior partners had been working on the acquisition with little success for several months. She'd been introduced to Mr. Poor in the elevator and, several hours later, was unexpectedly summoned to Ralph Emery's office and informed that, at Mr. Poor's request, she'd be taking over the negotiations for his purchase of Alaska Way Shipping, an acquisition that would enable Poor to dominate West Coast shipping from southernmost Mexico to the frigid Alaskan waterways.

Though the magnitude of the situation appealed to her, Laura had been somewhat repulsed by Mr. Poor— his threatening tactics and greed were legendary. And early in the negotiations she'd come to respect the mindset of John Lundgren, long-time owner of Alaska Way Shipping. Originally a small, family-owned business, Alaska Way had grown to dominate shipping along the Alaskan coast. Lundgren, like many lifelong residents of the state of Alaska, had grown increasingly concerned about the state's coastline. The Exxon disaster had succeeded in opening the world's eyes to the fragility of this precious national treasure, but years before the rest of the world became aware of the situation, native Alaskans were beginning to see the price their precious state was rapidly paying for its exploitation. Laura quickly realized that it was this environmental concern that had to be given foremost consideration in the negotiations. Poor, quite unhappily, had been upping the monetary value of his offer with little to no success, but Laura knew it was not the purchase price upon which the deal hinged. Her suggestion that an environmental fund be set up with 5% of the annual net proceeds—but with a corresponding substantial reduction in the purchase price— not only cinched the deal, but was hailed by all involved as nothing short of genius. Laura's reaction to all this was disbelief. Though she refrained from saying so, she had trouble believing that no one had picked up on the importance Lundgren attached to the environmental issue. To Laura, her suggestion was far from brilliant—it wasn't even imaginative. It was logical. But the establishment of a fund did make her feel better about the whole thing.

Used to working in the conservative, rigid atmosphere of business law, Laura was amazed by the working climate at Brooks. Though challenged by situations like the Alaska Way acquisition, Laura had been distinctly turned off by the closeminded, uptight conservatism that pervaded the business and legal world. The entertainment business, she soon found, had other vices, but stuffiness was not one of them. She'd almost forgotten how good it felt to laugh. At Brooks, laughter was an essential ingredient in every encounter. Her office adjoined Paul Brooks'—separated only by a wet bar and the executive bathroom, she deliberately left her door ajar most days to enable her to hear Paul's voice drift her way. He had, without question, the most distinctive, seductive, soothing voice she'd ever heard. More and more, as Paul's warm laughter drifted in, she'd find herself responding with a smile of her own. Usually it was just a smile she felt inside, but today as she sat drinking in his laughter, she apparently did not hide the pleasure the sound gave her, as Candy, who'd entered Laura's office unnoticed, looked more than a little irritated when she realized the source of Laura's smile. And Laura felt more than a little embarrassed to have Candy catch her reacting that way to the sound of Paul's voice.

Damn her, Laura thought. She and Candy had not gotten off to a good start. It was clear to Laura that Candy was in love with her boss. And it was clear to Candy that her boss was falling in love with Laura. Until today, however, Candy had felt quite certain that the feeling was one-sided. Laura had given no indication of an interest in Paul—Candy had been surprised, and immensely pleased, to observe that Laura seemed to be immune to Paul's charms. Until today, that is. That look on Laura's face today sent chills down Candy's spine. It also had unnerved Laura. She hadn't even admitted the attraction to herself until she'd been caught in the act.

As she negotiated the evening traffic, Laura's mood, which most nights these past weeks had been light, even slightly silly, was decidedly more pensive. By the time she pulled her car into the long drive of her beloved home, Laura had resolved to keep her distance from Paul Brooks.

* * *

Paul, however, had other plans. Ever since Laura joined the company, he just could not get enough of her.

He had always enjoyed his work. His devotion to

41

the company had, in fact, been a major source of conflict not only with his ex-wife, but also with the few women he'd dated for any length of time. But since Laura's arrival, work had taken on a whole new meaning. He arrived at the office early each day and lingered until he saw Laura's car disappear into the mass of automobiles that engulfed the Queen Anne area each afternoon at rush hour. At first he had sensed that Laura shared his feelings, but recently he'd had the feeling that Laura was avoiding him. He wasn't sure what to make of it. Still, Laura's presence on a daily basis gave him an unfamiliar sense of well-being. And at the same time that he found comfort in her company, he was also so aroused by her—her beauty, her subtle sensuality—that it took a mammoth effort on his part to focus on any business whatsoever in her presence.

This phenomenon had not gone unnoticed by his partner, Matthew, now trying to get Paul's attention.

"Paul, I'm afraid you're not taking our situation here seriously enough," started Matthew. "We need to get a commitment from Brubeck immediately, or our whole production schedule will go down the drain. We can't get started without an advance of at least two million. And from what Laura tells me, Brubeck's not even close to signing the agreement she drafted."

Paul's attention picked up at the mere mention of her name. Turning to Laura, he asked whether she agreed with Matthew's assessment of the situation.

"I can't speak for the numbers—whether it's two million or three that we'd need to get started, since I'm not involved in the production end of things—but it *is* true that Brubeck isn't about to advance us any money, much less commit to a total of nine million," Laura answered, feeling slightly uncomfortable seated there with Paul staring intently at her and Matthew seated at her side. She had the distinct impression that Matthew was studying both her and Paul. More and more, in fact, it seemed everyone at Brooks was unduly interested in the two of them. Though she'd been going to great lengths to avoid any unnecessary contact with Paul, when they *did* happen to be together, Laura always had the unsettling feeling that they were being observed.

"When I last talked to Bob Brubeck, he sounded very enthused about *After the Dance*. Why the change of heart? Were there problems with the terms of the contract?" asked Paul.

Matthew was relieved to see that Paul finally seemed genuinely alarmed by the possibility that the movie was in jeopardy. He'd been trying to get Paul to realize the gravity of the situation for some time now. When *After the Dance* was first conceived, Brooks' plan was to obtain bank financing for the production. With their first three movies, this had been no problem. Based on their confidence that the financing for *this* project would be just as easy to obtain, they'd blithely gone forward with hiring cast and crew and drawing up production schedules. But their earlier films had been low-budget productions— two to four million dollars at most. And when the budget for *After the Dance* came in at just over nine million dollars (still small by Hollywood standards), the bank turned them down. At that point, Paul had begun contacting some of the heavy hitters he'd come to know in the business, ones who'd shown a strong interest in Brooks and the critically acclaimed films they'd done to date.

Bob Brubeck had been his first call. Bob's response had been enthusiastic, so enthusiastic, in fact, that Paul assumed their verbal agreement was a done deal and had continued with pre-production work on the movie. As a result, Brooks had already expended hundreds of thousands of dollars on preproduction, and made commitments for over a half million. If something were to happen to impede the movie's completion and the movie never was completed, now a very real possibility if Brubeck failed to come through, Brooks Productions would be dramatically impacted by the obligations it had already incurred. And as word of its failure spread, future productions would be that much more difficult to get off the ground, not just because of financing considerations, but also because in the dog-eat-dog world of the film industry, it only took one such failure before most true talent, behind or in front of the camera, wouldn't touch you with a ten foot pole. As the reality of the situation began sinking in, Paul appeared somber. Still, looking at Laura now, waiting for her to respond, his mind drifted. He found himself appreciating the outline of her well-rounded, pert breasts. The sheer shell she was wearing was clinging to her, revealing her extraordinarily beautiful, feminine lines.

Painfully conscious of Paul's stare, Laura regretted having removed her blazer. She'd opened the window shades in her office earlier to enjoy the hot summer sun and had just taken the jacket off when Paul and Matt buzzed her and asked her to join them in Paul's office. Now, with Paul's eyes affixed to her chest, she was becoming a little flushed. She turned and directed her response to Paul's question more to Matthew than to Paul.

"None of the contract terms are a problem with Mr. Brubeck. I drafted a pretty standard production agreement for him—just made a few minor changes, at his request, and they were all basically changes in language. Nothing substantive." Matthew wondered why it was that Laura directed this to him, when the question had come from Paul. Besides, he and Laura had already discussed the situation earlier. Clearly there was something more than the situation with the movie going on here between his cohorts. Whatever it was, he was beginning to enjoy it. And Laura was looking especially sexy today. He halfway thought he could see through the cream colored blouse she had on.

Feeling utterly flustered now under both men's examination, Laura continued, but not without considerable difficulty. "What Mr. Brubeck *is* worried about is having Amy Griffin play the lead. He says she doesn't have enough box-office appeal. And the contract does give him explicit approval rights for all major roles."

"But we've already signed Amy," came Paul's response. "Besides, Amy's a class actress. She's perfect for the part."

"No, we *haven't* signed her yet," Laura corrected Paul, somewhat sharply. "At this point, everything we have on the movie—and I mean everything—is verbal. I've got her contract written but have deliberately held onto it. We shouldn't sign *any* contracts at all until we get our production agreement finalized. The repercussions would be enormous if we did and then we weren't able to get the financing. We'd have a big enough problem on our hands with all the verbal agreements we have. Signed contracts would just compound the situation." Laura paused, wondering if any of her admonition had penetrated Paul's skull. Her disapproval of the lax manner in which all the company's legal affairs had previously been handled was aggravated by her irritation at being on display—yet there was no denying the fact that she was also somewhat aroused by the situation. She flushed, visibly, as she realized this. It was becoming a struggle for her to retain her composure.

"By the way, Shawn Long has called several times today. I'm assuming he's wondering where his agreement is, too."

"You don't have to worry about Shawn," Paul responded. "I hear he's been doing some grumbling about things, but I can handle him. We go way back. I'll give him a call right away." Damn, I wish she'd worn something else today, he was thinking. Or maybe what I really wish, he admitted to himself, is that she'd just reach down, grab ahold of the bottom of that blouse and pull it over the top of her head. Paul found himself visualizing her doing just that and wondered what king of brassiere she was wearing. It looked to him like something French, with a little uplift to it. The kind Kim had always worn. God, stop doing this to yourself! his inner voice scolded. "I want someone to set up a meeting with Brubeck. Right away," he managed to say when his mind shifted back to reality.

"I've already set one up," came Matthew's reply. "He's flying in here next week, probably on Monday."

With that, the meeting was interrupted by Candy's voice over the telephone speaker. "Paul, I'm sorry to interrupt your meeting, but a Neil Roberts is one the phone for you. He says it's important."

"Neil Roberts..." muttered Paul. "Where have I heard that name?"

"He says he represents Mackenzie Montana," answered Candy.

46

Laura, flooded with a sense of relief at being able to escape, jumped up to leave the office as soon as Paul lifted the phone. Matthew, a little disappointed to see this meeting come to an end, followed.

That afternoon, Laura was in a bigger hurry than usual to get home. Once there, she ran into the house, kissed both the kids hello and headed to her bedroom. The moment she reached the privacy of her room, Laura removed her $80 silk Ann Taylor shell, wadded it in a tight little ball and tossed it in the wicker wastebasket next to her bed. Glancing first at the mirror's reflection of her standing there in her bra (a French push-up, the kind that Michael had loved), she reached into the closet for a T-shirt and muttered softly, under her breath. "Men!"

Then, before slipping into the T-shirt, she took one more long look in the mirror.

"Not bad!" she said, with a sheepish grin on her face.

*   *   *

Laura was just looking at her watch and thinking about calling it a day, when Candy buzzed her to tell her Corinne was on the phone.

Laura picked up the phone. "Hi. You just caught me!" She was clearly pleased to hear from her friend. "This is a nice surprise, hearing from you on a Friday afternoon. I would have assumed you'd be off with Mark by now. What's up?"

As soon as she heard the tone of Corinne's voice, Laura knew her friend was not in a good mood.

"That creep," came Corinne's response. "We were supposed to spend the whole weekend together. His wife and the kids had planned on leaving this morning for Vancouver. Then he calls me around lunchtime to say they'd had a change of plans. His son decided he'd rather stay home and go to a Mariners game with Mark, so two guesses who gets left high and dry?"

"Well, then, let's make *his* loss *my* gain," responded Laura cheerfully. "The timing is perfect. My kids are spending the weekend at my parents' house. I was just sitting here feeling sorry for myself about spending a Friday night at home alone. Why don't you come out and we'll order pizza?"

Corinne appreciated the fact that Laura was her one friend who never threw the "what do you expect with a married lover" line at her at times like this. Still, an evening at home with pizza was not exactly what she needed to get her mind off her troubles.

"I've got a better idea." Corinne's mood began to improve as her plans took shape. "How long's it been since you had a night on the town? Let's go out to dinner, then see what kind of trouble we can get into afterwards."

She jumped right in again when her response was greeted only by silence. "Laura, come on now. Do it for me. Okay? Please??" She knew her friend would be hard pressed to turn down this approach.

"What the hell," said Laura, rather uncharacteristically. "It'll beat sitting around alone feeling sorry for myself. I didn't really think I could talk you into coming back home with me. Besides, I'm kind of in the mood to let go a little. Let's do it!"

"Well, I'll be damned!" came Corinne's incredulous response.

*   *   *

They'd decided on Cucina, Cucina for dinner. A popular night spot on Seattle's Lake Union, it had been Corinne's favorite pick-up joint before meeting Mark. Most of the clientele were young, rather yuppyish professionals. Corinne seemed to know all of the staff and half the good-looking men hanging around the bar.

Neither women were heavy drinkers, so the bottle of Cabernet Sauvignon they downed with their dinners took its effect, and when it came time to leave, both Laura and Corinne had reservations about driving.

"Hey, didn't you say that your office is only a couple blocks from here?" asked Corinne, as they were debating their options.

"Yes. Why?" Laura wasn't following Corinne's train of thought at all on this one.

"And don't you have an employees' lounge there? Why don't we walk over there? You can show me the place. I would *love* to see where *the* Paul Brooks does his thing. And after that, if we still feel like we shouldn't be driving, we could even bed down there, couldn't we? Have our own little pajama party—only it would have to be an au natural party I guess, unless you keep nighties in your desk somewhere." She giggled, pleased with herself for coming up with this idea.

"That's not a bad idea." Laura answered enthusiastically. "I sure don't feel like hanging around here being eyeballed by these guys all night long. By the time we walk over and look around, I bet we'll feel fine. Besides, it'll be fun to show you around."

*   *   *

Corinne was more than a little impressed with Laura's set-up at Brooks. Observing her friend's reaction, Laura realized she was indeed very fortunate. Her office was large and bright, with a huge window overlooking Puget Sound. She worked with a wonderful, gifted group of people. She found her work stimulating and rewarding. And then, of course, she worked for Paul Brooks.

Despite Laura's efforts to maintain her distance from him, Paul was increasingly on her mind. She'd tried countless gimmicks to erase him from her thoughts. She now kept the door between their offices firmly shut. Still, his voice found its way to her when she was sitting there, trying with all her might to concentrate on a contract she was drafting or royalty statements she was reviewing. To avoid running into him, she tried not to venture out into the halls or reception area outside their offices unless she knew he was occupied in his own office or out of the building. If she absolutely had to talk to Paul about something, she tried to drop in when Candy was already in his office with him. *That* usually proved safe, as these days, Candy was not about to leave the two of them alone together.

Still, her mind drifted back to him regardless of the efforts she'd made, regardless of what pressing business she was tending to. Even at home, with Christopher and Hailey, she'd found herself constantly distracted by thoughts of him. It didn't help matters that Paul had taken Christopher under his wing. He'd shown an interest in her son all along, but this last month, ever since her decision to keep her distance from Paul, his interest in Christopher seemed to intensify. Though she appreciated it immensely and derived so much joy from Christopher's happiness, she worried that Paul's actions were not generated wholly by an interest in her son. She'd wished it had been someone else who'd succeeded in winning her son's affection. Just last night Chris had informed her that he and Paul were planning a camping trip for later in the summer. When it gave her beloved son so much joy to again have a man in his life, someone so much like him, who shared his love of sports and the outdoors, how could she possibly begrudge their relationship? The truth was that she didn't, yet their growing closeness terrified her.

"Earth to Laura!" Laura's thought were interrupted by Corinne's rendition of one of Christopher and Hailey's favorite expressions. "Didn't you tell me you had an exercise room here, too?"

"An exercise room and a sauna. They're both downstairs," responded Laura. "Want to take a look?"

"No," Corinne answered decisively. "Let's don't just look. Let's take a sauna."

Laura loved the idea. Before Corinne knew what was going on, Laura was running toward the stairwell, shedding her blouse and skirt as she ran. "Last one in's a loser."

It was a close race. They reached the door of the sauna simultaneously, but Laura declared herself the winner as Corinne, giggling, with briefcase in hand, was still struggling to unfasten her Frederick's of Hollywood brassiere while Laura had already succeeded in stripping down to nothing.

"That's what you get for buying that sleazy looking stuff," Laura laughed, grabbing a towel before stepping into the steaming sauna.

"Well, I can't afford that silk stuff you had on, so I guess it will have to do" Corinne came back. "Want to trade?"

As Laura made a crack about having to first spend a small fortune for implants in order to be able to fit into Corinne's generously proportioned bra, the two friends disappeared into the sauna.

Minutes later, when Hank, the janitor, walked past the locker room on his last round of the building, he was startled to hear laughter coming from the sauna. Damn, if that doesn't sound like Mrs. Kennedy, he said to himself. Just as he entered the room, his heart racing with the thought of Laura sitting in the nude (didn't *all* those young people sit in there stark naked?), he heard the blast of his wife's car horn signaling her arrival to pick him up. *Damn!* he thought as he turned reluctantly toward the stairs, the horn blasting again.

Hank would have a hard time sleeping that night.

*   *   *

Laura and Corinne were feeling tremendously relaxed and contented when Corinne suddenly squealed, "My phone! I can hear my phone ringing!" She dashed out of the sauna into the locker room, reached for her bag, extracted her cellular phone and answered it breathlessly.

After just a few minutes, she returned to the sauna.

"It was Mark," she explained, somewhat sheepishly, realizing how desperately she'd reacted to hearing the phone. "He just dropped his son off and wants to meet me. What do you think, Laura, would you be okay if he picked me up here and we spent some time together?"

Laura felt a pang of sympathy for her friend. "Of course I'll be okay. Go ahead and go. I can take a cab back to my car when I'm ready. But, you know, I'm enjoying this so much that I might just stay in the sauna a while longer."

"I'm not sure that's a good idea, Laura," Corinne responded. "I don't like to think of you here alone."

"I'll be fine, I promise. By now, there's a guard at the front door. His name is Tony. When you're leaving, why don't you just let him know I'll be here a little while longer?" When she saw the look of concern on Corinne's face, Laura continued, "Corinne, he's a dear old guy. I feel as safe with Tony upstairs as I would with my dad up there. Now go!"

Corinne was anxious enough to get to her lover that it didn't take much more assurance from Laura to get her going. As Corinne raced to get dressed, Laura settled back into the sauna and, for once, didn't resist, as sweet thoughts of Paul Brooks flooded her mind.

*   *   *

Paul was on his way home from the Fifth Avenue Theatre production when he decided, on the spur of the moment, to swing by the office and pick up some contracts Laura had asked him to review over the weekend.

As he approached the front door, Tony jumped up to greet him. "Evening, Mr. Brooks."

"Evening, Tony."

"Guess this is a popular place tonight, huh?" Tony went on.

"I don't understand, Tony. This place, popular on a Friday night?" Paul wasn't accustomed to Tony's kidding, which is what he assumed Tony was now doing. Intent on just grabbing the contracts and getting out of there without getting caught up in small talk, he hurried by the night watchman.

"Think I'll just head down and check on Ms. Kennedy," Tony continued.

At the sound of these words, Paul froze in his tracks.

"Yep, she's been down in that sauna quite a while

now. It's not healthy to stay in those things too long. Guess I'll just mosey on down there." Tony was enjoying this immensely.

"Tony." Paul's voice was firm.

"Yes, Mr. Brooks?" answered Tony innocently.

"*I'll* check on Ms. Kennedy."

Paul and Tony's eyes locked briefly, knowingly.

"Yes, Mr. Brooks," agreed the night watch man, a boyish grin breaking out on his kindly old face. "You're the boss!"

*   *   *

When she first stood, she felt lightheaded. Silently scolding herself for staying in the sauna too long, as she stepped out into the locker room, Laura automatically tightened the knot of the towel she had wrapped around her.

She was bending to pick up the pile of her clothing from the wooden bench, her back turned to the door, when Paul entered the room.

"Hey, Girl."

Laura whirled about, startled. "Paul..." The combined effects of the wine, sauna and the fact that she now stood before him wrapped only in a rather skimpy towel, left her speechless.

"What brings you here tonight?" Paul asked, as casually as if they'd just run into each other at the local Safeway.

Paul's demeanor gave no indication whatsoever of the utter chaos his body and mind were experiencing. Standing there opposite this woman whom he absolutely craved, he had to marshall every ounce of self-control and will power available to him to avoid letting his eyes feast on her long, lovely legs, the dewy skin of her exposed decollete. He shoved both hands in his pockets, and casually leaned against the doorway, hoping to hide, as best he could, her effect on him.

Oblivious to the true effect she was having on him, Laura thought Paul was acting so nonplussed that she wondered if maybe he were *used* to coming upon half-naked women unexpectedly. While his seemingly nonchalant reaction reassured and calmed her, it also irritated her.

In response to his questions, Laura explained how it was that she'd come to be there.

"Where are the kids?" Paul quizzed her further.

"They're staying with my folks this weekend," answered Laura, aware of the absurdity of her standing there wrapped in a towel, "chatting" with this man—a man who had been turning her world upside down and about whom, only minutes earlier, she'd been having the most erotic of thoughts. Something told her it was time to cut this conversation short and get out of there. Fast.

But Paul was in no such hurry. "Oh, that's too bad," he said. "I'd planned on asking Christopher to go to tomorrow night's Mariners' game with me."

"I'm sure he'd have loved to," answered Laura politely, turning to leave. But as she tried to step past him, Paul reached out and grabbed her wrist.

"Laura."

He tried to get her to look at him, but she averted her eyes and did not respond. It didn't escape his notice, however, that she offered little resistance to his grasp. Maybe it was this that emboldened him. Or maybe he simply ran out of will power. But what Paul did next came as much of a surprise to him as it did to Laura.

With the one hand still on her wrist, his other

55

hand reached up and, with a quick twist, unfastened the towel. It dropped silently to the ground.

Too shocked initially to even move, Laura, her eyes ablaze, was about to slap Paul across the face. But, as she lifted her eyes to glare at him, the look on Paul's face stopped her short.

He had stepped back, whether out of shock at his own actions, in an effort to escape her lashing out at him, or as a means of getting a better look, neither of them knew for sure. But as Laura recovered her senses and was about to strike out at him, she was so moved by the look of absolute reverence on Paul's face that she found herself motionless. She simply stood there, as Paul's eyes slowly, lovingly devoured her exquisite beauty; traveling from her firm, perfectly formed breasts, their erect little nipples clearly aroused by his examination, to her tight, flat stomach, still glistening from the sauna's heat, and on down to her soft, silk-skinned loins. Laura stood there watching Paul examine her, as moved by the look on his face as he was by the sight of her.

Finally, his voyage took him back to her face and they stood there, silently, looking into each other's eyes.

Without another word, his eyes still locked with hers, Paul reached for the towel, handed it gently to Laura, then turned and walked out of the room.

*   *   *

The flowers were delivered to Laura's house early the next morning—two dozen peach colored roses, with a card which simply said:

"You are lovely."

*   *   *

"You must have had one hell of a weekend," remarked Matthew, as Paul sat down at the conference table. "You look like shit."

It was Monday morning. Every Monday at 10 A.M. Paul held a staff meeting. In light of how he was feeling, he'd been tempted to call this one off, but realized that today's meeting was an especially important one.

"I *feel* like shit. I bet I didn't get more than four or five hours of sleep all weekend," responded Paul. In response to Matt's raised eyebrow, he continued. "It's not what you think. I spent the whole time alone, hardly even left my place. Just couldn't sleep—had a lot on my mind."

Matthew, assuming the movie was the source of Paul's insomnia, was pleased. Matthew knew Paul well enough to know that once Paul set his mind to solving a problem, he'd accomplish it, come hell or high water. For a while there, he'd been worried that by the time Paul began to take the situation with the movie seriously, it might be too late. He was therefore quite relieved to think that Paul had been so disturbed about the situation that he'd had trouble sleeping.

Concern over the movie, however, had played only a secondary role in Paul's thoughts over the weekend. Friday night's experience with Laura had been foremost on his mind. He realized that the situation with *After the Dance*, by all rights, should be occupying all his thoughts these days, but the last three nights he'd tossed and turned fitfully, working himself into an almost feverish state, the image of Laura standing there naked in front of him alternately torturing, then delighting him. He could not get the sight of her off his mind. He did not want to.

He'd picked up the phone to call her half a dozen times and had even driven by her house twice. But each time something had stopped him.

And now, as the room began to fill with staffers, Paul was feeling apprehensive about this morning's encounter with Laura.

He waited until well past ten, and when she still had not shown up, Paul started the meeting. Just as he asked Matthew to summarize the status of *After the Dance* for everyone present, Laura slipped quietly into the room.

There were two vacant chairs in the room—one next to Paul and another tucked in the corner, away from the table. Laura entered the room, quickly surveyed the scene and, avoiding any eye contact with Paul, pulled the chair in the corner up to the end of the table, out of Paul's line of vision.

Not a good sign, thought Paul.

Matthew was in the midst of explaining the movie's financing situation to the group. "At any rate, Brubeck has certainly not lost interest in *After the Dance*, but, according to Laura, we do have a problem. Laura, want to fill everyone in?"

Laura stood and addressed her coworkers. "Mr. Brubeck has actually been very reasonable to work with," she started. "The agreement we've come up with is basically just what we discussed here some time ago. But, as is usually the case, as co-producer and financier of the film, Mr. Brubeck has the right to approve, or disapprove, as the case may be, our casting for any of the movie's major characters. As you all know, we've always had Amy Griffin in mind to play Ashley, the investigative reporter. Well, Mr. Brubeck is adamantly opposed to Amy playing Ashley." Laura's eyes scanned those seated around the huge table as she spoke, but very noticeably skipped over Paul. "He seems to feel Amy's popularity is on the decline. Also, he thinks the role could use some spicing up. He's worried about the movie becoming too serious, too heavy. And until we get this one issue resolved, I'm afraid we won't be seeing *any* of that two-million dollar advance we've been anticipating."

"Well, what's being done to resolve it?" asked Laticia Rawlins, assistant production manager for Brooks.

"I've got a meeting set up with Bob Brubeck tomorrow morning," Paul spoke up. "I'm hoping to get him to agree to having Amy play that part. However, last week I did get a call that may prove to be timely. Apparently Mackenzie Montana has heard about the part and wants to have it. Her agent called me just the other day."

Paul's announcement about Mackenzie Montana stunned everyone.

"Mackenzie Montana—in the role of Ashley?? I don't think so, Paul!" Laticia was never one to hold her tongue. "Did you see her in *Busting Out*? *After the Dance* is hardly Mackenzie Montana's kind of movie."

"*I* saw her in *Busting Out*. Three times!" offered Randy, a cameraman. "Man, did I see her. Did you see that scene where the two of them make love in front of the office window—in the middle of the day. God, that was unbelievable." Clearly, Randy was not as appalled as Laticia by the concept of Mackenzie playing the lead in *After the Dance*. "I think she'd be fantastic."

"That's because you think with your crotch," shot back Laticia. "She's a slut. A beautiful slut, but a slut nonetheless. You're not seriously considering her, are you Paul?"

"Seriously? No, I'm not," assured Paul. "But according to her agent, this is just the kind of role Mackenzie is dying for. He tried to convince me that no one has begun to see this girl's real potential, that she's sick to death of being typecast in sexy roles and, if given the chance, can prove that she has the depth to become another Jane Fonda. I told him we'd already filled the role and were happy with our choice. What do you think, Matt?"

"It'd be interesting," answered Matt pensively. "There's no reason the reporter, Ashley Cowles, shouldn't be beautiful and sexy. Actually, I wish Amy looked today like she did six or eight years ago, when she did *On the Verge*. It never hurts you at the box office to have a looker in the lead role. But I'd have to be convinced Mackenzie has a hell of a lot more depth than we've seen so far. It'd be awfully risky. But if it did work, it would work big."

"Well, I made it pretty clear that we were not interested," continued Paul. "There are a lot of good actresses who could play this part if Brubeck refuses to agree to Amy. Mackenzie Montana is probably not one of them."

After more discussion of the progress on preproduction, Paul adjourned the meeting. He tried to catch up with Laura as everyone filed out of the conference room, but she'd hopped up and exited at the first sign the meeting was ending.

Paul approached Laura's office. As he walked by Candy's desk, which was situated between the door to his office and the one to Laura's, he told her to make sure that he and Laura were not disturbed. Candy, looking annoyed, shook her head in acknowledgment. Then Paul knocked lightly on Laura's door and entered.

She sat, staring out the window. She did not turn to acknowledge him, but as Paul approached, he could see tears in her eyes.

"Laura."

No response.

"Laura, we have to talk." His voice was gentle.

Turning to him, her eyes still glistening, Laura finally responded. "I know we do."

"You have to tell me what you're thinking," Paul pleaded. "I know that I should apologize about what happened the other night, but I can't, Laura. It may sound contrived, but I couldn't help myself. And I don't regret what I did. I'm sorry, but I don't. You must know by now how I feel about you, Laura."

"I'm not angry with you for the other night," Laura answered softly. "Maybe I should be, but I'm not. But I've given this a lot of thought, Paul, and it just won't work. You and I are all wrong for each other. And I'm just not ready for a relationship."

"What are you trying to say?" Paul had an ominous feeling. He felt helpless, unable to prevent the words he knew were coming.

"I'm trying to tell you that I can't do this anymore. I can't sit here day after day with you in the next room. I can't sit there in meetings with you. I can't..." Tears were streaming down her cheeks now. "I can't let myself love you, Paul." There, she'd said it. "So I'm leaving Brooks." Her voice broke as she uttered these painful words. "I'll finish up on the contracts for the movie. That should only take a few more days. Then I'll leave."

"Laura..." Paul searched for the right words, but before he could find them, she spoke again.

"Don't, Paul. Please, don't. Just go now. *Please.*"

As Paul turned and walked quietly to the door,

Laura buried her face in her hands. Paul turned back and looked at her just one more time, then slowly, sadly, he shut the door.

*   *   *

Neil Roberts grimaced as he prepared to tell Mackenzie about his conversation with Paul Brooks. She'd been vacationing at a producer friend's beach house on Grand Cayman Island the past week. As he stood at the gate waiting for Mackenzie to deplane, he silently rehearsed how he'd break the news that he'd had no luck in persuading Brooks to give the role of Ashley Cowles to her.

Usually when Mackenzie returned from one of her frequent trips, Neil enjoyed picking her up at the airport. Mackenzie always played any such public appearances to the hilt, and Neil had to admit that it was fun to be seen in the company of a gorgeous young star. He often wondered whether people assumed they were a couple. Today, however, the prospect of delivering the bad news robbed him of any of his customary pleasure.

These days Mackenzie flew first class only, so she was always one of the first passengers to deplane. Neil stood back from the crowd awaiting the arriving plane, until the sudden stirring and the sight of several people on tip toe, straining to get a look, signaled to him that Mackenzie had arrived.

She looked wonderful. Her glorious mane of wildly cascading, reddish curls was sun-streaked from days of lying on the beach. Her arms and legs, very much in evidence today by virtue of the skimpy spandex dress she wore, were browned, and her fragile face freckled. While Mackenzie's face exuded a wholesomeness and innocence, her body radiated unadulterated sensuality—a deadly combination. It was that body that gave Mackenzie Montana her start. Long, willowy legs—Mackenzie stood almost six feet in the highest of her heels—a tight, nicely rounded rear end, and full breasts, always prominently displayed— Mackenzie's body was the stuff that dreams are made of. For years the number-one lingerie model for *Secret*, a renowned mail-order catalogue, Mackenzie had become almost legendary well before she ever appeared on the silver screen. Back in her *Secret* days, her following became so great that she was recognized everywhere she went and treated like a celebrity. When she decided to try her luck at acting, her fans flocked to see their beloved Mackenzie in her first minor role. They were not disappointed, for if photographs captured Mackenzie's beauty, the big screen magnified it tenfold. As noted by Kevin Jensen, to view Mackenzie on the big screen was, in and of itself, worth the price of admission.

Flashing a handsome onlooker her dazzling smile, Mackenzie approached Neil, handed him her carry-on bag and, smile still in place, began barking orders, "You run ahead and get the car while I go to the bathroom. Then meet me out front. I'll wait in the car while you get my luggage. And hurry because I'm exhausted."

"Welcome home," muttered Neil sarcastically as Mackenzie disappeared into the ladies room.

When at last they were in the privacy of Mackenzie's silver Mercedes coupe, Neil took a deep breath before speaking. "Mackenzie, I'm afraid I have some disappointing news. I've talked to Paul Brooks and, though he seemed terribly pleased that you'd be interested in the part, they plan to go ahead with Amy Griffin." Looking straight ahead as he jockeyed for position on the busy airport drive, Neil was relieved to have an excuse for avoiding the glare Mackenzie directed at him.

"*I* am going to play Ashley Cowles in *After the Dance*," replied Mackenzie, scathingly. "No thanks to you, but believe me, I will play that part."

"I don't understand." Neil was not altogether comforted by this news. Clearly he was in the doghouse with his valued client.

"I suspected you'd be as ineffectual as ever in getting this part for me, so I've been doing a little campaigning myself." After a pause, Mackenzie continued, "I may not have it yet, but I have no doubt that I'll get it."

Neil was silent. Recalling Mackenzie's words when they first discussed her wanting this part ("You get it for me. That's what I pay you for. Or get yourself another meal ticket."), he began to perspire profusely as he waited for the axe to drop.

"Neil, darling. Relax." Mackenzie's demeanor actually softened somewhat upon seeing him so visibly distraught. "I'm not going to fire you."

Upon hearing her words, Neil's sense of relief was immediate and obvious.

"Not yet, anyway." True to form, she just couldn't resist one final jab. "But I may change my mind if things don't turn out right."

*　　*　　*

Paul's meeting with Bob Brubeck did not start off particularly well. Paul, his usual confident self, had gone into the meeting certain that he could persuade Brubeck that Amy Griffin was right for the role of Ashley Cowles. Early on in the discussion, however, he realized that he'd miscalculated the intensity of

Brubeck's feelings on the matter. And what really threw Paul off was Brubeck's choice to replace Amy.

"It comes down to this, Paul," Brubeck was now stating, "We've decided that we want Mackenzie Montana to play the part of the reporter."

Paul was dumbfounded by this announcement. He'd given the call from Neil Roberts some thought these past few days and had decided that Mackenzie was one of the last actresses he'd like to see in the part of Ashley Cowles. Not only was her image totally out of sorts with Ashley as he'd envisioned her, but Mackenzie also had a reputation of being difficult to work with. And certainly Brooks could not afford to pay Mackenzie anything close to the reported $1.5 million she'd received for her last movie.

Paul now sat silently, assessing all of these factors and wondering just what was going on. After talking to Neil Roberts last week, he'd returned Shawn Long's calls only to be told by Shawn that Amy Griffin was all wrong for the part. This news had come as a surprise to Paul, as he'd consulted with Shawn numerous times before approaching Griffin. It had actually been Shawn who first suggested Griffin and who reassured Paul, who'd initially planned on a younger actress for the part, that Amy's age would add credibility to the role. Shawn had not brought up Mackenzie Montana's name, but had told Paul that the film needed someone younger and more exciting, someone "hot," as he put it. The whole thing had left Paul puzzled, but now the pieces were falling into place.

Testing his theory, Paul finally responded to Brubeck's announcement. "Frankly, I think Mackenzie Montana is all wrong for the part, and I feel quite certain that Shawn would agree. In fact, I wouldn't be surprised if he refused to direct if Mackenzie were to play Ashley." Paul studied Brubeck's reaction. His suspicions were confirmed by Brubeck's reply.

"Actually, Paul, Shawn Long and I have already discussed this casting change, and I can assure you that Shawn would be delighted to work with Mackenzie. He and I are in complete agreement that Mackenzie will add an exciting dimension to the character, one that will ensure the commercial success of *After the Dance*. We both feel we'd be very fortunate to get Mackenzie to play the part of Ashley Cowles."

Paul's blood pressure was skyrocketing. "Commercial success! *Commercial success*! Is that all the fuck this movie's about to you? Whatever happened to *integrity*? You know, the word you've used to describe our films before? The thing you told me you respected most about our films? Suddenly it's *commercial success* that matters most to you!"

"Paul, before you..." Brubeck tried to respond, but Paul was not ready to stop just yet.

"Well, let me tell you something, Bob. *After the Dance* is not about commercial success. It's about AIDS. AIDS, for God's sake. It's about people dying—people like you and me, people like that beautiful daughter of yours. It's a movie with a message, Bob. An important message. Don't turn it into something about dollars and ticket sales." There was more he wanted to say, much more, but suddenly Paul looked defeated. He paused long enough for Brubeck to jump in.

"Paul, I appreciate your passion for this film. Believe me, it's your passion that made me listen to you when you first called me about backing you. And it was your passion that I tried to convey to the financing group when I presented *After the Dance*. But the cold hard facts are that none of us—and I've already told you that we're dealing with three other parties here, Paul, three lifelong friends of mine, people who are trusting my judgment on this—*none* of us is willing to come up with millions of dollars for passion's sake alone. This is a business deal to us, Paul. First and foremost, a business deal. And it had damned well better be a profitable one."

Paul resigned himself to listen as Brubeck continued. "I'll admit that Mackenzie Montana is no Meryl Streep. Shit, she's not even a Cher. But the lady does bring them out to the theaters." Brubeck looked halfway pleading. "Look at it this way. You want to get a message out. True, the message might have more impact with Amy Griffin playing the part. But what good is a message that no one hears? At least with Mackenzie, the message will be heard. In fact, handled right, and Shawn feels he can do it, the combination of Mackenzie Montana plus a message as current and as important as the one contained in *After the Dance* could make this the movie of the year, Paul. Think of what *that* will do for your message."

Seeing that Paul was still far from convinced, Brubeck decided there was no point in holding back. "The bottom line Paul, is that either it's Mackenzie Montana who plays the reporter in *After the Dance,* or your movie never gets made. It's as simple as that."

And with that, the meeting ended.

*　　*　　*

When she awoke, Laura felt a strange sense of relief. It took her just a few moments to realize what it was about. Just one more week, she now thought. One more week, then I should be done with Paul Brooks forever.

She lay in bed this sunny Sunday morning, reflecting on the events of the past two weeks. She'd been feeling as though her entire body had been placed in a slow-motion blender—whirling, churning at a pace that dizzied her.

It all began that Friday night, when Paul came upon her as she was leaving the sauna. She still could not believe what happened that night. What she *let* happen. Just thinking of it now gave rise to such strong emotions, such overpowering physical sensations, that she dared not dwell on it. Yet she did.

Thank God the kids were away that weekend. She wouldn't have known how to explain her behavior those next few days to them if they'd been around. She actually remained quite calm immediately after seeing Paul. Thinking of it in those terms now brought a slight smile to her lips as she lay there. She mentally corrected herself—after Paul saw *me... all* of me. She was pleased to realize that at least she could smile about it. She hadn't done much smiling recently. After seeing Paul, she'd calmly taken a taxi back to her car at Cucina, Cucina, then had driven home. But once home, it hit her. Like Paul, she'd spent the next nights tossing fitfully, reliving over, and over, and over again the glorious sensation of having Paul's eyes explore her. In her entire life, she'd never experienced anything remotely like it. Lying there thinking about it those sleepless nights, she had ached with such intensity, experiencing sensations she hadn't even realized existed. With Michael, lovemaking had always been warm, and gentle, and fulfilling, and wonderful—everything she had always expected it to be. But the feelings that this one moment of intimacy with Paul had given rise to, a moment in which they neither spoke nor touched, were feelings that overpowered and dizzied her. Her body had never ached so. Pain. Exquisite pain—those were the words that kept creeping into Laura's mind to describe it. Exquisite pain. A unique kind of pain that she did not *want* to go away, pain that she instinctively knew she'd been hungering for. Pain she could become addicted to. And *that*, that knowledge of the power that pain could exert over her, was the problem. That was the reason Laura had been so frightened that she'd finally done the only thing she could do to deal with her fear—she'd decided to quit her job at Brooks.

And he hadn't objected. When she told him, Paul had simply turned and walked out of her office.

Maybe she'd been wrong about Paul. Maybe she was just another challenge to his abundantly healthy male ego. Maybe the love she thought she'd read in his eyes that night had been little more than curiosity. At any rate, this past week he'd seemed as determined to avoid her as she was to avoid him. Until Friday, in fact, their only contact had been via the intercom. But Friday morning he'd come into her office and, rather formally, had asked her to stay on just long enough to finalize negotiations and draft an agreement with Mackenzie Montana.

That morning she sensed that Paul was experiencing the same pain she'd been feeling since she announced she was leaving. It was certainly nothing he said, as he'd been unusually businesslike that day. But something in the way he *looked* at her, ever so briefly, hinted at it.

Thinking of it now, though, she chastised herself for being so imaginative. Maybe she was kidding herself to think Paul Brooks had ever *really* been interested in her. What a fool she must have made of herself, that night in the sauna, then later when she confessed through her tears that she was falling in love with him.

Well, she'd done the right thing in quitting. Now she'd just finish up with the contract on the movie and put this whole episode of her life behind her, once and for all. She was not pleased that her leaving would be delayed by the change of actresses, but she felt that she owed it to Paul to draw up Mackenzie Montana's contract as soon as possible.

Then she would get on with her life.

Maybe she'd go back to Emery, Johnson. She knew that they'd welcome her with open arms. Yet the thought did little to cheer her. Despite her fears, despite her growing suspicion that Paul Brooks had already gotten over any feelings he may have had for her, Laura sensed that life at Emery, Johnson, or anywhere else for that matter—life without Paul Brooks— would be a life filled with pain.

An exquisite pain, which she would always cherish.

5

After the Dance had been a labor of love for Matthew O'Connor. The notion of writing a book to memorialize his little sister first came to him in Wyoming. After Colleen's death, he'd sold his Laurel Canyon home, traded in his Jaguar for a new Jeep Wrangler, taken an indefinite leave of absence from Encore Productions, the film company he'd helped establish years earlier, and headed out of Los Angeles for the mountains and wilderness of Montana and Wyoming.

But the first weeks of drifting aimlessly though his beloved Montana—from the northwestern most corner of the state, where he camped for nights in a solitary clearing just outside of spectacular Glacier National Park; to the shores of Flathead Lake, where he stayed in a lodge in the little town of Big Fork; and on down to the breathtaking beauty of the Gallatin Gateway—had done little to ease the pain he was so desperately seeking to relieve. The very mountains and rivers which as a child, and later as a young man, had given

71

him such inspiration and solace, now served only as painful reminders of the many happy summers he'd spent there in his youth, with his parents and sister. After spending several soul-searching days camping alongside the Gallatin River, a river which had in the past provided him with countless hours of the most satisfying, joyful fly fishing known to man, Matthew now felt betrayed. The very places which had always offered him an emotional anchor now left him with an ache that he feared would never dissipate. Maybe he'd been wrong to think that this trip could make a difference. Maybe nothing could. Except time, and given the snail's pace at which time was passing, this was not a comforting thought. Still, he was grateful for the solitude. And the beauty, the unbelievable beauty, which never failed to stir something deep within his heart. He was especially grateful that he could still respond to that. It gave him hope.

Matthew had always appreciated beauty. As early as four or five years of age, when the family made its first trip West and he'd laid eyes on the snow-capped peaks of the Tetons, he announced that when he grew up, he'd move to the mountains. While most children whined and crabbed their way across the country on family vacations, Matthew's enthusiasm and excitement about returning to the mountains each year buoyed the whole family's spirits. And as he entered adolescence and began to experience the anxieties and confusion of a spirited young man, it was often thoughts of the mountains that calmed and reassured him. The night that Nancy Able humiliated him by letting his friends read the love letter (his first) he'd written her, he'd pulled out every picture ever taken on their family vacations West, then lay in bed examining them until his troubled mind drifted into peaceful sleep.

His first solo sojourn to the magnificent states he'd grown to love as a child took place right after he graduated from Marquette University. He was feeling lost and confused—torn between following his heart by pursuing a career in filmmaking and pleasing his parents by accepting a scholarship he'd been offered to the University of Wisconsin's law school. The day after his graduation ceremony, he packed up his beat-up Volkswagen and headed out to his beloved mountains in search of answers. Weeks later, full of youthful enthusiasm and confidence, he returned to his home in Madison to announce his intention to enter USC's school of film production. Despite their disappointment over his move across the country to pursue a career that seemed, at best, iffy, his parents and Colleen became his greatest supporters in the next years. They soon also became his biggest fans, as his first films, low-budget movies, nonetheless featuring breathtaking photography, met with critical acclaim.

Many years passed between that first solo venture to the wilderness and the next, but just two years earlier he'd returned to his spiritual haunts—once again in search of answers—after discovering his wife in bed with a young cameraman who, ironically, had been given his first job by Matthew. That trip had also served its purpose, and, upon his return, Matthew had firmly but gently, ended his marriage of five years to a woman whom he loved and who dearly loved him, but who did not have the strength or self-confidence necessary to resist the temptations which constantly toy with the lives of those poor souls cursed with the fate of being young, beautiful and thrown—either by chance or design—into the vicious world of the entertainment industry. That, too, had proven to be the right decision as Matthew, once again single, flourished, enjoying his newfound solitude and spiritual rebirth, which began on that trip on a mountain top outside of DuBois, Wyoming.

So, it was natural that following the emotional service for Colleen, and after spending several weeks hovering over his parents to ensure that they were okay, Matthew once again returned to the emotional womb that the West represented—only to find that this time, his grief was so profound, so spirit-shattering, that even awaking to the sound of a gurgling mountain stream and the sight of a knobby-legged fawn was not enough to work its customary magic on him. Not enough, that is, until the morning he awoke in a tent in Wyoming, when over a cup of coffee brewed on his campfire, Matthew O'Connor looked out at the jagged peaks of the Tetons and was struck by inspiration. It was there, in the very campground that he and Colleen had seen their first awe-inspiring, heart-stopping grizzly bear, that Matthew first conceived of *After the Dance.*

The moment the idea entered his mind, Matthew knew that he'd found the answer that weeks earlier he'd set out to find. He would deal with his grief by memorializing his beloved younger sister in a book. And perhaps in doing so, he could save others some of the pain his family had endured. She would have liked that, Matthew reflected that morning by the campfire.

Not that it would change anything. He would never again lay eyes on her freckled little face, with its turned-up nose, nor would he be awakened at six A.M. by her childlike voice calling to tell big brother about the five adorable puppies her beloved mutt just gave birth to. Never again would he open his mailbox

74

to find one of her frequent ten page epistles, full of concern and motherly advice, full of her loving philosophy, her joy and optimism. No, he couldn't bring Colleen back. He could never erase the excruciating pain her absence would forever impose upon him, but by dealing constructively with his loss—by expressing the overpowering emotions, by paying tribute to her and by ensuring that her memory would live on—he instinctively knew that he could at least lessen the pain to where he might be able to learn to live with it. And, that was all he'd ever hoped to accomplish when he set out for the mountains.

He'd started the book that very day—sitting on a fallen log, basking in the Indian Summer sun, writing on the back of envelopes, paper bags, anything he had. That afternoon he drove into Jackson Hole and bought a dozen legal pads, returned to the campsite and, for the next week, wrote fervishly. On the fifth day, the fall rains started, so he moved into the front seat of his Jeep to write, but after two days of cramming his lean, athletic frame into his car, he'd decided to break camp. He drove further west. In Butte, Montana, he checked into the Capri Motel. ("Capri Motel—FIREPROOF" proclaimed several roadside signs on I-90 as Matt approached Butte—he couldn't resist checking it out.) It was from the Capri that Matt had called his lifelong friend, Paul Brooks. Upon hearing of Colleen's death and Matthew's undertaking, Paul insisted that Matt join him in Seattle. One long day's drive later, Paul Brooks greeted his unkempt boyhood buddy with open arms, and for the next five or six months, Matthew wrote his tribute in the comfort and serenity of Paul's cliffside home, in an office overlooking the soothing waters of Puget Sound.

When he wrote *After the Dance*, a movie had been the farthest thing from Matthew's mind. He was, in fact, totally unprepared for the immediate success of the book. With its timely subject matter, expressed in such a moving manner, *After the Dance* hit the *New York Times* Bestseller list within a month of its publication. Matthew became a much sought after guest on all the major talk shows. The audiences absolutely ate up this articulate, attractive, gentle young man, with his compelling story. Though he appreciated the warm reception and the outpouring of love and support for his family, Matthew hated this part of publishing and only agreed to two or three appearances at his parents and publisher's urging. He was relieved to have all the hoopla come to an end.

When it did end, Matt chose to stay on in Seattle. Paul had offered to bring him into the company and urged him to continue to share the roomy home he'd bought years earlier with his ex-wife. Though Matt had never spent any amount of time in the Northwest before, by now Seattle felt like home to him, with its spectacular scenery and earnest, friendly people.

Paul was thrilled to have his friend stay on. The two had been inseparable throughout their youth and remained in close touch despite the distance between them. Having his old friend with him helped fill a void in Paul's own life. Besides, as Paul saw it, Matthew offered Brooks Productions an incredible new dimension and talent. When Matthew came to Paul several months after joining Brooks and suggested that they make *After the Dance* into a movie, Paul had agreed, in a heartbeat, to undertake the project.

Paul's decision, however, was not a popular one within the company. *After the Dance* represented a departure from the artsy, environmentally oriented material Brooks had produced to date and would require a far greater financial commitment as well. Matthew was aware of that fact and greatly appreciated Paul's commitment to the film. While Paul set about finding financing and setting the technical process in motion, Matthew went back into seclusion to write the screenplay adaptation of his book.

Personally, Matt wasn't the least bit interested in whether the movie made any money—it was the tribute to his sister and his mission to have her death count for something that motivated him—but he was very concerned that Brooks Productions could suffer from Paul's decision to do *After the Dance*, a decision which he knew was motivated primarily out of loyalty. It was growing increasingly clear that Brooks had a lot at stake, and that without Mackenzie Montana playing the role of the reporter, financial backing for the movie would be virtually non-existent.

Paul was furious over this new turn of events. Just last night the two of them had discussed it over dinner at Cutters, the popular seafood restaurant located adjacent to Seattle's famous Pike Place Market.

"Let's face it," Paul stated, making no attempt to hide his disgust, "Brubeck's got us by the balls. He knows it's too late for us to start talking to someone else about backing. Basically, he can call the shots on who plays Ashley Cowles and he knows it. It's as simple as that."

As he'd done ever since the subject first arose, Matt downplayed his true reaction to having Mackenzie Montana in the movie. For his friend's sake, he even attempted to sound hopeful.

"Paul, maybe Brubeck and Neil Roberts are right. Maybe she's been given a bum rap and just needs a chance to play something other than some brainless bimbo." Even as he said it, Matt winced inwardly. "And if not, I'd like to think the movie is strong enough in and of itself to overcome any damage she might do to it." This, at least, was true. He did have that much faith in *After the Dance*. Of course, it was pretty hard for him to be objective about anything even remotely connected with the film, which was why he, too, was disturbed by this latest twist.

Now, as Matthew left his office and headed down the hall toward Paul's office for his first meeting with the infamous Mackenzie Montana, he wondered if it would be possible to continue to hide his true feelings about her playing the part of Ashley Cowles.

Paul had told Matt he wanted to spend a few minutes alone with Mackenzie and her agent. He asked Matt to join them fifteen minutes after the meeting was due to begin. Matthew was therefore surprised to find Paul still sitting alone at his desk when he entered the room.

"She's late!" Paul was fuming. "First meeting and she is already fifteen minutes late. Can you believe it?"

"Want me to leave, and you can buzz me when you're ready for me?" asked Matthew.

"No—stay. Let's just get this over with as soon as possible," answered Paul.

With that, in walked Candy with Neil Roberts and Mackenzie Montana.

Neil apologized profusely for their lateness, blaming it on their inability to find parking. However, his words were wasted, as neither Paul nor Matt were listening. Their eyes were glued to Mackenzie.

At Neil's urging, she'd worn a conservative, beautifully tailored olive-colored suit by the Italian designer Cerruti. It was Cerruti who'd transformed Julia

78

Roberts from a street walker to an elegant sophisticate in *Pretty Woman*. Neil was hoping for a similar transformation now.

It had been a major battle to get Mackenzie to agree to the attire, but finally, after repeatedly explaining to her the importance of looking the part of the reporter, she'd acquiesced. When Neil had arrived at her hotel room to pick her up, however, out she'd walked with the exquisite suit on and no blouse or bra underneath. A large portion of her breasts were exposed; the jacket barely covered her nipples. In fact, as they argued about Mackenzie's decision to forego the $300 blouse he'd purchased for her, Mackenzie's dramatic gesturing twice gave Neil a full view of her beautiful breasts. It had been difficult to argue convincingly with an annoying hard-on, but finally Neil prevailed. And fifteen minutes after their scheduled departure, Mackenzie truly did look stunning. Even classy, thought Neil with relief.

Now finished with his apology, and the rather unnecessary introduction of his client, Neil could finally sit back and watch Mackenzie go to work.

Despite her obstinate protests, Mackenzie had apparently taken Neil's words of advice to heart, for not only had Neil never seen her look so downright respectable, he'd never fathomed she could act so demure as well. In fact, his greatest fear now was beginning to be that Mackenzie would get carried away with this role she'd assumed. As he sat listening to her response to Paul as to why she wanted to play Ashley Cowles, Neil was silently willing Mackenzie not to overdo it.

"That's an easy question to answer, Mr. Brooks," Mackenzie was saying sweetly. "It's the fact that *After the Dance* is a movie about AIDS that first attracted me. I know there are a lot of stars who only get involved with popular causes for the good press they get, but with me, AIDS is a personal crusade."

Neil tried to get Mackenzie's attention before she continued. But she was too caught up to notice.

"You see, I've lost two dear friends to that hideous disease." At this, Neil was appalled to see her eyes fill with tears. "Two dear, dear friends. And I promised each of them before they died that someday, in some way, I'd do something to fight the spread of AIDS. Playing the role of Ashley Cowles will be my first step." Dabbing her eyes with a linen hankie, Mackenzie looked fragile and sad.

Paul was having a hard time keeping a straight face. Damn she's actually good, he thought wryly. And she's certainly not hard to look at. He glanced at Matthew to see his friend's reaction. Matthew was clearly enjoying this performance as much as Paul.

It was Matthew who spoke next.

"Mackenzie, it's very reassuring to us to know that this role would have some special meaning to you. It certainly is a project that is very dear to all of our hearts," he continued, never taking his eyes off the beautiful star. "But, frankly, we do have some reservations about you playing Ashley Cowles, and Paul and I both feel it's wise to be perfectly up front with you about them."

Now Neil spoke up. "Just what are your reservations, Mr. O'Connor?"

"Our biggest concern," started Matt, "is the fact that this role is so out of line with anything Mackenzie has done to date. Ashley Cowles is a far cry from any of Mackenzie's earlier roles..." Neil was clearing his throat to respond to this before Matt even had a chance to finish, but it was Mackenzie who interjected.

"Mr. Brooks," she turned and looked at Paul, "Mr. O'Connor," now turning to look into Matthew's eyes, "please, *please*, give me this chance. I know what you probably think of me, both as a person and as an actress." Her honesty surprised both Matthew and Paul. "Believe me, I know. That's why this part is so very important to me. I know that I can play Ashley convincingly. I will not rest until I do her justice. I give you my word." This time, Paul thought, her words actually seemed sincere. "I will do anything, *anything*," she repeated, "to get this role. Just give me the chance, please. Just give me the chance." Even Neil was half convinced of her sincerity.

The room fell completely silent.

Finally, it was Paul who spoke, "Well, Mackenzie," he said tentatively, "there's one more obstacle that we need to overcome. In light of what you just said, maybe it won't be that big a problem." He studied Mackenzie's face intently as he spoke these next words. "As you undoubtedly know, Brooks Productions is minor league, in terms of its financial clout. Our neck is stretched way out to here with this project," he stretched his long arm out to illustrate. "I'm afraid we have very little to offer you in terms of a salary. In fact, I suspect you'll find what we've budgeted for this role laughable after the millions you've been paid for your last films."

Mackenzie interrupted, him before he could continue. "Mr. Brooks, I'm prepared to take all my compensation off the back end of this film."

Paul and Matthew, incredulous, looked at each other. Even Neil looked shocked at this announcement. And none too happy.

Mackenzie continued, "In other words, I'll do this film for nothing more than a fair share of the profits. No salary at all." She knew by the look on all of their faces that her plan had worked. "Would that help things?" she asked in an innocent voice.

"It certainly would," answered Paul.

Again, there was a long silence.

"Well, Ms. Montana," Paul announced. "Here's your script."

"Welcome to Brooks Productions," he said somberly.

*　　*　　*

"Are you sad, Mom?" asked Hailey with a worried look on her little face.

Laura looked across the dinner table at her children. Christopher's face mirrored the concern in his little sister's. She *knew* she had been unusually quiet this past week or so, ever since the incident with Paul. Looking at them now she felt guilty. They were such loving, sensitive kids. She knew it hurt them to see her unhappy. Ever since Michael's death, she'd been so aware of that and had tried to hide her pain as best she could. For the most part, she'd felt she'd succeeded. Of course, in a way it wasn't difficult to do—she loved Christopher and Hailey so much that she inevitably did feel happier when she was with them. It was the time she spent away from them that had always been hardest.

But the turmoil she'd experienced since meeting Paul had been difficult to hide. She thought back to those first weeks at Brooks Productions, when she'd felt so happy again, so alive. One Saturday morning, she talked Christopher into walking the dogs with her. First she listened attentively to his play-by-play description of the basketball game he played in the day before. Then he challenged her to a race to the railroad tracks. As always, he beat her easily, but this time he sensed she'd really given it her all, which seemed to please him immensely. They'd laughed and teased and had a wonderful time. When they were nearing home, Christopher had put his arm around her and said, in the dearest voice, "Mom, I love it when you're happy." She'd been so moved by his deeply felt love and concern. But at the same time, she felt terribly sad for the pain her precious boy had been exposed to. She was glad she had her sunglasses on, as Christopher probably would not have understood her tears at that moment.

Laura knew that subconsciously the children played a significant role in her attitude toward Paul. But just exactly *what* their influence was, she was unsure. Perhaps that was because her love for them created ambivalent feelings. On the one hand, she suspected that the children were part of the reason she pushed Paul away. She had always been unusually close to her children, and after Michael's death, they'd grown even closer. The three of them loved their time together. At night, they'd all climb into Laura's big bed with a bowl of popcorn and watch their favorite television shows or a movie they'd rented. On weekends, they'd spend time outside together—Laura either doing yardwork or working with the animals, always with cheerful little Hailey by her side, while Christopher played basketball nearby. They frequently took walks together. They went shopping, or swimming at a nearby club. Laura knew that the children enjoyed their time together as much as she did. Often when she'd suggest that they invite a friend over, they'd respond by saying they just wanted to have "family time." They were so close that Laura suspected she inwardly feared that bringing in an outsider would offset the perfect balance they'd managed to achieve.

Yet, at the same time that she feared disrupting their closeness, she felt terribly sad that the children did not have a man in their lives. Especially Christopher. He was so all boy. He'd been a trooper about living with two females; in fact, he seemed to take pride in being the man of the house now. And he certainly had plenty of friends from school to offer him male companionship. But still, Laura knew that he missed his dad terribly. She hadn't realized just *how* much though, until he'd met Paul. He'd taken to Paul so quickly, so intensely. It was clear that Christopher adored Paul. But even that caused fear in Laura's heart. He'd already lost his dad. What if Paul drifted out of their lives as quickly as he'd entered? She'd never forgive herself if she subjected Chris to another loss. No, far better to nip things in the bud before Chris and Paul had a chance to become any closer. After all, this sadness that she'd been feeling would eventually go away, wouldn't it? Still, she wished she were better at hiding it so that she could spare her children the concern she now saw in their eyes.

"Mommy's just a little tired, Sweetheart," Laura finally answered. "Not sad, just tired."

"Are you still planning to quit your job?" asked Christopher, with the knowing look of an adult on his 12-year-old face. Sometimes Laura wished he did not know her quite so well.

"Yes, just as soon as I can finish up all the contracts for the movie we're making. I'm hoping I'll be through within a week or so," Laura answered.

"Maybe then you won't be so tired," offered

Hailey, her huge blue eyes peering over a glass of milk. This prospect clearly pleased Laura's little girl.

Laura chuckled at the simplicity with which Hailey viewed life. If only it were all that easy, she thought, but she tried to sound cheerful in her response. "I'm sure you're right, Sweetie. Mommy should be much less tired once I stop working."

"Good!" replied Hailey, a big smile lighting up her cherubic face.

It was moments like these that so warmed Laura's heart. As long as I have these two, Laura told herself, I'll be just fine.

*   *   *

Laura arrived at the office early the next day. She was scheduled to have her first meeting with Mackenzie Montana that afternoon and she wanted to have a rough draft of their agreement in hand for it. If all went well, she was thinking as she pulled into her assigned parking spot, she'd have everything finalized within the week.

She'd been uneasy about this meeting. It would be the first time she and Paul would spend any length of time together since she announced her departure.

It had been hard to read Paul this past week. One day she looked up from her desk to find him standing in the doorway, staring at her. Their eyes had met briefly. Then he abruptly turned and walked away. She sat there trembling, her heart racing. Just looking at him hurt. She didn't know if she felt relief or disappointment at his turning away, but the rest of the afternoon had been a total waste.

At least I'm prepared to see him this time, she reassured herself as she entered the building.

*   *   *

Paul had taken the long, scenic drive to work this morning. Whenever he felt a little down or stressed out, he took the slow, winding road that paralleled the Sound and offered travelers incredible vistas of its waters and the city's skyline. This morning he'd automatically headed in that direction—it was almost as if his car had picked up on his mood the moment he climbed in.

He loved the sight of the Winslow ferry crossing the Sound. Watching it now, cutting its way through a thin layer of early morning mist, he promised himself a ride on it soon. He often rode over to Winslow, disembarked, then turned right around to ride back to the city. He'd always been fascinated with the ferries. He even fantasized about captaining one some day. What a simple, pleasurable existence that would be, he now thought. Maybe I missed my calling, he said softly to himself.

It had been a tough week or two. Laura's announcement hadn't come as a surprise. He knew the moment she walked into the meeting that Monday—their first meeting since he saw her outside the sauna—that she would leave Brooks. Maybe he'd known it all along. Still, he didn't regret that night. If nothing else, at least he'd always have that image of her permanently etched into his memory. *Nothing* could erase that. Not an hour of the day went by without his thinking of her standing there before him. He'd known so many beautiful women, seen so many of them unclothed, yet never had he been so moved, so excited by one. Laura Kennedy, he now thought, you've definitely worked your magic on me. These days he wasn't even looking at other women. Even the beautiful Mackenzie Montana had failed to stir him.

With that thought, his mind turned to the day ahead. He was not looking forward to the afternoon's meeting. It would be difficult to sit there with Laura and conduct business as usual. Hell, last week when he'd stopped by her office just to say hello and ask about Christopher, he was so moved by the simple sight of her sitting there that he didn't even trust himself to speak.

At least Mackenzie would be there to provide some comic relief, he thought with a wry smile.

*　　*　　*

Mackenzie Montana was the one person who was looking forward to today's meeting.

She couldn't wait to see Paul Brooks again. God, he excited her. He was even better looking than her friend Angie had said. Sitting there opposite him that day, she'd remembered Angie's detailed description of her one passionate night with him. According to Angie, Paul Brooks was the best lover she'd ever had. Mackenzie sensed that day that Angie hadn't exaggerated. There was something so sure, so sensual about that man. And his size! I bet Angie didn't exaggerate about that either, thought Mackenzie with a giggle. Poor Angie. She'd been so crazy about him, it would probably hurt her terribly when she found out that Mackenzie had snagged him. Oh well, we were never that close anyway, Mackenzie concluded nonchalantly.

She was hoping to have some time alone with him today, but Paul had mentioned that the company's attorney would be in the meeting. I'll just tell him to get together with Neil later, she thought. That should get rid of him right away.

Yes, Mackenzie Montana was one happy lady as

she climbed into the taxi and ordered the driver to take her to Brooks Productions.

*   *   *

Things seemed to be going from bad to worse for Candy. It had been bad enough when Paul hired Laura, then proceeded to get that glazed look everytime he laid eyes on her. Candy had had a hard time dealing with that. For two years now, she's worshipped that man. And just before Laura arrived she'd begun to feel that maybe, just maybe, she was getting through to Paul. He'd even taken her to lunch on her birthday.

Then along came Laura. Candy took an immediate disliking to her. True, Laura had always been friendly and considerate to her (certainly more so than many of the others who worked at Brooks), and true, Laura didn't exactly seem to encourage Paul's attentions, but nonetheless, she knew that, deep down, Laura was out to get Paul. She'd seen it in her eyes. And that alone was grounds enough to hate her.

Still, the vision that moments ago had slithered by her desk and on into Paul's office made Laura Kennedy look like child's play. If Candy felt threatened by Laura, Mackenzie Montana was her worst nightmare come true.

After the considerable restraint she'd shown at their last meeting, Mackenzie was showing her true colors today. She'd been pleased that Neil had been called down to Los Angeles unexpectedly the night before. He'd stopped by her suite at the Four Seasons before leaving to give her another lecture and pick out another conservative suit for her to wear to the meeting. She'd assured him that she'd be a good girl and agreed to call him as soon as she and Paul were through. Only I didn't say through with *what*, she'd chuckled to herself this morning as she'd reached into her closet for her favorite dress. Thank God for spandex, she'd thought as she squirmed her braless form into the hot pink and orange number that left absolutely nothing to the imagination.

Scott, the ever horny cameraman, just happened to be standing at Candy's desk when Mackenzie entered minutes earlier. The look on his face as he stood there drooling over Mackenzie made Candy sick. He was living proof of her theory that most men were mindless fools when it came to sexy women.

She didn't even try to hide her disgust when she stepped into Paul's office to announce Mackenzie's arrival.

"There's some whore out there who says she's a movie star. She's here to see you." For some reason, Paul found her words quite humorous. The sight of him laughing at her misery irritated Candy so that she couldn't resist going on. "Laugh all you want, Paul, but I think having Mackenzie Montana play Ashley in *After the Dance* is what's really humorous here. No, on second thought, it's not funny, it's sad." Unfortunately Candy did not notice the fact that Paul's smile was fading fast. "To think that you're willing to trash something that meaningful with a..."

"Stop right there, Candy," came Paul's angry voice. Candy knew now that she'd crossed the line. She'd only seen that fire in his eyes once or twice in all the time she'd worked for him.

She tried to explain. "Paul, I'm sorry, but the woman makes me..."

Paul cut her off. He was in no mood for apologies. "Candy, send Ms. Montana in. Then let Laura know she's here." His tone was ice cold. "You and

I will talk after this meeting."

She started to speak again, but he gave her a look that actually frightened her. She turned and left the room.

Already off to a great start, thought Paul cynically as he stood to greet Mackenzie. "Welcome back, Ms. Montana," he said in as pleasant a voice as he could manage.

Mackenzie, oblivious to the conflict she'd just generated, ignored Paul's outstretched hand and planted a kiss on his cheek. "Now please, Paul, don't call me Ms. Montana," she said coyly. "We're going to be seeing much too much of each other for that." She batted her long lashes at him, arched her back and seductively lowered herself into the chair opposite his desk.

Paul was completely taken off guard, and more than a little irritated by the kiss. Wanting to set Mackenzie straight, he looked her right in the eye and replied, "Well then, 'Mackenzie' it is. Actually, though, I won't be that involved with production, so our contact will be minimal." He smiled politely, but his words were definitely not lost on Mackenzie. She looked like he'd just slapped her in the face.

Neither one spoke. Mackenzie's indignation was obvious to Paul. Seeing her reaction, he chided himself for being so forthright—especially in light of the fact that they'd not yet signed an agreement with her. Come on, Paul, he coached himself silently, you can do better than that. He reminded himself of how much this project meant to Matthew, and of Bob Brubeck's words. Getting on *this* one's wrong side could be a costly mistake. It was time to turn on the old Paul Brooks charm, whether or not his heart was in it. It wasn't.

Just as he directed a most appealing smile at Mackenzie, in walked Laura.

Mackenzie looked absolutely shocked when Paul introduced her as the attorney who'd be working on her contract for the movie. But Mackenzie wasn't the only one in shock. Though she was doing a much better job of concealing it, Laura, too, could hardly believe her eyes. She'd never been to one of Mackenzie's movies but she *had* seen pictures of her—since they were constantly plastered across the front page of tabloids and weekly entertainment magazines, it would be close to impossible to do your grocery shopping and not see pictures of Mackenzie. But Laura had assumed the sexy clothes and vampish look were little more than publicity gimmicks. It now took only one look at Mackenzie, sitting there seductively across from Paul, to dispel that belief and realize that Mackenzie took her image seriously. Very seriously. And from the smile on his face when she'd entered the room, it was clear to Laura that Paul took it seriously, too. She felt as though she'd interrupted and wished she could just disappear into thin air.

The sight of him looking at Mackenzie that way had hit her like a brick wall—she literally felt sick to her stomach, and her head spun so wildly that she feared she'd be unable to speak coherently. She was put to the test immediately, as Paul, anxious to get this meeting over with as soon as possible, jumped right in by asking her to review, for Mackenzie's sake, the major points of the preliminary contract she'd drafted.

Laura turned to Mackenzie and silently prayed that she'd be able to handle the situation. Her voice started off weakly.

"What I've drafted so far is pretty standard language for this type of agreement."

Paul looked at her tenderly at the sound of her strained voice. He felt touched by her vulnerability, something that he'd only seen in her once or twice before, when she'd let down her guard. His look did not go unnoticed by Mackenzie.

Once she got started, Laura was relieved to find that it helped to get down to business. She started by going over the more standard provisions she'd drafted, from a description of the role Mackenzie would play, to provisions giving Brooks exclusive artistic control over the production, to that all-too-common boilerplate language that is found in any legal document. By the time she got to those matters still left to be resolved between them, she was beginning to feel more like Laura-the-attorney again, instead of Laura-the-lovesick.

"If you're agreeable to all these basic contract provisions that I've just explained to you, then we really only have three or four other terms left to iron out." Laura looked over at Mackenzie for some indication of her response.

Throughout Laura's presentation, Mackenzie had been studying her intently. The sight of this beautiful, poised woman, an attorney nonetheless, who obviously owned a very special piece of Paul Brooks' heart, made her none too happy. Los Angeles was full of beautiful, sexy women, and usually Mackenzie found the competition quite enjoyable—rarely, if ever, did anyone outshine Mackenzie. But she instinctively knew that, with Laura Kennedy, she was up against an entirely new breed. She didn't know quite what to make of it all, but she *did* know that she wanted to get Laura out of there. As quickly as possible.

Her thoughts were interrupted by Paul. "Mackenzie?"

He had a quizzical look on his face. Was it his imagination or were both these women acting strangely?

Laura and Paul waited for some response from Mackenzie.

"I'm sorry, Paul," she finally said sweetly, ignoring Laura entirely. "But I was just thinking that I really should have either Neil or my attorney deal with Ms. Kennedy here. Maybe she could arrange to get together with one of them?"

Paul now turned to Laura. "Laura, how does that sound to you?" He tried to establish eye contact but Laura was trying equally hard to avoid it.

"I'd be happy to work with whomever Ms. Montana chooses," she replied. "As I said, there are only a couple things left to resolve. As long as she gives them the authority to speak for her, we shouldn't have a problem." Laura looked relieved at the prospect of working with anyone other than Mackenzie.

"Maybe you could give Mackenzie an idea of what still needs to be worked out," suggested Paul.

"The most important thing is compensation. You indicated that Ms. Montana's compensation would be based on a percentage of the profits. We need to agree upon a figure, a definition of profit and a time frame for payments," Laura answered.

Now Mackenzie spoke up. "Paul and I can come up with all of that, can't we Paul?" Paul didn't answer. "In fact, maybe we should just plan to have dinner together tonight to discuss it." She shot Laura a look that said she meant business. "Then I'll let Neil know what we've decided and the two of them can get together."

Laura couldn't take any more of this. Without waiting to hear Paul's response—in fact, not wanting to hear his response—she jumped up and said hurriedly, "Good. I'll just wait to hear from Mr. Roberts tomorrow." Turning to Mackenzie, she extended her hand politely. "It was very nice meeting you, Ms. Montana."

Mackenzie was pleased to see a wedding band on Laura's left hand. Maybe I'm wrong about those two, she thought hopefully. "I've enjoyed meeting you, too," she replied with just a hint of sarcasm in her voice.

Paul tried to catch Laura's eye as he walked past his desk. "Laura, we should plan to meet tomorrow morning."

"That would be fine, Paul," Laura responded a bit too politely. "My morning's wide open, so you can just call me when you're ready to get together."

"I'll do that," Paul said as he watched her walk away. His eyes mirrored the frustration he was feeling. Things had gone even worse than he'd feared. And now, on top of everything else, he'd have to spend the evening with Mackenzie. Trying not to reveal his distaste for her would be a challenge. They arranged to meet in the lobby of her hotel at seven o'clock that evening.

After Mackenzie had gone, Paul picked up the phone and dialed Laura's extension. He didn't even know what he would say, but he knew he had to talk to her, had to clear up any misunderstandings she might have from today. But the phone rang so long that finally Candy ran in from her desk just outside of Laura's office and picked it up.

"I'm trying to reach Laura," Paul told Candy gruffly. Hearing her voice reminded him of just one more unpleasant turn of events the day had brought him.

While Paul's desperate attempt to reach Laura

94

would ordinarily have prompted Candy to react angrily, she knew she'd already pushed Paul to his limit today, so instead she answered helpfully, "Laura left the office right after your meeting. She said she wasn't feeling well. Would you like me to try to get her on the phone for you?"

"Thanks but no," Paul answered unhappily and hung up.

I've probably really blown it now, thought Paul grimly. Damn. What a day it had been. And he had a feeling the night would be even worse, especially since he hadn't been able to reach Laura. He knew he'd be worrying about her all night.

He was sitting at his desk, thinking about driving out to Laura's house, when Matthew stuck his head in the door. "How about calling it quits a little early and going over to the club to shoot some baskets?"

Matt's suggestion worked an immediate transformation on Paul's face. "That sounds great!" He smiled at his friend. Matt had come up with the one thing that could get his mind off Laura and his troubles, even if only for a short while.

And for the next two hours as they sweat, huffed and puffed, bumped, jumped and twisted, Paul Brooks and Matthew O'Connor appeared to have no cares in the world.

*   *   *

Laura felt ill all the way home. I must be coming down with something, she thought to herself. Yet she knew that what she felt could not be blamed on any virus.

When a blue pickup changed lanes in front of her abruptly, nearly cutting her off, she laid on the horn and proceeded to make an obscene gesture at the driver. Then she suddenly caught a glimpse of herself in the rear view mirror. It was the simple sight of her reflection, so unbelievably angry, that caused her to burst into tears.

"What's happening to me?" she whispered. She felt frightened and out of control. Helpless.

She couldn't get the thought of Paul and Mackenzie at dinner that night out of her mind. Maybe I've been wrong all along, she thought. I should never have discouraged Paul. But it's probably too late to do anything about it now. No, now that Mackenzie Montana was on the scene, it was undoubtedly too late.

And with that gloomy thought, she pulled into her long driveway.

*   *   *

Mackenzie Montana was a quick study, a chameleon. And she was also quite perceptive and intelligent. After discovering, to her considerable shock and amazement, that Paul Brooks didn't seem interested in her, and then seeing the hold that Laura seemed to have on Paul, Mackenzie did what any intelligent woman of her nature might do. She decided to create a new character for herself, using Laura as the model. As she readied herself for her dinner that night with Paul, Mackenzie silently coached herself. Holding up the suit that Neil had chosen for her to wear for today's meeting, she decided it would be perfect. A suit that Laura Kennedy herself would die for, she thought sarcastically. But if that's what Paul Brooks wants, that's what he'll get. Tonight anyway.

Most people were wrong about Mackenzie Montana—at least about her acting skills. For the truth of the matter was that Mackenzie was, indeed, a very

good actress. Her performance tonight would be proof
of it.

* * *

Playing basketball with Matt was so therapeutic
that Paul lost all track of time. The two originally
planned just to shoot baskets and play a little one on
one, but before long, most of the regulars showed up
and a full-blown game developed. Paul had never
walked out on any game before it was finished, and
he wasn't about to do so for the first time now on
Mackenzie Montana's behalf. Besides, it was a very
close game and he was leading his team's comeback.

Still, after scoring the winning three pointer, Paul
looked a little worried when he glanced at the clock.

"You got a hot date tonight, Paulie?" His friend
Joe had noticed his look. "Anyone we know?" Having just lost the game, Joe was in the mood to give
him a hard time.

Paul ignored him, but Matthew couldn't resist
doing a little bragging for his friend. "If you call
Mackenzie Montana a hot date."

"He's shittin' us, right Paul?" asked Joe eloquently.

Paul still didn't speak. But he couldn't suppress
just a hint of a smile.

That was answer enough for the boys. They were
all over him. Mercilessly.

Though Paul acted annoyed with all the jokes,
incredulous questions (how on Earth did *you* get a
date with her?) and lascivious suggestions, many of
which did sound slightly exciting to him, he actually
got a kick out of all of it. And by the time he jumped
into his Porsche and headed to the Four Seasons to
meet Mackenzie, some 45 minutes late, he was in a

pretty good mood. Not unlike the sentiments that Laura often felt—that as long as she had Christopher and Hailey, she'd be okay—as he sped down Interstate 5 that night, Paul Brooks thanked his lucky stars for the ingredients that never failed to bring comfort and pleasure into *his* life—basketball and male camaraderie.

*   *   *

"Corinne's here!" little Hailey shouted, as she ran to get her mother. While she went to find Laura, Christopher ran out to greet Corinne's approaching car.

The kids loved Laura's friend, so their enthusiastic greeting was nothing unusual. Tonight, though, they were even happier than usual for this surprise visit, as Laura seemed upset about something when she came home from work that afternoon. They hoped that, as it usually did, a visit with Corinne would lift her spirits.

"Hi, Corinne," Christopher smiled as she stepped out of her flashy car. He wrapped his long, skinny arms around her in a sincere, but awkward hug.

Corinne gave him a big hug and kiss in return. "Hey, Guy, look what I brought you," she said, handing him a bag from his favorite store, the Locker Room.

Corinne inevitably came laden with gifts for Christopher and Hailey. She adored them as much as they did her. All her adult life she'd been firmly convinced that she did not want, or need, children. But since Michael's death, she'd grown extremely close to Laura's children and had even begun thinking recently that she might want to have a child of her own after all. The irony of it all, though, was that at the age of 42, and seriously involved with a man who already had children and made it absolutely clear that he was not about to start another family, Corinne was beginning to realize that she'd had her change of heart too late. So Christopher and Hailey were becoming all the more special to her.

As Chris was opening his gift, Hailey ran up and jumped into Corinne's arms for *her* hug. "Hi, Snookums," Corinne's voice emerged from somewhere within Hailey's bear hug.

Christopher slipped on the Chicago Bulls NBA Championship T-shirt that he'd found inside the bag. "This is sweet, Corinne!" he exclaimed, uttering the ultimate compliment. He modeled it for her. "All my friends have been wanting it, but I'll be the first to have one!" As usual, she'd known exactly what to get him.

Corinne wriggled her head out of Hailey's headlock grasp for some fresh air. "You don't think I forgot you, do you?" She put Hailey down and reached into the car for another package.

Hailey was as pleased with her "Tie-Dye" Barbie doll as Christopher had been with his shirt. "Love you, Corinne," she turned and shouted as she headed inside for the phone, anxious to call her friend Michelle and invite her over to play dolls. Christopher, already with basketball in hand, headed to the hoop.

"Love you, too," Corinne called back, just as Laura emerged from the barn.

"You're so good to them, Corinne," Laura said lovingly, giving her friend a hug. "We're all happy to see you. Especially today. A little time with my best friend is just what I need."

Seeing Laura's troubled look, it was Corinne who suggested a short walk before dark. After making sure the kids were safely inside a locked house, the two friends headed off with the dogs. Laura's orange-striped cat followed for a short distance.

They were a study in contrast—Laura, dark and lean, her hair tied back in a loose pony-tail, and in her usual attire of T-shirt, jeans and running shoes, and Corinne, blonde and voluptuous, wearing huge dangling earrings and a flashy jumpsuit. Yet walking down the quiet country road together, silently at first, the two women were completely at one with each other. As only two women can, they'd years earlier formed a bond that would see their friendship through a lifetime of trials and tribulations. As different as each woman's trials would be, as different as these two women were, both outwardly and inwardly, they each knew that the other would always understand, would always be there for the other. Though not born of the same parents, they were sisters, in the truest sense of the word.

Corinne often teased Laura by telling her she was an open book—that the reason she'd never be a good courtroom lawyer was that you could read her every emotion on her face. Today the book clearly was a sad one, and as they walked, Laura explained why, starting with what had happened that night at the sauna and ending with a description of Mackenzie Montana and the look she'd witnessed on Paul's face when she entered the meeting between him and Mackenzie earlier that day.

"Mackenzie Montana!" Corinne couldn't help but giggle a little, as insensitive as she knew it might look. "You really know how to pick them, don't you?"

Instead of being upset with Corinne's observation, Laura couldn't help but giggle, too. "Can you believe

100

it? I finally fall for someone and find myself up against a fucking movie star!" Laura was no goody-goody, but it was a rare occasion when the "f" word passed through her pretty lips. As that fact, combined with the irony of the whole situation, sunk in, first Corinne, then Laura, burst into laughter. And every time the laughter would start to taper off, one of them would look at the other, and it would start right back up. Finally Corinne plopped herself down on the grassy bank next to the road, holding her stomach, which was starting to hurt, and commanded both of them to stop.

"Okay, that's enough," she tried to say sternly. After all, this really wasn't a funny situation at all. Still, she always loved the fact that she and Laura found humor in most any situation. But she wanted to be able to help her friend work this out, and she suspected the short hour she had before she was supposed to meet Mark would be scant time to do so. Plus, she was dying to hear all the details. Leave it to Laura to get into a triangle involving Paul Brooks and Mackenzie Montana, she thought admiringly.

Corinne was trying to make sense of what Laura had told her. "So you've been discouraging Paul all along, right?"

"Well," hesitated Laura, "I guess you could say that."

"Let me ask you a few questions so that I can try to understand." Corinne felt like she was back in the office dealing with a confused client, one of the many who come in to see her on the pretext of wanting a divorce, but who, in reality, wanted desperately to save a troubled marriage.

"Are you attracted to Paul?" In light of her own opinion of Paul Brooks, this seemed like a preposterous question, but still, she and Laura were oftentimes like night and day when it came to this type of thing.

Laura's look said it all. She actually seemed pained to be thinking of him that way. "I'm unbelievably attracted to him," she finally said softly.

"And it's clear that he's attracted to you."

Laura didn't answer. Corinne continued. "Okay, then maybe it's something to do with the kids." She knew this would be a key issue. "Have they met?"

"Yes," Laura said, "they've seen Paul several times."

"And they don't like him?"

"No, actually they're crazy about him."

"But Paul doesn't like kids? Is that it?" Corinne felt she was onto something, but she wasn't sure what.

Laura's answer didn't help clear up anything. "Paul is wonderful with the kids. He seems quite taken with Christopher in particular. They've played basketball together several times now, and they're talking about taking a camping and fishing trip sometime. And he seems to think that Hailey is adorable, but I just don't think he knows quite what to do with a little girl."

"Okay," said Corinne, with a confused expression. "This is how I see things so far. You've got this incredibly wonderful man who seems absolutely crazy about you. You're very attracted to him. Your kids adore him. And he's completely taken with them." Pause. "And instead of letting him into your life, according to your plan, soon you'll be quitting your job at Brooks and never see the man again." Another pause. "Am I getting this right?"

"Corinne, I know how it looks to you, but it's just not that simple."

"So tell me. What *is* it?" Corinne truly wanted to understand this. "Just what is it that bothers you so much that you're willing to turn your back on what could turn out to be one of the best things to ever happen to you? And your kids."

"You just said the magic word." Laura answered. "*Could*. It's as simple as that. This *could* turn out to be a wonderful thing for me and the kids. But what if it doesn't? Frankly, I don't think I have it in me to lose again. And I *know* I don't want to subject my kids to it." She was on the verge of tears, but fought them back. "Losing Michael was enough. More than enough. We don't need to go through that again. Ever."

At last! Corinne's mind practically shouted with relief. At last I know where you're coming from!

She looked Laura straight in the eye. "Laura, what makes you so sure this wouldn't work? From everything you've told me, there's no reason for you to feel that way."

Laura finally voiced the concerns she'd not yet fully admitted, even to herself. "Let's face it, Corinne. Paul Brooks is not Michael." She paused to collect her thoughts. "That probably came out wrong. What I mean by that is that Michael was an unusually loving, devoted mate. He was content with me and our life together." Her words were spoken slowly, cautiously. "Paul Brooks is a sexy, adventurous man who has the whole world at his feet. He loves women. You yourself told me about his reputation."

"You don't trust him, do you?" Corinne interjected.

"Trust him? I'm not sure that's the right word. I'm just being realistic. And realistically, I can't see Paul giving up the exciting life he leads to become a husband and instant father."

Laura continued, "I do believe that Paul is falling in love with me. Or at least he thinks he is. And there's a part of me that wants to just enjoy that for all it's worth. Go along for the ride and probably have the time of my life. But inevitably, it's going to end, Corinne. Reality will sink in, and he'll either go, or he'll stay and be miserable. Either way, I couldn't take it." She looked resigned. "So I've just made the choice that will hurt the least. That's all there is to it."

"Laura," Corinne took her friend's chin gently in her hand and turned her face toward her. "You listen to me now. Please." Corinne drew in her breath and urged herself to be patient with her friend. "You're not making any sense. None at all. Don't you realize what an absolute treasure you are? And those kids of yours? Do you honestly believe that Paul's feelings for all of you could do anything but deepen as he gets to know you better? Michael was exceptional, I'll never deny that. But it was you and the kids who made him the loving, devoted family man that he was. Do you think you're being fair to Paul to jump to all these conclusions and never even give him a decent chance? What has he done to make you so sure he'd be any less devoted, any less loving to you and the kids than Michael was? And since *when* have you become so cowardly that you're not willing to expose yourself to even the slightest risk?" This seemed to bother Corinne as much as anything else. "Nothing in life is for certain, Laura. You of all people know that. But to just give up *trying* is pathetic. It's not fair, Laura. Not to you, not to the kids. And not to Paul."

As Laura lay in bed that night, Corinne's words came back to her over and over. She thought she had it all figured out—what she needed to do was to play it safe. But the result was that she'd been absolutely miserable ever since she started pushing Paul away. So what good was safe if you're still going to be unhappy, Laura asked herself. She thought back to how happy she'd been those first weeks at Brooks, when she and Paul were just getting to know each other. Life had seemed so wonderful, so full of promise again.

Maybe she was making too much of all this. Maybe it was as simple as choosing between being happy and being sad. Maybe she should learn to take things one day at a time and stop projecting so far into the future.

As she drifted off to sleep that night, Laura Kennedy felt confused. But still, for the first time in many a night, as she slept, a sweet smile crept onto her lovely face.

*   *   *

As he pulled up to the Four Seasons' entrance, Paul mentally braced himself for a scene. Somehow he suspected that Mackenzie Montana was not accustomed to having dates keep her waiting. He glanced around the lobby of the elegant old hotel. Mackenzie was nowhere to be seen. After quickly scanning the adjacent lounge, he picked up a house phone and asked for her room. She picked it up on the first ring.

"Mackenzie," Paul began apologetically, "I bet you're ready to wring my neck. I'm sorry not to have called to explain why..."

Mackenzie wouldn't let him finish. "No apology necessary, Paul," she said pleasantly. "I just came up to my room because I was feeling so conspicuous waiting for you down there—not because I was upset with you for being a little late."

This is one unpredictable lady, thought Paul with relief.

After a moment's hesitation, Mackenzie asked, "Should I come down or would you like to come up to my suite and have cocktails here before dinner?"

The red flag went up immediately in Paul's mind. Hoping to avoid what he assumed was a ploy to get him up to her room without insulting her again, he answered, "Maybe you'd better just come on down. I've got reservations for us at Prego's at eight o'clock. We're already running a little late."

Mackenzie answered good naturedly. "Prego's! Great! My favorite restaurant in Seattle. I'll be right down."

While he waited in the lobby for Mackenzie, Paul entertained himself by trying to guess what she would be wearing. He settled on—what else?—spandex. Black, he thought, probably backless. Or maybe topless, he chuckled.

When the elevator door opened he was surprised to see Mackenzie wearing a simple, elegantly cut, white suit. This was, without question, Paul's favorite look. He'd always been turned on by an attractive woman dressed in a simple jacket, short skirt and high heels. He loved the combination of femininity and professionalism. Very few women could carry it off. Laura often dressed that way for work, and he loved it. It showcased her incredible legs beautifully. Just thinking of her now dampened his spirits. But he had to admit that tonight, Mackenzie looked almost as lovely in her suit as Laura.

Not only did Mackenzie look wonderful, as the evening wore on, Paul was amazed to find himself enjoying her company. Maybe he was just relieved because he'd dreaded the night so. But Mackenzie truly was being attentive, even a little demure. The vulgar suggestiveness that was her trademark was nowhere to be seen.

He'd planned on getting the evening over with as quickly as possible. But after dinner, they'd lingered over their drinks, talking for over an hour. Paul felt in no hurry. He was enjoying Mackenzie's tales of her life in the limelight. Enjoying the fact that every head in the place had turned and men shot him envious looks when he and Mackenzie walked by. The evening's mood had also been enhanced by one of the most spectacular sunsets he'd ever seen over Elliott Bay. And not insignificantly, by the half dozen or so vodka and ices he'd already pounded down.

Still, Paul had every intention of calling it a night when the taxi deposited the two of them back at the Four Seasons shortly after midnight.

"Thanks for a nice evening," he turned to his movie star companion as the doorman held open the front door. "I enjoyed myself," he said sincerely.

He stopped just short of the elevator. It was clear to Mackenzie that he planned to see her onto it, then leave.

"Paul," she asked, almost shyly, "would you mind very much seeing me to my suite? I'd feel a lot safer if you did."

At any other time, Paul would have shrugged off her request and sent her on her way, unwilling to let her manipulate him. But he had enjoyed himself to-night. And how could he refuse when she put it that way—that she was apprehensive about entering an empty hotel room alone?

I'll just see that she's okay, then leave, Paul told himself as he stepped onto the elevator behind Mackenzie.

They were the only ones on it. As the doors closed, Paul reached for the panel and asked Mackenzie what floor she was staying on. As he did so, his arm brushed up against her jacket and the clasp on his watch caught in the embroidered trim that ran the length of her lapels. Mackenzie giggled as Paul tried to extricate himself. When he wasn't successful and started unfastening his watch to free himself, she stopped him.

"There's no need for that," she said with a mischievous smile. With that, she began unbuttoning the jacket.

Paul made a feeble attempt to stop her. "Mackenzie, that's probably not a very good idea..." were the words that left his lips, but his eyes—fixed to her partially bared chest—urged her on.

"Hush," whispered Mackenzie, her long, manicured nails continuing down the row of big white buttons, until the last one came undone. Then, with a motion as graceful and quick as that of a cat stalking its prey, she slid the jacket off. It hung for a moment from his wrist, still attached to Paul's watch. But Paul was completely oblivious to it.

Her breasts were cupped high by a lacey demi-bra. Her nipples, two hard, perfectly rounded pebbles visible through the sheer lace that stretched across them, offered themselves eagerly to Paul. Her chest rose and fell, visibly, with each impassioned breath. Paul stood, motionless, torturing her with his inaction. But when she reached inside her brassiere and lifted each breast out of the confinement of its cup, what remained of Paul's already weakened willpower evaporated.

He moved up against her and pressed his mouth, hard, against hers. His tongue probed deep into her

AFTER THE DANCE

throat, as his hands enveloped her breasts. She moaned
quietly as he twisted each erect nipple between thumb
and forefinger. Then, slowly, gloriously, his mouth
traveled down her long, graceful neck to her ripe,
aching breasts. She arched her back and whimpered,
and finally, willed his mouth to its destination. While
he sucked on her nipple, eliciting low moans from
Mackenzie, Paul slid his strong hands up her long,
muscled legs, over her tight rear end, and hiked her
skirt up around her waist. Then he stood and kissed
her mouth once more, while he backed her up against
the wall of the elevator.

This was the position the bellboy found them in
when the elevator doors opened. Muttering an apology
the teenager backed away, embarrassed but wildly
excited, his eyes glued to Mackenzie's heaving chest,
which she made no effort to cover. When the doors
closed again, Mackenzie reached out and pressed the
button to the penthouse floor. All the more aroused by
their brief audience, she pulled Paul hungrily to her.

By the time they'd reached their destination, Paul
had removed her thong panties, stuffed them into his
pocket, and, for the time being, erased all thought of
Laura from his dizzied mind.

6

Back at his apartment, Paul awoke with a bleak feeling the next morning. He felt oddly disturbed. Not exactly the response one might expect of a man who'd just spent an intimate evening with a gorgeous woman.

He rolled over slowly and glanced at the clock on his bedside table. Nine A.M. By now he was usually well into his day at Brooks Productions. Somehow that thought failed to get him moving. In fact, the very thought of going into the office today disturbed him. For a man who was usually up at the crack of dawn—in order to run his daily four miles before setting off, eagerly, to work—this was strange behavior. A man in constant motion, that was Paul. But not today. Today he just didn't have it in him.

As the significance of last night's encounter with Mackenzie Montana began sinking in, Paul realized that he was at a critical point in his life. He could continue on in the same manner he'd now practiced to the point of perfection, or he could do something to force a change that, somehow, he knew he deeply needed. With that thought in mind, this morning his deepest fear was that he'd already passed that critical point—the moment he'd given in to last night's stupor and ended up in bed with Mackenzie Montana.

It all had to do with Laura. These days, it seemed everything had to do with Laura. Just what was the hold that she had over him? A hold so strong that now, clear-headed for the first time since dinner the night before, the thought that last night's liaison with Mackenzie might jeopardize things with her absolutely terrified him.

Actually, deep down he knew the explanation for Laura's power over him, but had been unwilling to admit it. For the answer revealed too much about him, about his life, revealed a truth that he'd been unwilling to face for some time now—that something was wrong. That the Paul Brooks who seemingly had the world on a string, the one who was always laughing, carefree and upbeat, didn't feel quite so happy inside. That with Laura he might just be able to find a happiness and sense of peace that thus far had eluded him. The missing ingredient that could actually make his life as perfect, on the inside, as it had always looked on the outside.

Paul recognized from the very start that Laura had an effect on him that surpassed that of any other woman he'd known, but what he hadn't acknowledged—not surprisingly, since Paul was not a man disposed to introspection—was the subtle sadness, the longing, that had slowly crept into his life after all these years of either short-term, superficial relationships, or relationships that lasted longer, but still did not bring him true happiness.

Somehow his passionate night with Mackenzie Montana had suddenly, unexpectedly, crystallized the growing unhappiness within him.

When it came to matters of the heart or soul, Paul

had pretty much lived by a philosophy that said, if you don't acknowledge your problems, then maybe they don't really exist. Maybe they will just go away. Right? But this morning, he sensed he could no longer ignore what was troubling him. There was, indeed, a void in his life. More and more he felt it. It was subtle, but nonetheless very real. Lying there now he knew that it was time to reassess the course he was on, that to fail to do so could be costly. And instinctively he knew that the cost might very well be Laura Kennedy.

He reached for the phone and dialed the office. When Candy heard his voice, she sounded concerned. Protective.

"I was starting to worry about you." The alarm in her voice was genuine. Paul was moved by her unfailing affection for him. Why is it that the ones who would love you the most are never the ones *you* end up wanting? "You don't sound good, Paul. Is anything wrong?" Candy asked.

"Just a touch of the flu, I think," Paul answered. "Nothing to worry about, but I may not make it in to the office at all today, so if anything comes up, try to schedule it for tomorrow." Paul debated about asking Candy to put him through to Laura, but afraid that she would be able to read his mind just by hearing his voice, he immediately decided against it. "Please let Laura know that I won't be meeting with her today. Anytime that's good for her tomorrow will be fine with me."

Candy promised to take care of everything. She ordered Paul to rest and forget about work.

With a heaviness to which he was unaccustomed, Paul sank back into the pillows. He pictured Laura already at work at her desk and wondered what she was wearing today. He thought for a moment about Christopher and wished that he could see him again soon. And Hailey. He hardly knew little Hailey, but now that he was fearful he'd never get the chance, he somehow wanted desperately to get to know *her,* too. Then, though he tried to avoid it, his mind returned to the night before. To the sight of Mackenzie, nude, propped up against the headboard. To the sound of her cries of ecstasy. It was as if he had no control over his thoughts, as if his mind were determined to replay the night over and over again, sadistically reminding him of... of what? His *infidelity*? How was it that he felt this guilty when he and Laura were little more than employer/employee. Maybe he was overreacting. For a moment, all his old defenses resurfaced. So he'd given in to his labidinous impulses. It wasn't like this was a first. Why am I making such a big deal of this one night? Paul asked himself. Yet, deep down, he knew the answer.

Slowly, Paul got out of bed, lumbered into the kitchen and stuck a cup of water into the microwave. While he waited for the water to get hot enough for instant coffee, he stood staring out the kitchen's bay window, which, like most of the rooms in his house, looked out over the Sound. As was often the case in the mornings, he wore only his jockey shorts. His finely tuned body had the chiseled look of a sculpture. Broad shoulders, with long, muscled arms offset a tight, rippled torso and narrow waist. Paul's thighs were a cross of those of a running back and a sprinter—massive, yet long and rock hard. At the age of 38, he'd managed to maintain a level of fitness usually found only in that rare professional athlete who was still playing at that age.

Once he'd made his instant coffee and a piece of

toast, he went into the living room and stepped out onto its balcony, still undressed, into the crisp morning air. His spirits began to improve, as they always did when he gazed out across the waters to the majestic peaks of the Olympics. A huge black tanker streamed slowly across the Sound on its way into the city. Paul loved this sight. He'd found it's calming effect to be more effective than any meditation, massage or drug. When he'd first laid eyes on this hilltop home, with its incredible vistas, Paul knew he had to have it. And as was inevitably the case, what Paul Brooks wanted, Paul got. At least that had held true for most of his life, Paul thought now rather cynically. But slowly, over a period of time, maybe that was changing—at least the persistent longing he'd felt for some time now would indicate so. Or maybe, Paul thought, maybe I just haven't really known *what* it is I want. Not until now. Not until Laura.

Sitting there, half mesmerized by the view and the beautiful Indian Summer sun, Paul's unusually introspective mood led him to thoughts of his past.

He had an unusually happy childhood. Maybe it was too happy, too secure, a voice now told him—maybe that was at the root of the problem. He was a much-loved, only child. His father was a hard-working electrical contractor, very much the silent, strong type. He'd never been one to openly show affection to Paul, yet Paul never doubted for a moment the depth of his father's love for him. He knew, as well, that his father took great pride in all of Paul's accomplishments.

Any lack of affection on his father's part was more than made up for by his Irish mother. For Isabel Brooks, the sun rose and set in Paul. And, in return, Paul openly adored her. To this day, she was the one

114

woman to whom his saying, "I love you" came with ease, the only woman with whom a hug and a kiss were as natural as drawing his next breath. In his heart, his mom always was, always would be, the epitome of love and warmth.

His happy childhood evolved into an equally happy youth. By the time Paul reached high school, he was Madison's golden boy. Attractive, well-liked and an exceptional athlete, Paul's teenage years were every boy's dream. Six-foot-one by his freshman year, he started on the varsity basketball squad and helped lead the Trojans to their first state championship in 17 years. Paul was the first sophomore in its history to make McDonald's All American team, an honor bestowed upon the best high school players in the nation. By the time the scholarship offers started to roll in during his senior year, Paul had long since grown used to the attention and privileges lavished on talented athletes.

His mother never approved of that—the privileged treatment afforded Paul and others like him. Though she took great pride in his accomplishments on the basketball court, she frequently reminded Paul that his talent was a gift from God. True, it took great commitment and countless hours of grueling work on Paul's part to exploit that gift, but the basic raw talent was, nonetheless, a gift for which he could take no credit. She always impressed upon him the need to be sensitive and kind to those kids less popular or gifted than he. And Paul heeded her words. While friendships with the most popular kids were there for his asking, he much preferred the company of Stan, a shy, heavy-set boy who, when he lost his mother during their freshman year, turned to Paul for comfort and companionship, and Joe, who, as the only Hispanic student in the school, was often ostracized. Before each home game, Paul made sure that Stan and Joe were proudly seated immediately behind the team bench. And on more than one road trip, he coerced the coach into allowing one or the other of them onto the team bus.

Isabel Brooks repeatedly warned her son that the world he lived in, the fantasy world that the most talented athletes get lured into during their careers, was not real life. It was years before Paul realized just what she had meant; before he realized that his world was, indeed, a world not based on reality—at least not as it's known by of the rest of the world.

Paul's college career mirrored the same degree of success he'd achieved in high school. With full scholarship offers to several major universities, he'd finally settled on the University of Washington in Seattle. Back in the early '70s, the Huskies were a powerhouse of the Pacific 10 conference. By his sophomore year, Paul started regularly. At six-foot-four, Paul was one of the smallest shooting guards in the league, but under the tutelage of the legendary Marv Harshman, Paul's leadership carried the Huskies to two NCAA quarterly finals. A favorite of the fans, he became known as much for his sportsmanship and his tremendous heart as for his explosive jumpshot. He was plagued with injuries his final season, the most serious of which was a sprained ankle. While most players would have been sidelined by the pain with which he frequently played, Paul struggled through the entire season, never missing more than a quarter of play in any one game. By the time he graduated, with the character he'd consistently displayed on court and his off-court charisma, Paul Brooks had Seattle in the palm of his hand. And Seattle had wormed its way inextricably into Paul's heart. There was no question that he'd found a new home.

His attention drawn by their calls, Paul looked up to see a formation of Canadian geese just overhead. He watched their southward progress until they disappeared inland, fascinated, as he always was, by the beauty of their motion.

Paul resumed his reflection on his basketball career, which led, quite naturally, to thoughts of the women in his life. Perhaps that was because throughout his life, success with women had gone hand in hand with the success he achieved on the basketball court. Early on, he developed a reputation as a ladies man. Yet, despite the fact that he could invariably have had any woman he chose, the truth was that Paul had never been excessive when it came to women. In high school he'd gone steady with Janice Randall for two-and-a-half years. And his college sweetheart, Rebecca Hall, was the only woman he dated from early in his sophomore year through his senior year. While his teammates regularly took advantage of the starstruck female fans who are always available to a winning team, Paul was singularly loyal to Rebecca. Still, when graduation approached and Rebecca began pressing him for a commitment—she'd been offered a job in her field of audiology in Los Angeles but was more than willing to forsake it if Paul would only give her reason to do so—Paul backed away and encouraged her to pursue her career. Broken hearted, she moved to Los Angeles and for the next five or six years, continued to write and visit Paul. Their relationship did not come to an end until Paul married Kim.

The years after he graduated from the University of Washington flew by for Paul. Still recognized by fans and alums wherever he went, he managed to maintain his celebrity status well beyond most of his teammates. Not that that aspect had ever mattered to Paul. But it did bring him opportunities, and a life that was never boring.

Immediately after graduating, he was offered a position as a sports announcer for the local sports radio station. This soon led to his involvement in the production of several sports videos. Sports videos were a phenomenon just gaining popularity and would soon become a viable business in and of themselves. Correctly predicting this trend, Paul left his broadcast job and founded Brooks Production. Brooks was initially established to produce a string of videos, one for each major sport. Designed for children, each video featured an established sports star, giving instructions on the basic skills necessary for that sport. Sales far exceeded Paul's expectations, and before long, he was in the position to expand the business.

At the start of what was to become a decades-long environmental movement, it seemed a natural for Paul to combine his interest in the environment with his video know-how. Brooks Productions soon became a ground breaker in the environmental video business.

As he had with basketball, Paul threw himself into the development and growth of his own company with total abandon. While he dated a number of women in those days, he rarely saw anyone more than two or three times. Before long, this became a pattern. He'd meet someone to whom he felt some initial attraction, take her out once, maybe twice. Sometimes he'd sleep with them. But just as soon as that happened, he'd inevitably feel pressure to make some sort of commitment, and at that point, whoosh—Paul would do his disappearing act. It was not a pattern that he was especially proud of, but still, it was one that he'd been unwilling to change.

With the company's entry into the entertainment industry, Paul had the opportunity to meet and date a number of incredibly beautiful women. Yet even as he shunned one relationship after another, he began to feel a loneliness. It was easy to ignore in those first years of trying to get the company going, but after Brooks Productions was well-established and, therefore, less demanding of Paul's energies and attention, the void became more real. Harder to ignore. And it was at this point in his life that he met Kim.

Kim. Thinking of her was still painful for Paul. It wasn't so much that he'd been madly in love with her. Maybe if he had been, things might have worked out. No, years after their divorce Paul realized that her effect on him could be attributed more to timing than to his feelings for Kim herself. Undoubtedly she had recognized this. He was at a stage of life when settling down seemed appropriate. So many of his friends were now married. Several had even started families and seemed happy with their lives. Even Benny, the last of the die-hard womanizers on his old Huskie team, had a little baby girl and was amazingly blissful about the whole thing. Paul had just begun to think that perhaps he, too, could find happiness with a wife and family when he met Kim.

He'd gone down to Los Angeles for a screening of Brooks' second feature-length film, *The Earth's Gift*. It was a good year for Paul and the company. Their environmental videos had earned a tremendous degree of respect for their integrity, their unbelievable photography and the effectiveness of their message. Their first venture into big-screen productions had barely broken even due to the limited audience to which it appealed, but its reviews were universally

119

favorable. The movie, a film about an Indian child living on the Flathead Reservation and his struggle with poverty, had been a huge hit with environmentalists because of the powerful manner in which it conveyed the Native Americans' reverence for nature. Soon Greenpeace had approached Paul about producing several educational videos for them, and in the process of working with the fervent environmental group, Paul's idea for *The Earth's Gifts* was born.

The Earth's Gifts was based on the true story of a Greenpeace worker with whom Paul became close while working on the educational videos. The film dealt not only with the politics of the controversial environmental group and the hypocrisy of politicians who wave the environmental banner to get elected, then fail to do anything, but it also told one of the most moving love stories Paul had ever heard. It was a natural for Hollywood in the '80s, as more and more of the big stars were jumping on the environmental bandwagon. And, because of its environmental message, it was a film of which Paul and all of Brooks Productions were especially proud.

Kim Olson worked as an executive assistant to Jerry Gerschwinn, the Vice President of C.N.B., the distribution company handling the film for Brooks Productions. It was Kim who met Paul's plane when he arrived for the screening, and who accompanied Paul and Jerry to the screening and party afterwards.

Very young, just 20, and very beautiful, Kim had arrived in Hollywood just five months earlier from her hometown of Rapid City, South Dakota, with dreams of becoming a star. In the short time she'd been there, she'd already managed to become a familiar face at all the right places. It was at Spago's, a month after she'd moved to L.A., that she first met

Jerry Gerschwinn. Overweight and aging, Jerry was on the downhill slide, but still, he'd been around forever and knew how to play his position in Tinsel Town to his best advantage. Kim was to become one of a long line of young companions whom Jerry helped get established in the industry. Their relationship was not a sexual one. Jerry just enjoyed the company of beautiful young women and the ensuing respect that it earned him. In return, he was more than happy to help them skip a few rungs on their way up the tawdry and pathetic ladder of success which only a few, either very talented or very privileged, newcomers are fortunate enough to bypass.

The moment Kim laid eyes on Paul—the moment he stepped off the plane in his jeans and cowboy boots—she fell in love. In some ways still very much the unsophisticated country girl, she wore her feelings, for all the world to see, on her sleeve. Paul was amused and flattered by her attentions, but at first clearly uninterested. With his recent change of heart toward getting involved in a serious relationship, he was becoming more and more selective, looking at women from a whole new perspective. A 20 year old from Hollywood did not exactly fit the bill.

But still, he enjoyed Kim's company on that first trip. And after returning to Seattle, he did find himself thinking of her often. When she called and invited herself up for a week-end, he was surprised to find himself accepting, and even looking forward to her visit.

It's amazing how much power love, even the one-sided kind, actually wields, for in the three days that she was in Seattle, Kim managed to completely transform Paul's perception of her. She was so attentive, so unconditionally loving to him, so vulnerable and full of passion when they made love. By the time she left, Paul halfway believed that he was falling in love with her, too. Maybe he'd found the companion he'd been needing. Someone to settle down with, maybe even start a family with.

For the next couple of months, they pursued their relationship on a long-distance basis. Kim wrote two or three letters a week. They talked daily. She was very open about wanting to marry him, promising him a lifetime of devotion. Children. A happy, loving home. And for the first time ever, instead of running, Paul listened.

Still, it didn't feel completely right. Thinking about it now as he sat, still dressed only in his jockey shorts, gazing out at the water, Paul wondered why he'd just insisted on ignoring that—the fact that even then, something just did not feel right. But ignore it he did, and six months to the day after meeting, Paul Brooks and Kim Olson wed.

The first year was close to magic—coming home each night to someone, having someone to share each day's events with, making love after dinner, then dozing off and making love again when they climbed in bed. For the first time in his life, Paul felt complete, like he had it all. True, he'd never been all consumed by Kim. It was more a comforting, secure feeling than a wildly passionate one. But he felt at peace. At least that first year or so.

But then Kim started changing. She started feeling dissatisfied with staying home. He offered to bring her into the production end of the company, but Kim's response was that she wanted to be in *front* of the camera, not behind it. It wasn't until then that Paul realized they'd never really discussed Kim's plans, her dreams. Whenever he'd brought the subject up, her response had been that being Mrs. Paul Brooks was her only dream. He'd known she went to Hollywood hoping to break into films, but assumed that she'd now lost interest. After all, they were planning to have children soon, weren't they? It's tough enough to get any kind of break, even when you're able to give your all to a career in acting—to try to do so at the same time you're starting a family would be impossible, which is why Paul assumed Kim had given up these thoughts.

But the day the envelope from the Women's Clinic arrived, all of Paul's assumptions went down the drain. Along with many of his dreams.

It was addressed to Ms. Kim Brooks, but assuming it was a doctor's bill from last month—when Kim complained of the flu and had visited a doctor Paul had never heard of—Paul opened it. He was right. It *was* a bill. For an abortion that had been performed on Kim the previous month.

Paul's first instinct had been to call the clinic and ask if there had been some mistake, but even as he did so, he knew that there had been no mistake. At least not on the clinic's part.

The events of the days that followed were still too fresh, too painful for Paul to think about. For what Kim had done had not only destroyed all of Paul's feeling for her, but had destroyed a part of Paul, as well, the part that had let someone in, that had dared to dream.

Kim's anguish at Paul's insistence on an immediate divorce soon turned to bitterness. Then greed. Though no legal grounds for support payments existed, her lawyer threatened a long, drawn out battle if Paul would not agree to Kim's demands. Wanting to put Kim and all that she represented behind him as quickly as possible, Paul agreed to a generous settlement whereby Kim would be comfortably supported for a period of five years. The divorce was finalized in record time, but the time it took for Paul to get over what had happened with Kim would take far longer.

Though outwardly Paul managed so well that his friends and colleagues marveled at his resiliency, on the inside, Paul was a changed man. For a year after the divorce, he didn't date at all. Instead he immersed himself in his business and in physical activity—every evening he could be found at his sports club. First he'd head to the gym to play some basketball. Sometimes he'd just shoot alone, but more often than not, a couple of the guys would show up, and soon, a heated game would ensue. Then after basketball, he'd work out with weights, relax for a while in either the sauna or Jacuzzi and finally, when he was too exhausted to think—*that* was the key—he'd head home and literally drop into bed.

After a while Paul began dating again, but he'd become so wary of women that it became virtually impossible for any of them to penetrate the thick walls he'd built up around his innermost self. Still, woman after woman would try.

Evenings like the one last night with Mackenzie Montana were always there for his asking. But they were strictly for physical pleasure. That was all he would let them be. And the deeper he fell into this rut, the harder he worked at maintaining his distance, the lonelier he grew.

Then one day last spring, in walked Laura Kennedy. Something happened to Paul that day. Something stirred in him again. It wasn't just physical, though Lord knows there was a chemistry between them. Paul could sense that she'd felt it, too. He sensed that it frightened her. Yes, the physical attraction was immediate, and intense.

But Laura Kennedy had also stirred something else in him, something that could only be described as spiritual. Something that Paul had begun to believe only existed in fairy tales, not in real life—at least, not *his* life. The truth was that Laura had stirred within him the most dizzying combination of erotic, passionate feelings, along with feelings of romance, warmth and hope. Hope. Maybe that was the single most significant response that she'd evoked in him. She'd given him reason to hope.

But now, by his own actions, Paul may have jeopardized that hope.

With a sigh, he stood. Resting his large hands on the balcony railing, he leaned into the late morning sun, face turned upwards, eyes closed, drinking in the energy it offered him. He let it soothe and calm him. Inspire him.

Last night had been a mistake, possibly a costly one. One that he alone must take responsibility for and accept. He was ready to do that.

But even this darkest of clouds had a silver lining, for Paul now knew, with absolute clarity, what it was that he wanted. And though the uncertainty regarding the final outcome was unsettling, there was, at the same time, a great sense of peace that came with his newfound knowledge.

Even if his dreams of a life with Laura were never to come true, today, with great relief, Paul Brooks realized that he was, after all, a man still capable of dreaming.

And *that*, in and of itself, was a gift for which he was grateful.

7

Shawn Long slammed on the brakes, cursing the lowslung Ferrari in front of him. With traffic on the Santa Monica Freeway now at a complete standstill, he reached into the glovebox of his Jag and extracted a roll of Tums. He could feel a case of heartburn coming on.

It had been another bad day. It started off with another battle with his wife, Joan, then nothing but problems on the set of the movie he was just finishing. Now this. God, how he hated this traffic.

Just as he was reaching for his phone to call Joan and try to smooth things over before he arrived home, it rang. He shuddered when he heard the voice on the other end. It was Mackenzie Montana.

"Shawn, Sweetheart!" exclaimed Mackenzie. "You'll never guess where I am."

"Not at home, I assume," answered Shawn, not anxious to get sucked into playing her little game.

"Hardly." Mackenzie sounded even more smug that usual.

Shawn knew instantly that this call spelled trouble. He popped another pill into his mouth and chewed

126

frantically as she continued.

"I'm up in Seattle. Finalizing things on my contract for *After the Dance*. I'm having the most wonderful time!"

Shawn did not respond.

Sounding a little hurt, Mackenzie asked, "Don't you want to hear about it?"

It was the last thing on Earth he felt like doing, but Shawn knew that he'd better rise to the occasion and humor her. "Of course I do, Mackenzie. I'm just a little distracted right now. Caught in one helluva traffic jam. I didn't mean to sound disinterested. Tell me, what's happening up there?"

"Right now, not much. But what happened last night was sensational!" Mackenzie answered, and with that, she launched into a detailed account of her evening with Paul. When she reached the part about the incident in the elevator, she paused just long enough to ask, "Are you jealous, Shawn?"

"You *know* I am," he lied. "So maybe you should spare me any more pain."

"No such luck, Sweetie," she answered, then she proceeded to chronicle the events that took place in her suite. The only thing she had to embellish was the part about Paul spending the night afterward. She hardly wanted Shawn to know the truth—that after the two of them had made love, Paul had turned quite somber and departed hastily.

When she was done with her story, Mackenzie's thoughts turned to the movie. "You know we're going to need you up here pretty quick, Shawn." The 'we' did not go unnoticed by Shawn. "I'd like to start working with you as soon as possible, get some time in together before we actually start shooting."

Shawn didn't know whether she meant this as a

request or a command. He suspected it was the latter.

"Have you seen the script yet?" he asked her, deliberately avoiding having to respond to her suggestion that he rush up to Seattle. The thought of one-on-one time with her, before they actually started filming, was quite disturbing. He knew that he would eventually come to regret having urged Bob Brubeck to insist on Mackenzie instead of Amy Griffin for the role of Ashley Cowles. He just hadn't expected it to happen so soon.

"I just finished it yesterday. I've penciled in a number of changes that it needs. Nothing major, but some of the dialogue they've given me had to go." Mackenzie sounded pleased with herself.

Shawn was appalled, but he tried to temper his response. "Just what makes you think you're going to be able to make changes in the script?" he asked.

He knew she was testing him. While some directors do at least give lip service to allowing input from actors, it was common knowledge that Shawn Long insisted upon total control on the set. Fortunately for him, he'd been successful enough that this did not deter even the biggest of names from wanting to work with him. He was furious to find himself in a position where some mediocre actress like Mackenzie Montana thought she could start pushing him around. Yet, the truth is, he admitted to himself, that's just what she'd been doing for some time now. Ever since the incident at Cannes.

"What makes me think I can change the script?" Mackenzie shot back in a snotty voice. "You know perfectly well why I think I can. Besides, I'm quite certain that Paul will be happy with my suggestions."

"You and Paul are that tight, huh?" asked Shawn sarcastically. He'd known Paul long enough to know that a one-night stand with Mackenzie Montana was very unlikely to evolve into anything more.

"Let's just say that I plan on spending a lot of time in Seattle from now on," Mackenzie answered. "In fact, I just may start looking for a place here. Maybe a condo downtown... or one on this wonderful little lake—I think it's called Lake Union. It's right in the heart of the city. Yah, Lake Union would definitely be nice," she said, almost as if she were talking to herself. Then, she offered, "When you come up, I'll show you all around."

"That'd be great," Shawn replied hollowly. "Say, listen, Mackenzie, I'm going to try to wind my way out of here and get off on the exit ramp just ahead. How about my giving you a call tomorrow? Where can I reach you?"

"I might be hard to find. I'm sure I'll be with Paul somewhere, but we haven't discussed our plans yet. Why don't I call you instead?" Mackenzie suggested. "Besides, if I leave it to you, I know better than to think you'd actually call. You can be so bad, Shawn. Really." She loved to give him a hard time. But her words echoed Shawn's own thoughts—that it'd be a cold day in hell before he'd call *her*—even as she said them. "But I'm in a good mood. No, let's make it a *great* mood, so I'll let you off the hook. Take care, Sweetheart!" And with those cheerful words, she hung up.

Shawn sat there, mired in the afternoon L.A. traffic. There was no exit in sight. That had just been an excuse to end the agony that every encounter with Mackenzie Montana imposed upon him. For what must have been the thousandth time, he chastised himself for ever getting involved with her.

It had all started five years ago, 1988. Of course,

back then, no one even knew who she was. When she'd shown up at Cannes that year, everyone was taken not only with her beauty, but with her charm as well. He'd brought Joan along, but they'd done nothing but fight the whole trip. That afternoon by the pool, when Joan had suggested attending the screening of some French film, he'd been ready for a break from her. And she was apparently feeling the same way, as she was all too agreeable to going with one of the other women in their group when he begged off.

After she'd gone up to the room to get ready, Shawn looked up to see that Mackenzie was eyeing him. At first, he assumed he was mistaken. But she was so obvious about it that, before long, he had to admit it. She was definitely checking him out. He smiled at her once, and before he knew it, she came over and slithered into the chaise lounge next to his.

She was very direct. And he was all too vulnerable to it. That night, she arrived at his room—for some reason she insisted it be his room, an oddity he never stopped to question until much later—at seven p.m. on the dot, which is when the film Joan was seeing was scheduled to start. He'd never experienced anything quite like the next two hours with her. It was so extraordinary, so inebriating, that even though he'd *known* when it was time for her to leave, he hadn't stopped. And then he heard the key turn in the door.

At least he had had the presence of mind to slide the dead-bolt in place when Mackenzie first arrived, which meant that Joan's key wouldn't open the door. As she stood outside, calling his name, they scrambled to pick up Mackenzie's clothes. It was Mackenzie who thought of hiding out on the balcony. Finally, with Joan becoming more and more agitated out in the hall and Mackenzie Montana, wrapped in a towel, out on the balcony, Shawn opened the door.

He told Joan that after a couple margaritas in the hot afternoon sun, he'd suddenly grown ill and had come up to the room to lay down, thus hoping to explain the fact that the bed was unmade. "Unmade," however, would not be adequate to describe the condition of the bed, with the blanket and sheet ripped free and hanging over one side, and pillows at both the head and foot of the bed. No, it had taken only one look at that bed for Joan to know the truth. As Shawn babbled on about being in the bathroom, sick, when he finally heard her knocking, Joan furiously searched the bathroom, then one by one, each closet. Nothing. Finally, her eyes came to rest on the door to the balcony. If he had a gun in his hands, Shawn would have shot himself before she made it out that door. But, having no such escape, he simply stood helplessly watching as she stepped out onto the balcony. He saw her look each way, then turn, and with a puzzled look, she re-entered the room.

Joan's mind was whirling. None of it made sense. Certainly she and Shawn were having trouble, major trouble, with their marriage. But he had always been faithful. Of that, she was certain. And despite the condition of the bed, and the fact that the door had been dead-bolted, if someone *had* been in there with him, where could she possibly have gone? And he did look downright ill, she thought, turning to examine him again.

Shawn was in shock the rest of that night. And jumpy. He kept expecting Mackenzie to pop out of a closet. When Joan went into the bathroom a little later, he even dashed out onto the balcony and looked down the eight stories to the ground, half expecting to see

Mackenzie lying there in a heap.

The next day he ran into her in the lobby. Joan was in the gift shop buying some stationery. Mackenzie walked right up to him, a huge smile on her face. The proverbial cat who swallowed the mouse.

"You and the Mrs. have a good night last night?" she asked playfully.

Nervously watching for Joan, he asked, "What happened to you?"

"Well I didn't want to get you in trouble, Sweetie. Especially after you'd shown me such a good time," she looked at him seductively. "So I just got myself dressed and climbed onto the balcony next door. I must say, your wife looked a little distressed when she came out onto your balcony."

"You mean, you saw her?" Shawn sounded appropriately incredulous.

"Of course. And she saw me." Mackenzie's delight in telling her story was obvious. "I was just sitting there, as if it were my room. Just enjoying the view from my balcony." She laughed. "Apparently it worked, didn't it? My biggest problem was getting inside the room next door. The door was locked. Luckily some nice man came out on the next balcony and called for a bellboy. I just told them I'd somehow locked myself out there." She clearly found the whole situation extremely funny.

Not seeing the humor in any of this, Shawn hadn't joined in the laughter, but he did feel grateful for Mackenzie's actions. This was one crazy lady, he thought—nothing would get me to climb over that railing, eight stories up in the air. He felt indebted to her, and he told her so.

"Don't you worry about it, Sweetheart. Mackenzie will think of a way for you to repay her," she promised. And with that, she turned and sashayed away.

Much to his chagrin, over the years that followed, Mackenzie made sure to stay in touch with Shawn. But, though she reminded him regularly of the debt he owed her, until recently she hadn't actually *asked* anything of him.

Then, last month, after his telling her about his plans to start work soon on *After the Dance*, she called in her marker. Apparently Mackenzie Montana had her heart set on playing the reporter in *After the Dance*. And when Shawn had reacted with considerable reluctance to her suggestion that he persuade Bob Brubeck to give the role to Mackenzie instead of Amy Griffin, Mackenzie made it clear that she was willing to go to Joan with the truth about that night in Cannes if Shawn didn't use his influence on her behalf. In short, he'd been emotionally blackmailed.

And because he loved his wife and was still trying to salvage their ever-precarious marriage, Shawn, against his better judgment, called Bob Brubeck and did just what Mackenzie had asked of him.

He'd been ashamed of it ever since. He, a director respected for his "integrity" and vision, had just jeopardized the success of a movie, one that he'd been enthused about making. One that was much more than just another project to the people involved. He knew both Paul Brooks and Matthew O'Connor personally, knew the story behind the movie. He, in fact, had been so touched by it that recently he'd even refused another film that had been offered him—one that he'd hoped to have the chance to direct—in order to do *After the Dance*. And now, on top of having to live with this his guilt, he'd also have to live with Mackenzie Montana. He wasn't sure which was worse—the shame he felt or the prospect of working with her.

Isn't it absolutely amazing, Shawn observed bitterly, as he sat chewing his Tums, how much havoc one moment's indiscretion can wreak on your life? I really thought I was different. Took great pride in the fact that I'd always been faithful to Joan. Just who was I kidding? All it took was a little attention from one cunning bimbo and I was willing to risk it all. Guess I got just what I deserve. Sad thing is, though, that now it's affecting other people as well. Not sure I can live with that.

Suddenly needing desperately to hear his wife's voice, Shawn picked up his phone and dialed home.

"Hello?" She had a beautiful, strong voice.

"Hi, Babe. It's me. I'm on my way home."

She could tell he was upset. Recently something had been troubling him, but he hadn't wanted to talk about it. He really sounded blue to her now.

"Is something wrong, Shawn? What is it?" she asked.

"Just needed to hear your voice," he answered. "Still mad at me?"

Though she had been angry with him all day long, hearing him now, sounding so wistful, she no longer felt anything but love. It had always been this way. Theirs was such a stormy marriage, yet, when the chips were down, they'd always been there for each other.

"No," she assured him. "I'm not mad at you. Just hurry home."

"I love you, Joan." He almost never called her by name like that. Somehow it frightened her now.

"I love you too, Honey," she replied. Then, needing to help him in whatever way she could, she said, "Shawn, whatever it is, it's going to be okay.

I promise. We'll *make* it okay."

"I hope so," he said softly, almost in a whisper. "I hope so."

*   *   *

As soon as he arrived at the office the next morning and sat down at his desk, Paul picked up the phone and dailed Laura's extension to set up a meeting with her.

She sounded unusually happy to hear his voice and agreed to come right in. As he sat waiting, his mind raced back over the events of the last couple of days—his evening with Mackenzie followed by yesterday's tumultuous day of introspection. Ever since that rather painful self examination, he'd felt a sense of peace and comfort. He was very concerned about Laura's reaction should she find out about him and Mackenzie, yet, overall, the realizations he'd come to yesterday had given him a great deal of hope. And this, in turn, exhilarated him and strengthened his resolve.

And the miraculous thing was that when Laura walked into the office a few minutes later, he immediately sensed a difference in *her* attitude as well. For the first time in weeks, she allowed herself to look him straight in the eye. She entered the room, smiled warmly at him and then—standing before his desk, arms wrapped around her clipboard like a schoolgirl, making her appear fragile, vulnerable—she stood silently for a moment and simply looked at him, deep into his eyes... and into his soul. And he'd known, without a word having been spoken, that for Laura, too, something had happened. Instinctively, he knew that she would no longer fight him, push him away. It had been as simple as that. One soul-baring look, and somehow, magically, he knew that he hadn't lost her. The rush of emotion that he felt at that moment had almost overwhelmed him. His desire to reach out and pull her to him was so intense that his fustration at not being able to do so was physically painful to him. Yet he'd never felt happier.

Laura, too, was overwhelmed by the moment, the unspoken surrender that they both so obviously, so suddenly felt. After months of agonizing, avoiding, denying, it was suddenly so clear to her. So simple. And so right. Whatever the risks, whatever her fears might be, she had finally realized that the thing she feared most was the prospect of a life without Paul Brooks. Standing there looking into his beautiful, gentle eyes, the thought of how close she'd come to just that—pushing Paul out of her life once and for all—gripped her with panic. She longed to touch him. To feel his touch. Her entire body ached for him. She felt the pain—the exquisite pain that only Paul Brooks could bring her. A pain that now filled her with incredible joy and anticipation.

The meeting was brief, with only cursory attention given to business. It was difficult for either of them to even pretend to have any interest in contracts at the moment. And Paul was anxious to avoid any discussion of Mackenzie Montana, so he concentrated instead on inquiring about the status of Shawn Long's agreement to direct *After the Dance*. Finally, he suggested, as casually as possible, that Laura talk to Neil Roberts about Mackenzie Montana's agreement.

At the mere mention of Mackenzie's name Laura's expression darkened. Panic gripped Paul at the sight. For a moment neither one spoke, and then, before she could respond to his suggestion, he reached into his desk and held up something he'd bought the day before for Christopher. It was a video—a basketball video that Chris had mentioned wanting. Paul's relief was visible when Laura chose to go along with this diversionary tactic. She even suggested that Paul drop by that evening to give the tape to Chris in person.

"Better yet, why don't you just follow me home after work tonight and join us for dinner?" she asked.

Paul's eyes immediately filled with relief. He could tell by Laura's expression that the subject of Mackenzie Montana was a painful one. She was obviously concerned about the two of them. She could easily have turned to ice at the mention of her name, and for a moment, that's just what Paul expected to happen. Certainly Kim would have. Her jealousy had forced Paul to censor himself at all times—even the mention of a casual female friend or business acquaintance would send her into a tailspin. But Laura chose not to let this moment be destroyed, and Paul felt incredibly grateful for that. And incredibly sorry, incredibly stupid, for having lost his head with Mackenzie. A sense of dread began to creep over him. But for now, all that mattered was what was happening between Laura and him. And something was definitely happening, no doubt about it.

The rest of the day passed as a blur for both Laura and Paul, with each of them glancing at their watches every few minutes. Mackenzie Montana phoned several times, but Paul instructed Candy to say he was unavailable. Finally it was time to call it a day.

They agreed to meet in the parking lot. Paul followed Laura to her house in his own car. When he pulled into her driveway behind her and parked, she was standing, waiting for him. She smiled at him as he got out of the car. He was struck with her beauty, her grace, and with the fact that her eyes, sometimes

137

so filled with pain and conflict, looked so beautifully alive, so warm and inviting. She wore a short pleated black skirt and a deep blue silk blouse, black hose and heels. Her thick hair, shining in the late afternoon sun, hung loose down her back, with her long bangs and shorter wisps framing her exquisite face. She looked as if she'd stepped off the page of *Vogue* or *Cosmopolitan*. Hardly like a 39-year-old mother of two returning from a day's work.

Laura's horse, Spencer, knickered loudly at the sight of Laura from behind a fence adjoining the driveway. She laughed and walked over to him, softly stroking the velvety skin of his muzzle. He stretched his long neck and tried to stick his nose into her briefcase. Gently, she pushed him away and scolded him, a look of absolute delight on her lovely face.

Paul could have stood there watching her forever. Just looking at her filled him with pleasure. When Laura turned back to him and realized he'd been studying her, she looked slightly embarrassed.

"He was looking for an apple," she explained almost shyly. "I'm afraid I've developed some bad habits with him. He's getting a little too used to my having treats in hand. The other day he even nibbled at Hailey's fingers. Didn't hurt her at all, but it *did* make me stop to think. The new rule is that all treats go in his bucket. But he's not sure he likes it." She felt silly, like she'd been babbling, but Paul was thoroughly enjoying it.

As they approached the house, Christopher emerged from the front door. "Paul!" he shouted upon seeing them. Then, mysteriously, he turned and headed back into the house, only to return seconds later with a huge smile on his face and a basketball in hand.

Paul laughed, handed Laura the video he was

138

carrying and held up his hands for a pass. With that, the two of them took off for the basketball hoop.

After greeting Hailey, who was parked in front of the TV watching cartoons, Laura started dinner—a chicken casserole she'd frozen over the week-end, a big green salad loaded with carrots, broccoli, cucumbers and tomatoes, garlic bread and, the kids' favorite, Jello. Then, while the casserole baked, she took a glass of wine into the living room and sat on the floral couch, from which she had an almost unobstructed view of the basketball hoop and Paul and Christopher's lively game. At first, the sight caused her pain. How many times, she thought, did I sit here watching Michael and our son doing the very same thing? Seeing the two of them playing together had always filled her with joy. They'd been so close—two peas in a pod. For a moment, she regretted asking Paul to dinner, chided herself for thinking she could ever go on with her life, could even think about another man after Michael. Her instincts told her to get up and block the sight from her mind, but another part of her made her stay and watch. And slowly, just slightly, the pain started to ease. Her heart just could not help but respond to the sight of Christopher hustling around his imaginary basketball court, looking so alive, so incredibly happy. And the sight of Paul, so strong and agile, so handsome, as lost as her twelve-year-old son in the game the two of them played. She couldn't help but be moved by watching them, yet at the same time, she felt stirrings of loneliness, fear, and perhaps, more than anything else, guilt.

She didn't realize that her eyes had filled with tears until Hailey's soft little hand touched her cheek.

"Why are you crying, Mommy?" Her dear little

girl climbed onto her lap and wrapped her arms tightly around her. Then Hailey's eyes turned to the activity outside the window. "Are you thinking about Daddy?"

"Yes, Sweetheart, I was," Laura answered in her usual honest manner. "I was just missing him. But I'm fine now. Don't you worry about it. We're all going to have a nice night together." She smiled at Hailey and kissed her little nose.

"Is Paul going to stay after dinner?" Hailey asked.

"I imagine he will, Honey. At least for a little while. Would that be all right with you?" She wasn't sure how Hailey felt about Paul's being there.

Hailey hesitated and then said, "Yes. I *like* Paul." She laid her head on Laura's shoulder then. Laura held her tight and stroked her long hair.

Just then Paul and Christopher erupted into the room, laughing and teasing each other, both of them dripping with sweat.

"I beat him, Mom!" Chris gloated. "Just barely, but I did it!" His face was beet red, his hair matted down and wet, and his shirt looked as though he'd been standing in a rain shower. He had a grin from ear to ear.

Laura and Hailey couldn't help but smile at Christopher's happiness. Laura knew that he would have that same look whether he'd won or lost out there—that the real source of his enthusiasm was having Paul there, doing the things with him that his dad and he had always done. She was happy to know that Christopher wasn't experiencing the same guilt she'd just felt. Maybe kids have it right, she thought, watching Paul and Chris head into the kitchen for a drink, with little Hailey trotting behind, wanting in on the fun. Maybe we adults should learn from them, stop making everything so complicated, so gut-wrenching. She vowed to snap out of the thoughts she'd been having.

Actually, that wasn't very hard to do with Paul there. Somehow it felt so right, so natural to have him there. He was remarkably at ease with all of them. And the kids clearly were enjoying him—at dinner they'd both talked non-stop. Laura worried that her unusually animated, enthusiastic kids might be a little overwhelming to someone unaccustomed to being around children, but Paul appeared to be enjoying himself.

After dinner, while Paul and Christopher sat down to watch the Michael Jordan video Paul brought Chris, Laura took Hailey upstairs for her bath, then tucked her in bed and read her a short book before turning out the lights.

When she returned downstairs and told Christopher it was time for him to go to bed, too, Paul stood up and reached for the sports coat he'd thrown over the back of a chair.

Christopher walked over to the two of them and gave Laura a kiss. "Night, Mom. I love you." Laura was touched that Paul's presence didn't alter Chris's nightly expression of affection to her.

"I love you, too, Christopher," she said. "Sleep tight."

Paul was moved by the love these two shared, the openness with which they expressed it. He reached out and ruffled Chris's hair. "Night, Big Guy," he smiled.

Chris smiled, thanked Paul for the video, then said good night. He started toward the stairway, but then turned abruptly, hurried back to Paul and gave him an awkward but sincere hug. "And thanks for playing basketball with me."

141

Laura halfway thought she saw Paul's eyes moisten. In a voice that sounded a little muffled, Paul called out to Chris as he ran up the stairs, "Don't forget. You promised me a rematch!"

"Any time!" Chris's happy voice replied.

Laura looked at Paul, debating briefly about whether to ask him to stay a while longer. At that very moment, she felt so much love for him that it frightened her. The thought of his leaving and this wonderful evening coming to an end was enough to make up her mind.

"Why don't you stay a while longer?" she suggested, her smokey blue eyes looking deep into his.

For the second time that day, their eyes locked. They found themselves staring at each other in silence. Their looks conveyed feelings of such incredible intensity, such passion. Feelings that they obviously both shared. Feelings that had been suppressed for too long now.

Still gazing into Laura's eyes, Paul reached out and softly stroked her silky cheek. Then, lifting his other hand to her face as well, he pulled her gently to him. After months of his studying her beautiful, full lips, yearning to feel their touch, their lips finally met—sweetly, delicately, almost *reverently* at first. But as Laura stepped toward Paul, pressing herself against him, she unleashed the passion within them both. Paul's tongue parted her willing lips and met with hers. While one of Laura's hands grasped the back of his powerful neck, clinging, pulling him closer, closer to her, the other traveled almost frantically along his back in an effort to bring their bodies, already pressed tightly together, even closer. She moaned as his tongue, now filling her mouth, probed deeper, into her throat.

In one graceful movement, their lips never parting, he reached down, swept her into his arms and carried her to the darkened living room. Slowly he sat down on the sofa, still cradling her in his arms. Both knew that with the children asleep upstairs they would not, could not, have each other, so they sat in that position, never speaking, just holding each other, and slowly explored one another—with their hands, their mouths—until they were physically and emotionally spent.

Finally, feeling a peace she'd not experienced since before Michael's death, Laura drifted off to sleep. Paul held her head against his shoulder, thought about the evening, while inhaling her sweet fragrance, cherishing the warmth and delicacy of her body. Aching to have her. He felt as if he'd been born to love this woman. She was already, inexplicably, a part of him. Sitting there holding her, he knew, beyond a shadow of a doubt, that this woman was his destiny. The aching he'd lived with for so long was simply gone. He knew that it always would be, so long as he had Laura.

And that evening he vowed to himself that no one, not Mackenzie Montana, not *anyone*, would come between the two of them. Ever.

* * *

It was a glorious day in mid-October.

Seattle's winters and springs are every bit as dreary and wet as they're made out to be, but what is not universally recognized is that summer in Seattle—which in most years does not really get its start until early July—does not observe the rest of the country's calendar. For the most part, it ignores entirely the September 21st deadline and dawdles well into October. Seattlites, so starved most of the year for a little blue sky, appreciate every sunkissed day with a zest only they can understand; but never is this more obvious than this time of year, when each such day might well turn out to be the last. As a result, a phenomenon, an unwritten rule peculiar to this part of the country alone, has evolved. On days such as these, picture-perfect days, it is acceptable to play hooky—to skip out of work when, after giving it at least a token effort, one can no longer resist the temptation that beckons from outside an office window.

Thus, in the early afternoon of this sensational day, instead of sitting in her office at Brooks Productions, Laura sat perched atop a boulder-sized rock in her back yard. She'd shed her blouse and felt free, in the privacy of her yard, to soak in the sunshine in just her bra and the jeans she'd quickly changed into upon arriving home. A short, midmorning break to get a latte at Deli Joe's, a deli and espresso stand near the office, had been transformed into most of the day off, when, on impulse, Laura cruised right on by Deli Joe's and continued on to the freeway. And then right on home.

At her feet lay her beloved dogs, Jake and Cheyenne, both in a state of drugged-like, sunsoaked bliss—the ancient Cheyenne snoring softly, Jake's athletic legs occasionally stirring in his sleep. Laura smiled. She strongly suspected her lab was in the midst of a dream, one in which he was no doubt chasing a ball. Only a yard or two away stood Spencer, eyes closed, head slightly lowered, ears in the airplane position—flopped to the sides. One hip dropped slightly. His chestnut tail gave an occasional swish.

It gave Laura an incredible sense of serenity and wonder to sit there with these magnificent creatures, knowing they were so at peace in her presence. She felt honored to have earned their trust and loyalty; safe and protected in their presence. Throughout her life, whenever reality started to take its toll on her faith, her hope, her usually indefatigable optimism, she'd always been able to replenish and restore it with moments like these. These goofy, majestic, loving creatures consistently managed to stir something god-like in Laura's heart and soul, reminding her always of the basic beauty and goodness of life. Life without stress, without heartbreak. Life at its simplest and, in many ways, most real level.

She sat for a long while, then stood and walked over to Spencer. His eyes flickered open, acknowledging her nearness, but he did not move. She stroked his long, muscled neck. It shone in the afternoon sun and was hot to the touch. She laid her face against it then, her arms wrapped around him. He let out a contented sigh.

She closed her eyes, suddenly overwhelmed by this feeling of well being.

Silently she thanked God for this moment. For Christopher and for Hailey. And... for Paul. It some-how seemed a natural thing for her to do, yet she realized even as his name formed in her mind that just acknowledging Paul that way, actually including him in a prayer, was a landmark for her. To Laura, prayers were sacred, never formed impulsively, with-out thought. Even as a child, only the purest of her thoughts and emotions were revealed in prayer. Some-how this signified an acceptance on her part, a com-mitment, that previously hadn't existed.

With her face still pressed tightly against Spencer's skin, eyes still closed, Laura asked God for His blessing, guidance, and forgiveness for the fact that as she aged, these conversations with Him were becoming so very infrequent.

The last thing that she asked Him was to take good care of Michael.

And please, dear Lord, she continued, please, tell him how dearly we all love him. How dearly we will always love him.

Somehow, at that moment, standing there in a bra and jeans, hugging a sleeping horse on a sunny October afternoon, Laura Kennedy knew that everything was going to be all right. That with Michael's spirit always beside her and his love always in her heart, she could, and would, go on. She had grieved and lived in the past long enough, and now, it was time to live, and to love again.

And *finally*, she had the strength to do just that. Yes, it was indeed a glorious day.

*   *   *

8

In many ways, Charles Cunningham's office was not unlike that of other successful, high-priced attorneys. To a piece, the furniture was oversized and masculine, slightly ostentatious. On the inside wall, solid mahogany bookshelves, floor to ceiling, housed the requisite volumes of legal case law and statutory codes, *California* and *Federal Codes and Regulations*, *ALR* and *Corpus Juris Secundum*. From where she now sat, the floor-to-ceiling window that ran the length of the wall behind Cunningham's imposing marble topped desk gave Amy Griffin a sense of being suspended in midair, some twenty stories above the busy Beverly Hills streets below.

But the wall of pictures that Amy Griffin next turned her attention to could not be regarded as standard fare for just any legal office. Looking out at her, one silver framed photograph after another, was one smiling, dapperly dressed Charles Cunningham after another—here a picture of him on the golf course with ex-president Reagan; next to that, Charles with his arm draped around a younger, slimmer Liz; a group shot of Charles with Sinatra, Martin, and Davis;

two shots of him with Merv Griffin, one of which included Zsa Zsa nestled happily between the two men; more recent photos with Clint Eastwood.

Amy studied the wall, trying to figure out what it was that bothered her so about those photographs—made her feel even more uneasy than she'd already felt before arriving 30 minutes earlier. She felt like a child trying to solve one of those riddles: What's wrong with this picture? Before she could attempt to answer, her thoughts were interrupted by Sol's voice.

"Amy," he was asking, sounding exasperated with her for her inattention, "would you mind answering Mr. Cunningham's question?"

Amy looked at Charles Cunningham, now leaning back haughtily in his black Naugahyde chair behind his desk, a smelly, lit cigar in hand, and apologized. "I'm sorry, Mr. Cunningham, I was just admiring your photographs. I'm afraid I didn't hear that last question."

Clearly pleased to have her acknowledge his wall of "trophies" (as he had long ago privately labeled these mementos), Charles was willing to forgive her inattention. "Yes, they're quite impressive, aren't they? All major personalities whom I've had the pleasure of representing over the years. People with great integrity, class. A dying breed, don't you think?" he asked, with total sincerity.

That's it, Amy suddenly realized. The answer to the riddle. But not having time to formulate her thoughts further, she answered, in her typical forth-right manner, "Guess it depends on your definition of class."

Sol rolled his eyes, as if to say, here she goes again. Charles looked shocked. Neither spoke for a moment, until Amy repeated her admission.

"I'm afraid my mind was wandering a moment ago. Would you mind repeating your last question?"

Charles cleared his throat and took a long drag on his cigar. As it often did, the cigar now came in handy. It gave him a chance to clear his increasingly foggy mind, or, as in the situation at hand, a chance to get a grip on his anger.

Sassy little bitch, he was thinking. You don't deserve to have Charles Cunningham represent you, to keep company, even figuratively speaking, with the likes of those esteemed legends staring down at you. Still, business had slowed down lately. All those young, liberal, yuppy types moving into the area, dying to rub elbows with the stars. Classless, totally classless. Yet, they'd started to make a real dent in his practice. More and more, the only new clients he got were those who were represented by his old buddies, like Sol here. And the Sol Greenberg's of this world, world-class agents, were hurting these days, too, so they were channeling fewer clients to him as well. Charles was, in fact, quite surprised to see Amy represented by Greenberg. She had a reputation for being one of those political-type actresses, real liberal—an activist. Not exactly Sol's type of client either. But these days neither he nor Sol had the luxury of picking and choosing clients.

So despite his indignation at Amy's putdown of his revered clientele, while he puffed away on his cigar, Charles counseled himself, reminding himself of the fact that he could use this case, this client. Amy Griffin, though not the hot star she was five years ago, was still an attractive account for any entertainment lawyer. Might give his practice a real shot in the arm. Get him some much-needed press.

With that sentiment in mind, Charles smiled con-

149

descendingly at Amy and repeated his query, "I was just asking you to recount all of your communications regarding *After the Dance*. Before I can advise you as to what, if any, legal recourse might be available to you, I'll need to have a good understanding of just what has transpired to date between you and Brooks Productions."

Amy sank deep into thought. She was not, by nature, a troublemaker. With as many contracts, verbal and written, as she'd been a party to since breaking into the business 20 years ago, she'd never even seen the inside of an attorney's office before. Everything had either been done with a handshake, or, once she got big enough for an agent, by Tom, with nary a problem.

Tom was Tom Price, her agent for ten years, until his death from AIDS two months ago.

It was at her father's insistence that she hired Sol after Tom's death. He'd represented her dad, an actor, too, his entire carreer. Years earlier, the idea of Sol Greenberg representing her would have been unthinkable to Amy. But her dad was not well. And she was doing anything these days to please him. Besides, she'd grown savvy enough over the years to halfway believe she didn't even need an agent. She felt competent enough to handle her own affairs—she was certainly competent enough to oversee Sol's handling of her career. At least until her father passed away, which from the latest prognosis, could well happen any day now. Besides, let's face it, Amy reflected, these days there wasn't a hell of a lot to oversee, was there?

Amy was not your typical movie actress. To start with, publicity and popularity had never been of any importance to her. She truly was motivated solely by her love of acting—not by vanity or insecurity or greed. Problem was, if you weren't young, spectacularly beautiful or popular with movie goers, none of which described Amy these days, the parts that came your way were few and far between. Though universally acknowledged as a fine actress, she had been less and less in demand these past few years. Maybe if she played the games and courted the press even a little, she'd have had more opportunities. But she hadn't, and the few scripts that had come her way recently were dismal. She'd rather not work, rather struggle along on her dwindling savings, than find herself reduced to accepting the crap she'd had offered her the last couple of years.

But all of that looked like it might change when Shawn Long had called her about a new movie he had just agreed to do.

The screenplay Shawn sent her for *After the Dance* moved Amy like no other she'd read in years. It was ironic that the script arrived at her home the very day that Tom Price was buried.

Over the years, she and Tom had become much more than agent and client. In a sense, they were soul mates. Theirs was a relationship as loving and comfortable as perhaps only a friendship between a gay man and a woman can be. Tom was the brother she'd never had. She was the sister he'd once had. The one who'd stopped acknowledging his existence the day he informed her he was gay.

In a very real sense, Tom's battle with AIDS had been Amy's too. From the moment he disclosed his diagnosis as HIV positive to her, through the relatively good years before he developed full blown AIDS, and through the last two years of incomprehensible pain and suffering—the memories of which would never ever leave her—Amy had been by Tom's side. Tom's long-time companion had died of AIDS in 1985. Tom's family disavowed him shortly thereafter. Had it not been for Amy, he would most likely have struggled and died pretty much alone. She could not spare him the pain. She could not remove the anguish from his heart. But never in his struggle did Tom feel alone. Amy was there for him—physically, emotionally, in every sense of the word, there for him—every step of the way.

As would be expected, the entire experience changed Amy. It enriched her. It enraged her. It gave her a perspective that is unique to those who have experienced immense pain. It also gave her renewed purpose. But just how to go about fulfilling that sense of purpose, she hadn't yet figured out. And then Shawn Long called.

The opportunity to play the reporter in *After the Dance* seemed the answer to a prayer, divine fate at work. Not only was the part of Ashley Cowles the first substantive, challenging role Amy had been offered in years, of even more importance was the chance she would have to work through her grief in the only way she really knew how—through her craft—and the chance to contribute her unique understanding to the telling of this powerful story.

But suddenly Brooks Productions was planning to have Mackenzie Montana, of all actresses, *Mackenzie Montana*, play Ashley Cowles! Amy was stunned when Paul Brooks called and explained the switch to her. As disappointed as she was, she halfway felt sorry for Paul that day. He was so embarrassed and seemed truly sorry. In fact, though he never cast blame on anyone else—just made vague references to a "joint decision to go with a more marketable name"—

Amy, an especially perceptive person and very familiar with the inside workings of the industry, was convinced that this decision was not the work of Paul Brooks. In fact, she'd be willing to wager that Paul had fought to keep her in the role.

Comforting as those thoughts may have been to her, and as sympathetic as she might feel toward Paul, the bottom line was that she no longer had the role she desperately wanted, even needed.

So, when Sol telephoned, for the third time, insisting on her seeing Charles Cunningham, a highly visible "lawyer to the stars," she finally agreed to at least go talk to him.

But the moment she'd stepped foot in Cunningham's office, she had second thoughts. Sitting there now, with both men staring at her, waiting for her response, the riddle popped back into her mind. What's wrong with this picture? She looked up at the wall of photographs. With the exception of Liz and Clint Eastwood, both of whom Amy had tremendous respect and admiration for, the faces on that wall were those of conservative, old school politicians or entertainers. The personification of Hollywood. Everything Amy had spent years trying to escape, avoid. Everything she strived *not* to be. What was wrong with this picture? *She* was. She realized that, for many reasons, she did not belong there. It went against her every fiber to be sitting there, to even be contemplating a legal battle over a part in some movie. Still, Amy thought, this role is more important to me, on a personal as well as professional level, than any role I've ever gone after. And I'm here now. Might as well at least hear what old Charles here has to say on the matter.

Finally, she turned her attention, somewhat reluctantly, from the wall of photographs to Charles and, in her usual no frills, succinct manner, recounted the events that led to this meeting. "A couple of months ago, I was sent a copy of the screenplay for *After the Dance*. It was Shawn Long who sent it to me. Shawn and I worked together on *Outlaw* and have talked about working together again ever since. I read it, loved it, called Shawn and said I'd do it. Soon after, I got a call from Paul Brooks. We talked about the movie, the part of the reporter. I made it clear I would do the part. And by the time we hung up, it was my understanding that I had it."

Charles questioned her extensively. Exactly *what* had been said by both her and Paul in that conversation? What contact had she had with him since? Any letters? What about contact with Shawn Long? What actions, if any, had she already taken to prepare for this part? On and on it went.

Amy had little patience for it, especially in light of her instinctive distaste for bringing a suit for breach of contract. Yet, despite these feelings, she sat there, answering Cunningham's ridiculously detailed questions, listening to him espouse legal doctrine on contract law. For as she sat there, she realized that as strong as her distaste for bringing suit—indeed, her distaste for the legal system in general—her desire to play the reporter, Ashley Cowles, in *After the Dance* was even stronger. She sat there, a woman totally in conflict, trying to weigh two deeply felt beliefs, which, in this situation, were totally at odds with each other. With both men's eyes baring down on her, awaiting some response to the options Cunningham had just outlined for her, she finally spoke.

"This is the shits, isn't it?"

Charles and Sol exchanged looks of indignation

and disgust. Charles, hand trembling slightly, lifted his cigar to his mouth to calm himself and hide his contempt for this classless young woman sitting opposite him. Whatever happened to breeding? Grace? This was a sad state of affairs, indeed. *I probably should have retired years ago.*

But with her next words, just two simple words, Amy was able to make amends, to redeem the tarnished image Charles Cunningham had just formed of her.

She was able to do all this with just two beautiful words: "Let's sue."

*   *   *

Neil Roberts was about to hang up the phone, after letting it ring more than a dozen times, when he finally heard Mackenzie's voice on the line. Either the connection was bad or Mackenzie had been drinking—her voice sounded distant, and a little bit fuzzy. The only other time he'd heard her sound this way was the night she'd called to tell him that Ricky Mo had just left her. It had been clear to Neil that night she'd had too much to drink. He hurried over to check on her and found her half passed out on her bathroom floor. With that sobering memory in mind, he silently hoped that this time the telephone connection was to blame for his barely being able to hear her.

"I've been calling you all day," he started, a false cheerfulness in his voice. "I'd begun to think maybe you'd already headed back here to L.A., without my knowing it. Where ya' been?" He held his breath waiting for her reply, knowing even before he heard it that his worst suspicion was true.

Mackenzie giggled, then quickly turned somber. Neil knew immediately that she was drunk. "Where have I been?" she answered in an amused tone. "What the hell business of yours is it, where I've been?" Though she feigned anger with him, she was actually very relieved to hear Neil's voice. It had been a bad day. Somehow it was reassuring to know that someone, anyone, had been looking for her. Maybe even missing her.

"Mackenzie," Neil answered, "what is it? What's happened?" He sounded genuinely concerned.

Mackenzie wasn't about to level with him, to tell him that after her passionate night with Paul Brooks, she hadn't heard so much as one word from him. He hadn't even returned her phone calls. As well as Neil knew her, which was undoubtedly as well as anyone knew her, she still couldn't bring herself to tell him how humiliated and hurt she felt.

"I've been out with a realtor all day," she lied, "looking at houses." Actually, this wasn't too far from the truth, she thought, as she *had* spent the morning in bed pouring over the want ads, and a real estate magazine she'd picked up in the hotel lobby. It had been the one bright spot in her day. There appeared to be an abundance of wonderful homes and condominiums in the area, many of which were either right on the water or had unobstructed views of either the Sound, Lake Washington or Lake Union. And the prices were unbelievable. No wonder half the state of California recently migrated up here. Yes, that had cheered her somewhat. Now she just needed to figure out what was going on with Paul.

This news only made Neil more nervous. "What do you mean—looking at houses?" This woman would undoubtedly be the death of him. You'd think by now he'd have grown used to her unpredictability. Sometimes he halfway suspected that he might even *like* this aspect of working for the fiery star—that perhaps he even thrived on it. Life with Mackenzie Montana was never boring, and if there were ever anything Neil sought with all his soul to avoid in life, it was boredom.

"Looking at houses," she snapped back at him. "You know, those things people live in." This response struck her as unusually clever and witty. Even drunk, especially drunk, Mackenzie Montana was her own best audience. She chuckled for some time before explaining. "I've decided I'd like to make Seattle my home. At least, for part of the year. I'll keep my place down in Beverly Hills, but I'll spend plenty of time here, too."

Neil was alarmed at this news, but he knew better than to argue with her, or even question her judgment or reasoning right now. He decided that the best tactic was to change the subject. He was sure she'd be pleased with his news about the contract for *After the Dance.*

"Listen, I just received the final draft of your agreement for the movie. I knew you'd be anxious to get it signed, so I was just calling to tell you I'd be Fed Ex-ing it to you in the morning for your signature."

Mackenzie did not respond. Neil sensed his words had only served to aggravate the situation, but he did not understand how that could be true. Just the other morning, the morning after she'd apparently had a cozy night with Paul Brooks, she called him and told him to call Laura Kennedy and finalize the agreement. She'd been in an unusually good mood that morning. So good, in fact, that she told him just to get the best terms he could for her, without bothering to get into extended negotiations—that she trusted his judgment on this one. Anything he was agreeable to would be fine with her. "Let's just get something signed right away." Those had been her words.

The irritation in Mackenzie's voice at his news was unmistakable. "You certainly don't expect me to just blindly sign an agreement that I've never even seen. What kind of a manager are you? You've never even told me what my points will be!"

"But Mackenzie," Neil answered, "you told me you'd trust my judgment on this." He knew he was walking on thin ice to correct her, but he wasn't about to let her turn the tables on him. "Anyway, I'm sure you'll be pleased with the deal we've struck. You'll be receiving seven and a half percent of the proceeds. The *take*, Mackenzie, not the profit. This could well turn out to be your most lucrative movie yet."

"I want *ten* percent," the young star announced. "Seven and a half isn't enough."

"You want WHAT!!" exclaimed Neil in disbelief. "Not even Streisand gets ten percent, Mackenzie. You've got to be kidding. Do you actually expect me to go back to Laura Kennedy and hold out for ten percent?" It was his turn to be incredulous.

"No," Mackenzie answered quickly, "I don't expect you to go back to that bitch and do anything of the sort. In fact, what I suggest you do is call the lady and tell her that from this point on, I'll be dealing with Paul Brooks myself on this agreement. I don't need you, and I certainly don't need *her* to negotiate my agreement." She paused and pondered this new train of thought. The more she did so, the more pleased with herself she became for coming up with this strategy. "Yes, I'll just work this out with Paul myself," she repeated. She was not about to give up the only leverage she apparently had over Paul Brooks.

He may have chosen to avoid contact with her on a personal level after their evening together, but she knew he could not afford to jeopardize the movie by avoiding contact with her—contact that she would insist upon—on a business level. And, though her ego was somewhat bruised by his apparent rejection of her, deep down she knew she could get to him. All she needed was the opportunity to spend a little time with him. They were sensational together the other night, and there was no denying Paul's attraction to her. She just needed a little more time with him to wear down his resistance. She thought, for what must have been the twentieth time that day, about a future with Paul Brooks. Here, in Seattle. It was too beautiful, too perfect, *not* to happen. Yes, without doubt, she and Paul would be together. It might not happen as easily, as quickly, as she once assumed, but it would, no doubt, still happen. Of that she suddenly felt certain. Her thoughts continued to drift.

"Mackenzie?" Neil's voice snapped her out of her stupor. "Are you still there?"

He'd have to catch the next plane up there and find out just what the hell was going on. He'd known all along that this movie was a bad idea. Maybe he could still talk her out of it.

"Of course, I'm here," Mackenzie replied testily. "But I'm tired, Neil. I can't talk any longer."

She did sound tired. Sleep was probably just what she needed. And by the time she wakes up, I should be back up there, Neil thought.

"You go ahead and get some sleep then. Don't worry about anything for tonight."

Mackenzie did find his voice, his *concern*, comforting. Even if, as she suspected, they were motivated more by his own self interest than by any real

159

affection for her. At least someone cares, she thought as she lay back on her pillow and drifted off peacefully.

At least *someone* cares.

The last face she saw before losing consciousness was that of her beloved father, who had died when Mackenzie was only five years old. He had been the one person in her life who had truly loved her, truly cared.

As he hurried to throw some clothes in a suitcase, Neil Roberts couldn't help but feel for his crazy, irritating client. Couldn't help but think of her lying alone in some strange city, an empty bottle of wine no doubt on the bedside table.

Couldn't help but be haunted by the thought that what he'd heard her mumble just before placing the receiver back on the hook, sounded very much like a garbled, "Night, Daddy."

*   *   *

It was just before noon. Matthew, running shoes in hand, walked into Paul's office and plunked himself down on the leather couch situated to one side of Paul's desk.

"Ready?" he asked his friend and partner, as he tied the laces on his high tech Nike shoes.

Leaning back in his chair, Paul lifted a foot into the air. The running shoes he'd already changed into indicated his readiness. "I'm one step ahead of you," he grinned at Matthew. "Figured I could at least beat you at that!" he added, referring to the fact that inevitably Matthew, an accomplished track star in college, outran his long-legged friend.

Matt grinned back. He could tell Paul was in a good mood. He always enjoyed his friend's company—in good times and bad. They were always there for each other. But when the two of them were both in good spirits, their time together was incomparable. In addition to sharing many common interests and values—from sports to films to a passion for nature and the environment—they enjoyed a similar, rather offbeat perspective on life, often reflected in their sense of humor. Perhaps most significantly, they shared a long history, one which gave each of them a unique understanding of the other. There was a sense of ease between them, a total lack of the usual jockeying for position that frequently takes place when two or more men are together.

Ever since Matthew joined Brooks Production, they made a point of running together during the lunch hour at least once or twice a week. Not only did these runs provide both of them with a strenuous workout, they also provided a forum for some of their most productive or enjoyable conversations—about work, women, life in general.

Stepping out into the cold, damp Seattle midday, both men automatically adjusted their clothing—Paul pulling the zipper on his nylon jacket all the way up to his neck and Matthew throwing the fleece hood of his sweatshirt loosely over his head. They decided early on that the weather would not be a factor in whether or not they ran.

After crossing Elliott, a rather ugly, congested major thoroughfare, its only saving grace the fact that it affords drivers an occasional glimpse of water, they headed south along the footpath that runs along the Sound, down to Seattle's famous waterfront piers that house a number of seafood restaurants, some touristy shops, the ferry terminals and the Seattle Aquarium. The waters were shrouded with a particularly heavy

APRIL CHRISTOFFERSON

mist, lending an eerie feeling to the sight of a massive tanker suddenly breaking through the fog as it cruised slowly into its destination on Pier 90.

As was often the case, they ran along in silence at first, waiting for their rapid pace to settle in, to become comfortable enough for conversation.

Matthew spoke first. "You've seemed in unusually good spirits recently. What's going on?" He glanced sideways at Paul. Paul smiled at his friend's recognition of his frame of mind. He never could hide anything from Matt. Even as a kid, especially if something was worrying him, Matt was always the first to pick up on it. This hadn't particularly pleased him at times, for Paul had never liked discussing his problems; yet inevitably he'd found that he felt a little better after talking to Matthew. He respected Matthew's opinion and more often than not found his advice to be appropriate. Still, the process had never been easy for him.

Today, however, was a different story. There was no one he'd rather share good news with than Matthew, and he hadn't had a chance to talk to his friend for some time—not since before he and Laura had started seeing each other.

"I *am* in good spirits," he answered. "I'm in love, my man. Madly, passionately, *totally*, in love." Only with Matt would he dare to express himself this freely.

"Oh yeh?" his friend responded, with a gleam in his eye. "With who?"

Paul gave him an exasperated look and answered, "With Laura, asshole."

Matt laughed. "Well, *that* comes as no surprise. As far as I could tell, you've been in love with her since the first day she stepped foot in Brooks' door," he teased, his pleasure for his friend obvious in his smile.

"It's been that obvious, huh?" asked Paul with a grin.

"Let's just say no one at the office will be shocked at the news. But I assume from your mood recently that your relationship has developed into something more than it was."

Paul looked over at Matthew and said, "I finally got through to her, Matt. It took long enough, but I finally did it." He paused again, then continued thoughtfully, "You know, all my life I've been running from women..."

Matt chuckled. "Tell me about it! While you've spent years trying to avoid them, I've spent years looking for the right one."

"That's what I mean, though," Paul continued, slightly out of breath by now, as they'd run over two miles already. "It wasn't just that I didn't want to get involved. The real problem was that I never found the right woman. Until Laura."

"Laura's pretty special. I'll admit that," Matthew replied. "I have the feeling this is serious."

"As far as I'm concerned it is. I can't speak for Laura though. I'm taking it slow—I sense that I have to with her. She's still not completely over losing her husband. Maybe she never will be—completely. But I'm willing to wait as long as it takes for her to be ready for a serious relationship," he said resolutely.

"What about the fact that she has kids?" Matt asked. "Are you really ready for that?"

"You know," answered Paul thoughtfully, slowly, "even *that* seems right to me. Deep down I've always wanted a family—basically, I think that's all that Kim was about to me. But these last few years, I began to think that might be an impossibility for me—if I learned anything with Kim, it's that having a partner you love and want to be with comes first, before having kids. Before I met Laura I was starting to wonder if I'd ever find someone I could feel that way about."

Rain fell steadily by this point in their run. The two men, now thoroughly drenched, ran in place as they waited for the traffic light to change so that they could cross back over Elliott and head up toward Pike Place Market. "Now that I have found someone who I want to be with—for a long, long time—I'm finding the idea of kids appeals to me more than it ever has. And her two kids are great, Matt. Really, great."

"Then I'd say your hooked, my friend," Matthew kidded. "Never thought I'd see the day." He reached out and patted his friend on the back. "I'm happy for you, Paul. I really hope things work out for you two."

"Thanks. I do, too." Paul suddenly turned somber. "There's just one thing that's hanging over me— one thing that could really screw things up with Laura."

Matthew looked puzzled. "What is it?"

"Not *what*," answered Paul. "*Who*. Mackenzie Montana."

Matt stopped dead in his tracks and turned to look at Paul.

"Tell me you didn't!" he challenged his friend.

The sheepish, pained look on Paul's face made an answer unnecessary.

"You did! You dirty dog!" Matthew laughed, then realized immediately that this was definitely not a humorous subject for Paul. They started to run again, and he continued. "I am a little surprised, Paul. Only

164

because you'd seemed so turned off by her after that first meeting we had. But, still, I can't say I blame you."

"Well *I* blame me," Paul responded, making his regret over his actions absolutely clear. "I still can't figure it out. You're right, I could hardly stand her. But I had too much to drink. I was feeling discouraged about Laura. And she was great that night Matt—she looked fantastic, and she couldn't have been much nicer to be with. She was like a completely different person than who we saw before. Still, it was a stupid thing to do. An incredibly stupid thing to do. And I have the feeling I'm going to pay—*big*—for it."

"Does Laura know?"

"No. And I still haven't decided what, if anything to tell her." Paul was obviously very troubled by the situation. "I'm afraid if she knew she'd be gone, once and for all."

"It's not like you and Laura had made any kind of a commitment to each other, Paul," Matthew pointed out. "In fact, had you even begun seeing her when you slept with Mackenzie?"

"No, actually, at that point I'd almost given up hope on Laura. But still, something tells me that Laura couldn't handle it—that she *wouldn't* handle it." He thought for a while, then said, "No, the more I think about it, the more I think I have to make sure she never finds out."

"That may not be so easy. You know how those things get around. Especially with someone like Mackenzie Montana." He hesitated, then added, "And especially if she wants it to get around. Just what's going on with Mackenzie now?"

"Nothing. And that's the way it's going to stay," answered Paul. "She's called several times, but I haven't called her back yet—so I'm not really sure *what* she's thinking. But somehow I just know that she's going to be trouble. Guess I'll find out soon enough."

They both fell into a silence as they continued their run, Matthew digesting the information Paul had just given him, and Paul, his mood visibly darkened by talk of Mackenzie Montana, lost in his own thoughts.

As they rounded a corner and caught sight of their building, Matthew couldn't resist asking his buddy just one question.

"Well?" he looked over at Paul, his eyes full of mischief.

"Well *what* ?" Paul scowled at him.

"Well..." there was a long pause. But Matthew just couldn't stop himself. "How was it?"

At first, from the expression on his face, Matthew thought Paul might just pop him one. But Paul's look softened immediately as he realized that if he were Matt, he'd probably be asking the same question.

He thought for a moment, then, finally, chuckled softly and responded, "Not worth it, my friend. Definitely, not worth it."

Somehow Matthew was pleased to hear that answer.

*　　*　　*

When Paul approached, Laura and Matthew were seated next to each other in his office, both bent over a Far Side cartoon that Matthew was holding. Paul stood silently at the door, observing Laura. More and more these days, he found himself doing just that— sitting back and simply looking at her.

Matthew had torn the cartoon from the Far Side

calendar he kept on his desk. Laura sat reading it, her lovely legs crossed at the knees, leaning with ease and familiarity into Matthew, a smile growing on her face. She and Matthew dissolved into laughter. They were still laughing, when Paul broke his silence. Laura and Matthew looked up.

"Okay, you two," he said. "Let's see that." He really wasn't much in the mood for silliness, but he wasn't about to be left out of the fun either.

Matthew handed the cartoon to him as Paul seated himself behind his desk. As Paul read it, the stern look he'd been wearing slowly gave way to a smile. But as his mind turned to the letter in front of him, he quickly grew serious again. He explained that the purpose of the meeting was to let Laura and Matthew know about a letter he'd just received from a Charles Cunningham. It seemed Mr. Cunningham, a Beverly Hills attorney, represented Amy Griffin. Apparently Amy decided that in replacing her with Mackenzie Montana, Brooks Productions had breached a contract with her to play Ashley Cowles in *After the Dance*. Paul handed Laura the letter as he concluded, "The bottom line is, Cunningham says either we reconsider and give Amy the part of Ashley Cowles or they'll sue."

Laura took the letter and read silently for a few minutes. Again, Paul took advantage of the chance to observe her. He loved to watch her at work. He found her especially sexy at times like this, when she was lost in concentration. His desire for her was growing daily, especially since the other night when he'd first kissed and held her. That night had confirmed for him something that he'd suspected since the day he first saw Laura—that she was an unusually sensual, passionate woman. There'd been no question that night

167

about the intensity of her desire for him. Thinking of it now, he felt himself becoming aroused. He'd never wanted her more. Still, he vowed to himself after that night that he would not pressure her—he understood her need to take things slowly. But some days just sitting there with her in the same room was enough to drive him mad.

Laura looked up and realized that he had been watching her. She smiled fleetingly at him before speaking.

"Well," her tone was all business. "We may have a problem on our hands."

"But neither of us ever signed a contract," Matthew responded. "Or did we?"

"No, Matt, we didn't," Laura answered. "Thank goodness for that. But that won't necessarily save us. Employment contracts, especially this type, where the services are to be performed within a year, don't need to be in writing. However, oral contracts are harder to establish than written ones, so at least we have that going for us. Still, if what this letter says is true, Amy may have a decent case against us." She turned to Paul. "Paul, I wasn't around when you first started talking to Amy. I'd appreciate it if you'd spend some time thinking about your conversations with her and making notes about them. Everything you can remember about them. Try not to leave anything out. Once I've had a chance to see that and talk to you some more, I'll have a better idea of whether or not she really has a case against us or whether this is just threatening talk, designed to scare us into either hiring Amy or settling with her."

"You seem to think there's at least some reason for concern, then?" Paul asked.

"When you get a letter like this, there's always

reason for concern," Laura answered. "As I said, there are a number of factors that a court would take into consideration. Until I know all the facts it's hard to form an opinion. If it's true, as this letter states, that Amy turned down another part in reliance on having a firm agreement with Brooks, we may have a problem. A lot depends on just what terms you discussed and agreed to with her. On how specific your conversations were. Oral contracts are not enforceable if the terms are too vague. That's why I need you to write down absolutely everything you remember about your talks with Amy." She paused, then continued hesitantly, "At least we haven't signed anything with Mackenzie Montana yet..." Her voice trailed off. She immediately regretted her words.

Both Matt and Paul looked startled at the mention of Mackenzie's name. When Paul remained silent, Matthew spoke up.

"Just where do we stand with Mackenzie?"

"To be honest, I don't really know," answered Laura. She looked at Paul. "I was planning to talk to you about her contract today, Paul. I'd talked with her agent, Neil Roberts, several days ago. We'd come to what I thought was an agreement on all the basic terms. I'd gone ahead, based on the talk you and I had last week, and offered her the seven-and-a-half percent you'd authorized since she was willing to defer her compensation for doing the film. Neil seemed very pleased. Then I finalized the agreement, incorporating those changes and mailed it to him."

"And has she signed and returned it yet?" Paul asked. It was clear that he was uncomfortable discussing Mackenzie Montana, even in a strictly business sense, with Laura.

"No, that's why I wanted to talk to you," Laura

169

answered. "When I didn't hear back from him, I called. He hemmed and hawed, then said that Mackenzie was having second thoughts about some of the terms. He seemed to think that now she's not satisfied with the seven-and-a-half percent, among other things." Laura hesitated, then looked pointedly at Paul. "He said that from now on, Mackenzie insists on working these things out directly with you, Paul. She wants Neil and me out of the picture."

Paul's discomfort turned to visible panic. Matthew immediately jumped in to distract Laura.

"Then, what you're saying is that we don't have a binding agreement with Mackenzie Montana?" Matt asked.

"Not yet," Laura answered quietly.

She suddenly felt frightened and weak. It was impossible not to notice Paul's response when she'd informed him that Mackenzie wanted to negotiate the contract directly with him. When Neil had told her that, she'd been annoyed, perhaps even slightly concerned, about the significance of this request. Still, she'd been fairly successful in shrugging the whole situation off by attributing it all to Mackenzie's unrequited interest in Paul. But Paul's reaction just now shook her up. Clearly there was more to his feelings for Mackenzie Montana than Laura had assumed—if mere discussion about her rattled him so visibly. All of the fears she'd discussed with Corinne, fears about Paul and his inability to give up playing the field, suddenly resurfaced. At that moment all she wanted was for this meeting to come to an end. So that she could go home and be with her kids.

Matthew sat there watching both Laura and Paul going through their own private hells. He wanted for things to work out between Paul and Laura. Yesterday when Paul confided his fears about how Laura would react to his sleeping with Mackenzie Montana, Matt had been inclined to think Paul was overreacting. But sitting there today, observing the tension at the mere mention of the star's name, he realized that Paul's fling with Mackenzie *did* stand to jeopardize Paul and Laura's relationship—a relationship which he fully believed could, at long last, bring his friend true happiness. His mind raced, trying to find a way to help his friend. *Both* of his friends. Paul cleared his throat and was about to speak, but Matthew beat him to the punch.

"Paul," he looked at his friend in an unusual way. "I think it's time to level with Laura about Mackenzie Montana. To tell her what's going on."

Laura and Paul both looked startled at his words. Before Paul had regained enough presence of mind to try to silence him, Matt went on.

"Laura, I know that Paul didn't want to upset you, so he's tried to hide the fact that Mackenzie has been trying to make life miserable for him," he paused, needing some time to think about what he was doing. "She has some crazy idea about the two of them becoming involved and Paul, of course, has no intention whatsoever of becoming involved with her. I can attest for the fact that he's been doing everything he can to avoid her." Now he turned to Paul and continued, "Paul, obviously you're going to *have* to return Mackenzie's phone calls. I know how much you hate dealing with her, but apparently it's not going to be possible to keep avoiding her altogether."

Paul, having observed a visible relief in Laura's expression at Matthew's words, was once again composed. "I'm sorry, Laura," Paul's voice was somewhat tentative. "I know that I haven't handled this very well, that I should have come right out and discussed what was happening with you, but I didn't want to upset you. And I wanted to believe that the whole situation would eventually just go away. I thought that having you and Neil Roberts working on this would solve the problem. I never imagined that it would come to this—to Mackenzie's insisting that we work this out without your being involved."

To Laura, Paul still looked too uncomfortable. And why had it been necessary for Matthew to explain the situation for Paul? But she wanted—desperately—to believe what she was hearing—that Paul's discomfort was based solely on the fact that Mackenzie had been pursuing him, and that he'd just been trying to hide the situation from her. Although something still did not feel quite right to her, Laura still managed a half-hearted smile.

"Don't worry about it," she said quietly. "Please."

Paul felt tremendously relieved. Still, he saw the hurt in her eyes and felt sick. And ashamed of himself.

Matthew decided to bring the meeting to an end as quickly as possible. "Well, let's get back to business. I guess all that's left, then, is for you to make the notes for Laura about your talks with Amy," he said to Paul, a false levity in his voice. "Guess there's not much more we can do right now, is there?"

"No, there's not," Paul answered. He turned to Laura. "I'll get you those notes in the next day or two," he said. "Okay?"

She'd already stood to leave.

"Sure. Just give me a call when you're ready to go over them."

With that, Laura left the room.

Matthew and Paul sat there looking at each other.

Finally Paul shook his head and said, "Thanks, Buddy."
He looked miserable.

"You don't look too happy," Matthew observed.
"I think she believed it, Paul—that Mackenzie is after
you. I really do. Shit—actually it *is* the truth, you
know. I just didn't tell her the *whole* truth."

"I hate lying to her, Matt."

Paul paused.

"But maybe not as much as I'd hate for her to
know the truth. I couldn't stand for her to know what
really happened between Mackenzie and me." He
looked pensive, sad. "But I really hate lying to her.
She doesn't deserve that."

When Matthew left, Paul picked up the phone and
dialed Laura's extension. When she answered, he
winced at how childlike and sad her voice sounded.

"Laura," he said, almost pleadingly. "I have to
see you tonight. Please."

Laura was silent for a moment.

"Why don't I come over to your place after
dinner?" she finally suggested.

"Only if you let me pick you up," Paul answered.
"I don't want you driving into the city alone at night.
You've never been to my place. It's a little hard to
find."

"Okay."

Paul couldn't quite read her mood, but she didn't
sound herself.

"Why don't you pick me up at eight o'clock?"

"See you at eight," Paul answered.

He was pleased that she was willing to see him,
but she definitely sounded strained. He wasn't sure
what, if anything, to make of her suggesting they go
to his house.

After a few minutes more of trying to assess what

might be going on in Laura's mind, Paul finally came to a decision. Despite what he'd told Matthew, despite how fearful of her reaction he was, he *had* to tell Laura about Mackenzie. The thought of losing her—which he felt was a real possibility once she learned the truth—killed him. Yet, somehow, he knew he couldn't live with himself if he lied to her. She deserved nothing less than complete honesty.

Yes, tonight he would tell Laura everything.

*   *   *

Paul felt grim, but resolute. Even his customary work-out at the gym failed to lessen his feelings of doom.

As he showered and dressed, he rehearsed how he would tell Laura about his night with Mackenzie Montana. When nothing he came up with sounded right, he gave up. No amount of rehearsing would make it easier.

On the way out of the city, he stopped and bought an expensive bottle of wine—Duckhorn Merlot, his favorite. He figured that soon he'd either be drinking it with Laura, which would definitely warrant a special wine, or, he'd be drinking it alone—in which case *no* wine would be adequate enough to soothe him.

*   *   *

Laura was waiting for him when he arrived. The kids were nowhere to be seen. She explained that they were spending the night at their grandparents' house. Paul watched as she called her two dogs into the house, then locked the patio door leading out to the deck just off the kitchen.

She looked especially beautiful, in an oversized,

soft, white angora sweater, sleek white stirrup pants and suede ankle boots. He ached just looking at her. Though she smiled at him sweetly when she answered the door, her demeanor was noticeably restrained. She looked even more delicate than usual. He wanted to reach out and hold her.

Laura had noticed rain beginning to fall, so she excused herself to get a trench coat. After she left the room, Paul noticed a framed photograph on the sofa table and walked over to take a closer look. It was a family picture—Laura, Christopher, Hailey and, standing with an arm draped around Laura's shoulder, a man, apparently Michael. He'd never seen a photo of Michael before. Seeing him now was unnerving. He'd never before tried to picture the man whom Laura had obviously loved so deeply; the man who had fathered her children. He was struck by Michael's enormous smile, by the happiness that seemed to radiate from him and infect the rest of his family. He was of medium height. Dressed in a T-shirt, Levis and cowboy boots, he looked lean, and very masculine, with a ready, engaging smile and clear green eyes that danced with life. While one arm was draped casually around Laura's shoulder, the other rested on Hailey's head. The little girl, in turn, was wrapped quite snuggly around one of his legs, a big grin lighting up her cherubic face. Christopher, not quite up to Laura's shoulders at the time, stood smiling in front of Laura, who had her arms wrapped loosely around his neck. If he'd been casting a movie about a young, happy family, Paul thought rather wistfully, he would look no more. What struck him most about the photograph, however, what *hurt* most, was the look of utter contentment, utter joy, really, on Laura's face. Since he'd known her, he'd only seen vague hints of that look.

He suddenly felt defeated. Empty. Then he sensed Laura's presence. She was standing next to him, studying his face. He turned to her. His eyes were full of pain. Without saying a word, she reached up and placed her hand, gently, sweetly, on the side of his face. Then she stood on tip toe and kissed his cheek. He pulled her to him and held her, her head pressed against his pounding chest. Neither spoke, but somehow, at the same time they each experienced their own confusion, their own pain, a slight healing also took place.

The ride back into the city was a quiet one. Paul looked over at Laura from time to time, trying to gauge her mood, her thoughts. She was not in a talkative mood. Nor was he. He reached over and took her hand. She didn't resist, but she didn't really respond either. He felt as though he were on an emotional rollercoaster—waiting for that one stomach-turning, head-spinning drop that surely awaited him. Before they reached his house, he made up his mind that he'd tell her about Mackenzie as soon as they got there—he just couldn't stand the anticipation anymore. The sooner he got it over with, the better.

When they finally arrived at his house, Paul gave Laura a brief tour. Usually he enjoyed showing a guest around, as the house was his pride and joy. But this time he hurried through, not even making mention of the views—which by now, were of little more than faint lights of the city's skyscrapers and the vessels moving across the Sound.

Laura said all of the appropriate things when they walked through the house, complimenting him on his decor and admiring the open, airy feel of the house. But there was no mistaking the reserve she was feeling. It only served to make him that much more apprehensive about discussing Mackenzie Montana with her. But as much as he dreaded it, he still had not lost his resolve to come clean. He had to tell Laura the truth.

When they reached the living room, he invited Laura to sit down. Laura watched him as he walked to the wet bar and opened the wine he'd bought.

She, too, was feeling confused and full of anxiety. Ever since their meeting with Matthew that afternoon, she'd been struggling with her feelings about Paul and Mackenzie Montana. His reaction to the discussion about Mackenzie had been so strange, so pronounced. When she'd tried to analyze it, to understand its significance, she'd begun to feel physically ill. She'd finally decided that perhaps it was better to just let it go. Still, it wasn't easy to do.

Seeing Paul helped. Especially seeing that pained look when she caught him examining the picture of her and the kids with Michael. She had no doubt now that Paul loved her. None whatsoever. And she now realized that she loved him with all her heart. It was too late to fight it, even to think about going back. As she sat watching him cross the room to her, two goblets of wine in hand, she knew what she had to do, what her heart was telling her to do.

Paul handed her the wine, then seated himself next to her. "Laura," he started off, his eyes averted, "there's something I want to say to you. To tell you." He paused, trying to summon the courage to continue.

"I know I acted strangely today, during our meeting, when you told me about Mackenzie wanting to deal directly with me from now on..." He paused again, not knowing how to say, how to put into words, something that might well spell the end of the

177

only relationship he'd ever truly cherished. Finally realizing that there were no words that could make it any easier, he blurted out, "I want you to know the truth about Mackenzie and me, to know what really..."

"Paul, stop," Laura said softly, reaching up and touching his lips, forbidding them to say another word. "Please. Don't say it."

He turned to look into her beautiful eyes, which at that moment conveyed to him such a myriad of emotions—feelings of pain, of fear, but most of all, unmistakably, feelings of great love. She withdrew her fingers from his lips and reached tenderly for his hand.

Still looking into his frightened eyes, she continued, "I don't want to hear it," she said almost in a whisper. "I *can't* hear it." She continued to stare, lovingly, at him, while tears filled her eyes. "I appreciate your wanting to be honest with me. I really do. But some things are better left unspoken. Whatever there is between you and Mackenzie Montana, I won't let it affect us. I don't even have a choice, really." She laughed softly at the irony of it, then quickly grew serious again. "You see, I'm already in love with you... It's too late for me to worry about Mackenzie Montana. Or anyone else for that matter... And nothing you say to me, *nothing you've done*, is going to change that." A tear was trickling slowly down her cheek, but she had a peaceful smile on her face. "So, please, don't say another word. Just hold me."

Paul set the glass of wine he'd been holding down on the coffee table, then took the glass from Laura's hand and placed it on the table next to his. Feeling a tenderness that bought a lump to his throat, he took her exquisite face in his hands, looked into her eyes and said, "I love you too, Laura Kennedy. I'm not very good at expressing these things," his voice grew suddenly hoarse, "but, God, how I love you."

When he took her in his arms and kissed her, he knew—the time had come. He'd have to wait no longer to have her. She returned his impassioned grasp with a fire, a surrender, that sent shivers throughout his body.

"Laura, Laura," he whispered, pulling her closer, closer, until, sliding off the couch and onto the plushly cushioned carpet, their bodies touched, writhing and grinding against each other, entwined from head to toe.

She whimpered softly, and as he lifted her sweater over her head, she frantically tore at his shirt, needing to see him, to feel his bare skin against hers. When they were both naked from the waist up she lowered herself unto him, pressing her warm breasts into his massive chest, revelling in the sensation of their skin-to-skin contact. They kissed slowly, deeply, consciously trying to slow themselves. Gently, Paul rolled Laura over onto the floor, then raised himself up to look at her. He'd seen this image of her in his mind's eye time and time again, ever since that day in the sauna, yet now, looking at her lying half-clothed alongside him, he felt an awe, an arousal that exceeded anything he'd ever experienced.

She let him look at her for a while, then she pulled him back to her. The passion of their next kiss led them to shed their remaining clothing. Finally naked, they luxuriated in each other sensually, passionately. Then Laura drew away. Now it was her turn. She knelt next to him and slowly, lovingly surveyed him lying there.

"You're beautiful," she whispered. Never before had she been so moved, so excited as she was at the sight of him. She shivered and moaned in anticipation as he pulled her back down to the floor, gently rolled her onto her back, lowered himself on top of her, and whispered in her ear, "So are you."

As the weight of his body parted her long, beautiful legs, Laura closed her eyes momentarily, lost in an anticipation that dizzied and delighted her.

"Look at me, Laura," his voice commanded, softly, almost in a whisper. He wanted to see the pleasure he was about to give her, to be able to read it on her face. And as he at last entered her, as their bodies became one and they discovered in each other a pleasure and a passion beyond their wildest dreams, her eyes told him what he wanted to know.

The climax he brought her to reverberated throughout every fiber of her body, forcing her to cry out in ecstasy, as she clinged to him, pulling him deeper and deeper with every thrust, clinging to him with a force, a strength, that surprised and excited him. Their bodies, moving now in perfect synchronization, accelerated in rhythm until his grasp, too, grew tighter. She felt him catch his breath and, finally, heard his moans, as he exploded inside her.

They lay, completely spent, for several minutes, still clinging to each other, each feeling the other's pounding heart. When Paul raised himself up to look at Laura, he saw a trail of tears down each of her cheeks, but one look in her eyes and he knew that they had been tears of immense pleasure and joy—tears of unparalleled passion, not of sadness.

Her eyes welling up again, Laura looked at him and said quietly, emotionally, "Thank you."

His finger traced the wet path from her eye to the

pillow he'd moments earlier pulled off the couch and placed tenderly under her head. She smiled at him, then reached up and gently stroked his face.

He pulled a soft afghan off the arm of the couch, covered her as she lay curled on her side, and slid up against her under the blanket.

Then, nestled together like a couple of well-fed newborn kittens, they drifted off to sleep.

9

Now that the filming of *After the Dance* was set to start within the month, Matthew O'Connor was totally immersed in pre-production planning. For many weeks, he'd been putting in 16 to 18-hour days, scouting locations in Seattle, where most of the scenes from the movie would be shot, and flying back and forth to L.A. to help in the casting of the film's major characters. He was exhausted, but happily so.

In the months between finishing the screenplay and starting pre-production, he'd grown increasingly anxious and frustrated. Though very cerebral in one sense, Matthew had always had a need to stay busy, to be productive. Never had that need been more pronounced than during the last couple of years—since Colleen's death. And as emotionally involved as he was in making *After the Dance*, the idle time between writing the screenplay and actually beginning work on production had driven him crazy. So—though he was feeling the physical strain of the long days he'd been putting in for the past few weeks—mentally, emotionally, he was thriving on finally getting started on the project.

One Monday morning in early November, he sat on an airplane bound for Los Angeles, poring over the sports page of the *Seattle Post Intelligencer*. If everything went as planned, this was to be one of his final trips to Los Angeles. He'd already flown down to observe screen tests for the roles of his mother and father, as well as one for the role of himself—that had been a little unsettling, he admitted, reflecting upon the actors that had been cast so far.

Overall, he was very pleased. Marjorie Shane, an experienced and much respected character actress in her late 50's had been cast as Mrs. O'Connor. Though physically Marjorie did not bare any resemblance to Matthew and Colleen's mother, there was a quality about her—a gentleness and compassion—that reminded Matthew so much of their mother that he was able to overlook the physical differences and immediately gave his approval for Marjorie for the role. After she'd been cast, Marjorie asked Matthew if he'd be willing to spend some time with her, to help her learn all that she could about the O'Connor family. Matthew arranged for his mother to fly down and spend time with Marjorie the following week, but Marjorie seemed especially eager to learn about the O'Connor matriarch from one of her children, so he'd spent the better part of the next three days with her, answering the most detailed, often intimate, questions about his family life as a child. By the end of their time together, Matthew was not only thoroughly impressed with Marjorie's professionalism and insight, but he'd grown very fond of her as well. Yes, he thought now, as he stared out the window of the airplane at the sight of an eerie looking, flat-topped Mt. St. Helens below, Marjorie was perfect for the role of his mother.

Casting the role of his father had been somewhat

more difficult, but overall, Matthew again felt that they'd made the best choice in settling upon Tom Brady. Tom actually did bare a striking resemblance to Matthew's father. What troubled Matthew most about Tom, however, was that, in contrast to his affable father, Tom had come across as quite reserved when Matthew first met him in Bob Moore's office.

Bob Moore was the casting director. Matthew had stopped by his office the day before the screen tests were scheduled to begin, just as Bob happened to be interviewing Tom Brady. Matthew's first impression of Tom was not that favorable; however, two days later when he viewed the three screen tests Bob filmed for him, Matthew had to reevaluate his opinion of Tom Brady. On film, he'd come alive, and Matthew had been impressed not only with his physical resemblance to his father, but with Tom's newfound warmth and animation as well.

For Matthew, the most difficult part to cast so far was that of himself. All of the actors Bob Moore lined up to play his part were relative unknowns, and all of them seemed quite talented. But Matthew had trouble identifying with any of them, either finding them too handsome, too frail, too... Let's face it, he chuckled to himself, you're a tough act to play. Finally, not able to trust his own objectivity, he left the matter in Bob's hands, and now, some two weeks later, he'd grown more used to the idea of seeing the young man Bob eventually chose to portray him in the movie. After all, his role was really not a pivotal one. Clearly, the major roles were those of Colleen and the reporter, Ashley Cowles.

With this in mind, his thoughts turned to Mackenzie Montana. While he certainly was not *happy* with the turn of events that resulted in Mackenzie playing

Ashley Cowles, curiously Matthew's reaction to the idea had never been as negative as Paul's—or as that of any of his other cohorts at Brooks Productions, for that matter. He'd wondered why this was true. If his only criteria were choosing the best actress for the role, certainly Amy Griffin would have to be Matthew's first choice. In light of what this film meant to him, of the fact that it portrayed such a personal, emotional story for him, one would think that that criteria would be the single overriding one for Matthew. Yet, after meeting her, he had to admit that his resistance to Mackenzie was at least slightly diminished. For in truth, Mackenzie Montana had struck a chord somewhere deep within Matthew. Matthew was such a believer in the good in life, in the inherent virtue of every human being, that despite what he'd seen of Mackenzie thus far, he sensed that deep inside, well hidden by her crass and calloused demeanor, lay at least a few grains of decency, perhaps even of vulnerability. And there was something in him that made him want to dig down and find those grains, to nurture them. Her beauty and raw sexuality made that challenge all the more appealing to him. And so, though professionally he knew that Amy Griffin, by all rights, should be playing Ashley Cowles in *After the Dance*, on a personal level a part of Matthew wanted to believe things would work out all right with Mackenzie.

But the role with which he was most preoccupied today was that of his sister, Colleen. The purpose of this trip was to view two screen tests Bob Moore had filmed the previous week. Matthew and Bob had held numerous meetings and long distance conversations over the past few weeks in which Matthew described his sister at great length and tried to communicate to

Bob the attributes he felt to be of utmost importance in the actress who played Colleen. He'd appreciated the fact that Bob took this assignment to heart—so much so that he'd interviewed well over 50 young women before finally narrowing it down to the two whom Matthew would view on film today. Though Bob sounded characteristically restrained in describing these two to Matt over the week-end, Matthew sensed a particular excitement when Bob spoke of one of them, Sherry Falconer. Matthew was both nervous and enthused about today's screening. So much rode on this one role. If neither of these girls met with his approval, it was likely that the start date scheduled for shooting would have to be delayed. And that could prove catastrophic.

He was scheduled to view the two screen tests later that afternoon. Glancing at his watch he decided that he had plenty of time to check into his hotel and have lunch before heading over to Bob Moore's. As usual, he'd carried both his bags onto the plane, to avoid having to wait for them at the other end. Stepping out into the unusually warm November air, he flagged down a cab and instructed the driver to take him to Century Plaza.

The Plaza was Matthew's favorite hotel. Today he was staying in the Tower, a recent addition to the grand old establishment. His room, on the twenty first floor, was situated in the southwest corner of the building, providing Matthew magnificent views from both balconies. Though a distinct layer of smog hung over the city, the hot midday California sun was more than Matthew could resist. He shed his shirt and pulled a chair out onto the balcony for a few minutes of sun and relaxation.

Immediately below him, workmen were putting

the finishing touches on what looked to be very exclusive, absolutely massive, homes. Their adobe style exteriors and red terra-cotta tiled roofs epitomized the chicest in Southern California architecture. Matthew was struck by the contrast between these showy homes and the architectural styles he'd already grown used to in the Northwest. He wondered just what outrageous price tags would be put on these new structures. Whatever the price, someone would no doubt be willing to pay. This was high-end real estate. Very high end. Beverly Hills. Somehow he felt out of place, and his life there—his years before Colleen's death—suddenly seemed unreal, almost like it had never really happened. While he'd been enjoying his recent trips back, he felt fortunate to have escaped. Had it not been for his sister's death, he probably never would have. Thanks, Sunshine, he silently whispered to his sister.

He was startled out of his reflections by the phone's ring. It was Shawn Long. Matthew was pleased to hear from him. The two men had gotten to know each other quite well since starting work on the movie. They'd hit it off right from the start.

"Just thought I'd see if you'd like a ride over to the screenings," Shawn offered, after they'd greeted each other.

"I'm not quite ready to head over to Bob's office yet," Matthew responded. "I was just about to run down and get a quick bite to eat. I wouldn't want to hold you up, so why don't I just take a cab and meet you there?"

"Nonsense," Shawn replied. "I haven't eaten yet either. I've got to swing by a sporting goods shop in Hollywood on my way to Bob's. Why don't I just pick you up now, and we can grab a quick lunch at the Roosevelt? I'll call Bob and tell him we might be a few minutes late." He hesitated, then added, "Actually, this way, we'll have a chance to talk a little bit, too."

"Anything wrong?" Matthew asked, picking up on an underlying strain in Shawn's voice.

"Let's just wait til I see you," Shawn replied, confirming Matt's suspicions. "Why don't you meet me in the lobby? I'm already in my car—probably only five minutes away."

"I'll be there," Matthew answered.

As he rode the elevator down to the lobby, he wondered what might be bothering Shawn. He'd heard that Shawn was a true perfectionist, that he could be very difficult to work with; however, so far Matthew had found him to be an especially easygoing, cooperative person. Of course, we haven't really started filming yet, Matthew reminded himself. Maybe I'm about to see the side of Shawn I've only heard rumors about so far.

While he waited for Shawn to arrive, Matthew admired the opulent decor of the grand old hotel. Not exactly his taste, he thought, but still he could not help but appreciate the fine art and extravagant touches that greeted his eyes wherever they roamed. It almost reminded him of a museum, or even a castle. While waiting for Shawn, he enjoyed the opportunity to people-watch—after all, people-watching at the Century Plaza was people-watching at its best. His previous visit, he'd ridden up the elevator with the Prince Aga Khan, then the next evening dined at a table next to that of ex-President and Mrs. Reagan. The lobby, especially in the evening, was always adorned with glamorous looking couples—most of whom appeared to be part of the movie industry. But Matthew was particularly fascinated with people of great power, like the Prince—far more so than he was with movie people. Perhaps that was because he'd been in the industry a while and had become somewhat jaded. After all, the movie industry was saturated with attention-hungry egos, and beautiful faces and bodies striving to be recognized. And, with the exception of the very few who truly were not in the business for the fanfare, most in the industry were pathetically transparent about their need for attention. To Matthew, the truly powerful—be they politicians or people of great wealth—many of whom frequented the Century Plaza, had a greater sense of mystery about them.

Before long Matthew saw Shawn hurry through the lobby. He'd double-parked his sleek black Jag in the hotel's drive. Extending his right arm to greet Matthew with a firm handshake, he steered Matt back outside and into his car.

While driving, their conversation was light. They talked a bit about the actors they'd cast so far. Shawn, like Matthew, was pleased with the casting. They discussed the previous night's Lakers' game—Shawn was a season-ticket holder and entertained Matthew with first-hand stories of "Show Time."

They headed toward the intersection of Hollywood and Highland, then parked near a sporting goods shop. While Shawn ran inside for his package, Matthew walked up one side of the street, then crossed over and returned to the shop, all the while reading the names of Hollywood legends engraved in the stars imbedded in the sidewalk. As long as he'd lived in the Los Angeles area, he'd never taken the time to stroll the world famous Walk of Fame. Feeling very much like a tourist, he nonetheless enjoyed himself and was quite impressed. Bing Crosby, Charlie Chaplin, Jim

Healy, Marilyn Monroe, the recent addition of Sophia Loren... The star-studded sidewalk extended as far as his eyes could discern, reminding Matthew of the incredible talent of these people and the tremendous fascination the public had with them.

When Shawn emerged from the shop, he was smiling. "What do you think?" he asked, holding up a Lakers' jersey, with the number 32 on it. As Matt looked closer, he could see an autograph scrawled across the left shoulder. "Magic" was all that it said, but that one word said a lot. Magic Johnson—a basketball legend whose retirement in 1991 had stunned and saddened the world. Now, as a spokesperson for AIDS awareness, Magic was a bigger hero than ever. There was talk that he would one day be back with the Lakers—either as a coach or owner. Matt was suitably impressed.

"How'd you manage to get that?" he grinned back at Shawn, who was clearly pleased with himself.

"I'm friendly with the owner of the shop, who just happens to have gone to high school back in Michigan with Magic," he said, nodding in the direction of the door he'd just exited. "Paul called me a while ago and asked me if I could get Magic's autograph. I guess he knows some kid who's a big fan. So I asked my friend here, Joe, whether he could help. Last week I saw Joe at the game, and he told me to stop by and pick something up. I was hoping this was the something." He surveyed it again, then handed it to Matthew. "Here, why don't you take it back with you and give it to Paul?"

"Sure," said Matthew, folding the shirt and sticking it under his arm as they began walking down the street toward the Roosevelt. "I'm sure I know who Paul got this for." He smiled at the lengths to which

Paul was willing to go to please Laura's son.

Noting the look on his companion's face, Shawn asked, "Anyone I might know?"

"No," answered Matt. "Paul has a new lady friend. She's the company's attorney—a really great lady. I'm sure it's for her son. Paul seems really fond of him."

"Well, that's not quite the picture Mackenzie's been painting for me," answered Shawn, looking more than a little surprised by this revelation.

"Mackenzie?" It was Matt's turn to be surprised. "Do you mean to tell me Mackenzie Montana has been talking to you about Paul?" He hesitated for a moment, then sighed, "I should have known she wouldn't keep her mouth shut."

"I'll say she's been talking about Paul," Shawn continued. "Plenty. In fact, that's one of the things I wanted to talk to you about. To hear her tell it, the two of them are ready to settle down together. She's told me she's moving up there to Seattle. Every other sentence is about her and Paul." He paused. "But, you know, it just didn't sit right with me. I could never see Paul getting serious with someone like that. But you never know. The thing that really gets me is she's been using that—her relationship with Paul—to play heavy-handed with me. Sticking her nose into things that she has no business getting involved in, all under the guise of being Paul's girlfriend, his 'partner.'" Thinking of Mackenzie's manipulative games, Shawn grew angrier by the moment. "That bitch is enough to..."

Matthew looked at Shawn, but remained silent. It struck him as odd that Shawn had let Mackenzie go as far as he apparently had. This certainly was not the Shawn Long he'd heard so much about.

Over lunch, Matthew came to realize just why Shawn was as upset as he was by Mackenzie. Shawn, feeling he could trust Matthew and also needing a confidant, confessed his dalliance with Mackenzie and disclosed her veiled threats to tell his wife what had happened between them. He went on to tell Shawn of the numerous calls he'd received from Mackenzie recently. She'd been making his life miserable, holding their secret over his head (with that leverage buttressed by her imagined relationship with Paul), using it to meddle in his directorial decisions, always trying to inject her own interests into them.

"Hell, " Shawn added, as he was concluding his story, "she even insisted on being at the screen tests for the role of Colleen—as if she had some voice in the casting. I gave Bob Moore firm instructions not to give her any information whatsoever on who's being tested and when. But knowing her, it wouldn't surprise me one bit to have her show up today at the viewing."

The strain he'd been feeling as a result of Mackenzie Montana's blackmail was very obvious.

Matt sat there taking in Shawn's story thoughtfully. He felt sorry for Shawn. He was clearly a good man, one who, in a weak moment, had done something he'd lived to regret for years. But Matt's real concern at that moment was for Paul. Clearly, Mackenzie Montana could be big trouble. When Paul had said just that, Matt had thought he was overreacting. But now he was alarmed. Alarmed for Paul and for Shawn. And concerned about what havoc she might wreak on his cherished movie. For a movie to be successful—especially this movie—there needed to be true harmony on the set. True, there was an occasional exception to this rule—he'd heard rumors about

192

the nightmares on the set of *Hook*, which turned out to be successful enough. But Matthew suddenly felt a foreboding about the fate of *After the Dance*. Mackenzie Montana had to be stopped.

After more discussion of the situation, Matthew and Shawn decided it was imperative that Shawn fly up to Seattle in the next few days to meet with Paul. They discussed the advisability of including Bob Brubeck in that meeting, but they decided to wait and hear Paul's thoughts before dragging the movie's financier into the picture.

As Matthew and Shawn climbed back into the car and headed over to see the films of the two screen tests, each was lost in thoughts revolving around Mackenzie Montana and the commotion she was causing in so many lives.

Matt was relieved to get to Bob Moore's offices, ready to be distracted from the worries his conversation with Shawn had prompted. Bob seemed in an unusually good mood, greeting them each with a hearty handshake and ready smile. He wasted no time in ushering them into the small viewing room down the hall from his office. He was clearly anxious to get started.

Matt felt better already, felt a strong sense of anticipation, of excitement, as the room darkened and the screen lit up. The words "Screen Test, *After the Dance*, Role of Colleen O'Connor—Sherry Falconer," flashed before them. Then, suddenly, Sherry Falconer's image filled the screen. Matthew caught his breath. She was absolutely lovely, with clear, expressive eyes, a sprinkling of freckles across her cheeks and up-turned nose, and a halo of shoulder-length auburn waves. A true Irish beauty. The resemblance to his little sister was so strong as to cause him to shiver.

He sat spellbound, watching her enact a scene from the movie in which Colleen was getting dressed for her Senior Prom. He was overwhelmed with emotion. Bob Moore, who had been shooting anxious glances at him ever since the room darkened, knew at once that his instincts had been right. They'd found Colleen.

Matthew was so overcome that, when the room's lights first came back on, he was unable to speak. Both Shawn and Bob recognized this and excused themselves from the room to give him a moment of privacy. He sat there for some time, unable to control the wave of sentiments stirred up by the performance he'd just witnessed. He'd expected to be moved today, but he hadn't prepared himself for the strength of this reaction. For a moment, the pain he felt was as pointed, as fresh, as the agony he'd experienced immediately after Colleen's death—what he'd just seen had brought it all flooding back so intensely that he was frightened by it. Yet, as unsettling as it had been to sit and watch this realistic portrayal of his beloved little sister, it was equally exciting to him. Matthew always believed that the actress who played Colleen held in her hands the power to elevate this movie from mere entertainment to a message—and a powerful one at that, perhaps one of the most important messages of the decade. And that had always been Matthew's most fervent wish for *After the Dance*.

When Shawn and Bob returned after several more minutes, Matthew had regained his composure. He looked up, smiled at Bob and shook his head in astonishment. Then he addressed him.

"What can I say?" he asked, reaching out and resting a hand on the casting director's shoulder. Looking Bob straight in the eye, with a look that conveyed both wonder and gratitude, he said, "She's perfect, Bob. Absolutely perfect."

Bob's usually serious face erupted in a huge smile. "I was hoping you'd be pleased."

"Pleased!," laughed Matt. "Pleased? I'm *thrilled*!"

"So am I," offered Shawn. "You've done a great job, Bob."

The conscientious casting director was touched by both men's response. He always took each project he worked on to heart, but never more so than this one. The affirmation he felt at this moment, the thrill of finding the perfect person to give life to a script, was the reason he was in this business.

He looked at the two men and asked, "Want to take a look at the other one?" referring to the second screen test he'd filmed. In his heart, he'd known all along that Sherry Falconer was right for the part. He'd struggled for some time with the decision of which test to run first and had finally decided to go for the impact of running Sherry's test first—strongly suspecting that the second test would never even be seen.

He was right. Without a moment's hesitation, the other two men chose not to view the second test. In their minds, Sherry Falconer already *was* Colleen. To try to visualize anyone else in the role was now inconceivable.

*   *   *

Two days later, as he once again sat on an airplane poring over a sports page, this time the *L.A. Times*, Matthew paused to reflect on what had transpired on this trip to Los Angeles. He felt tremendous relief at having cast Sherry Falconer in the role of Colleen. And he was pleased with casting for the other members of his family, himself included. But he was not without apprehension, for he sensed a storm cloud hanging over the movie. A storm cloud in the person of Mackenzie Montana.

And soon he would learn that his premonition was, indeed, valid. Little did Matthew know what had transpired in his absence.

10

Amy Griffin knelt on the floor of the giant auditorium, the vast quilt extending before her. As she reached out and touched a blue square in front of her, as she read the words someone had so lovingly embroidered: "Beloved son, brother, uncle, friend," she choked back a sob. A hand reached out and patted her on the shoulder. She looked up into a stranger's face and saw compassion and understanding. She smiled into the kind face. Seeing that she was okay, he smiled back at her, then moved along, looking for another person in need of a gentle touch. He was dressed all in white.

In November of 1985, at a candle-light march in San Francisco, the idea of the international AIDS Memorial Quilt was born. The NAMES project soon became a reality, as mothers, fathers, siblings, lovers and friends left behind by those who have died of AIDS began sewing their panels, heartfelt remembrances bearing names of people from around the nation who lost their lives to the disease. Now comprising well over 15,000 panels, the vast, colorful mosaic could fill a space the size of several football fields, all contributors united by a common bond, a tragedy shared, all seeking a means of dealing with it, wanting to do something to bring the rest of the world to its senses, to make it take note. Hard not to once you've seen this, thought Amy, looking around the cavernous exhibition hall, which was so full of people, yet so silent. She was struck by the expressions on the faces surrounding her, by the gamut of emotions they revealed. Some were stunned, as if they were unable to process the enormity of what they now saw. Some were sad, openly grieving. Some were calm, seemingly at peace—often these were the faces of the volunteers, all dressed in white, who were there to lend support. Some were angry. And the faces of those who chose to focus on the celebration and love reflected in the quilt, on the hope that this outpouring instilled in their hearts, actually looked joyous. Amy felt a little of each of these emotions as she examined each panel. The love, the devotion, the pain reflected in each panel overpowered her. The face of a young man, arm around his canine companion, cat in his lap, stared out at her and brought tears to her eyes, as did the "Bye Mom" written on another panel. By the time she left the exhibit, some three hours after walking through the gymnasium's doors, she felt changed.

She drove back to her small West Hollywood house that evening, climbed into bed and sat quietly in the dark, trying to understand something beyond understanding, something of which little real sense can be made. She thought of Tom Price, her beloved friend and agent. Somehow she felt comforted for the first time since his death. They say that misery loves company—was that it? She hoped not, that she was not guilty of taking comfort in the knowledge that others suffered also. No, she quickly decided, the comfort came not from other suffering, but from the tremendous love and compassion she'd felt that day. Never before had she experienced anything quite like it.

Her thoughts turned to *After the Dance*. She'd had second thoughts about the letter that Charles Cunningham sent to Paul Brooks. Second and third and fourth thoughts. She hated even the thought of litigation. She was growing to hate Charles Cunningham, with his pompous attitude and his greed. But what she hated most was the thought of Mackenzie Montana playing Ashley Cowles in the movie. Each time she'd thought about calling Paul and withdrawing her threat to sue, it was that thought—the thought of Mackenzie Montana—that stopped her. Maybe if it had been someone else, someone she respected, whom she trusted to do justice to the role. Maybe then she'd be willing to back off and chalk it all up to her ongoing streak of bad luck. But not when it was Mackenzie Montana who would end up in the movie.

And today had reaffirmed her decision. No one who walked through that hall today, who viewed that quilt, would leave untouched, unaware of the reality of AIDS. But just how many people would actually *see* that quilt? How many people will leave the comfort of their homes to subject themselves to the painful reality brought home by that quilt? The truth is that the vast majority of those there today, and those who will view the quilt in the future, have already been touched by, are already painfully aware of the reality of this disease. It's the *others* that need to be reached, Amy thought emotionally. And *After the Dance* represents a precious opportunity to do just that—to reach people with the reality of AIDS. The reality that sweet young girls like Colleen O'Connor are dying from

AIDS.

The very thought that this message would be weakened, might be lost or, worse yet, satirized by having Mackenzie Montana play the reporter was enough to make Amy crazy. Crazy enough to retain Charles Cunningham to represent her. Crazy enough to sue, if she has to, to stop them.

As she finally slid down between the sheets and rested her head on the pillow, Amy's mind drifted back to the photograph of the young man with his pets. He looked so gentle, so kind, so full of love and life. She thought of her dad—her feisty, funny little father who was fighting so valiantly to stay around a little longer. What keeps him going, she wondered? What keeps us all going in this day and age? She knew that she didn't have the answer, but there *is* something. She knew that for sure. Felt it stronger than ever today, and tonight, sitting there in the dark. Life can be ugly and cruel and lonely and painful, but still we cling to it. Somehow, we still have enough intelligence to realize that it is unbelievably precious. Every single day of it—the ugly days and the monotonous days, as well as the joyous days. They are all precious.

And I, for one, vowed Amy before turning her weary mind off for the night, plan to make something of mine. Make my life count.

And *After the Dance* is where I start.

* * *

The same morning that Matthew got on the plane to California, Paul arrived at his office to find a wooden crate sitting on the floor next to his desk. When he asked Candy what it was, she informed him that someone from the Kenneth Behm Galleries had delivered it first thing that morning.

"I thought maybe you'd ordered something else for your house," Candy offered, watching with great curiosity as Paul used his letter opener to pry off the top of the large box.

"I've had my eye on a bronze I saw there last month, but decided I couldn't afford it," he answered. He removed the lid and reached into the small sea of popcorn-like styrofoam that filled the crate. Suddenly his hand met with a hard, sharp object. He scooped several handfuls of the little white marbles to reveal a small cowboy hat. He dug a little deeper until he found the base, then started to lift the object out of the crate. It was surprisingly heavy.

"Wow!" exclaimed Candy as the last pieces of styrofoam fell to the floor.

It was the bronze that Paul had just spoken of. An original. Standing about 14 inches high, it portrayed a weathered old cowboy, hat pulled down over his eyes, leaning up against his sturdy horse. The detail was incredible, from the expression on the cowboy's tired face to the crumpled shirt, belt (even the buckle), chaps and scuffed up boots. Every strand of the horse's mane looked real enough to brush. He stood alert, ears pricked, eyes wide, as if watching guard over his tired companion, who'd stopped to rest. Paul had been fascinated by it, by the artist's ability to convey a story, a relationship, a *lifestyle* by capturing just one ordinary moment in their day. He'd been back to the gallery twice to admire it. Ordinarily he'd have purchased it at first sight. It was perfect for his house, and Paul had grown accustomed to spending freely. But in light of the still uncertain situation with financing for the movie and the $15,000 price tag on the figure, he'd refrained. Still, he promised himself that once finances for *After the Dance* were in place, he'd return to the shop and buy the bronze sculpture that now stood before him.

"It's incredible, Paul," gasped Candy, appreciatively. Though Candy was no expert on fine art, she clearly realized that the tiny figures were extraordinary. "I thought you said you'd decided you couldn't afford it?"

"I did," he answered, a puzzled look on his face. "And I can't. I have no idea why they sent this to me."

Candy looked at him in surprise. "You mean you didn't buy it?"

"No, I didn't," answered Paul.

"Well apparently someone is trying to win you over—someone with good taste, I might add."

"Don't be silly. Who is going to go out and spend that kind of money to win *me* over?" Paul responded. But even as the words left his mouth, the realization struck. Mackenzie Montana. Of course. It had to be from Mackenzie. Then he thought back to their conversation at dinner. She'd been so attentive, so interested in every detail of his life. She'd asked him about his house, his taste in art. As he remembered that he'd actually told her about the bronze, about being so tempted to buy it, he let out a groan.

Candy looked startled. "Paul, what is it?" she asked.

He walked over to his desk and slumped into his chair, a weary look on his face.

"Get me Mackenzie Montana's phone number," was all that he said.

*   *   *

Candy returned several minutes later and informed

Paul that Mackenzie was still staying at the Four Seasons. Damn, he thought. He'd assumed she was back in L.A. by now and that he could deal with her on the phone. Now he'd undoubtedly have to *see* her to clear things up between them. With a sense of dread, he picked up the phone and dialed the hotel's number.

The switchboard put him through to Mackenzie's room, but there was no answer. Paul left a message that he'd called, then sat back, feeling somewhat relieved not to have reached her.

Just as he hung up the phone, Laura walked in. She smiled at him, then, noticing the opened crate on the floor and the bronze sitting on his desk, she said, "Looks like you've been shopping." She turned the small statuette to face her. "This is lovely, Paul."

Paul wasn't sure how to respond. The last thing he wanted Laura to suspect was that the bronze she was admiring was a gift from Mackenzie Montana. Yet, as he'd already experienced, he found it very difficult, almost impossible, to be deceptive with Laura. With other women, he'd never thought twice about telling little white lies. Not that he'd ever been deliberately deceptive with them, but he'd frequently opted for the easiest way out. If that meant distorting facts slightly—or simply failing to disclose facts—in order to avoid conflict, he wasn't above doing just that. As far as Paul could tell, all men were like that. He'd never even stopped to question the morality of such an attitude. But somehow, with Laura he had this compulsion, this *need* to be completely honest and open. It was a new phenomenon for Paul, one that he was not altogether enthused about. Especially at times like this. But this time, Paul was spared his moral dilemma by an interruption from Candy, who'd just opened the door and stood looking at the two of them. As usual, she looked less than pleased to see Laura in Paul's office.

"There you are," she said, addressing Laura. "Your daughter's school is on the phone. Line two."

Laura looked alarmed. Paul handed her his phone, relieved to have had her distracted from the bronze, but hating to see the look of panic on her face.

Moments later, he heard her ask, "How high is it?" Then, after a short pause, she said, "Please tell her I'll be there in thirty minutes. Thanks so much for calling."

"What is it?" Paul asked her when she'd hung up the phone. "Is everything okay?"

"Hailey's running a slight temperature," Laura answered. "Last night she didn't feel well, but then this morning she seemed just fine. She insisted on going to school. Paul, I hate to do this, but I'll need to take the rest of the day off. I want to get her home and in bed right away, maybe even take her to the doctor later, if he thinks he should see her."

Paul assured her that her leaving wouldn't be a problem.

"We have to sit down soon and talk about that letter from Charles Cunningham," Laura reminded him, as she stood to leave. "We've only got a few more days to respond. Have you had a chance to make those notes I asked you to?"

Paul reached for a legal pad sitting on the corner of his desk. "Right here, Ma'am," he answered. "But for now, you just worry about Hailey. Okay? Tell her I said hello."

Laura shot him an appreciative glance before opening the door. "I will." She smiled at him. "And thanks, Paul," she said.

"For what?" he asked.

"For being you," she said lovingly.

He suddenly had this irresistible urge to throw her to the floor and have her, but somehow suspected that, under the circumstances, this would not be an appropriate response. So instead he just smiled back and watched as she disappeared out the door.

* * *

Later that same day, Paul was getting ready to leave the office and head over to the gym when he noticed activity outside his half-opened door. A glorious mane of flowing strawberry-blonde hair caught his eye. Mackenzie Montana.

She was standing at Candy's desk, her profile to Paul. Dressed in tight blue jeans, hand-tooled leather boots and a short fur jacket, it was no wonder Paul had noticed her. She commanded as much attention in jeans as she did in the skin-tight dresses that were her usual fare. But looking at her now, Paul's appreciation of her appearance was considerably diminished by two factors: the fur coat and thoughts of the scene with her that he knew awaited him.

He felt like slipping out of sight, maybe into the bathroom adjoining his office, but he also wanted to get this over with. And Laura was gone. Better to see Mackenzie now than risk her coming into the office some other time, when Laura was around. With that thought in mind, he stepped out into the reception area and greeted Mackenzie politely.

She looked relieved to see him, as well as slightly embarrassed, as if Paul could tell that she'd rushed right over after getting the message he'd called—determined to catch him at the office and not give him a chance to avoid her any longer. Now standing face to face with him for the first time since their night together, she felt uncharacteristically shy. It didn't last long.

Paul invited her into his office. The opened crate still sat on the floor next to his desk. He'd placed the bronze back in it earlier in the day. Mackenzie looked at the box, then at Paul.

"Is that it?" she asked, motioning toward the box. Seeing the Kenneth Behm Galleries logo on the outside, she went on, "Is it the one you told me about at dinner that night? Did I get the right one?" She was obviously excited about the gift. It was clearly very important to her to know that she had pleased Paul. All of which made it that much more difficult for him to say what he'd planned.

"Yes, you did get the right one," he said, then immediately regretted his choice of words. "What I mean is you *did* get the one I told you about. And it is fantastic, Mackenzie. Really, fantastic." He paused here. Mackenzie stood just inches away now, looking for all the world, thought Paul, like an eager little puppy. It was strange to see her like this. Damn her, Paul couldn't help thinking. He halfway wondered if this weren't just another attempt to manipulate him, divert him from saying what he was about to say. This woman drove him absolutely crazy. She infuriated him. But at the same time, every once in a while he saw something... something almost childlike in her. And it was this side of her that stared into his eyes now. He felt like a complete jerk, but, determined, he continued anyway.

"I'm afraid I can't accept it," he said, stepping back, trying to put some distance between them. He didn't like the look on her face upon hearing him refuse the gift, but he didn't let it stop him. "It would

be totally inappropriate for me to accept it. Really."
There, he thought, I've said it. None too eloquently,
but at least I've said it. She stared at him. He noted
that she no longer looked like a puppy. Feeling
extremely uncomfortable, he stammered a few more
words, "It's not that I don't appreciate it, Mackenzie,
but..."

"What about fucking me the other night?" Her
voice had changed. She'd been transformed from a
puppy into a Doberman pinscher. "Was that 'appropriate'?" Pause. "And what about the fact that I've
called you at least a dozen times since then and,
finally, *two weeks later*, you get around to returning
my call? How's that for 'appropriate'?" She laughed,
a hard, almost scary laugh. "I'm just curious, Paul.
About what your definition of 'appropriate' is."

She waited for an answer. But Paul was none too
eager to give her one. He was collecting his thoughts,
trying to react calmly. He didn't like this. No, he
didn't like this at all. This being attacked. He'd never
been too patient with it—with women giving him grief
for what he did or didn't do. They were all the same
(all but Laura, that is). Thought you owed them
something. God, once you've slept with them, you're
really in deep shit. True, he'd admit that it had been
insensitive of him not to least return her calls. Usually
he was good at least for a call afterwards—in an
attempt to leave off on good terms. Trouble was, it
never worked that way. The minute they realized there
was no "relationship" in the cards, they hated you.
But at least he usually went through the motions. This
time he hadn't though, and it was *this*—this slight
guilt he'd been feeling for not doing what his own
peculiar code of decency dictated—that kept him from
blowing up at her now. That, plus the fact that—as

of now anyway— Mackenzie Montana was still very much a part of *After the Dance*. No, as much as he felt like blowing up at her now, his better judgment restrained him.

"I'm not going to answer that," he finally said. "And let's not go for each other's throats, okay? There's nothing to be gained by that." He pulled a chair up for Mackenzie. She gave him an icy look, but cooperated by lowering herself into it. He went around to the other side of his desk and sat, too.

"Mackenzie, I can't say I blame you for being upset with me. I should have called. I don't deny that. But let's just say I didn't much look forward to having this conversation with you, so like the coward I must be, I put it off. For that, I apologize."

She did not respond. Clearly she expected this to be his show. Thinking that the worse was behind him, Paul was now trying to repair some of the damage.

"I want you to know that I enjoyed our night together very much. You're an incredible lady. A man would have to be crazy not to feel that way about you. But I should never have let things go as far as they did. I accept responsibility for my actions. I wanted you. That night I felt I *had* to have you." Looking at her now, he tried to block out the images of that night that were starting to pop, uninvited, into his mind. She was definitely a beauty. And incredibly sexy. But in such a sleazy way, he quickly reminded himself.

"But I should never have acted on those feelings. It was wrong. For many reasons. It just shouldn't have happened."

He couldn't tell just how much damage he'd done, but suspected it was considerable. Her icy expression never changed. She hadn't so much as blinked throughout his discourse. Having said about all he was willing to

208

say, about all he felt obligated to say, he finished with, "I hope none of this will stand in the way of our working relationship."

That last comment got a response. She laughed again. The same brittle, caustic laugh.

"Working relationship?" she asked. "*What* working relationship?"

She reached into the tan leather portfolio she'd carried with her and withdrew a copy of the contract that Neil Roberts had given her. It was the contract Laura sent days earlier.

When she pulled the contract out, it was with the intention of ripping it into pieces before Paul's very eyes. She'd show him. She'd known for some time now that the one way she could get to Paul was through *After the Dance.* Her initial instinct had been to dramatically rip the contract up and walk out the door. See what *that* does to your fucking movie, she'd have said. But as she reached for the thick bundle of paper, something stopped her. Somehow she suddenly knew something that even Paul did not fully realize— that walking out on the movie was just what Paul wanted her to do.

So instead of tearing the document in half and throwing the pieces in his face, she calmly reached inside her bag for a pen, signed the last page, tossed it onto Paul's desk and, giving him one last soul-withering look, moved toward the door.

"You'll be sorry," were her only words as she sashayed out of the room, her hair cascading down her back, blending with the streaked fur.

As it always did, the sight of a woman clothed in fur sickened Paul.

But, watching her exit, he couldn't help but admit that she had a really fine rear end. Yes, definitely, Paul thought. That woman has a great ass.

11

It was Thursday morning, three days later. Matthew had returned from his trip to Los Angeles the night before. Anxious to meet with Paul and discuss the conversation he'd had with Shawn Long about Mackenzie Montana, he'd been keeping a watchful eye on the front of the door since arriving a little before eight. When Paul strode into the building some fifteen minutes later, he followed him into his office.

"How was the trip?" asked Paul, as he hung his leather jacket on a brass and oak coat tree sitting in the room's corner. "You sounded pretty excited about the girl Bob Moore found to play Colleen."

Matthew sat down on the couch situated under the big window opposite Paul's desk. The couch had been one of Paul's first purchases upon furnishing his office. He had a remarkable ability to cat-nap—oftentimes at the drop of a hat. Candy was always amazed when she'd have a conversation with Paul, then moments later, enter his office to find him sound asleep on the couch. For a man with as many responsibilities and demands as Paul had to deal with on a daily basis, not to mention his being such a physical man, this talent came in handy. It undoubtedly helped him in maintaining the energy level and enthusiasm that were his signatures.

Sitting on that couch now, Matthew did not look relaxed. He was leaning forward and speaking in an unusually animated matter.

"She's incredible, Paul," he shook his head, as if in disbelief. "Absolutely incredible. You know, with all the characters, I was worried I'd have trouble accepting anyone who played the part. After all, this is my family. It's *me*, for crying out loud. It just seemed to me it would be pretty damned hard, for me anyway, if not for the rest of the world, to buy into anyone's portrayal of any of us. But it's been the weirdest thing." He scratched his head and stared straight ahead, trying to express what he'd been feeling.

"A lot of the time, it's like I can actually separate myself from the story. Like I can become just another objective person in the audience. That's how professional all these people are." Now he looked right at Paul, a real gleam in his eye. "But with this girl, Sherry's her name, I don't know whether I'm being objective or not. All I know is that to me, sitting there watching her during the screen test, she *was* Colleen. Not some actress playing Colleen, but Colleen herself." He hesitated, clearly shaken by the recollection. "I'll tell you, Paul. It was really a powerful experience."

Paul looked at his friend with a mixture of pleasure and concern. Pleasure to learn that the casting had gone so well, but concern at the obviously emotional response the whole process had evoked.

"I'm really happy to know things went so well," he said. He hesitated for a moment, not wanting what he was about to say to come off wrong. "Listen, Buddy, are you sure it's a good thing for you to be so close to this? I mean, we obviously can benefit from your involvement in every aspect of this movie, but I don't want it to put you through any more than you've already been through. Know what I mean?"

Matthew looked at his friend with affection, then teased, "Don't worry. I'm not going to go over the deep end." Then, knowing Paul's concern was genuine, and deeply felt, he grew serious. "I don't want to worry about that, Paul. I've given it a lot of thought and just keep coming to the same conclusion. Yes, this movie is going to stir some strong emotions in me. Obviously some really painful ones. But overall, it's going to be therapeutic for me. It already is. I need this movie. You know that. I need to be as involved in it as I can possibly be, without becoming a giant pain in the ass to everyone, that is." Both men chuckled, knowing that such involvement oftentimes did create hard feelings amongst cast and crew. "But thanks for being concerned, Paul. I appreciate it."

He wanted to thank his friend for more, much more. To tell him how much he appreciated his decision to do the movie in the first place. And his ongoing commitment to it, and to doing it right. But such heartfelt words did not come easy. They'd already come dangerously close to getting downright emotional with each other, so he stopped right there. It seemed a good time to sober things up by bringing up Mackenzie.

As Matthew related to Paul what he'd learned from Shawn Long, Paul shook his head with disgust and anger. When Matthew was finished, Paul took his turn, telling Matthew about his scene with her the other day, about how it had ended with her signing the contract and storming out of his office. Paul had felt a cloud hanging over his head ever since. Hearing what Matthew had to say, Paul could see the situation was clearly out of hand. This woman was capable of even more despicable actions than Paul had imagined. She'd been blackmailing Shawn! At last he understood Shawn's about-face, his insistence on having Mackenzie in the movie.

He and Matthew discussed the situation for well over an hour. They were in a real dilemma. Apparently at Shawn's insistence, Bob Brubeck had basically decided that either Mackenzie Montana was to play the role of the reporter or he'd refuse to finance the movie. At this stage of the game, with even more money having been sunk into preproduction—as to date, they'd not received any of the advances promised by Brubeck—they faced monumental consequences if Brubeck backed out. Yet, to have Mackenzie Montana star in the film was not only morally repugnant to Paul, Shawn, and now, even Matthew, they all also knew well enough what the antics of one crazy star could do to an otherwise outstanding movie and production crew. They were conceivably in a real no-win situation and they knew it.

Finally, after kicking around ideas for some time, Paul announced decisively, "We can't do it, Matt. We absolutely cannot allow Mackenzie Montana to play the role of Ashley Cowles. Tomorrow morning I'm calling Bob Brubeck and asking him to fly up. You get ahold of Shawn and make sure he's here, too. The three of us are going to sit down and reason with that man."

He sounded sure of himself, but looked anything but.

"Think we can do it?" asked Matthew.

"We can sure as hell try," answered Paul. "As far as I can tell, we really have no choice."

They both left the meeting feeling apprehensive and concerned. So much was at stake, and in a way, they were powerless to do anything. Anything but plead their case, anyway. While Matthew headed for, the studio to seek out the cameramen who were helping him scout locations, Paul felt a sudden need to see Laura.

He walked down to her office. It was empty. He felt ridiculously disappointed. Almost panicked. Maybe she wasn't coming in at all today. She'd asked to cut back a little on her hours recently, feeling her long days were becoming a hardship on the kids. She'd been taking work home with her and working on her wordprocessor there. Workwise it created no problems—Laura was responsible to a fault, so Paul wasn't worried about work going undone. But he did miss her at the office. Had she told him she wasn't coming in today? The thought disturbed him.

But then she walked in. She was wearing a tailored, olive-colored pantsuit. He was disappointed not to see her legs, but he found himself thinking how very feminine she appeared in what looked almost like a man's suit. She smiled upon seeing him—looking surprised, but happily so.

"Hi there!" She touched his arm. She wanted to kiss him—at least a quick kiss on the cheek, but she was still uncomfortable with their relationship in the workplace. Enough so that recently, she'd been wondering whether it was such a good idea to continue working there. Still she'd promised to see things through with the movie. And she loved her work. She thoroughly enjoyed this new twist her career had taken—enjoyed the field of entertainment law and the people at Brooks. And she absolutely adored working with Paul. Every day was full of thrills for her, like this, walking in and finding him there, obviously waiting to see her. Clearly *needing* to see her. She felt so alive again, so incredibly alive.

Frustrated by the inadequacy of a mere touch from her, needing more, much more, Paul suddenly announced, "We're taking the rest of the day off."

Laura looked at him and smiled. The smile cinched it. "Just what do you have in mind?" she asked curiously, maybe even a little seductively.

"Never you mind, Girl," came his response. "Just meet me in my office in five minutes." He glanced at his watch. "Better make that *two* minutes," he said as he headed for the door.

"Paul..." Laura called after him.

"Don't forget who's boss around here," he responded, without looking back. "And don't be late."

It was a spectacular winter's day—a cloudless blue sky, brisk air, snow-capped mountains in every direction, with Mount Rainier reigning supreme. Paul hustled Laura into his car and hurriedly headed toward the waterfront. They had just five minutes to catch the Winslow ferry.

Theirs was the last car on. Once they'd parked, they left the car and headed up the stairs to the main enclosed cabin, where commuters can sit back and enjoy the incredible scenery streaming by in warmth and comfort. But the view this morning was so sensational that they walked right on through the lounge, out onto the deck. They stood with a handful of other cold but appreciative souls and looked at the skyline of Seattle as the ferry drew away from the dock. Standing with his back against a somewhat sheltered wall, Paul opened his long camel hair coat and drew

215

Laura to him. She wrapped her arms around him and hugged him affectionately, then, still wrapped in his coat, turned and stood with her back pressed against him. They stayed like that, wrapped in their little cocoon, and silently watched the city fade.

Finally, when the cold wind threatened to numb their exposed faces, they reluctantly returned to the cabin. While Laura settled into one of many empty booths that line either side of the massive vessel, Paul went in search of coffee. When he returned, coffee cups in hand, he sat down next to her. But Laura immediately moved to the opposite side of the booth and seated herself facing him. It was a tough decision for her—whether she most preferred being seated *next* to him, where they could hold hands and touch, or whether she would rather sit *opposite* him, where she could look directly at him. Looking won out. Laura absolutely loved to look at Paul. Little gave her more pleasure than just the sight of him. She loved to look into his beautiful eyes, to read them as best she could, to communicate with him without saying a word. Most of all, she loved it when he was unaware of her studying him. Loved to observe him, his posture, his expressions. His hands. She *loved* his hands. More than anything else, looking at him reminded her of that overwhelming adoration a young mother feels when looking at her newborn infant. When every little patch of peach fuzz, of newborn skin, every little curled finger and toe, and every wrinkled, expressive face can, in its unsurpassable beauty and wonder, move a mother to tears. That was the effect that Paul Brooks had on her. That was how dearly she loved this man.

While Paul would have much preferred to have Laura at his side, he was beginning to understand her, to appreciate the intensity and depth of her quiet love for him. She fascinated him in her complexity—he was finally realizing that her need for distance somehow did not dispute her great love for him. In fact, he suspected that the intensity of her feelings may well have given rise to the need for separateness. Did that make any sense? So while he couldn't even begin to know the thoughts she was having now, sitting there opposite him, he did know that her actions were likely prompted by love. Her kind of love, which was—of this, he was dead certain—a very special kind of love.

Upon reaching the other side of the Sound, a ride of about thirty minutes, Paul and Laura climbed back into Paul's Porsche and drove into the quaint little village. Paul was clearly in charge this day. Though he'd had no time to plan the day, he already had a very definite agenda. He thought back to the many times he'd taken this very trip alone, always subtly aware of his loneliness at not having someone to share it with. Today he wanted to retrace all his customary steps, knowing that the pleasure this trip usually gave him would be magnified by Laura's presence.

They started at the little coffee shop. It was as inauspicious a restaurant as Laura had seen, the kind her dad always called a "greasy spoon." Paul seemed to think it was something really special, though. She loved that.

It didn't take long to see why he was so enthusiastic. The only seats available were at the counter, looking directly into the kitchen, where three friendly faces called out a greeting to them. The cafe's ambiance, which in Laura's eyes grew by the moment, was in large part attributable to these three. They kept up a cheerful banter the whole time they went about their business of waiting and cooking.

Though it was nearing the lunch hour, Paul and Laura ordered breakfast. While Laura, who was usually a light eater, would normally have settled for some fruit and a cup of coffee, she went along with Paul's urging and ordered their specialty—blueberry pancakes. Paul ordered the pancakes and an enormous Western omelette.

Paul was clearly in his element. His pleasure at sharing this day, this restaurant, even the pancakes with Laura was obvious. While he'd seemed disturbed by something when she first found him waiting for her in her office that morning, Laura noted that Paul now seemed completely relaxed. After downing every last bite of their breakfast, which Laura agreed was superb, they sat back and basked in each other's company—kidding each other, chatting freely about themselves. There was still so much to discover, to learn, about each other. The beauty of this little cafe was that they felt free to linger. Every once in a while, the heavy-set waitress would stop and pour some more coffee for them, but it was clear she didn't mean to hurry them. The truth is, she—and many of the other customers who noticed Paul and Laura, which was hard not to do—was getting great pleasure from watching these two. It was obvious to everyone that day that they were in love. And though they were surrounded by the hustle and bustle of Winslow's most popular eating establishment, they felt completely alone, free to express themselves and their affection for one another. It was a welcome change from the restrictions they sensed at the office, and even at Laura's house, with the children present.

After answering many of Paul's questions—on topics ranging from her childhood, to her first boyfriend, to why she'd recently become a vegetarian—

Laura decided it was time to turn the tables. She knew that Paul loved basketball and that he'd played it—played it exceptionally well—in college. Christopher had shared that with her. But Paul, being modest to the extreme, had never so much as mentioned his athletic history to her.

"Now, it's *your* turn," she said, reaching for his hand. "I want to hear all about your basketball career."

Paul laughed. He looked slightly embarrassed, but replied, "There's not much to tell, I'm afraid." The look on Laura's face told him she wasn't going to buy that. He realized she'd need to hear something in order to placate her. For some reason, it had always been very difficult for Paul to talk about his prowess as an athlete. It was one of the things the press and fans had loved about him. In his own mind, he did not even think he was exceptional, but on another level he couldn't help but realize that he possessed extraordinary talent. And, in truth, though his involvement with the game was now limited to his pick up games at the club, basketball was still a big part of him. It was still part of who Paul Brooks really was. But unless you grew up with a ball in your hand, grew up with that round ball practically ruling your life, how could you possibly understand? Still, it was clear that Laura was truly interested, so for the first time he could recall, he talked about his basketball career, his passion for the sport. He started off slowly, but as he saw Laura's response, her eagerness to understand, even share, his passion, he soon found himself revealing more about himself than he'd ever dreamt possible, to the point that he even detailed his performance in the game of which he was most proud. It was his junior year at the University, the last game of the season, when his 20 footer, followed closely by a beautifully executed drive to the basket for a left-handed lay up—all in the last 20 seconds of the game—brought the Huskies back from behind and gave them the win that sent them into the NCAA quarterlies.

As he ended his story, he realized, with a deep, uncharacteristic blush, how absorbed in reliving that moment he'd become. He apologized for what he was sure Laura would perceive to be boasting on his part. But Laura responded by telling him the story thrilled her. She seemed sincere. She was sincere. It had thrilled her to hear his account, not just because she appreciated his obvious talent. She'd watched enough basketball to appreciate the talent he must have had to be able to turn that game around, to even be playing at that level. But what thrilled her even more was the trust Paul showed in her, for though some might not consider such talk to be very intimate in nature, clearly Paul had revealed something very personal to him, very emotional. Basketball was, indeed, a passion for Paul. Laura could recognize this, perhaps because she'd already recognized it in her son. Some people are born to write. Some to paint, or act. And some to play basketball. She appreciated Paul's willingness to share that with her. Somehow she knew how rare and special it was for him to do so.

The rest of the day was equally meaningful and joyful. They drove around the peninsula, stopping on a quiet, dead-end road to admire yet another incredible sight—the snow-capped mountains, the waters of Puget Sound and, in the distance, the Seattle skyline. Then they'd made love—right there in the car, throwing all caution to the wind, and feeling like a couple of lovestruck teenagers.

Finally, they took a late afternoon ferry back to the city. On this trip, they never even got out of the car, preferring to sit there, holding hands, looking at each other. By now, they were pretty much talked out. They felt content. Happy. Sorry that the day was about to end. Very much in love.

Driving home that night, Paul reflected upon the day, from the anger and apprehension he'd felt that morning after talking to Matthew about Mackenzie Montana to the peace he now felt, after spending the day with Laura. Deep down, he knew that a storm was brewing, but for the time being, at least, he was a happy man.

*   *   *

The meeting with Bob Brubeck took place later that week. It was not pleasant for anyone.

Paul was not eager to confess his dalliance with Mackenzie Montana. As far as he was concerned, the fewer people who knew about it, the better. He was hoping it would not be necessary to tell all, but that seemed unlikely, as their relationship was an integral part of the story of what had transpired to bring him to this point—to calling this meeting, the purpose of which was to get Brubeck's approval to oust Mackenzie. He was in a difficult position. He knew that Brubeck's financial backing for the movie was at stake, and that if Brubeck were to back out now, the company could be financially devastated. In a very real sense, the future of the company itself was at stake. It was imperative that they convince Brubeck to make the change and that they not lose his backing. If that meant admitting his fling with Mackenzie, so be it.

At least he'd scheduled the meeting for a morning when Laura would be working at home, so he was

221

assured she would not be present if it became necessary to lay all his cards on the table.

And the fact that Amy Griffin had threatened to sue was helpful. Before the meeting he'd held some hope that that fact alone might be persuasive with Brubeck, might be enough to convince him to give the part back to Amy. He'd daydreamed of a meeting where, in response to the news of Charles Cunningham's letter, Brubeck insisted on reinstating Griffin. But he'd underestimated the job Shawn had done on Brubeck in selling him on Mackenzie Montana. When Paul opened the meeting with news of the letter from Charles Cunningham, it was immediately clear from Brubeck's reaction that Amy Griffin's threats alone were not going to sway him. He still wanted Mackenzie.

Paul was also very much aware of another obstacle with which they might have to deal, which was, of course, the fact that they now had a signed agreement with Mackenzie Montana. Paul had never signed it for Brooks Productions. He wasn't exactly sure where that left them, legally speaking. Ordinarily he'd have gotten an answer on the matter, in anticipation of their discussing it at this meeting, but he hadn't wanted to discuss any aspect of this situation with Laura. Besides, as far as Paul was concerned, with or without a contract, he was willing to go ahead and fire Mackenzie. What the hell, he thought—the way things were going, either way they'd probably end up being sued by someone.

None of this made the task at hand—persuading Brubeck—any easier.

But if the meeting could be said to be "uncomfortable" for Paul, it was to be downright painful for Shawn Long. He'd struggled with what explanation he'd give Brubeck for his sudden change of heart—for

222

why he was now asking to go back to Amy Griffin, when not more than two months ago he'd been the one to suggest—no, really, to insist on—switching to Mackenzie Montana. To tell Brubeck the truth about Mackenzie and him would be admitting the undue influence he'd allowed her to have on him, influence which had in turn led to Shawn's influencing Brubeck on Mackenzie's behalf. The consequences of such an admission could be catastrophic. Would he ever direct another picture?

And so, while neither Paul nor Shawn were happy about being placed in a position of admitting their flings with the sexy Ms. Montana, both now had to weigh the costs of doing just that against the prospect of making the movie with Mackenzie Montana in it.

And before the meeting was over, both men would decide that ridding *After the Dance* of this time bomb was worth placing themselves on the line.

Brubeck's reaction to both men's stories was a mix of incredulity and disgust. The fact that his own amorous antics were almost legendary in entertainment circles did not stop him from getting on his moral high-horse. He railed on and on about their lack of ethics and character, their stupidity—accusing them of thinking not with their heads but with another part of their anatomy. This man, who'd bedded almost every attractive female ever featured in a film he financed, and who'd been looking forward to getting to know the lovely Ms. Montana, chastised them soundly for their inability to draw the line between business and pleasure.

During his tirade, Paul and Shawn sat quietly, shifting uncomfortably under his penetrating gaze. For the most part, they figured they had it coming. Neither man was proud of his actions; neither made any attempt to defend them. At one point, it appeared inevitable that they'd lost his backing, but just as Paul began a panicky tally in his mind of the money he'd already sunk into preproduction, money which he stood no chance to recover if Brubeck walked away, just as Shawn began thinking that he'd never direct again, Brubeck grew silent.

He looked at Shawn, long and hard. Then he spoke.

"Do you still believe in this movie?"

"Enough to risk telling you what I just told you," was Shawn's simple, heartfelt response.

Then Brubeck turned to Paul.

"And you," he said, a look of genuine curiosity now replacing the anger that moments earlier had dominated his face. "Just what makes you willing to risk the scandal and negative publicity that you must know this will give rise to... maybe even a lawsuit—which, by the way, you damned well better indemnify me against if we do go back to Griffin—just to get rid of Mackenzie Montana?"

Paul looked at Matthew. Then he looked at Shawn, who'd just put his entire career on the line for this movie, and the answer came easy.

"We can make this movie with Mackenzie Montana and people will come to see it. There's no question about it. We'd make some money," he answered candidly. "For the same reason that Shawn and I ignored any good judgment and ended up in bed with her, people would come to see the movie. But with a real actress, with Amy Griffin, what we'll make will be much more than another profitable movie. It will be THE movie of the year. Maybe even of the decade. I promise you that." He looked Brubeck straight in the eye, then continued. "But what's more

224

important than that, more important than the money, or lawsuits, or the fanfare, will be the difference that this movie can make—*if* we do it justice. A difference that will be measurable in lives. Not dollars, not awards, but *lives*."

Paul searched Brubeck's face to see if he understood, to see if any of what he'd just said had gotten through to him.

But if Paul was looking for an emotional response, he was out of luck. Bob Brubeck was, first and foremost, a businessman. And the decision as to who would play the reporter, Ashley Cowles, in *After the Dance* was strictly a business decision.

Brubeck's face registered no emotion whatsoever as he finally proclaimed, "Let's go with Griffin."

* * *

Number five across had him stymied. A seven-letter word that meant "stroll." Second letter "a."

Though he was finding more and more time for crossword puzzles these days, Charles Cunningham had the disturbing feeling that the time it took him to solve them had been steadily increasing of late. He used to be such a whiz at them.

His secretary's voice interrupted these troubling thoughts. "Paul Brooks on line one." They rarely had need of a second line these days.

Cunningham picked up the phone. "Charles Cunningham here," he announced busily.

"Hello, Mr. Cunningham. This is Paul Brooks, from Brooks Productions," Paul started.

"I must say, Mr. Brooks," Cunningham responded in what was even a more arrogant tone than usual, "you appear to be unusually casual about the prospect of a major lawsuit against your company."

"How so?" responded Paul, forming an immediate dislike for the person at the other end of the line.

"Did I not give you two weeks in which to reply to my letter? And unless I'm mistaken in my mathematics, today makes day number 16. Does it not?" Cunningham leaned back in his chair smugly. It felt so good to be in the saddle again—Charles Cunningham, negotiator extraordinaire! The great intimidator, that's what he'd always called himself.

You prick, thought Paul. Then, reminding himself that it was Amy Griffin they were actually dealing with, he held his tongue. "You're absolutely right, Mr. Cunningham. We are a day or two late in responding. The truth is, we've been trying to reach Ms. Griffin for the past couple of days and haven't been successful. You see, we wanted to be able to give her the news personally, but since we haven't been able to reach her, we thought we'd better notify you."

"The news?" Cunningham straightened in his chair. "Notify me of what, Mr. Brooks?"

"Notify you that we would like to reinstate Amy in the part of Ashley Cowles in *After the Dance.*" Paul was disappointed to be giving this news to Cunningham instead of Amy. With Amy, he'd planned to give a more in-depth explanation of their decision, to exercise his considerable diplomatic skills to ensure her that they all got off to a good start with her. He still would do so, but he'd quickly decided that there was no need to waste words with this chump.

"I see," Cunningham finally responded. "A wise decision, Mr. Brooks. Very wise, indeed. For if it had come to a legal battle, I assure you things would not have worked out to your liking." God, this felt great. He hadn't lost it, after all. "No, I'm afraid you'd have found yourself out of your league if you'd been foolish enough to test us."

While Paul could be a great diplomat, and while he was, by and large, a very easy-going guy, he did have his limits. Charles Cunningham was pushing them. "Cut the crap, Cunningham," Paul snapped. "For your information, your letter, your threat to take us to court, had absolutely nothing to do with this decision. This decision was based solely on our reassessment of who was best for the part. And we've decided Amy is the best actress to play Ashley Cowles. If you think for a moment that you played any part in our decision, you're a bigger fool than you sound." He suddenly felt a little guilty for jumping on this guy. But just a little. "If you would kindly give Ms. Griffin the news and ask her to contact us as soon as it's convenient, we'd appreciate it very much. Goodbye, Mr. Cunningham." With that, he hung up.

Just what is this world coming to, wondered Charles, as he sat back and lit one of his cigars. It's no wonder they don't make quality movies like they used to. All these crass, classless people in the industry today. And I'd heard such favorable things about this Brooks character.

He shook his head in disgust, then smiled as he caught sight of his dapper reflection in the mirrored wall across from him. No sense letting Paul Brooks' rude behavior steal his thunder. No, nothing should be allowed to diminish this moment. It had been a little while since he'd had a victory this sweet, but he hadn't forgotten the feeling. He still had it. Charles Cunningham, attorney extraordinaire, lawyer to the stars. He still had it.

He picked up the phone and called his secretary. "Kelly, get me Susan Lance of the *L.A. Times*."

Susan wrote the local gossip column that was always heavily filled with names of the biggest stars. Yes, soon word would be out, and they'd be standing in line again for his services.

He put the phone down and puffed on his cigar. Then, almost as an afterthought, he picked it back up. "And you'd better give Amy Griffin a call, too."

Yes, we mustn't forget to call Amy.

* * *

Mackenzie Montana was still registered at the Four Seasons. Paul had left several messages for her there since the meeting with Brubeck but had not yet heard back from her. Finally, he decided to try her house in Beverly Hills. Neil Roberts answered.

After exchanging cordial greetings, Paul asked to speak to Mackenzie. Neil informed him that Mackenzie had not been feeling well the past couple of weeks and had checked into Cedars Sinai the day before for tests. The doctor had assured them it was nothing serious, probably just a touch of the flu, he told Paul. Nothing that would delay the start of *After the Dance*.

"That's why I called, Neil," Paul responded. "It's about *After the Dance*..." he was not sure how to proceed, especially in light of this news about Mackenzie's health. This whole situation stunk. As desperately as he'd wanted to get rid of Mackenzie Montana, he couldn't help but feel some sympathy and concern for her. He wished he didn't. But as well as he knew by now, wishing something just didn't make it so. Now this. He envisioned her lying in a hospital bed, being told she'd just been canned from *After the Dance*. As much grief as she'd already given all of them, he still couldn't help but feel a little sorry for her. But he really had no choice. He had to tell

228

Neil about their decision.

Neil responded to the news professionally, politely, but he also let it be known that they considered the part Mackenzie's and that they were not about to take this news lying down.

While the conversation ended on a somewhat cordial note, with Paul asking Neil to wish Mackenzie well, Paul hung up knowing that this was by no means the last he would hear of Mackenzie Montana. No, intuitively, he just knew that it would be a good long while before he could breathe easier about her.

*   *   *

Paul knew what was wrong the moment he saw her walk into his office. Like a child, he'd been trying to avoid her the past couple of days. But he'd known that a confrontation was inevitable.

Laura stood and faced him. This conversation was a standing-up kind of conversation. She was too agitated to sit.

"I'd like an explanation." She was trying to remain calm, reasonable. "I've just heard that the decision was made two days ago to fire Mackenzie Montana and reinstate Amy Griffin. I'd like to know why the hell, as company attorney, I've not been involved in any of this? Why I haven't even been made aware of any of this?"

Paul had been waiting for this. He was beginning to feel like he couldn't do anything right. Every move he made got him in trouble with someone. He knew that as the company's attorney, Laura should have been involved in the meeting with Brubeck and any communications with Charles Cunningham, Neil Roberts or Mackenzie Montana. He knew that she'd react just as she was now to being excluded. But he'd handled it the best way he knew how, choosing to risk her anger in order to insulate her from the whole Mackenzie Montana mess.

And deep down, even as she stood there demanding an explanation, Laura already knew what Paul was trying to do. And, the truth was that, on some level, she was relieved and grateful to be protected from the truth. Yet on another level, she felt betrayed.

Paul's response was honest and direct.

"I don't blame you for being upset. As our attorney, you *should* be involved in this. And if that were all you were—the company attorney—you would be. I think you know that. But because you're the woman I love, Laura, I did not want you to be involved." His eyes searched hers for forgiveness. "I honestly thought that was what you wanted, too. And I apologize if I was wrong. I apologize for this whole sorry mess."

She just stood there. It pained Laura to see him looking so sad and defeated. She knew he was trying to protect her. He was just doing the best he could with a difficult situation. But *damn* him. He was the one who'd gotten them into it in the first place. Just the thought of what they were tiptoeing around—the thought of him being with Mackenzie Montana—brought a pain to her gut.

She didn't trust herself to speak. And so, though she wasn't trying to punish him, though she truly appreciated the pain he felt—and his good intentions— she had no choice but to turn and walk out the door. Without saying another word.

And nothing could have punished him more.

12

Matthew was nervous. He stood, tightly gripping a steel pole as the underground shuttle that took passengers from the main terminal of SeaTac Airport to the facility's north wing, where the United Airlines gates were located, rocked passengers back and forth. The lurching motion called for a good hold, but as he watched a little red headed girl swing round and round the next pole, he realized that his grip was excessive. That's how he knew he must be unnerved by the prospect of meeting Amy Griffin within the next few minutes.

It wasn't the fact that she was a movie star. The truth was that he'd met and rubbed elbows with enough "stars" in his days in Los Angeles to have quickly dispelled any false illusions he may once have had about celebrities. And Amy Griffin, though once one of the hottest young stars in Hollywood, had long since fallen into relative obscurity. Still, he'd never forgotten her performance in *Outlaw*. He'd fallen in love with her after seeing that movie. Saw it at least four or five times. Maybe six. She'd played the decent, strong-willed high school sweetheart of an

Italian lothario who'd later risen to become a drug kingpin. A man who could have had any woman he wanted, but who always came back to Amy's character. Trouble was, though, that once she'd discovered how it was he earned his phenomenal income, Amy's character would have nothing to do with him. And soon his only mission in life was winning her back, which, of course, led to his fall from the good graces of the mafiosa and, eventually, his death. But not before Amy Griffin had rewarded him one last time with her own sweet brand of love. At least the Outlaw died a happy man.

For weeks after seeing her performance, Matthew had not been able to get Amy out of his mind. It wasn't just the performance. In those days, Amy was a great beauty. Actually, she was one of those women whom some men found rather plain, but to others, and Matthew belonged to this group, her natural, athletic looks, her straightforward, non-beguiling demeanor, were incredibly appealing. Most screen beauties were the stuff of fantasies, with the faces and bodies that, during lovemaking, men superimpose over wives or girlfriends who long ago lost the ability to excite them. But, for the most part, that was the only way men envisioned these screen goddesses, lying there, hot, panting, begging for more of it. Once it was over—the lovemaking, that is—most men would just as soon drift off to sleep at the side of a real person. Somehow Matthew could never imagine eating breakfast across from Kim Basinger. Or taking the garbage out with Cindy Crawford. But with Amy Griffin, it was a different story. For Matthew, Amy was a woman who could inspire the most erotic of feelings—no superimposing over that face, that body— and afterwards, take out the garbage with the best of them. Yep, Matthew thought Amy was some woman back then.

But that had been, what, maybe ten years ago? He'd long ago gotten over his thing about Amy. For years now, she'd been pretty much out of the public eye. In fact, until yesterday when he'd talked to her on the phone, he'd all but forgotten he'd ever had a giant crush on her. When they'd initially made the decision to go with Amy in the role of Ashley Cowles, Matthew's support of the choice was based not on his old feelings but upon his recollection of her intensity as an actress and her ability to bring depth and emotion to otherwise lifeless scenes. Amy Griffin did not just walk though a part. She had incredible presence. And that had been why he wanted Amy to be cast as Ashley.

But something about talking to her yesterday had stirred old feelings in him. It was her voice. And her mannerisms. Straightforward, but polite. Kind. She had a very kind voice. And she was so... so... reasonable. That was it. She'd been so goddam reasonable. Here they'd almost really screwed her over. Given her what might well be one of the best female roles of the year, a part that had the potential to revive her career, then, without warning, without any wrongdoing on her part, they'd pulled the rug out from under her. Not intentionally. In fact, he'd tried to explain that to her yesterday. To explain why, because of Bob Brubeck's ultimatums, they'd gotten into this whole Mackenzie Montana mess in the first place. She'd listened quietly. Then she'd said, without so much as a hint of resentment, that, as far as she was concerned, that was behind them. In fact, she apologized for the threatening letter her attorney had sent. All she wanted to do now was get started.

She wanted to fly up right away and spend some time with Matthew to prepare herself for the role and to learn as much, firsthand, as she possibly could before they started shooting in two weeks. Before they'd hung up she'd told him, "You won't be sorry about this, about giving this part back to me." And he knew, with absolute certainty, that they wouldn't be.

The plane was actually a few minutes early. He'd planned on being at the gate when Amy deplaned, but when the train's doors opened and Matthew stepped off, Amy was already riding the escalator down from the gate area. After sighting her, he stood and waited at the base of the moving stairs. He felt his hands getting clammy and nonchalantly wiped the palm of his right hand before introducing himself, hoping that he'd been successful in wiping the moisture off. He could feel himself sweating profusely.

But if she noticed anything, Amy did a good job of hiding it. She smiled warmly. He found himself staring at her. She had definitely aged, but the added years hadn't really diminished her appeal. The smile could still mesmerize. She still looked like an ex-athlete, the kind of woman who lounges around the house in men's sweats—no designer, high-tech gear for her—but still manages to look sexy in them. Part of it was the way she moved. She was strong and graceful. Very determined looking. Sure of herself. And, in spite of all this—no, maybe *because* of all of this, thought Matthew—utterly feminine. In a different kind of way. A way that might not affect many men, but that really did something for Matt.

His rather uncharacteristic self-consciousness did not last long. Despite Amy's warmth and easy social graces, it was clear she was anxious to get down to business. By the time they'd reached the luggage carrousel and stood waiting for her bags to appear, she'd already begun grilling Matthew with questions, and he became engrossed in the task at hand—that of giving the actress the background information necessary for her to develop her role, insight into the O'Connor family, their ordeal, and the community's reaction. Her questions were blunt. Right to the point. Almost insensitive. Like, "Weren't you, down deep inside somewhere, really ticked off at her? I mean, for doing this. For putting all of you through all of this?" Matthew could tell that when Amy Griffin got down to business, all rules of etiquette were tossed aside. But he didn't really mind. He knew that her lack of tact was not born of a lack of caring. Besides, no amount of tact or diplomacy could make the subject of Colleen and her battle with AIDS any easier for him to discuss. He'd just as soon talk straight about it.

They talked all the way through the airport, in the car, and all the way to her hotel, the Edgewater. She'd stayed there years earlier and, the day before, when he'd asked her if she had any preference, she told him without hesitation that she wanted a room at the Edgewater. There were plenty of luxurious, new hotels downtown, but for a certain type of traveler, the Edgewater was a hotel without rival. Situated on the waterfront, literally *on* the waterfront, the old hotel offered rooms that gave guests a feeling of being suspended over water. Years earlier, in fact (Amy had told Matt yesterday), she had fished right out of the window of her room there. The hotel didn't even discourage it. In fact, they supplied her with the fishing pole.

Several years ago, the Edgewater, in an attempt to compete with the construction of a new downtown

Sheraton, the ever popular and prestigious Four Seasons, and numerous other hotels, underwent extensive renovation. Fishing from one's window was no longer permitted, but the atmosphere hadn't changed. And now, in addition to the loyal customers who'd patronized it for years, it was also attracting its share of the new business. It was "in" again. The waterfront room with a balcony that she was now surveying enthusiastically had not been easy to get.

"It's wonderful!" she exclaimed, that million-dollar smile rewarding him many times over for his efforts.

In spite of the rain and cool temperature, she headed right for the sliding glass door and stepped onto the deck. A ferry was streaming by, and closer, maybe only 25 yards from where they stood, the *Spirit of Puget Sound* moved quietly through the waters. Amy waved at the passengers sitting inside the vessel. Several arms waved in return.

"I do love Seattle!" She laughed heartily, then turned toward him. "Was that a gym bag I noticed in the back of your Jeep?"

Matt looked a little confused. "Yes. Why?"

"You look like a runner. Are you?"

"A serious runner? I used to be." He was still puzzled by this new line of questioning. "Now I just do it to stay in shape."

"How about going for a run with me?" Amy asked.

"Now? In the rain?"

"I love rain." That smile again. "And this way we can keep talking. How about it?"

As he trotted out to his car to get his running gear, Matthew had a feeling that life was about to get real interesting for him. He'd promised Amy he'd make himself available to her as much as possible over the next two weeks, before filming was scheduled to start. Before meeting her, that had caused him some anxiety. But at this very moment, he was looking forward to the next two weeks immensely.

* * *

Matthew could never forget it—the moment his parents informed him that his little sister had tested positive for HIV. That one moment where you suddenly know that life will never be the same.

He'd come home from L.A. for the holidays. He was still doing that in those days—coming home most Christmases. It was before he'd married. He'd really been looking forward to this trip—to being with his family, to having a white Christmas, getting out of L.A. for a while. But he'd sensed something was wrong. The couple of times he'd talked to them in the week before his trip, his parents hadn't sounded right. They said all the right things, acted enthused—maybe even too much so—about his visit, but he couldn't help but feel there was something wrong, something they weren't telling him. Both times he called, he'd asked to speak to Colleen. Maybe she could tell him what it is, or, better yet, tell him that he was imagining things and that everything was great. But both times they'd said she was out, which was a little unusual for her. It had been fairly late when he'd called. It always was. Maybe 10 or 10:30. Colleen was a fourth-year student at the University of Wisconsin and still living at home. She was a serious student, one who rarely went out at night. But that week she apparently had lots of social activities. Probably Christmas parties, Matt told himself, pleased to think of his little sister getting out a little. He'd always worried about her, wondered if she was such a homebody out of choice or lack of it. She was such a great kid. He absolutely adored her. Couldn't wait to see her and hear all about college life.

He was really surprised when Colleen wasn't at the airport to pick him up. That was a first. Hers had always been the first face he'd see upon arriving. He used to tease her by asking why she didn't just rush onto the plane to find him the moment they opened the doors. Later he would learn that she just couldn't bear to be there when the news was first broken to him.

Between the fact that she wasn't there and the look on his parents' faces, he knew immediately that something really was wrong. Seriously wrong. With Colleen. He tried to remain calm, but felt like he might lose it when he asked, "Where is she?" He halfway expected them to break down, to tell him she'd died in some freak accident. SOMETHING WAS SERIOUSLY WRONG. Just let her be alive, he prayed in that instant before they answered.

"She's at home, Honey," his mother answered gently. "She can't wait to see you."

Though he felt hugely relieved, her controlled response signaled to him that his instincts were right. Something was, indeed, very wrong. With Colleen. With his baby sister. He didn't ask anything else while they walked through the airport. Didn't trust himself to speak. At first, his parents attempted small talk ("You look great," "How was the flight?") but soon they all fell silent. Until they reached the car. Once they were all seated in the car, still in the parking garage (in row 5G—for some reason, that had always stayed with him, maybe because he sat staring at the big "5G" stenciled on the cement column in front of the car the entire time his mother spoke), his father turned to him and said, "Matthew, we have some bad news. About your sister."

At that point, the man whom Matthew had never seen so much as a tear out of, buried his face in his hands. His shoulders shook in big, silent sobs.

"Oh, God," said Matthew as he turned to stare at the "5G." Oh God, don't let this really be happening, he thought, having no idea what it was that was happening.

Then his mother took over. Told him that two weeks earlier they'd heard tragic news—that Bobby Folsum had died. She asked if Matthew remembered him. He answered that the name sounded vaguely familiar, but he couldn't really place it. It irritated him to be talking about this guy, this Bobby Folsum, and *his* tragedy, when there was obviously something wrong with Colleen. Then his mother told him what it was that killed Bobby. AIDS. Suddenly Matthew remembered. Remembered where he'd heard that name. Bobby Folsum had been Colleen's prom date her senior year in high school. Actually, Bobby Folsum had been her *only* date in high school, so the name was not that easy to forget. Hadn't he moved away right after they'd graduated? His mother nodded in the affirmative, but even as she did so, it hit him. No, he practically shouted. NO. NO. You can't be telling me this has anything to do with Colleen. Tell me this is some kind of bizarre joke. AIDS was already everyday news down in Los Angeles, where the list of casualties in the entertainment business grew daily. But this was Madison, Wisconsin, for Chrissake, not Hollywood. And even more significantly, this was his sister. The one who, in high school, didn't know the first thing about boys, who'd asked him to teach her

239

to slow dance before that date with Bobby.

But it was true. They sat talking, crying, explaining for over an hour. They told him that a couple of weeks earlier, Colleen had heard—by chance, as it turns out—about Bobby's death. Shortly after their prom date, a week after their graduation, Bobby Folsum's family had moved to California. Colleen hadn't heard from, or of, him since. But two weeks ago, she'd run into an old friend of Bobby's on campus. Bill Arnold. It was Bill who told her the news of Bobby's death. At first, when he explained the cause of death—that unbeknownst to everyone, Bobby had contracted the AIDS virus from a blood transfusion he'd been given following knee surgery his junior year—Colleen failed to appreciate the significance. She was terribly shaken and saddened. Bobby had been very special to her. More special than anyone had known. But it wasn't until she was riding home on the bus that afternoon that the realization, the significance, struck her. After all, in those days AIDS was only striking IV drug users, homosexuals and those who'd received unscreened blood transfusions. At least, that's what the average person believed. So it wasn't surprising that Colleen failed to make the connection right away. But by the time she'd walked through the door that day, fear had overshadowed the grief she'd felt upon hearing the news about Bobby, and her mother could tell immediately that something was wrong. Once she heard the news about Bobby, she understood. Or at least she thought she did. Colleen was such a sensitive, compassionate young woman. It didn't surprise her to see her so shaken by the news that an old friend had died.

But that night, Colleen knocked on the bedroom door and asked to speak to her mother, in private. When the two of them were alone, what she told her mother shook her to the core. Trembling and in tears, Colleen told her mother that she and Bobby Folsum had made love following the prom. Over and over again, she repeated, "I'm sorry, Mama, I'm sorry," while her mother held her and soothed her. With a calm that totally belied her feelings, her mother had taken charge, reassuring Colleen that they were not disappointed in her, that all that mattered now was for Colleen to be tested. That the odds were in their favor. When she asked whether they'd used a condom, her daughter's renewed sobbing gave her all the answer she needed. "We didn't plan for it to happen, Mama," was all Colleen could manage to say.

And this, then, was how Matthew learned that because of tainted blood Bobby Folsum received in 1978, because in a moment of abandon, two naive, inexperienced teenagers, trying to discover their sexuality, had awkward, unfulfilling sexual relations in the back seat of a car, because of a world that was all too often anything but fair and just—because of all this, his sister had tested HIV positive just two days earlier.

They were all still pretty much in a state of shock. This was 1983. For people like the O'Connors, AIDS had not yet become a reality. It was a hideous disease that they'd read and heard about, but not one that they felt threatened by. Not one that they could imagine, in their wildest dreams, touching their lives. Their hearts had gone out to those afflicted with the disease. Colleen had been especially touched by stories of children who'd tested positive and who had subsequently been isolated by the community, refused admission to school, even taunted. A disease made all the more hideous by its double whammy—not only did it ultimately rob its victims of life, it also stripped them of their dignity. Made them outcasts, sometimes because of a lifestyle they'd long ago chosen, sometimes because they just happened to get that one (in how many million?) pint of blood that slipped through undetected.

At least there had been some comfort, some security in knowing that, if one were not a drug user, not a homosexual, had never received a blood transfusion, one need not worry.

And then, Colleen and the O'Connors, and soon the rest of the world, would slowly come to the realization that AIDS is here and now. It is *not* some other person's disease. AIDS is real. For everyone. For homosexuals, for heterosexuals. For young and old. For the promiscuous, for the sexually inexperienced. In today's world, this is fast becoming common knowledge—subject matter for school kids—but on that day in 1983 when Matthew O'Connor learned that the sister he cherished, the one he'd spent a lifetime trying to protect, had contracted this disease, it was a startling revelation. A revelation that, quite literally, broke his heart.

His planned one-week visit became a month-long stay. The first week remained a blur to him. He vividly remembered the moment he first saw Colleen—he'd opened the front door to see her standing there, waiting for him. He'd dropped his bags and held out his arms to her, and she'd fallen into them, sobbing.

"It's okay, Collie. It's okay," he'd said, repeating his nickname for her over and over again, tears streaming down his cheeks.

All he could remember of the rest of the day was their constant physical contact. They sat pressed up against each other, watching movies late into the night. He talked to her non-stop. Soothing talk. Telling her everything was going to be all right, that they would beat this thing, that he'd never let anything happen to her. Then, after she'd drifted off to sleep on the couch, he locked himself in the bathroom and cried until morning. The rest of the week passed in a fog. There were visits to the doctors, long walks in the bitter Wisconsin cold. More tears. Moments of incredible anger. Moments of disbelief. Sleepless nights.

Then, toward the end of that first week, something happened. When he awakened, he heard her singing. "Stuck on You" by Lionel Richie. She loved that song. And despite the fact that her high, squeaky voice managed to render it almost unrecognizable, Matthew had never heard anything quite so beautiful.

That morning at breakfast, Colleen announced to them that they'd all grieved enough—too much, really. That there were two ways they could respond to what had happened: They could either be depressed, bitter and miserable from this day forward, or they could let what had happened have a positive influence on all of their lives. She, for one, had just chosen the latter. And from this day forward, she had every intention of giving, and getting, as much joy as humanly possible out of each and every day. Starting with that very day. She informed them that after they ate the breakfast she'd prepared them, they were all going sledding together. And that's just what they did. And basically, from that day on, this was her attitude. One of joy and gratitude for the treasures that each day brought— be they an early morning walk or a beautiful sunset, a visit with a friend, or the laughter of a loved one. Colleen concentrated on making each day count, on cramming as much living and loving into the rest of her life as she could.

And it was this unshakable spirit that later, when he wrote about the experience, Matthew focused on. Matthew had two missions in writing *After the Dance:* One was to warn the world that unprotected heterosexual intercourse can result in AIDS. The second was to memorialize Colleen and to show the world how one brave young woman chose to deal with the cards that had been dealt her—namely, with courage, joy and optimism. To let the world know that a diagnosis of HIV positive does not mean that meaningful, joyful life ends right then and there.

Not that there wasn't plenty of pain—physical and emotional—that the entire family would experience in the years to come. Matthew tried to convey a realistic portrait of the next few years of all of their lives, the years leading up to Colleen's death in 1991. But, as his sister would have wanted him to do, he chose *not* to focus on the pain.

His struggle to follow Colleen's example was aided by a journalist, Ashley Cowles. Ashley was a young, struggling writer with the *Madison Sun Times* when she first came into the O'Connors' lives. A recent graduate of the University's School of Journalism, she'd learned of Colleen's diagnosis from a mutual friend. When she approached the family about the possibility of a series of articles chronicling Colleen's experience, her parents' initial reaction bordered on anger. Their pain was personal. And although Colleen had insisted upon telling her friends, all of whom had been tremendously supportive, they were fearful of the consequences to Colleen if the community at large were to know. But it had been Colleen who sat them down and told them that she planned to cooperate with Ashley. She hoped they'd understand, she said, and she apologized for any pain it might bring them, but, even at the risk of being ostracized, she felt that by telling her story, someone else might just be spared her fate.

And so she began talking to Ashley Cowles. At first it was a weekly meeting, but soon Ashley became a regular face at the O'Connor dinner table. And tastefully, sensitively, always with Colleen's approval, she allowed the city of Madison a glimpse into the life of a young woman struggling with the uncertain future that an HIV Positive diagnosis brings, always somehow managing to capture the beauty of Colleen's spirit, her ineffable joy of life. The O'Connors were tremendously relieved to find that they had underestimated their fellow Madisoneans. With some painful exceptions, the public reaction to Colleen's plight was warm and supportive. Later, when she developed AIDS and struggled to go on, the cards and letters that poured in as a result of Ashley Cowles' passionate portrayal would provide Colleen and her family with comfort and inspiration.

And when Colleen O'Connor finally passed away, on February 16, 1991, some eight years after learning she had been infected, the grief that Ashley Cowles experienced was very nearly as profound as that of Colleen's brother and parents.

*   *   *

When Matthew finally grew silent, Amy Griffin just sat watching him, trying to compose herself, gather her thoughts. His story had touched a chord in her. He was such a fine, kind man, so gentle—yet there was no denying his quiet strength. Or his wonderful spirit and compassion. His adorable sense of humor. The past week with him had been unlike any other she'd experienced. Despite the painful subject that had brought them together, they'd still managed to laugh until her sides ached, run until her legs refused to cooperate any longer, and talk until she grew hoarse.

But this disease. This fucking disease. Sometimes seeing his pain and knowing that there was this incredibly special young woman whom she would never get to meet because of it, it was all too much for Amy.

The week before, she'd read a horrifying list of some of the people from the arts community whose lives had been claimed by AIDS. Howard Ashman, whose magical lyrics graced *The Little Mermaid,* Michael Bennett, who choreographed *A Chorus Line* and *Dreamgirls.* Perry Ellis, Halston and Willi Smith, designers. Rock Hudson. Liberace. Anthony Perkins. She read of one actor who spoke of the emotional toll taken by one month in 1986 when he lost 35 friends. Imagine that, 35 friends in one month!

The death of Arthur Ashe in February of 1993 had especially stunned and saddened the world.

And the tragedy is not limited to our losses today, thought Amy. This disease's toll will ultimately include the countless books that will never be written, the basketball games that will never be played, the performances never seen. The Colleen O'Connors of this world who will never have the opportunity to teach, or to mother, or to love.

Amy wiped a tear from her eye. What an insane world it was becoming. Just when would it be enough?

Finally, softly, she reached out and touched Matthew's arm. He placed a hand on top of hers and smiled. He has a goofy smile, she thought. Goofy, but sweet. It had been a long time since she'd met a guy like this.

"Tomorrow's the big day, isn't it?" she said. Shooting was to begin in the morning.

"Nervous?" Matthew asked.

"Always am," she replied.

"You're going to be sensational," he said with absolute conviction.

"Thanks." She flashed him that smile, then grew serious again. "It's been a long time. Hope I've still got it."

"Oh, you've still got it all right," he kidded, throwing her an admiring look.

She leaned toward him and kissed him lightly on the cheek. "Thank you, Matthew. For that, and for the past two weeks. It's been wonderful."

Oh you definitely still have it, he thought. No doubt about it.

* * *

The first scene was being shot at an old school that, years earlier, had been abandoned as a schoolhouse and put into service by the YMCA as a youth rec center. They had been very cooperative, willing to give the crew free reign for the two weeks Shawn predicted it would take to shoot the scenes with Colleen and Bobby Folsum—the ones where he asks her out and then, the actual prom date. The setting was perfect—a huge red brick building, two stories, just like the one Matthew, and then, six years later, Colleen attended in Madison. Matthew drove around just about every neighborhood in the city of Seattle to find it. They were able to recruit plenty of extras to play all the other students from among the kids who utilized the facilities.

As executive producer, Paul was hurrying about, introducing cast and crew, and seeing to the last-minute things they hadn't foreseen. Candy, who'd pleaded with him to be given the role of his assistant, followed closely behind, jotting down notes on her legal pad as he gave orders.

Shawn Long hovered with Sherry Falconer and the young man they'd cast as Bobby Folsum, as they pored over their scripts. Cameramen checked lighting and positioned their equipment. At the last minute, Shawn succeeded in getting Michael Boyd to take over cinematography. It was a real coupe, as Michael was considered the best.

Matthew and Amy Griffin sat in the background. Amy wouldn't be involved in shooting at all that day, but she was the kind of actress who could be counted on to be there every day, every scene. As they talked, observing the hustle and bustle all around them, Laura walked up and greeted Matthew.

"Laura, what a pleasant surprise!" Matthew smiled warmly. He stood and hugged her, genuinely pleased to see her. "I didn't expect to see you here."

"I probably shouldn't be," she answered sheepishly. "I didn't plan to come. At least, not today, as hectic a day as I imagined it would be for all of you. But Paul insisted I be here to see things get started. It seemed to be important to him." She smiled at Amy.

"I'm glad he did," Matthew responded. Then, realizing that Laura and Amy hadn't met, he apologized and introduced them to each other.

"I don't need to have Amy introduced to me," laughed Laura. "I'm a big fan, Ms. Griffin. It's a real honor to meet you."

"Please, call me Amy," the actress responded warmly. "So you're the company attorney. It's my turn to be impressed."

Matt was pleased to see the immediate rapport

between the two women. Sensing they were comfortable in each other's company, he excused himself to see if he might be of help to either Paul or Shawn.

"Hey, Paul," Matthew said, upon finding his buddy helping a prop man position some classroom furniture, "did you know that Laura's here?"

Paul didn't respond, but gave a few quick instructions to the prop man, then joined Matt. He looked somewhat frazzled, preoccupied with the myriad of details on his mind, but Matthew knew he was in his element.

"Almost like the rush of a game, huh?" Paul's look reminded Matt of the intensity he used to see on Paul's face before a big game. Actually, it was the same look he still saw often enough, even when the game was just a friendly pick-up game at the club. Paul Brooks loved a challenge. He seemed to thrive on pressure.

But the news that Laura had dropped by softened his expression. "Where is she?" he asked, anxious to get a look at her again. He hadn't seen her since last night, and that was too long. It was getting to where he hated going home alone at night without her. And he didn't understand why it had to be that way. As far as he was concerned, he was ready to move right in with her. Of course, that wasn't even an option with Laura. Too fast. And there were the kids to consider.

As Matthew steered him to where he'd left Laura and Amy, they noticed a stirring on the far side of the big gymnasium. The entire crew had, in unison, stopped what they were doing and stood, gaping. It was Mackenzie Montana.

"Holy shit!" was all Matthew could think of to say.

Then she spotted them. Followed closely behind

249

by Neil Roberts and another well-dressed, middle-aged man, Mackenzie marched right over to where Paul and Matthew stood. By now, Shawn Long had gotten word of her arrival, and, none too happily, he also headed toward them. There was enough tension in the air to ignite a bonfire.

Before Mackenzie could open her mouth, Paul took charge.

"Hello, Mackenzie, Neil," he nodded to her agent. "I'm afraid I don't understand why you're here." He was trying to stay calm, but Matthew could tell he was nearing his blast-off point.

Mackenzie stood facing him, a fiery look on her face. But somehow, Paul thought that she did not look right. Something was different. Though she had dressed as she always did (seductively), had pranced over to them as she always did (with an exaggerated sway of the hips), and now faced him with a familiar expression (bitchy), something did not feel quite right. Usually all of those traits seemed so natural to her—she was so *good* at them. But somehow, today he sensed that the whole act was requiring a great deal of effort on her part. That perception took him aback a little.

"I'm here to shoot *After the Dance*," Mackenzie finally said, actually quite civilly. And before she could continue, the man who'd accompanied Neil and her spoke up.

"Let me introduce myself, Mr. Brooks," he said in a very polished manner. "My name is Lenny Coleman. I'm an attorney. I represent Ms. Montana."

Once he'd revealed his name, no further explanation was necessary. Paul and Shawn recognized it immediately. Mackenzie hadn't screwed around with finding an attorney. She'd gone right to the top.

"Well, Mr. Coleman," answered Paul, "it's a

pleasure to meet you. But I'm still confused as to why Mackenzie is here. I spoke with Mr. Roberts over two weeks ago and informed him that the part of Ashley Cowles is being played by Amy Griffin."

By now, both Amy and Laura had walked over to see what all the commotion was about. Once they sighted Mackenzie Montana, they dropped back and watched from near the stage. Both women looked upset. Amy was visibly angry, as though she were ready to do battle. Laura looked shaken. Paul was afraid to glance in her direction.

Coleman spoke again. "I'm aware of that conversation, Mr. Brooks. It's unfortunate that you had a change of heart. But I'm afraid Ms. Montana had a binding legal agreement with you to do *After the Dance.*" He spoke with confidence. Authority. "Now she is here today. Ready to start shooting."

He looked at Paul as if to say, "So what do you intend to do about it, Buster?"

Paul was glad Laura was out of earshot. He knew that, had she heard Coleman, had she even known he was Mackenzie's attorney, she'd have felt obliged to get involved. All he could think of now was that he had to get them out of there before that happened. Why had he been stupid enough to practically insist she come today?

"Mr. Coleman," Paul started, not completely sure of what he was going to say, "we intend to begin shooting *After the Dance* today. And we intend to shoot it *without* Mackenzie Montana. Now, I can only tell you that you all are most welcome to stay and observe the goings on," (Why on Earth would I say such a thing? he asked himself), "but, let me warn you, that if you in any way interfere with our production, if you so much as cause a moment's delay in our schedule, you'll be out of here so fast it'll make your head spin."

He was sure he'd said all the wrong things, but he didn't want them to know that's what he was thinking. So he added, "Have I made myself clear?"

"Perfectly clear, Mr. Brooks," Lenny Coleman said politely. "And I will tell you this, Mr. Brooks," he continued, "you can expect to see us in court." Then, wanting to hit Paul where it really hurt, in that place where he knew every producer was vulnerable, he added, "I just hope, for your sake, that your budget has the financial wherewithal to withstand a major lawsuit."

Ouch. That did hurt, but Paul's face didn't betray him.

With Coleman orchestrating, the trio turned to leave. Out of the corner of her eye, Mackenzie caught Paul throwing a worried look into the shadows. She stopped dead and stared. Then she saw them—Amy Griffin and Laura. When Paul saw the recognition register on Mackenzie's face, he cringed and prepared himself to dash over and protect Laura from her, as if he half expected Mackenzie to pull a knife and lunge at her.

But Mackenzie just stood and stared. Paul's fear turned to shock as he looked into her face—instead of seeing the crazed, hateful look he'd expected, she looked like she was about to cry. He felt sick.

Neil Roberts, who had seen the look, too, grasped Mackenzie's elbow and gently steered her toward the door they'd entered. With Lenny Coleman on one side, and Neil, dutifully, on the other, Mackenzie was led out of the gymnasium without further incident.

And so went the first day of shooting of *After the Dance.*

13

The situation with Mackenzie Montana was starting to take its toll on Laura and Paul's relationship. Both of them were striving to not let it interfere, but it just kept rearing its ugly head.

They'd been shooting now for three weeks, keeping Paul extremely busy. But he tried to set aside as much time as possible for Laura and the kids, heading right over to their house as soon as each day's shoot was over, joining them for dinner, and staying until the kids went to bed. Usually that was when Laura kicked him out. Good naturedly, but firmly. There was a definite strain between them. Paul knew better than to push.

After leaving their place, he'd head to the office for meetings with Matt until well into the morning. Then a couple quick hours of sleep and back on the set in the early A.M.

They'd been served with the complaint yesterday. At Laura's request, Paul called for an extended lunch break from shooting and met her back at his office to discuss it.

Mackenzie Montana vs. Brooks Production. The

complaint alleged, not too surprisingly, a breach of contract on the part of Brooks Productions. Just the standard legal jargon alleging harm done as a result of Brooks' failure to recognize their alleged agreement. In the Prayer for Relief, there were vague references to lost opportunities, and detrimental reliance on Mackenzie's part. Nothing they hadn't expected. Still, it was unnerving.

Paul knew he could no longer keep the matter from Laura, but he was still determined to minimize her involvement.

"I just think it would be wise to let Winnifred and Barry handle it," he was saying. Winnifred and Barry was an old, established Seattle firm. They'd handled the company's affairs before Paul hired Laura.

Laura acted incredulous. "Just what am I here for?" she wanted to know.

"Laura," Paul said in as soothing a voice as he could muster when his stomach was so tied in knots, "you know that I believe you are more than capable of handling this lawsuit. You know that. So please don't act as though this were an affront to your abilities. I just don't want this to affect us. I refuse to let it."

"But, Paul," answered Laura, "pretending this situation doesn't exist just won't work. It's here. It's not going to go away. Believe me, I hate it every bit as much as you do. But I'm not going to run away from it." She looked away for a moment, as if running away was just what she wanted to do, but then redirected her gaze to him. "And I'd like to think—no, I *know*—that I am enough of a professional to separate my personal feelings from my responsibilities as this company's lawyer."

She hesitated again. Then her voice grew softer.

"Don't you see, Paul? It's something I *have* to do. I'm a big girl. A professional. I can't let you protect me from a situation that I have to learn to deal with. That, from a professional viewpoint, I feel a responsibility to deal with. It's a precedent that I just can't let you set: Let's see, this is a legal matter that might upset Laura... or, gee, Laura might get pissed off if she sees how stupid I was in this situation, so I'll just give this one to Winnifred and Barry."

She wasn't trying to be sarcastic, but she knew she was right. Even if she wished she weren't.

Paul still didn't speak. He looks so sad, thought Laura. She wanted to walk over to where he sat and press his face against her chest. Stroke his hair. Murmur comforting words to him.

He sensed her feelings, realized that he was causing her pain. More pain. The one person in the whole world he wanted to spare pain—she'd already had more than her share before he ever came into her life—and he just kept hurting her.

"You're determined to handle this, aren't you?" he asked resignedly.

"I promise you that I'll do my absolute best to avoid letting it affect us," she answered with utmost sincerity.

"Starting with letting me stay a while tonight after the kids go to bed?" Paul asked, a slight smile finally creeping into his eyes.

"Starting with that," she responded, more than willingly.

*   *   *

Christmas came and went in the blink of an eye. It turned out to be the best Christmas Paul could remember.

255

The holiday spirit was heightened by the fact that things were coming along great on the movie. After the rocky start they'd had, courtesy of Ms. Montana, things had settled right down. The dailies looked great, and the atmosphere on the set was one of great anticipation. They'd finished up with the high school scenes and were now introducing the audience to Ashley Cowles. In the book Ashley did not make her appearance until she'd already learned of Colleen's diagnosis. In the screenplay, however, Matthew chose to build up that first meeting with Colleen by first giving the audience a chance to know Ashley Cowles in her position as an inexperienced, somewhat naive, but undeniably talented, reporter. It was an effective technique that added impact to that first meeting.

Amy Griffin was brilliant. Her performance in her first scene already had people talking about an Oscar nomination. With her understated, dignified manner, she was capable of conveying more passion with a single look, or a subtle gesture than most actors could muster up working with the most eloquent and moving of dialogues. What's more, her intensity and professionalism were lifting other cast members' performances to a higher level.

Everyone knew that in *After the Dance,* they had a winner on their hands.

More than once, Paul and Shawn shuddered to think of what production might have been like had Mackenzie Montana played Ashley.

Even that situation seemed to have abated somewhat. Laura had filed an answer to the complaint already. So far, they'd not heard anything else. It actually seemed to be helping the situation between Laura and Paul for Paul to have agreed to going along with her handling the suit. In retrospect, Paul decided

that trying to shelter her had been just one more
situation in which he'd exercised poor judgment. So
what else was new? At any rate, they were now
dealing with the Mackenzie Montana situation on a
strictly business level—not giving it any undue attention. At least so it seemed to Paul.

Back to Christmas. It had been wonderful. He'd
never spent a Christmas around kids before. Never
realized what sharing it with them, seeing it through
their eyes, could do to his own enjoyment of it.

By now they'd pretty much gotten into a routine
where Paul spent evenings and week-ends with Laura
and the kids, though he always slept at his own house.
But on Christmas Eve morning, when he was out with
Christopher and Hailey doing some last-minute shopping for Laura, the kids were telling him about their
Christmas morning rituals—about waking up, usually
before dawn, to run down and check out what Santa
had brought—when little Hailey looked at him (her
looks were beginning to melt him—he wondered if she
suspected as much and used it to her advantage at
times) and asked, "You'll be there, won't you?"

"At five or six in the morning?" Paul had answered incredulously. "Sorry, Munchkin, but that's a
little early for me to make it over there."

"Why can't you just spend the night?" she persisted. "Then you'd already be there." Made perfect
sense to her. It sounded pretty good to Paul, too.

"Yeh!" chimed in Christopher. "You can stay in
the guest room. Then we can play with my Genesis
all morning. I know I'm getting that NBA Jams I told
you about. That's a great idea, Hailey... for a change!"
His smile let her know he was kidding.

"Just what makes you so sure you're getting a
new video game?" Paul teased. He'd already helped

Laura buy the game but wanted to make Christopher sweat it at least a little. "Your mom didn't tell me anything about buying you a video game."

"I *know* she got me one." Clearly he didn't buy Paul's act. "She always gets me my top three things and that was number one. What about it Paul, will you spend the night?" He loved the idea, too.

"I'm not the one you need to ask that question, guys," Paul answered. He was pleased that they seemed to want him there, to share such a special family day with them. It especially pleased him that Hailey had been the one to come up with the idea. Their relationship was finally taking off. The first couple of months he and Laura were seeing each other, it was clear that Hailey had mixed feelings about Paul hanging around. But now her enthusiastic greetings, constant chatter when he was around, and the increasing number of hugs he got from her signaled he'd finally met with her approval. It meant a lot to him. Not just because he knew how important it was to Laura for both kids to feel good about them, but also because he'd grown awfully fond of the little girl. She was a real character, an absolutely beautiful little girl who was very sweet and loving, but one who also had a lot of spunk. And incredible curiosity. It had been, in large part, Paul's patience and willingness to answer her never-ending stream of questions (on anything from why dogs have such long tongues, to why the word "know" has a "k" in it, to his all-time favorite: "Why is it dark in noses?") that had won her over. At a loss at first as to how to relate to a little girl, Paul finally realized that the best way was simply to listen. And it had worked, for in Hailey, he'd found a real talker, one who greatly appreciated a good listener.

When they got home from shopping, both kids

rushed in and pleaded with Laura to let Paul spend the night. She'd put up no resistance. And that was how it came to be that Paul's one-night stay (in the guest room), became a seven-day stay over the holidays.

The only hard part had been his having to leave after New Year's Day.

Still thinking back over the holidays, the only other thing that troubled Paul was the fact that Laura received some strange phone calls, mainly just hang ups, but once, she'd heard breathing. When he realized what was going on, Paul grabbed the phone from her and said "Hello" in as menacing a voice as possible. He wanted to make sure whoever it was knew there was a man around. It always bothered him that Laura and the kids were alone out in the country like that, but now he was really worried. And a woman like Laura was bound to attract male attention. It didn't make him feel better knowing she had the two dogs. They were good barkers, but that was about it. They'd be more apt to lick someone to death than to actually attack. So, after the second call, Paul arranged to have a security system put in. He'd love to get his hands on the creep who'd been calling. He'd make sure he thought twice about calling again, or coming anywhere near Laura and the kids.

But the funny thing was that, when he grabbed the phone away from Laura, he heard what sounded almost like a gasp of surprise.

And he could have *sworn* the voice on the other end was that of a woman.

*   *   *

With other women, Paul's experience had always been that after the initial rush, he quickly grew bored. Restless.

That had not happened yet with Laura. And he was beginning to believe that it never would. No, he'd pretty much concluded, life with Laura would be anything but boring. She was far more complex, unpredictable, than he'd expected. Full of surprises. Today had been one of the best.

He'd left the set early and went back to the office about five p.m. to return phone calls and review numbers for the budget. He'd seen her in the hall when he first got there.

About half an hour later, Candy came in to say good night. Then he heard David and the guys from shipping leave. He was just wondering why Laura hadn't bothered to say good-bye when she appeared at the door. She looked great, wearing a blue sweater and short, tight skirt, black high heels, and no hose. He was surprised to see her bare legs. Surprised he hadn't noticed when he'd run into her in the hall. After all, he'd admired her legs as he watched her walk away. Could have sworn she had colored hose or tights on. Her hair was piled loosely on top of her head—like she'd put it up neatly earlier in the day, or maybe even the night before, then forgotten about it. Several long wisps tickled her neck and shoulders.

She'd been working on a recording agreement for Blue Moon. They were doing the sound track for the movie, and she'd spent the better part of the past four days working out the contract with them.

"How's the contract with Blue Moon going?" he asked her, his eyes wandering to her legs as she stood leaning against the doorway.

"Just finished it," she answered in a tone that Paul thought indicated she was pleased to have it behind her. Behind her, he thought. That's just where I'd like to be. Then he mentally chastised himself for being so single minded. Typical horny male, but he couldn't help it. Sometimes just looking at her made him so damned excited. And there was something about the way she was standing there, something that made him pretty sure she was having thoughts not unlike his.

He decided to test his hunch. Starting with her eyes, then traveling slowly downwards, he surveyed her with a look whose message could not be mistaken. When he reached her legs again, he commented, "No hose today, huh?"

"Not now," she answered. Immediate erection. "No panties either." God, he must be dreaming. He was hard as a rock.

She closed his door and twisted the lock, then turned to him with a Cheshire-like smile. He sat, blood rushing to all the right places, and waited for her to approach him. He couldn't believe it. What about their rule about the office?

Before he knew what was happening, she was kneeling before him, between his legs, unzipping his pants. She took him into her mouth. His head swam. He leaned back in his chair. When she heard him moan, she stopped. "Not yet," she said. She climbed onto him then. Skirt hiked up around her waist. High heels still on. She hadn't been kidding. No panties. He'd never been so turned on. Slowly at first, then with increasing tempo, she ground herself into him. He could see their reflection in the darkened windows opposite his desk. It wasn't easy, but he held himself back until her undulating hips reached a frenzied pace and her pleading voice called out, "Now!" And then, holding her down at the waist, he gave it to her, hammering her with a force he'd never before shown her.

When it was over, he was halfway afraid to look at her. Afraid she might regret what had just happened, or worse yet, be angry with him. But she sat, still wrapped around him, and held him close. Then she giggled.

"What's so funny?" he asked her as she loosened her grip on him and leaned back to have a look at him. She smiled. No sign of regret, or hurt. Just a big, satisfied smile. He felt relieved.

"When I was leaving my office, I saw Tony," she answered, giggling again. "He was just starting his rounds of the building. I figure by now, he's back at his post." Which happened to be practically right outside Paul's door. Definitely within earshot. And they hadn't exactly been quiet.

Minutes later, when they opened the door to leave, there he was, sitting at his desk, a big grin on his face.

"You folks have a good night now, you hear?" he said cheerfully. Laura thought she saw him wink slyly at Paul, but she was too embarrassed to look.

When they got to the parking lot, they burst into laughter. Paul's office was just one story up. As they kissed and nuzzled each other before parting ways, they suddenly noticed the lights going on in the darkened room above them. They could see Tony standing there in the doorway of Paul's office, the grin still fixed to his face, studying the room. Laura was more than a little shocked to be able to see into the room as well as they could. The thought had occurred to her earlier, but the truth was at that moment, she hadn't much cared. Now, however, she felt slightly unnerved by it. Thank God the lot was empty.

But as she climbed into her car and waved goodbye to Paul, she shuddered.

Suddenly she had an eerie feeling that maybe they hadn't been alone after all.

14

"Listen to this," Amy Griffin commanded, as she stepped into a group that consisted of Paul, Matthew and several cast and crew members. It was midmorning, and she'd just arrived to observe shooting of a scene that did not involve her. The others were taking a short break, while Mike Boyd worked on lighting for the hospital scene they were in the middle of.

She had a Seattle newspaper in one hand, a latte from Starbucks in the other.

She read to them from an article on the front page: "The best and brightest high school students in the United States have become more aware of the dangers of AIDS but are doing little more to protect themselves against the deadly disease."

Looking up, her expressive face full of alarm, incredulity, she asked, "Can you believe it? It says that even though they know it's out there and they're aware of it—aware that they can contract it through unprotected sex—even though they're actually worried about it, finally at least they're worrying about it, THEY STILL AREN'T PRACTICING SAFE SEX!

They think they're fucking invincible! That's what this article says. Can you believe it?!"

She shook her head and looked around with a pained, bewildered expression that practically begged for relief, for someone to snap their fingers and wake her from a bad dream.

No one else spoke. What, really, is there to say about news like this? By now, each and every person involved in making *After the Dance* had been touched by the story of Colleen O'Connor. There was not an actor, prop man, makeup artist, or wardrobe person for whom this movie was just about working, about making a living. To a person, *After the Dance* had taken on added meaning and had given them a sense of being part of something bigger than the production of just one more source of entertainment for the American public. They all felt, to one degree or another, the mission that had inspired Matthew to write the book and screenplay and Amy Griffin to fight for the role of Ashley Cowles. No one was more outspoken about it, more articulate on the matter, than Amy, but she knew they all felt it too.

"This is what this movie is all about. You see that, don't you?" Her piercing look studied the faces turned to her. "You see how important it is, how imperative it is, to reach them? The kids? The ones who responded to this survey were bright kids. This article calls them 'the best and the brightest kids.' They're all high school students, listed in *Who's Who Among American High School Students*. Intelligent kids. Kids who seem to know all about AIDS, but *still* aren't doing anything about it. And what about the kids that aren't so smart? What about them?" She looked close to tears, overwhelmed. Matthew walked up to her and put an arm around her shoulder. "The ones who don't even know of the danger?"

Now her eyes filled with tears. "I'm sorry, Guys. I don't mean to get all melodramatic on you. I know this stuff gets to you as much as it does to me. But I read this shit, and I just go nuts. Fucking, stark raving, nuts. We've just got to make them listen. That's all there is to it. We have to make them listen."

She finally smiled. She felt a little foolish, but sometimes she just couldn't help herself.

The group dispersed, still silent. Matthew's arm was still around her, supporting her. He didn't say anything at first because he didn't trust himself to speak. He knew what she was feeling. He'd read an article over the week-end about a very small, rural Texas town in which one healthcare worker claimed to know of six teenagers who'd acquired the HIV virus through heterosexual activity. It had sickened him. Brought back all the old feelings and memories, the disbelief he'd felt upon learning about Colleen. But that had been ten years ago! Ten years had passed, and this disease was still not being taken seriously by mainstream Americans. It was insane. His only solace was the hope that *After the Dance* would have an impact. If only a handful of kids take note and actually let its message affect their decisions, it will all have been worth it. And somehow, he knew that with Amy Griffin's passion and her incredible talent, his goal was not only realistic, it was very modest. This movie could conceivably impact the actions of thousands, perhaps tens of thousands.

He was so moved by this woman standing beside him. Touched by her passion. But, as men often do, Matthew found it easier to find something to joke about than to share the emotions overwhelming him.

Gesturing toward the Starbucks cup in Amy's hand, he accused her of "going Seattle" on him. She'd only been there a matter of weeks but had already fallen victim to one of Seattle's greatest frenzies—the espresso frenzy. Every corner had an espresso stand or shop on it, and at every shop could be found a line of trench coat-clad Seattlites waiting for their fix. "Give me a single, tall, non-fat, mocha. Decaf, please. And hold the cream (whipped cream)....oh, and make that iced." It had become a language in and of itself. And serious business in this rain-soaked region. Espresso stands were popping up in the grocery stores, and gas stations. Matthew could only shake his head when one was installed in his office supply store the week before. He'd often thought it would make good material for a *Saturday Night Live* skit.

So breaking the somber mood with a joke about her latte was a natural. And it worked. Amy's eyes warmed immediately.

"God, why do I do that?" she asked, smiling at him wistfully. "Next time I get up on my soapbox, will you kick me or something?"

"Depends," Matt responded.

"On what?" Amy asked.

"On what the 'or something' is," he replied.

Amy looked at him thoughtfully, playfully. Her female antennae were up. He was testing her. She studied him for a moment. He was such a sweet guy. It was just a game they were playing, but one that she knew he took seriously. She'd hate to see him get hurt. She knew they were on the verge of crossing a line. And before it was crossed, she wanted to be as sure of her feelings as she could possibly be. That was why her answer was so long in coming.

Finally, she said, "I think *that* should be up to

you."

It was an answer that pleased him immensely.

* * *

Laura was on her way to meet Corinne for lunch. They hadn't seen much of each other recently, and Laura had been feeling a little guilty about it. Corinne was such a good friend to her, and over the past couple of years, since Michael's death, had always made such a point of sharing time with her.

She'd been instrumental in getting Laura through that period of intense grief, had practically lived from with her from the day she received the call at work until the funeral two days later. And, even more importantly, after other friends had all but disappeared—everyone is always right there in those first few days and weeks, but before long, the tugs and pulls of their every-day lives lure them into thinking they are no longer needed—it's easier to tell themselves that the grieving family is doing just fine. It's then—that period after all the connecting, the togetherness, when life gets back to "normal"—that the panic really sets in for those left behind. But Corinne had been there for Laura then, too. Which is why Laura had been feeling no small amount of guilt for the fact that, since Paul's arrival on the scene, she'd had far too little time for her dear friend. Last night, lying in bed, she'd realized just how self-absorbed she'd been in the past few months. She'd picked up the phone right then—it was almost midnight, but knowing Corinne, she was watching *Almost Live*, a bottle of wine, perhaps even Mark, at her side.

Revealing not even a hint of hurt feelings, Corinne squealed in delight at hearing from Laura, at the news of her and Paul's blossoming relationship. They'd promised each other a long lunch together the following Monday.

Now, behind the wheel of her Jeep Cherokee, sitting almost at a standstill on the traffic-logged Evergreen Point Bridge into the city, Laura smiled as she remembered the first time she met Corinne. She'd just been hired at Emery, Johnson. It was a Monday morning staff meeting. She was being introduced to the partners and associates. Until Laura's arrival, Corinne had been the firm's resident hot stuff. Though not a classic beauty, Corinne's status was well deserved. She was an extremely striking woman. Her voluminous blonde hair framed a wonderfully animated face. Her more than ample chest—always tastefully, but prominently, displayed—was accentuated by a tiny waist. She was tall, with regal bearing, and long, shapely legs. She was obviously a woman used to getting an abundance of male attention. And before Laura's arrival, she pretty much had a corner on it—the male attention—at Emery, Johnson. Corinne didn't even attempt to hide her displeasure that morning, upon seeing the lovely vision upon which all eyes were focused. No, Laura Kennedy was not a welcome sight to Corinne. And as she was introduced around the table, and stretched her hand out in Corinne's direction, Laura made a mental note to watch her step around that one.

But she'd underestimated the blonde bombshell. For if Corinne was anything, she was a good sport. And she soon found out that it was actually pretty nice to have a true cohort at the office. An accomplice. Someone who found Old Man Emery's sexual innuendos, his casual brushing up against her, as disgusting and pathetic as *she* always had. (Now, they both agreed, they didn't actually mind it so much with

Drew Freeman. No, old Drew could brush up against them til his hunky Southern heart was content. But old man Emery, *that* was disgusting). Someone who was as turned off as she was by Bill Eagan's incredible arrogance. Who could understand when, two days before her period is due, she feels like telling Bob Olson, a senior partner, to fuck off, when all he has done is politely ask her to get him another copy of the Arnold brief she'd written for him.

No, it wasn't long before Laura and Corinne became thicker than thieves.

The truth is that pretty women often times have difficulty establishing close female friends. Both had learned that good looks can be an albatross in relationships, one that makes the person with the "good fortune" of being attractive have to work that much harder to prove she is just a regular person. Bend over backwards to be nice. Downplay her attributes. Over the years, Laura had become adept at doing just that, but now, approaching the hard-earned age of 40, she was becoming more than a little tired of having to stand on her head in order to be liked. Yet, perhaps out of habit, she started out playing the same old games with Corinne. But, fortunately, Corinne's own self-confidence and rich sense of humor soon made the extra effort unnecessary.

Once in a while, two women like Laura and Corinne manage to get through all the bullshit and connect. And in this case, the bond that resulted would provide one of the richest, most satisfying relationships of Laura's and Corinne's lives. A relationship between two mature women who truly understood each other, who had experienced life—it's disappointments, its thrills—and who knew that what lay ahead might well exceed, in its depth and capacity for joy, any fairy tale illusions they may have formed as girls. Women who knew that what really matters in relationships was not being as pretty as the other person, but was simply having that other person to walk with, side by side, through the insane journey. As only two women can do, Laura and Corinne found in each other a camaraderie, a spiritual bonding that male-female relationships simply could not offer them. And at 42 and 39 respectively, Corinne and Laura were at a new stage in their lives, one that they'd been conditioned to look forward to with dread, but one that they were slowly learning held the promise of being the absolute best. They were no longer young, dreamy girls—what a relief. They were now women, productive, self-confident women, who knew what they wanted in life and who had slowly and, often painfully, learned what was really important in life. Women who could laugh—who *loved* to laugh—at themselves and at the ironies of life and who no longer worried about attaining a physical perfection, but who now valued their experience and hard-earned wisdom far more than their looks, and yet, had never looked better. Women who knew the value of fun— who could talk about sex without feeling the word "love" had to follow closely behind—who had the security of knowing they could, if necessary, do just fine, thank you, without a man in their lives to "take care of them." Women who had made plenty of mistakes, "mondo mistakes," as Corinne would say, but who even liked the fact that they'd made them, seeing that every mistake, every misfortune, had been an opportunity for growth. Not that they'd taken advantage of all the "opportunity." Not even close. But at times they had. And they were that much richer for it.

Laura and Corinne were two women who absolutely cherished the gift of this other person, this one other friend who truly understood what being a woman—what being a 40-year-old woman—in this day and age meant. These were the thoughts behind the smile on Laura's face as she inched her way forward on the freeway.

She ended up being fifteen minutes late for their lunch date at Palomino's. Corinne was in the midst of a lively conversation with a handsome young waiter when she arrived, so Laura knew her lateness had not been a problem.

They talked like magpies, both so eager to hear what was going on in the other's life. Laura made Corinne go first. She heard all about Mark and their relationship, now at a turning point. Corinne was tired of playing second fiddle to his wife and family. She'd been making herself less available, even accepting occasional dates. It was driving Mark crazy. He was truly miserable at home, but he was a kind man, one who found it very difficult—maybe, they were finding, even impossible—to hurt a family, a wife, who loved him very much. Corinne felt sorry for Mark. She was not angry with him, and her new attitude was not a ploy on her part. She was just beginning to lose hope. To worry about her own needs, not so much at present, but in the future. After all, she could still pretty much pick and choose between a number of men. For example, Philip here—the dreamy young thing with GQ looks who was serving them drinks. She had a good ten years on him, but there was no mistaking his interest in her. But, characteristically philosophical, she pointed out the inevitable fact that one day soon that might not be true. And though, she could certainly get by, and most likely happily so,

272

without a lifelong companion, she'd never abandoned the dream of finding one.

Laura offered what advice she could, knowing full well that, in the final analysis, Corinne would handle the situation as she saw fit, which undoubtedly would be just as it should be handled.

Now the conversation turned to Laura and Paul. Corinne was dying to get the low-down on their relationship. One would think, by the look of absolute glee on her face, that it was *her* good fortune they were discussing, and not Laura's. That was the kind of friend Corinne turned out to be. She wanted to hear everything—how the kids felt about him, how much time they spent together, what they did, how the movie was coming along, and finally, *especially,* what kind of a lover he was. Laura was not comfortable going into any kind of detail, but her response was enough to satisfy, and amuse, her curious friend.

"I never knew orgasms could last that long," she said, an amazed look on her face. It was all she needed to say. As Philip approached the table with their salads, they dissolved into laughter.

So went the rest of the meal. They laughed, commiserated, counseled each other and thoroughly enjoyed the comfort that their time together always provided.

As they were leaving, walking toward the elevators to the parking garage below, Laura offhandedly remarked, "You know, I had the strangest feeling today."

Corinne looked at her. "About what?"

"When I was driving in to town," Laura continued. "I had the feeling I was being followed." She laughed. "Isn't that silly? Like someone would have a reason to follow me around."

"Laura," Corinne answered, clearly concerned about this announcement, "Dear. You, of all people, stand a chance of being followed. Listen, Laura, there are a lot of creeps out there. You better not take any chances that some sicko guy might catch you off-guard sometime."

"But, that's just it," answered Laura. "That's what's so silly about this whole thing. The car I thought was following me wasn't driven by a man. A woman was in it. I'm almost sure of it. She had a hat on—one of those glitzy baseball caps, the kind with fake stones all over it—but I'm just sure that it was a woman."

"Well, then," responded her friend, "maybe you *are* being a little paranoid."

And with that, the two women laughed, hugged, and bid each other goodbye.

* * *

Sometimes he was sure it was deliberate—that she was *trying* to drive him crazy. Like now. Finally, for the first time in over two weeks, Neil Roberts was talking to Mackenzie Montana. He'd been trying to reach her at the Four Seasons and had left countless messages. Lenny Coleman had called at least half a dozen times—he sounded really angry the last time Neil answered her phone. How the hell did Neil know why she hadn't returned his calls? She wasn't even returning Neil's calls. And this new script he'd been wanting to tell her about was hot. If she didn't jump right on it, she could probably forget it. When Stan Crowe first called him with it, he told him he had Mackenzie in mind for the lead, but Neil had since heard Goldie Hawn was after the part.

He couldn't believe Mackenzie's reaction when

he'd told her about it.

"What do you mean, don't bother sending it up there?" he was now asking her, incredulous. "It's a great part. Why wouldn't you want to take a look at it?"

"You're WHAT??" he responded. "You're not interested!! Give me a break—how the hell can you say you're not interested when you haven't even seen it yet?" Neil usually showed a great deal of deference to his client, but his patience was wearing thin. As was his bank account. Now that *After the Dance* had fallen through, he'd begun to feel more than a little anxious about their next project. True, Lenny Coleman sounded confident about their suit against Brooks, but it would be some time before that was resolved. And he and Mackenzie hadn't yet addressed what his share of any recovery would be. He assumed it would be his standard 25 percent, but with Mackenzie Montana, it was never safe to assume anything. This new script was as important to Neil as it should have been to Mackenzie. Problem was, she didn't seem to share his way of thinking.

"I'm not interested because I'm not planning to do another movie for a while," she answered curtly. "I'm taking some time off."

"You're WHAT?" This was too much. She couldn't possibly be serious.

"I'm taking a few months off. Maybe even a year," Mackenzie responded, "so there's no need to send me any scripts for a while."

Neil was silent. Goddamn her, he thought. How dare she play with him this way. Just what did she think he'd do during her little vacation? Maybe she could afford the luxury of time off, but he certainly couldn't. Which is why he decided to back off a little.

He knew her only too well—pushing her now would only end in disaster. Sometimes, not often, but *sometimes*, he'd been able to reason with her. Hopefully, this would be one of those times. Right now, he dare not let her know what he was thinking—of her plans. Of *her*. No, better to fall back on tact. What he really needed was to spend some time with her.

"Mackenzie, I understand," he finally responded. "You're feeling a need for a little break. You worked your rear end off last year. Then all the problems we've had with *After the Dance*... I know how upsetting this whole thing has been for you. It's no wonder you want to take some time off. I'm all for it."

He wished he could see her face. He knew her so well. If they were together now he'd know immediately what she was thinking. But, since the only measure of her response was an acute silence, he had no choice but to continue.

"I'll tell you what. I'll just fly up there. Spend a little time with you. Make sure you get some well deserved R and R..."

"Neil?" her voice interrupted him.

"Yes?"

"Nice try," she laughed. "But *can* it. Will you? Oh, and don't even think about coming up here. When I need you, I'll call."

"But Mackenzie..."

"Goodbye, Neil. Gotta' run!" she said tauntingly, as she placed the telephone back on its receiver. Then, after looking out the window to check on the weather this late morning in Seattle, she called the bell captain and ordered her rental car brought around to the entrance.

* * *

What started off as a great day for Laura ended in near tragedy.

Paul had asked her to spend some time on the set with him. Though he was always encouraging her to, she hadn't gone near there ever since that first day of shooting, when Mackenzie Montana made her appearance. But many weeks had lapsed since then, and she had to admit that she was curious. She kept hearing how great things were going. The initial tension and apprehension surrounding everyone involved with the movie had been visibly transformed into a form of elation, and Laura was beginning to feel left out. So yesterday, when Paul asked her to visit, she did feel tempted. Paul could see that, and with just a little more urging, she happily accepted his invitation.

Some of the scenes were being shot in a rented warehouse in West Seattle. It was little more than a huge metal, windowless structure situated in an industrial area of the city, but once she stepped inside, Laura was transported—via a sophisticated soundstage— into a vibrant newsroom, where Ashley Cowles sat arguing with the editor about the merits of an article she'd been working on for the *Madison Sun Times*. It was 1983. A young student at the University had discovered that she was HIV Positive. With the student's cooperation, Ashley wanted to chronicle her experience with this relatively new disease. After all, most of the world was still under the impression that this was a gay person's disease. Or an IV drug user's. This young woman, an honor student—heterosexual, nonpromiscuous—was startling evidence of the fact that AIDS might pose a threat to a much wider segment of the population than was previously thought vulnerable to it. Ashley was passionate about this story, about its significance, but her editor was less than enthusiastic. She'd just been informed that he'd relegated the story to the University area edition only— to page 24 nonetheless, where it was doomed to oblivion. The harder and more adamantly Ashley argued her case, the more he dug his heels in on the matter, until finally, Ashley stormed out of the newsroom in a fit of anger.

In the final scene of the sequence, the camera zooms in on Amy's face, as she leans against the door to the newsroom—the one she'd just slammed shut— to reveal a look of pure anguish and frustration. But as the lens lingers there, slowly Amy's expression changes. One can see a determination emerge, grow, and, finally, swallow up the despair that defined the young reporter's mood moments earlier. It's a look that tells the audience that somehow, some *way*, the reporter will make sure the story not only gets told, but heard, a look that smacks of confidence in her eventual triumph. It was one of those subtle but unmistakable messages that Amy was famous for conveying without so much as a single word—a nuance of expression that only a handful of the world's finest actors could attempt without falling flat on their faces.

While the earlier scene between the two of them in the newsroom had to be shot a number of times, Shawn Long knew that he could not improve upon the first take on this closeup of Amy. It was only two o'clock, but they'd already accomplished the day's goals and, since the next scene was to take place in the O'Connor home and would take several hours for the crew to set up, they decided to call it quits for the day. Besides, things were going so well, that Shawn, in an uncharacteristically benevolent mood, announced that the cast deserved a little free time as a reward. The crew would not be so fortunate. They would find themselves working on the next set into the early morning hours.

After congratulating Amy on the fine job she'd done, Paul and Laura walked out together. Paul suggested they grab a late lunch, but Laura answered that she was anxious to get home to the kids—if she hurried, she might just be able to meet them at the bus. That was always a treat for all of them.

"Why don't you come on out and say 'Hi' to them?" she asked Paul when she saw the disappointment on his face. It was clear that he wasn't ready to part with her just yet. "I'll fix you a sandwich. Maybe you and Christopher can get a game in, too—he's been asking when you're coming out. I think he's got some new moves to show you."

Paul loved the idea. "You know I can't resist an invitation like that—you and playing a little b-ball with Chris," he answered cheerfully. "I'll follow you out."

Since rush hour in Seattle doesn't usually start until 3:30 each afternoon, their trip across the bridge was a quick one. Paul, who was no slouch himself in fast cars, hadn't realized that Laura had such a heavy foot—as he trailed her at speeds well over the posted limits, he found himself keeping a watchful eye for police traps. Guess she really is anxious to see those kids, he chuckled to himself.

When they reached the turn off to her house, Laura checked her watch to see whether they'd made it in time to meet the bus. It would be close. Instead of heading to the house, she decided to drive right over to the bus stop.

The street the kids were dropped off on was usually fairly quiet, but traffic picked up each afternoon about this time—a combination of parents returning from picking kids up from school, high school students driving themselves home, and some people just getting off work.

As her car turned onto the street where the bus stopped, the one along which the kids walked to get back to the house, Laura noticed a great deal of commotion just ahead. Traffic had slowed and several people had pulled over and were jumping out of their cars. Laura's heart stood still, as for one agonizing moment, she wondered if something had happened to Hailey or Christopher on their walk home.

Then she saw him. It was Spencer.

The big powerful horse was running along the street, heading in her direction. She saw a man several cars ahead of her, who'd jumped out as he saw the horse head in his direction, and was now reaching out and calling "Whoa, Boy!" But Spencer, thoroughly spooked to find himself in the midst of all this commotion, ran right on by as the concerned passerby lunged and tried to grab ahold of his halter. Laura slammed her car into park and jumped out. Paul, immediately behind her, did the same. After starting off in another direction, only to be faced with more strange faces, Spencer suddenly turned and began running back in Laura and Paul's direction. Laura positioned herself directly in the horse's pathway. At the last moment the big horse recognized her and looked less panicked, like he would stop at her outstretched arm and the sound of her voice calling his name. But just as he slowed, as he approached within only a few feet of her, a car heading in the opposition direction whizzed by and sounded its horn! The horse was now hemmed in on both sides—the line of slowed cars on one side, a fence that ran alongside the road on the other. Laura stood directly in front of him. When the horn sounded, he did what any startled horse would do—he bolted, in the only direction which offered him any hope of escape—which was exactly where Laura stood. Paul, who was several feet behind her and could see what was about to happen, dived in an attempt to tackle Laura before Spencer reached her. But he was too late. Laura took the full force of the massive 1,200-pound animal head on.

Upon impact, she collapsed to the ground, face down. Paul scrambled over to her and frantically rolled her over, then gasped at the sight of her face. Trying to avoid colliding with Laura, at the last moment Spencer had actually attempted to jump over her. As she fell back, one of his front steel-shoed hooves came in direct contact with the side of her face, literally raking it with its metal.

At first she appeared to be unconscious, but within seconds she opened her eyes. She looked stunned, but managed to ask, "Is Spencer okay?"

She tried to sit up, but immediately fell back into Paul's supporting arms.

Paul's relief upon hearing her speak was so great that it was difficult for him to respond. He looked up to see what had happened to Spencer. He could see that down the street a short distance, the helpful man who'd earlier attempted to stop Spencer now had him firmly in hand—the resourceful good Samaritan had removed his belt and was using it to lead the horse back in their direction.

Still holding Laura as she lay next to the road, Paul asked a young woman who'd stopped to offer help to call an ambulance from his car phone. By now, a good-sized group had gathered, including a neighbor whom Paul recognized from one of their walks. He asked her to meet the kids, and drive them home, via another route. The last thing he wanted Hailey and Christopher to come upon was the sight of an ambulance attending to their mother. Instinctively he wanted to spare them that.

When Laura saw Spencer being led toward them, she struggled to get up. Suddenly Paul found himself losing his temper. He yelled at her and demanded that she just lie still. He was feeling a tremendous sense of relief. It appeared Laura would be okay, though her face would bear the reminder for some time to come. He wasn't surprised when he later learned that she sustained a mild concussion—he'd seen the force with which Spencer's shoulder, then hoof had come in contact with her head. But even as relief was settling in, a feeling of intense anger was growing within him. With the immediate matters needing his attention, he could not afford to indulge in any such thoughts right now. But in the back of his mind, something—something extremely black and troubling—was already nagging at him.

But for now, Laura needed his undivided attention, so he forced himself to shrug it off.

Laura had grown silent. Paul wasn't sure whether it was a response to his anger or whether she might be going into shock. Hoping it was the former, he knelt over her, kissed her forehead, took her hand gently in his and apologized for his outburst. She smiled and said, "I'm sorry for worrying you like this. I'm fine, Paul. Really." She squeezed his hand. "But is he okay?" She still needed to hear that her beloved horse was safe.

After thanking the horse's rescuer and giving him directions to Laura's house, Paul returned to Laura and assured her that Spencer was fine. She smiled, then closed her eyes. Paul feared that she was on the verge of losing consciousness. A panicky feeling began to rise in his chest. He silently cursed the ambulance for being so slow. If anything happened to her... He stroked her forehead gently. Then the nagging image he'd been trying to suppress came back to him again. The car, a sporty, bright red number, whizzing by just as Spencer appeared to be stopping, and the sound—the unbelievable sound of the blaring horn. His heart pounded, whether in anger or worry at the sight of Laura lying there, he did not know.

When the ambulance arrived several minutes later, he identified himself as Laura's husband and climbed in back with her. He suspected that as a boyfriend, he might not be allowed to accompany her on the ride to the hospital, and he wasn't taking any chances that he might be excluded.

Laura remained quiet on the ride and as she was admitted to the ER at Evergreen Hospital. Whenever possible—when no one was taking her blood pressure or pulse or testing her pupils for dilation and whatever else they were looking for—she reached out for his hand. He tried to look calm and reassuring whenever their eyes met. In the ambulance, she told Paul she was worried about the children hearing what had happened. She pleaded with him to head right over to the house and be with them. Paul promised he'd go, but not until he had a chance to talk to her doctor. The moment they reached the hospital, he called the kids. Breaking the news wasn't easy. The fear in their little voices broke his heart. He reassured them that Laura seemed just fine and promised that he'd be there shortly. He felt torn. He wanted to stay with Laura, to not let her out of his sight. But at the sound of the fear in their voices, he also wanted to rush to them.

For an hour Paul sat waiting in the lobby outside the ER. He was just about to barge in and insist on being with Laura when a young doctor came out. He told Paul that, all in all, Laura was doing well. She had a slight concussion, however, which would necessitate her being hospitalized overnight for observation. He was confident, however, that she would be released first thing the next morning. And, best of all, Paul could go right up to her room and see her.

Paul rushed toward the elevators, then turned suddenly and hurried back to the telephone booths. He dialed the kids' number. It didn't surprise him to hear the phone picked up on the first ring. At first, Christopher did not respond when Paul told him what the doctor had just said.

"Did you hear me, Buddy?" Paul asked. "She's going to be just fine... Are you okay?"

He heard a sniffle, then in an emotional, broken voice, Chris finally said, "I'm just glad she's okay."

Paul had to struggle to maintain his own composure. "She's fine, Chris. I promise. In fact, if you'd like, I'll check with the doctor and, if he says it's okay, I'll come right over and bring you and Hailey back in to see her. How does that sound?"

Paul sensed it was extremely important to Christopher, and undoubtedly to Hailey, to see for themselves that their mother was all right.

Christopher was noticeably cheered by this idea. Before they hung up, Paul asked to speak to Hailey. She, too, was eager to see Laura. He told them he'd be out to see them just as soon as he checked on Laura, and then hung up.

Minutes later, he pushed open the door to her room, to see her lying quietly on her side. Sensing his presence, she turned, reached out her hand to him, and gave him a big smile.

"Hi, Handsome," she said.

He tried to think of something lighthearted and clever to say, but as he climbed onto the bed beside her, he could feel his arms shaking as he reached for her. He wrapped them around her and lay rocking her, stroking her hair, totally overcome by emotion. Unable to speak.

It was Laura who broke the silence.

"I love you," she whispered, holding him close.

After a moment, she pushed away from him gently and asked whether he'd talked to the kids yet. He winced inwardly as he saw the left side of her face, which was a shocking combination of colors— red, purple, black. Amazingly, however, she hadn't needed stitches. She was terribly bruised, but aside from superficial abrasions, the skin had hardly been broken.

He told her he'd just talked to both Christopher and Hailey and that they were fine, but they were anxious to see her. That's when she put her hand up to her swollen face and asked, "How bad is it?"

"You're beautiful," he answered sincerely.

A few minutes later, the doctor stopped in to check on her. He gave them the go-ahead for the kids to visit. Laura hurried Paul out the door to get them.

*   *   *

In the taxi, Paul was able to relax for the first time since the accident. Though his primary feelings were relief and a sense of eagerness to see the kids, to reassure them, these feelings were being involuntarily overridden by the fury that had been growing within him over the image of the car, the little red sports car, and its horn, which had caused Laura to be injured. Who in their right mind would lay on the horn in a situation like that? As hideous as the thought was, his gut instinct told him it had been deliberate. But why? Who would do such a thing? And how on earth had Spencer managed to be out on that busy road in the first place?

The taxi deposited him at his car, still parked on the side of the road where he'd left it. He hopped in and hurried the few blocks to Laura's house.

When he pulled into the driveway, the kids flew out the door. Both of them headed right for his outstretched arms. Picking Hailey up in one arm, and wrapping the other around Christopher's shoulders, he ushered them toward the barn, telling them they'd head right back to the hospital, but first he promised Laura he'd check on Spencer.

He wanted to believe that Spencer had broken out through a rotting segment of the fence—one that he and Laura had inspected weeks earlier and planned to repair. But as they headed into the barn, what Christopher was saying blew that theory to pieces. "When I got home, before that nice man brought Spencer back, the gates were wide open," Christopher announced.

Paul turned and looked at him. "*Both* gates?" he asked.

"Yep," answered Chris. "Wide open. I thought Mom had gone out riding, but it seemed strange 'cause usually she takes Spencer out through the barn, not the gates. And her car wasn't here."

Disturbed, Paul walked into the stall to check on Spencer. The horse was still skittish, but aside from a five or six-inch long scratch on one of his shoulders, a superficial wound which didn't look as though it

286

would need a vet's attention, he seemed not too much the worse for his experience. Paul gave him an extra helping of oats, checked all the gates and doors into the barn, then, leaving all the lights blazing, climbed back into the car with Hailey and Christopher.

*   *   *

The kids' visit with Laura reassured them immediately. They both climbed onto the bed with her and examined her colorful face. Hailey, the eternal optimist, tried to find something cheerful to say.

"It looks like a butterfly, Mom!" was what she came up with. That tickled Laura.

By the time they left her, as her dinner was being served, everyone looked immeasurably happier. As Laura watched the three of them leave her room, after first getting big hugs and kisses from each of them, her heart felt so full of love, so full of a joy in life—*her* life—that the night ahead of her, the dull ache in her head, and the unsightly bruise on her face seemed utterly insignificant in the whole scheme of things.

Laura had planned on calling her parents down from Bellingham to stay with the kids, but when she mentioned her plans, Paul offered to stay with them instead, and the kids made it clear that they liked *that* idea a whole lot better. Despite the circumstances, it would end up being a thoroughly enjoyable night for the three of them. They were all so relieved by Laura's condition and good frame of mind, and having Paul there was a treat for the kids, not unlike the week-end evenings they frequently spent together. They stayed up late watching a movie, eating popcorn, and talking. As close as Paul had been growing to the kids recently, this night sealed their relationship.

After he'd gotten them bedded down, Paul sat for

some time in the darkened living room—the spot where he first held Laura—and tried to come to grip with the many thoughts and emotions the day had given rise to. Some were frightening—the sight of Laura lying so still in the road and the long wait for some word at the hospital. Some were heartwarming and inspiring—the realization of the depth of his love for this woman. And her two kids. And of their unquestionable love for him.

Some emotions were almost too troubling, too dark, for him to want to deal with. Two gates opened in the middle of the day? While Laura was away and the kids were at school. He sat in the dark racking his brain for a legitimate explanation, wanting desperately to believe that it had been an accident. Careless, maybe even negligent, but still, just an accident. Tomorrow he would look into it. Maybe the house's oil tank was back that way? Laura had mentioned needing to get it refilled. Perhaps someone from the oil company had been the one to open the gates, and who left them open? The thought comforted him somewhat.

But then there was that car. That fucking red sports car that could easily have caused Laura far more serious injury than a slight concussion. If he could get his hands on the bastard... Why was it that he sensed the two were connected? The gates being opened and that car blasting its horn? Was he overre- acting? Becoming so protective of her that he'd lost his ability to reason? He almost hoped that that were true. But somehow he knew better. And something about that car—he'd seen it before. But where?

Finally, exhausted, realizing these thoughts would get him nowhere, he got up to go bed. He'd planned on sleeping in the guest room, but as he walked by

Laura's room, he stopped and turned on the light. He
looked around at the signs that were all so unmistakably Laura—fresh flowers in a vase next to the bed;
pictures everywhere, of kids, family and beloved pets;
a lacy bra flung across a chair. Her briefcase next to
the door.

Then, stripping down to his silk shorts, he climbed
into her big, warm bed, took another look around
before turning out the light, and finally, drained by
the emotional day, fell into a deep sleep.

* * *

To say that Mackenzie Montana was growing
impatient was an understatement. She was unusually
nervous already. Ever since that afternoon. Now this.
What the hell was taking this joker so long? She'd
been standing in line at the luxury rental car counter
down the street from SeaTac Airport for at least
fifteen minutes. If this guy in front of her didn't get
moving, she stood a chance of missing the night's last
flight to L.A. And they'd just told her the flight was
booked and that she'd have to fly stand-by for Christ's
sake! She could hardly believe it. She wouldn't even
be able to fly first class. And when she made her
displeasure known to the old hag behind the counter at
Northwest, she'd had the nerve to respond that even
movie stars needed to make reservations in advance if
they wanted to be guaranteed space on a flight!
Mackenzie made a mental note of the bitch's name.
Her supervisor would hear about this. How could
Mackenzie have known she'd have to get out of
Seattle so fast?

This is the type of thing I need Neil here for, she
was thinking. Standing in line. Returning cars. At
times like this she wished she'd let him stay with her

in Seattle, like he'd wanted to. When the refined looking gentleman in front of her finally walked away with keys to a Mercedes in hand, Mackenzie threw down her keys and announced, "I'm returning my car. And I'm in a hurry."

The young man behind the counter recognized her immediately. He'd been lucky enough to be working the counter that night about a week ago when she arrived. He'd never forget it, not just because he'd followed her career ever since her days as a lingerie model, but also because it had been no small chore to locate a car that would satisfy her.

He asked her for a copy of her rental agreement, and after glancing at it quickly asked, "I notice you're returning the car quite a bit earlier than planned, Ms. Montana. I hope there weren't any problems with it?"

"No. Just a change of plans," she answered brusquely. "I'm leaving town earlier than I'd expected. The car was fine."

As he watched the flamboyant actress walk away, the star-struck young man looked at her longingly. Then, since there were no other customers in sight, he stuck a sign on the counter which read, "We'll return in just a minute," and headed out to drive the car she'd left at the curb into its assigned space in the lot behind the building. There was a young high school kid whose job it was to do this, but he couldn't resist the chance to park this one himself. It was such an awesome car. And maybe she'd left something in it that he could keep. A memento of Mackenzie Montana.

As he slid behind the wheel of the expensive car, he took a deep breath and inhaled the sweet fragrance of the new car, and of Mackenzie Montana's perfume. He sat for a moment, eyes closed, imagining her next to him. But his fantasy was cut short by the sound of a car pulling up behind him.

Finally putting the car into gear, he couldn't resist pushing down on the gas pedal just a little harder than normal. And with the squeal of rubber against asphalt, he pulled the little sports car—the shiny, red Ferrari—away from the curb.

15

At Amy Griffin's request, Shawn called a production meeting. Now, as Paul, Matthew, Shawn and Amy sat around the table in the conference room at the offices of Brooks Productions, all eyes were on Amy, who was about to explain the reason behind her request.

Realizing that it was highly unusual for an actress to be calling such a meeting (and perhaps even more unusual for her request to be granted), Amy hesitated, choosing her words carefully, before speaking. A reassuring smile from Matthew helped to get her started.

"I want you all to know that I'm thrilled to be in this film," she began, "and I feel like things are going well—extremely well—so far. I say that because I want you to understand the spirit in which my next comments are being said. Because this film means so much to me. To all of us."

"The screenplay was beautifully written," she continued, turning to direct this comment at Matthew. "It is one of the most touching, powerful scripts I've ever read—I knew the moment that I picked it up, it would

292

be the choicest role of my career. As far as its artistic
value is concerned, I truly believe it cannot be im-
proved upon. But, as most of you know, I've been
interested in AIDS for some time now. I do a lot of
reading about it. And, as good as the script is, it fails
to address some important issues. Women's issues."
Her look was still directed at Matthew. "I know that
we all see this movie as a chance to educate the
public. We have a vehicle here which might have
some impact, which can actually make a difference, to
women in particular."

Matthew looked puzzled, "I'm not sure I follow,
Amy. Colleen was a woman, and she had AIDS.
That's what this movie's about. So how is it that
we're not addressing issues dealing with women and
AIDS?"

"True," Amy answered, "this movie will further
the interests of women in regards to AIDS simply by
the fact that we are dealing with a woman here. But
there's so much information that is specific to women
that never gets addressed in the script. For example,
did you know that transmission of the virus is seventeen times more likely to occur from a male to a
female? And that women infected with the HIV virus
usually go undiagnosed much longer than men who
are infected because their early symptoms are less
easily identified as being HIV-related? During the first
three to five years after infection, women frequently
get vague symptoms, such as vaginal yeast infections,
sinusitis, diarrhea, fever—subtle conditions that can be
easily blamed on a number of other factors. This
means they're frequently misdiagnosed until later stages
of the disease. And the fact that they're diagnosed in
later stages of the disease means they start life-pro-
longing treatment later than most men who are

293

infected."

It was Shawn's turn to speak up. "Assuming all of that is true, how would you propose going about introducing that information? Have you given that any thought?" He sounded exasperated. He hated it when actors tried to meddle with scripts. And, sooner or later, they all did it. True, this actress and this subject matter provided more compelling arguments than any others he'd dealt with, but still, this was always a pain in the ass.

Matt had other concerns. "At the time of Colleen's illness, was this information even known? I rather doubt it. I know that I've never heard those statistics before ..."

"I doubt very much that this information was even available then," Amy admitted. "There were so few women diagnosed with the disease back then that very little was known about if, and how, this virus might affect women differently. But women are now the fastest-growing group of people with AIDS. And still, they're not getting the attention they need. Women with AIDS simply have not been given the medical attention—the research, money, etc.—that men have. Did you know that, to date, there have been no studies involving solely women who are HIV-positive, or who already have AIDS? How can we be providing women with the ultimate benefit—with the most advanced treatments—if we haven't even thoroughly evaluated their situations?" She looked around the table. "Do you see what I mean?"

Shawn returned to his earlier concern. "But just how would you suggest incorporating this information into the movie?"

"Maybe we have her doctor saying it. In a consultation session with Colleen and her family," Amy answered. "If we..."

"But, if this information didn't even exist back then, we can't have a doctor—or anyone else for that matter—saying it," interrupted Matthew. He, too, did not looked pleased. But his tone remained professional, courteous. "Look, Amy, it's important that we be true to the facts. I've gone to great lengths to accurately portray what happened. To start throwing in information that wasn't even available when Colleen was alive would only deprive us of credibility."

Paul was quick to join in. "I agree. We can't start playing with the facts. Especially at this late date."

Looking around, it was painfully clear to Amy that she was outpowered *and* outnumbered Three against one. Three *men* against one *woman*, she noted mentally. So what else is new?

Actually, though, she had to admit that these were three men she admired and respected. All for different reasons. Shawn Long was a tremendously talented director. She felt privileged to be working with him.

Paul Brooks was, well, *Paul Brooks*. Every woman's dream. Probably deservedly so. Plus, he was just being loyal to Matthew. She really couldn't blame him for that.

And Matthew. Dear Matthew. This movie meant so very much to him. Understandably so. She wasn't surprised that he'd reacted as he did to her attempt to alter his painstaking work.

No, she really couldn't be angry with any of them for their response. Still, she wasn't about to give up on this. But her better judgment told her there was nothing to be gained by pressing her point further at this meeting today. Something told her that another approach might stand a better chance.

With that idea in mind, she thanked the men for

the opportunity they'd given her to discuss her concerns with them and wished them all a good night.

Then, catching up with Matthew as he left the building several minutes later, she asked whether he was free to join her for dinner that night. Feeling somewhat guilty for the way he'd responded during the meeting, he was more than happy to accept.

As they walked up the street to Duke's to get a bite to eat, Amy slipped her arm into Matthew's comfortably. She was pleased to have a chance to be with him. And the fact that she didn't intend to give up her crusade just yet was only *one* of the reasons.

*   *   *

The morning after the accident, Paul was at the hospital by nine A.M. He'd dropped the kids off at their respective schools and headed right in to the city to see Laura.

She was sitting up in bed, looking in good spirits. He winced upon seeing the ugly bruise on her cheek, but still, he thought she looked beautiful, hospital gown notwithstanding.

She gave him a huge smile and hug. She wanted to go right home. The doctor had already visited and given her the go-ahead.

They were back at her house by midmorning. Paul made her climb into bed. He fixed a tray of everything he thought she could possibly need for the hours before the kids returned—coffee, cereal, fruit, chocolate-covered biscotti (her favorite), a newspaper and several magazines. He had to get back to the set—Shawn had called with a minor emergency—but before he left he wanted to talk to Laura about something.

"What is it?" she asked, looking concerned upon

hearing the serious note in his voice. "Is everything at work okay?"

"Let's forget about work, Girl," he answered, reaching for her hand. "Right now, *work*, the movie, is about the last thing on my mind."

"Well, then, what is?" Laura asked, anxiously. "On your mind, that is?"

"You," he answered, looking into her beautiful blue eyes. "Us."

She sat there, propped up against several pillows, in her white, Chantilly lace gown, and looked to Paul like a vision out of a magazine ad. Until she turned and displayed her bruise. The sight of it made him reach out and tenderly touch it.

"Does it hurt much?" he asked.

"Nothing hurts me when you're here," she answered truthfully.

He felt a rush of emotion and knew he needed to go ahead with what he wanted to say, before he became overwhelmed.

He took her delicate face in both hands and said in a hoarse voice, "Laura Kennedy. I love you. If I ever had any doubts, which, believe me, I have not had since the day you first walked into my life, yesterday would have dispelled them forever."

He looked so incredibly handsome to Laura, so incredibly strong. And right at that moment, so vulnerable.

"And after yesterday, all I've been able to think about is, what if I'd lost you?" He stopped, the very thought so disturbing to him that he had to pause a moment before continuing. "Maybe I'm being overly dramatic, but that's the effect it had on me. And last night, lying here in your bed, with your two kids, who I love now almost as much as I love you, asleep in the next rooms, all I could think is that I don't want to waste another minute without you. Without *all* of you."

He looked into her eyes, her very soul, with a look so intense, so emotional, that Laura suddenly felt engulfed by him, by his love for her.

"What I'm trying to say is...will you marry me? Please. Will you marry me?"

Her eyes brimming with tears, Laura placed her hands gently on top of his. As the tears spilled over and trickled down her face, onto both of their hands, she answered softly.

"Yes, Paul, I will marry you. Nothing in this world could make me happier."

He took her in his arms and held her.

Then he laid her back down on the bed, and gently, ever so gently, Paul Brooks made love to his future wife.

*   *   *

Once in a while, however fleeting the moment may be, life seems absolutely perfect. Times when, even if it were possible, there would be nothing, absolutely *nothing*, one would change about his current lot.

For Paul, the weeks after Laura and he became engaged were like that. And it was clear that Laura was experiencing similar bliss. Two people very much in love. Perfectly in sync. Yes, at times like these, life was unbelievably good.

Progress on the movie was remarkable. Paul had just viewed the dailies from a scene between Matthew and Colleen. It had been an especially emotional one. He wasn't sure how much of his response could be attributed to his affection for those involved and how much was due to his own heightened emotional state, but Paul had been so moved by the scene that he'd simply sat quietly for several minutes after the film stopped, grateful to have been alone at the time. Increasingly, he and Matthew were convinced that the film was fated to succeed. In every sense of the word. Both agreed that the cinematography was some of the finest they'd ever seen. Usually work of this caliber, artful work that made each and every scene an unforgettable visual experience, could only be found gracing extremely high-budget movies. But Mike Boyd, through his creative use of lighting and angles, was transforming each scene into a visual feast.

Then there was the casting. It had been so right on. Amy, in everyone's opinion, was carrying the movie. But the lesser actors, in particular Sherry Falconer as Colleen, were also convincing and natural. Neither Matthew nor Paul had worked on enough films to appreciate just how unusual it was for an entire cast to be so well selected. But Shawn Long commented on it a number of times. He, in fact, had spent a great deal of time analyzing it. What he had here was a director's dream, one that he hoped to be able to reproduce again in future films. At first it hadn't made much sense to him. After all, aside from Amy Griffin, he hadn't been especially impressed initially with any of the actors. But that wasn't unusual, especially given the budget they were working with. But, remarkably, he'd soon found each and every one of the cast to be more than effective. And after considerable thought about how that could be true, how a movie could be so perfectly cast, he'd come to a conclusion—that it wasn't so much the *actors* involved as it was the movie. It was the emotional commitment that each of these people had made to this film. True, as it turns out, he'd been blessed to be working with very talented, very competent actors, but what really made the difference, he finally decided, was the emotional commitment they'd all made. He'd never worked on a movie where that element was so universally present.

Paul knew Shawn Long shared his confidence in the film's progress, and that he was extremely pleased with the work of Mike Boyd and the cast. Yes, Paul was sure now the movie would be a success. And that felt good, very, very good. It had been a big gamble. Brooks Productions could well have gone under if it had failed. But he knew now that that wasn't going to happen. And that knowledge gave him a sense of satisfaction that was almost like the euphoria he used to experience after a big win on the court. He remembered how, back in his last year of college, he'd begun worrying about his basketball career coming to an end. Worrying that life would never again be able to provide him with as sweet a feeling as that one he was left with after each victory. It had been a huge, nagging fear for him. He'd awakened in a cold sweat more than one night over it. After all, basketball had been his life. What on Earth could ever replace it? Replace that feeling, that sweet, sweet feeling, of going out there game after game and doing that for which he was born? After a lifetime of that kind of high, he was finally finding that there were *other* ways to achieve those feelings. Well, maybe not quite as intense, and rarely as satisfying, but sometimes, as with the success of *After the Dance*, he could come close.

And then there was Laura. Now that he wasn't worried about her, about losing her, about the Mackenzie Montana thing, now that they were planning to be married, the Laura Kennedy high was unquestionably a match for the old basketball high. With other women, he hadn't known that was even possible. True, more than once he'd felt the initial excitement, the adrenalin, or hormones, or whatever it could be attributed to, that accompany a new relationship, but nothing that could ever be said to rival the thrill of his basketball days. Nothing that he wouldn't gladly trade to be back on the court again. But with Laura, the feelings were so intense, so profoundly a part of him, that once again he was waking in the night in cold sweats at the thought that they, *she*, might not be forever.

And with Laura, there was something else. Something maybe even more meaningful than the excitement and passion she'd brought to his life. With Laura, there was a gentle peace, a comforting feeling within him that even basketball had never been able to provide.

Yes, Laura Kennedy satisfied that something deep inside him that craved the challenge, the excitement. Something that made him feel extraordinary—*that* had always been critically important to him. And extraordinarily blessed. And at the same time, she provided him with a security, a calm that he hadn't even realized he needed.

It had been just this combination of feelings— intense excitement coupled with satisfaction and peace— that dominated his emotions these past weeks. Ever since the accident. Ever since their engagement. With *After the Dance* moving along so smoothly. Life was as good for Paul right now, as close to perfect, as he'd ever dared to hope it could be. And Paul Brooks was smart enough to realize that, to appreciate it for what it was worth.

And to know that it might well be fleeting.

301

16

Lenny Coleman was losing his patience. He'd tried to reach Mackenzie Montana several times now. Left a message each time. Once Neil Roberts had answered. He'd promised he'd have Mackenzie call, but she still hadn't phoned him back.

He wasn't used to this. A client who didn't return calls? Usually they hounded *him*. But this one really surprised him. Based on her reputation, he'd expected Mackenzie Montana to be a royal pain in the ass, like most of the successful entertainers he'd represented, the type who called and made demands all the time and complained about how slow things were going. No, she'd certainly not been guilty of that. In fact, if anyone were guilty of slowing things down, it was her. He had to get a response filed to their request for a deposition today or he could be found in contempt.

She was a tough one to figure out. The part in this movie seemed to mean so much to her, yet she'd chosen not to go for an injunction. If they were successful, that would have forced a halt in the shooting until the case was decided. It would have been her only chance to actually play the part of Ashley Cowles in *After the Dance*. And it would obviously have been an effective bargaining position for them to be in. Faced with total inactivity on shooting until the matter was decided by the courts, there was a chance Brooks would have given her back the part right then and there. But there had been no convincing her to go that route, which left them with only one other course of action to pursue—suing for damages. Not that that was such a bad route to take. Many actors might well have chosen it. In a sense, it was the easy way out—get the money without doing the work. But the thing that puzzled Lenny about Mackenzie was that the part itself, not the money she'd have earned, seemed to be what mattered to her. It was easy to see just how much she wanted it, yet for some reason she was not willing to fight for it. Maybe she had some underlying fears that she'd fail miserably. Blow her one chance at establishing herself as a real actress. Maybe *wondering* whether she could have pulled it off was preferable to finding out that the talent really wasn't there. Who knows what goes through the minds of these people, thought Lenny. Thank God I'm just their attorney, not their shrink.

When she finally returned his call—after his leaving a rather scathing message that morning—it was from her car phone. She informed him that she was en route to the airport, on her way to an extended vacation in the Bahamas.

"How extended?" Lenny quizzed her, none too happy to hear this news.

"I haven't any definite plans right now," was all she could tell him. "But I suspect I'll be out of the country for a good long while."

"Mackenzie," Lenny responded testily, "you mean to tell me you're about to leave the country, for an extended trip, and you didn't even think to advise your attorney of that fact? When you're in the middle of a lawsuit?" The more he thought about it, the more worked up he was becoming.

"Gee, Lenny, I'm really sorry," she answered caustically. "I didn't realized it was necessary to get my attorney's approval for all my actions. Why don't you just get one of those tracker things and put it around my neck? Then you can know where I am twenty-four hours a day. Shit, I bet you could even wire me some way or another—that way you can listen in on all my conversations. What is this? Did I ask you to file a lawsuit for me or to be my fucking caretaker?"

Now THERE was the Mackenzie Montana he'd heard so much about. He was almost glad to see she could get so stirred up. He always wanted his clients to have some fire. Of course, too much was dangerous, but a little bit was very helpful. And he'd begun to wonder if this one had enough. He was happy to see that she did. But right now, he certainly didn't want to let her know that. No, clearly, it was time to set down some rules with this one. He was not about to spend his time running down some off-the-wall movie star. Either she played by the rules—*his* rules—or he didn't play. True, this was a good case. And it wouldn't hurt his reputation to be able to tout Mackenzie Montana as a client. But he wasn't about to let a client start jacking him around like this. No, no case was worth that much to him.

"Well, Ms. Montana," his tone was controlled, very official, "if that's the way you feel, I'm afraid you've come to the wrong attorney." He let his words settle in for a moment before continuing. "I thought you wanted to give this case its best shot, which means getting the best there is to handle it. And let me assure you, I am the best. But, you see, because of that—because I am the very best there is—I can pretty much pick and choose my clients. And I can tell you this: I choose not to work with smart-ass rich folk who don't feel a need to cooperate with me. Who think I get paid to take whatever it is they feel like dishing out. My time's too valuable to play those kind of games. I have too many truly appreciative clients to be wasting time on someone with your attitude. So I suggest that you pull out the Yellow Pages and get yourself another attorney to handle this matter. Good day, Ms. Montana." And with that, he hung up.

He looked at his watch and bet himself that it would be five minutes, no, *two* minutes, tops, before she called back. The phone rang almost before he could start timing. Seconds later, his secretary buzzed him. Ms. Montana was on the line.

He picked up the phone. She began pleading with him before he even got a chance to say hello.

"Lenny, Mr. Coleman, please. Don't do this to me." She sounded desperate. "I apologize. For being so rude. For not being more cooperative. It won't happen again, I promise. It's just that I've been having a pretty rough time." She did sound terribly distraught. "I mean, this thing with the movie, with losing the part, has really gotten me down."

"It's not too late to go for an injunction," Lenny interjected.

"No, please," she said. He was happy to hear the word 'please.' His hardball tactics had obviously worked. "I still feel the same about that. No injunction. But I don't want to give up on this suit. And I want you to handle it."

"And you'll give me your absolute cooperation?"

He wanted a clear commitment on her part. Nothing less.

"Absolute," she answered dutifully. "One hundred percent."

"Good," said Coleman. "Then I'd be happy to continue representing you. Now, let's get down to business..."

He told her that Brooks had filed a request for her deposition and explained what that involved, the kind of questions she could expect to have to answer. She asked where it would be done, and by whom. The where could be negotiated, he responded. The who would be their attorney, a Laura Kennedy. Of course, he explained, he'd be there, too, to look out for her interests.

Mackenzie balked and said she didn't get it—she'd have to appear in court, wouldn't she? So why would she have to go through all that *twice*?

Patiently, Lenny explained that the deposition was an important tool of "discovery." (He never tried to talk down to his clients, always using the correct legal jargon.) He explained that it was useful for both sides in developing their cases and preparing for trial. Sometimes it could cut down on the court time it would take to try the case. He added that he was still hopeful they could settle without going to trial, and the deposition could help in that regard. The bottom line, though, was that they had no choice but to cooperate.

Before he could pin her down on the deposition, she wanted to know when the case would come to trial.

"That depends," he told her, "on how the Washington court calendar looks. At least a year," he answered, "probably longer."

She seemed pleased. Almost relieved. That both-

ered him. Most clients seethed when they learned
they'd have to wait that long to get a trial date. She
actually seemed pleased that the trial wouldn't take
place before then. A red flag went up in Coleman's
mind. Something was wrong. After 15 years in the
profession, most lawyers develop a sixth sense for a
client who's hiding the truth. Maybe Mackenzie Montana had a hidden agenda. Or maybe she was just
another weirdo. Either way, he'd better find out. He
wasn't altogether sure he should continue to handle
this one. He had kind of a funny feeling about it.

But he couldn't help but be affected by the desperation in her voice. And the fact that she was
ravishingly beautiful had to be taken into consideration
too. He made a mental note to do a little digging,
check out her and her story out on his own. Until he
discovered something that dictated otherwise, he'd
continue to represent her.

He guided the conversation back to the deposition.
Despite her promise of cooperation, Mackenzie was
determined to delay it.

"But can't you explain that I'm out of the country?" she asked. "Please. This trip is very important
to me. I need it."

"I'll buy you as much time as I can," Coleman
finally conceded, "but once a date is set, I'll expect
you to be there. If not…"

"I know. If not, you'll drop this case," Mackenzie
finished the sentence for him.

"Precisely," he affirmed.

As Mackenzie accelerated her Jaguar, she looked
very unhappy. Nothing in her life seemed to go as
planned anymore. Yesterday she'd decided to leave
the country—spend the next few months on the islands. Of course, she hadn't told anyone that. Espe-

cially not Neil. He'd have known right away that something was up. He already suspected something. Nothing she did made any sense to him anymore. He'd been surprised by her coming home from Seattle so suddenly. And he couldn't understand why she'd refused to go after that part—he was still annoyed with her for that. Had tried to lay a guilt trip on her telling her if she didn't get something going soon, he'd have to consider taking on other clients. In a way she didn't blame him. She couldn't very well tell him the truth—that she couldn't take that role, or any other role for that matter. At least not right now. So she'd told him to go ahead—she wouldn't stand in his way if he wanted to take someone else. And that had really confused him.

It was after their talk that she'd realized that she would have to leave town. If she stayed in L.A., she'd forever be doing just that—answering questions from Neil, from reporters, trying to avoid all those assholes who loved making her life miserable. That thought was unbearable. And she couldn't go back up to Seattle. No, definitely, she had to stay out of Seattle. At least until her house was done. They'd said it would take about six months for it to be finished. That was about right. She'd leave the country, go down to the islands, lie in the sun, and just veg out until it was safe to return.

Thinking about the house she'd just bought in Seattle brought a smile to her troubled face. Her house in Seattle. She loved the sound of it. She signed the papers yesterday morning. They'd start the remodeling right after the closing, probably sometime next week. And by the time she got back, it would be ready for them to move in. It had seemed the perfect plan yesterday.

But now this. This deposition. It would mean she'd have to come back. Have to sit there answering Laura Kennedy's questions. The bitch. Just the thought of her made Mackenzie livid. The thought of what she'd seen that night—Laura and Paul in his office, screwing their brains out. She was the worst kind. Acted like such a classy, dignified, haughty thing— like the grieving widow. But underneath it all, she was just another whore. One with an education—that was the only difference between her and me, thought Mackenzie. Couldn't Paul see that? Maybe not yet, but eventually he would.

Once on the plane, she settled back and did that which Mackenzie Montana did best. She closed her eyes and began to daydream. She'd always been good at that, ever since she was a child—closing her eyes, to block out reality, and creating her own little fantasies, her own little dreamworlds. Dreamworlds that became so vivid, so powerful, that sometimes, to Mackenzie Montana, they actually became real. Even after she'd opened her eyes.

She pictured her new Tudor home, sprawled along the eastern shore of Lake Washington. Pictured lying in bed, looking out at the water, across the lake to Seattle's skyline, both of which were framed so beautifully by the master bedroom's windows. Pictured lying there next to...

"Excuse me," a voice interrupted her fantasy. She opened her eyes to find a large, spectacled man now seated next to her, leaning toward her, into her space, a silly look on his face. He smelled of alcohol. "Aren't you Mackenzie Montana?"

Mackenzie looked disgusted. It was her pet peeve. Used to be that first class offered her some assurance of privacy. Half the time, it was almost empty, and even if there were some other travelers in that section, they usually left her alone. Sure, she could tell they recognized her, but they had enough class to pretend they didn't.

These days, though, first class rarely had an empty seat in it. And the flyers occupying the seats looked, and often times acted, like a bunch of hicks just off the bus. This guy was a case in point. He was already fumbling in his pocket—undoubtedly groping for a pen and paper for her to sign. An autograph for a friend. Or nephew. It was always for someone else.

She sat watching as he finally extracted a business card and asked her to autograph the back. She gave him a look that, had he been stone cold sober, would have stopped him in his tracks. But, blissfully oblivious to anything but the cleavage he was literally drooling over, he persisted, sticking the pen and card right in her face. He didn't even notice her reaching for her high heel and removing it. Well, actually, he did notice her leaning over, as it gave him an even better view of her breasts. He knew they were big, but in person, her knockers were even more impressive. What a set! Wait 'til the guys at the office hear this one.

No, until she drilled the heel right into his thigh, he hadn't noticed a darn thing about Mackenzie Montana except her chest.

But the "Buzz off" and the hole in his slacks, the hole in his leg actually, finally alerted him to the fact that she hadn't appreciated being disturbed.

For the rest of the trip, he kept his eyes directed straight ahead. He didn't dare look at her again, not even when the male flight attendant, equally mesmerized by the star's cleavage, proceeded to spill the drink he was passing her all over the two of them.

310

No, he never so much as glanced her way again.

If he had, he'd have seen her sitting there, eyes closed dreamily, a wicked smile on her face. Finishing up her little dream, right where she'd left off.

Before she'd been so rudely interrupted.

*   *   *

"Paul!" she called to him as she stepped out of the conference room and saw his lanky form ahead of her in the second floor hallway of the Brooks building.

He turned, smiling, upon hearing her voice.

"Yes, Ma'am," he answered. "What can I do for you?" As he got closer, she could see the glint in his eyes. "Want to have a little nooner with the boss?"

"You're such a classy guy," she laughed. "I need to talk to you."

He felt foolish around her at times. Here she was, the company attorney, and the president went around horndogging her all the time. He knew Laura was too professional to be treated like that, but he just couldn't help it.

"About Mackenzie Montana," Laura explained. Ouch. That brought Paul's dreams to a crashing halt.

She followed him into his office and, once they were both seated, told him she had a feeling something funny was going on. She'd been trying for over a month now to get a date for a deposition set with Mackenzie's attorney and had met with nothing but excuses from him. It didn't make sense, she explained. They're the ones who filed the suit. As plaintiffs, they should be most anxious to keep things moving right along.

Paul was visibly uncomfortable. This news about a deposition surprised him. "Is it really necessary to take her deposition?" he asked, hoping he sounded a lot more casual than he felt.

"I'd be remiss not to," answered Laura. Her tone made it clear that she didn't want to discuss the old Mackenzie Montana thing again. That was her new policy. This lawsuit was strictly business, she told herself over and over. Paul knew how Laura felt. Still, he felt slightly ill at the thought of the two of them—Laura and Mackenzie Montana—in a room together.

Laura continued, explaining that she didn't understand what Mackenzie stood to gain by delaying things. And the more thought she'd given it, the more anxious she was becoming to get the case moving. She still had hopes of settling, perhaps even getting them to drop the suit altogether, once Lenny Coleman saw their case. She was concerned about the affect the suit might have on the upcoming release of the movie, and about the attendant publicity that could result if they hadn't resolved the case by then.

She was right, Paul thought. He hadn't really thought about *that*. Of course, sometimes that type of thing and the publicity it engendered, just sold more tickets. But sometimes not. And *After the Dance* could make it on its own, without any attendant gossip to bolster it. No, definitely, it would be better to get the case resolved. But this deposition thing really bothered him. He suddenly had the feeling that the old storm clouds were rolling in again, slowly but surely.

Laura told Paul that she planned to call Lenny Coleman one more time. If she didn't get a firm date set for the deposition this time, she would file a motion to compel with Judge Harley. That would most likely result in a court order, forcing Mackenzie Montana to appear for a deposition.

Paul's uneasiness was fast becoming terror.

Before Laura left to make the call to Coleman, they discussed legal strategy a bit. Actually, with his mind on the upcoming deposition, Paul was having difficulty concentrating on the conversation, but Laura didn't seem to notice. She explained to him that the basis for their defense, that they did not have a binding agreement with Mackenzie Montana, was two-fold. First, Paul had never signed the agreement. And secondly, after sending Neil Roberts the first agreement she'd drafted, Laura talked to him and was told that the seven and one-half percent they'd agreed to earlier was now insufficient compensation for Mackenzie. At that point, in an effort to expedite things, Laura sent a new agreement, leaving this provision blank. Once they'd agreed on a figure, Mackenzie could have simply filled the blank in, then signed the agreement. It had been *this* agreement, with the percentage compensation still blank, that Mackenzie had signed that day in Paul's office. And Laura would therefore argue that, since an essential term was missing, the proposal did not constitute a valid offer. Therefore Mackenzie Montana's "acceptance," evidenced by her signature, did not create a binding contract.

Laura went on for some time, explaining other arguments she expected Lenny Coleman to make, but while Paul heard bits and pieces (phrases like "partial performance," "detrimental reliance," "terms that were implied in fact"), basically all his mind could focus on was the image of Laura and Mackenzie Montana facing each other in a deposition.

When Laura finally left to make the call to Coleman, Paul broke into a sweat. When Candy walked in without knocking moments later—which was not an unusual thing for her to do—Paul practically bit her head off. It was then that he decided to head over to the gym. He needed to let off some steam. A good work out was definitely in order.

Meantime, Laura was already drafting the motion to compel. When she talked to Lenny Coleman just minutes earlier, he had apologized about the difficulty they'd been having trying to get this "damn thing" scheduled, and promised to contact his client and get back to Laura "soon," But Laura was not in the mood to wait any longer. She meant business. She suddenly realized she was actually looking forward to deposing Mackenzie Montana, to sitting across from her and grilling her. This motion she was working on practically insured that it *would* happen. After all, if she didn't cooperate now, she'd be found in contempt. That thought lightened Laura's mood considerably.

And so, while Paul took his aggressions out on a leather ball and state-of-the-art breakaway hoop, Laura sat and plotted her own game plan.

Trouble is, neither one really knew what they were up against.

*   *   *

Amy Griffin was still working on Matt. About the script changes she wanted. She knew how protective of his work he was, how difficult it would be to convince him to make the changes, but he did seem to be weakening a bit.

It had become a matter of routine for them to run together at the end of each day of shooting. The clocks had just been moved up an hour, and courtesy of day light savings, it was now staying light until 7:30 p.m. Their favorite route was the one along Elliott Bay. First they'd head north for a while, up to the Magnolia bridge, then retrace their steps and head

down toward the piers and Pike Place Market. That
gave them a good four miles under their belts before
they'd hit the Sports Cafe at the edge of the market.
As its name indicated, it was a place where sweats,
and sweat, were acceptable. Even chic. Usually Amy
and Matthew would stop and have a drink, sometimes
a light bite to eat. Then, depending on whether they'd
had wine or Evian, they'd either trot slowly back to
Amy's hotel or stroll.

Tonight called for walking. It was dark by the
time they'd finished their sandwiches and beer. Thinking she looked chilled, Matthew draped his arm around
Amy. As they walked, they resumed the conversation
that had begun at the restaurant.

"But adding valuable information to the script
should do nothing but *add* to its credibility," argued
Amy. "I mean, one of our goals is to educate, isn't
it? How can you resist including information that's so
valuable?"

Matthew looked at her and smiled. "You're never
going to let up on this, are you?"

His tone was affectionate. She was definitely the
most determined woman he'd ever known. Headstrong. Oftentimes irritatingly so, but he admired her
commitment, the passion she brought to the film, and
undoubtedly to everything in her life. And he had to
admit, she did have a point. The information she
wanted to include in the movie was important. He
couldn't deny that. But that didn't change the fact that
in the 1980's it wasn't even available. How could he
incorporate it into Colleen's story without impairing
the movie's credibility?

As important as the information might be, he still
was not ready to write it in. But his resolve was
weakening. Tonight, however, he'd just as soon put

the whole subject—in fact, the whole movie and everything related to it—out of mind, for a while.

Looking at Amy as they approached the Edgewater, he sensed that she, too, was ready to call a truce.

"Hey, you've never seen my houseboat. How about tonight? Want to come over? On the way, we can stop at Pacific Desserts and get some of those insane chocolate concoctions you were drooling over the other day."

Amy would have agreed to go anyway, but the chocolate cinched it.

Matthew lived in a community of houseboats moored on the eastern shore of Lake Union. What had once been the domain of squatters, early in Seattle's history, was now high-end real-estate—though with the exception of a common dock, as far as Matthew could see no actual real estate existed. Funny thing was, from the pictures Matt had seen, the appearance of the structures hadn't changed much since the early squatter days. While the high price of rent and astronomical selling prices might indicate otherwise, the vast majority of the houseboats were old, very funky, one or two-bedroom structures, which on land, would be considered fit for little more than rustic mountain cabins. Still, nowhere else he'd looked had offered even a trace of the ambiance found on these docks. His houseboat was not located on the most exclusive docks found toward the south end of the lake. Rather, the common dock upon which his houseboat was situated, populated primarily by young professionals, many of whom, surprisingly, had young children, had an even more decidedly youthful, bohemian air to it than the others. Along all the docks, well-tended flower boxes, full to overflowing with their springtime blossoms, abounded—evidence of the value residents placed upon such aesthetics. Houseboat living in Seattle was a world, a way of life, all its own.

It was a world that Matthew could tell Amy appreciated at first glance. She squealed upon seeing the postage-stamp sized playground which parents had squeezed in at the foot of the ramp to the dock. She climbed onto a tire which hung from the big wooden structure and ordered Matt to push. Instead of pushing her, swing-style, he twisted her round and round until the rope, finally wound tight, refused to go any further. Then, giving Amy and the tire one big push in the opposite direction, Matthew stood back and watched, laughing, as Amy whirled madly around. Around and around and around. Squealing, laughing, hurling choice epitaphs at him.

When she finally dismounted, she fell a half step sideways, giggling, hair tousled, head still spinning. He stepped up against her to steady her, and pressed himself into her. And when she responded by turning her face up to his, he kissed her. Long, hard. Passionately.

When they got to his houseboat, he invited her upstairs. His bedroom was up there, but despite the unmistakable fire in her returned kiss, Matthew would not have presumed to take her right to his bedroom. At least not for *that*. No, what he wanted was for Amy to see the view that only this second-story room provided. From the window, the city lights to the south looked so bright and so near on a night like this—an incredibly brisk, clear night—that one might think he could reach right out and grab them. The view of the night sky, marinas and restaurants across the lake on its western shores, and twinkling lights of cars moving along the Ballard Bridge to the north, was unparalleled. At least that had always been Matthew's experience.

But, by her own initiative, Amy never got to experience the view. At least not that night. And by the time they awoke the next morning, Seattle was already fogged in.

The Chocolate Decadence they had for breakfast lived up to its name, but still wasn't nearly as sweet as the night before had been.

And the view would just have to wait.

17

The party was being held in an elegant suite on the 11th floor of the Four Seasons. After four-and-a-half months, shooting was over, and now cast and crew were gathered to celebrate, reminisce, and say goodbye. Though considered a celebration, these final wrap parties were oftentimes touched with sadness.

The mood of the participants tonight was decidedly mixed. There was more than the usual sadness, as this group had become an especially close-knit one. Though they would have occasion to gather again when the film was released, for the most part, cast and crew would now go their separate ways, rarely, if ever, seeing or even communicating with each other again. And while the end of filming was always accompanied by a collective sigh of relief, it was also then that the uncertainty of the business, of when the next job might come along, grew most acute.

Shawn Long, with wife Joan on his arm, walked around the room, working it like a polished politician, thanking his stars, lesser actors, and each and every member of the crew for the dedication they'd shown to this project, the brilliant work they'd all contributed. True to his nature, his praise of make-up artists and stagehands was no less effusive than that of Amy Griffin and Sherry Falconer, both of whose performances had stood out. He looked tired, but even the grueling schedule of the past months could not diminish his pride and sense of accomplishment at this moment. Shawn's work would not actually be done until the editing process was finished, but still, his relief was evident.

And there was more to it than just having finished shooting. A week earlier he'd confided in Matthew— told him that he and Joan had turned a corner. After the trauma surrounding the casting for Ashley Cowles, and the experience of being blackmailed by Mackenzie Montana for the role, he'd decided he could no longer live with his indiscretion hanging over his head. He confessed his infidelity to his wife. Joan responded that she'd known all along. She didn't have to be a V.I. Warshawski to figure out what had gone on that night in Cannes. It had been written all over his face when he'd finally come to the hotel room door. Only thing she couldn't figure out, at first, was where the culprit had gone, but once she'd stepped out onto the balcony and seen Mackenzie Montana, a big smirk on her face, sitting on the next balcony, even that was clear.

It wasn't that she wasn't hurt and angry—she was. But she'd realized that she'd played a role in their problems, too. And instinctively she knew that he'd never screw around on her again, not after she'd seen what a basketcase he'd been after the Mackenzie Montana thing. She was actually as relieved as he was to finally have it out in the open. The two had pledged a renewed commitment to each other. After editing was done, they were taking a long trip. To

Cannes. No joke. Matthew hadn't known whether to laugh at their choice of destinations, but since Shawn's intensity hadn't lessened at this announcement, his better judgment told him not to. At any rate, tonight Joan's happiness looked equal to that of her husband.

Looking at them, Matthew felt a little surge of renewed optimism. He'd been feeling that more and more these days. These little glimmers of hope, faith. Like maybe the world wasn't such a sad place after all. Reminders of how he viewed life before Colleen's illness. As emotionally draining as shooting had been for Matthew, more and more, slowly but ever so steadily, he realized that he was regaining his appreciation of life. He looked over at Amy, who was deep in conversation with Mike Boyd, and knew that there stood, in large part, the person responsible for his rebirth. She was really something. They'd battled for a solid week about the script changes she wanted. Finally, he'd relented. Not without misgivings, but he wanted—no, maybe *needed* was closer to the truth—to get beyond it and get back on solid ground with her. More and more she was becoming the focus around which his life revolved, especially once they'd made love.

They decided to take it slow. Tomorrow Amy would be returning to Los Angeles. She was anxious to see her father. And there was talk of another part for her. But she promised to return soon. And often. And Matthew knew he could count on her to keep her word. After all, she was as much in love with Seattle as he was now with her. And the houseboat was a definite plus. Amy *loved* the houseboat. After their first night together, she'd pretty much moved in with him. He'd given her free reign and, in just a few weeks, she'd managed to brighten up the place considerably, painting walls vibrant Acapulco sunset colors, adding playful touches—interesting old bottles, Indian blankets, weathered picture frames and boxes. No, thought Matthew as he continued to stare at her, Amy Griffin wasn't about to give up that houseboat now.

His gaze scanned the room, finally coming to rest on Paul and Laura. Paul Brooks was in his element. He, too, was a changed man, noted Matthew. And for Paul, it was clear that Laura was his magic. The fact that all three of them—Shawn, Matthew and Paul—could attribute their enhanced well-being to a woman did not escape Matthew's attention. Three completely different types of men. All of them successful, strong, and, in Matt's and Paul's case, quite independent. Shawn had never been the bachelor type, but Paul and Matthew had both been single for all but a very few of their years. So long that they'd both begun to believe that was their preferred state. Three very different men, yet tonight Matthew could draw a direct correlation between the heightened happiness of all three and the women in their lives. And that said something to him. *What* he wasn't exactly sure—it would be good food for thought later. Despite Matthew's firmly held belief that it wasn't necessary to have a mate in order to be a whole, happy person, and an even *stronger* belief in the foolishness of being with the wrong person just to avoid being alone, there was unquestionably something about the human condition that made facing the world as half of a partnership— half of a *good* partnership—a whole lot more palatable, a whole lot more beautiful, than facing it alone. Trouble was finding that good partnership, then appreciating it enough to be willing to work your butt off to keep it. From the looks of things tonight, thought Matthew, both Paul and he may now have been lucky enough to have found it, but so far, only Shawn's relationship had withstood the second test. The real test—that of time.

Paul and Laura had seen Matthew standing, solo, in the corner and were now walking over to him, big smiles on both their faces. Laura looked stunning in a pink silk halter dress, aglitter with beads and sequins. Her hair was swept onto her head to enhance the bare effect of the backless, curve-hugging dress. Paul was wearing a sleek double-breasted suit tailored to perfection to accentuate his broad shoulders and narrow hips. He exuded strength and power, yet the subtle good taste reflected by his choice of suits tempered the effect somewhat, giving an overall impression of great dignity. They were as good looking a couple as Matthew had ever seen. A perfect compliment to each other.

Laura hugged Matthew and asked where Amy was.

"Yeh," echoed Paul, "and what are you doing over here by yourself, with a room full of lovely ladies?"

"She's over there with Boyd. Probably trying to get him to reshoot some scenes in black and white or something," Matthew answered good naturedly. "Actually, I was just checking you two out. You caught me."

"And?" asked Laura. "Do we pass?"

"With flying colors. In fact, in addition to looking great, I couldn't help but notice how happy you both look tonight."

Paul put his arm around Laura, squeezed, and answered, "How could I not be happy with this lady by my side?" When they looked at each other, Matthew saw so much love pass between them in a single wordless exchange that, for a moment, he felt embarrassed to be intruding on them. Just then, Amy approached.

"Hey," she said cheerfully, "looks like this is where its happening!" She flashed her dazzling smile at Paul. "Paul, it's a great party, but I think a little music might be in order. Don't you?"

Paul agreed, and the two of them went off to locate a compact disc player, leaving Laura and Matthew alone together.

"She's really great, Matt," Laura said sincerely. "Looks like the two of you are doing great, too." She said it with a slightly raised voice, as if it were really a question to which she hoped for a response. She wasn't trying to pry, but Matthew knew how important it was to Laura that he be happy. They'd grown increasingly close over the past year. Both greatly valued the other's friendship. And opinion.

"I'm really glad you like her," answered Matt. "She's sure made a difference in my life. I'm going to miss her when she's down in Los Angeles. Miss listening to her crusades. Miss having her run my butt into the ground. And eating all the chocolate I keep trying to hide from her."

They both laughed at what was a pretty accurate description of life with Amy Griffin. Yet Laura knew he meant what he said. He *would* miss Amy. She hoped he wouldn't get hurt. But as little as she knew of Amy, Laura's sixth sense told her Matthew was safe in opening his heart, and his houseboat, to her. She was a little eccentric, but solid. Laura suspected that Amy had given her relationship with Matthew a great deal of thought before ever becoming involved with him. In a way she envied them, for taking their time. As much in love with Paul as she was, as much as she wanted to spend every waking moment with him, as *all-consumed* as she was with him, something frightened her about the speed at which everything was happening. Yet, even if given the opportunity to slow it all down, she knew she wouldn't. The closer she and Paul became, the more of him she wanted. She'd long ago stopped listening to her fears and given herself completely to him.

Lost in these thoughts about Paul, she didn't realize that Matthew was speaking to her. "Laura?" he had an amused look on his face.

Laura blushed. "I'm sorry, Matt!" She felt as though he'd been reading her mind. "I didn't mean to go blank on you. Now what was it you were saying?"

He took her hand and squeezed it gently. "Please. Don't apologize. It gives me a great deal of pleasure to see both you and Paul like this." Her blush grew deeper. "I hope you know that. I was just asking you your plans. Paul told me yesterday that you two are planning a trip to my favorite state!"

Laura was happy to change the subject. "Yes. We're going over to Montana next week. To White-fish!" She was clearly enthused about their plans.

"Why wait 'til next week?" asked Matthew. "Paul could easily get away now. We'll be busy editing for a while. No reason he has to be here for the initial editing phase. He'll need to see the final cuts, but that will be weeks from now."

"Well, actually, I've got a deposition scheduled on Monday. We have to stay here until that's done."

Something about her abrupt change in expression alarmed Matthew.

"A deposition?" he asked, hoping she'd volunteer more.

Laura simply nodded, and made no attempt to

elaborate. He really didn't need to ask who it was she was deposing. Her expression gave it away. Fearful of ruining the upbeat attitude they'd both been enjoying just moments earlier, he returned to the subject of Montana, playfully inviting himself to go along. Laura, not wanting to spoil the evening's mood any more than did Matt, was happy to cooperate, telling him that they'd only arranged for one bed. But it was a king size, so he was most welcome.

"God, don't tempt me like that," he teased. "Paul and I have been friends for a long time. Shared a lot of experiences. But somehow I don't think *that*'s one he'd want me in on." Laura giggled. "So," he continued, "tell me more about your trip."

"We're staying in a beautiful lodge on the mountain for a couple of days. Then the kids are joining us—my mom and dad are putting them on a plane and we'll all spend a couple days exploring Glacier National Park. We're really looking forward to it. Paul and I could both use a break, and you know, we've never really had a chance to spend concentrated time alone together." Just the thought brought a wonderful look into her eyes. She and Paul had agreed to keep news of their wedding secret until their plans were more definite, but at that very moment she felt so happy, and so very close to Matthew, that she confessed. "Actually, one of the purposes of the trip is to make arrangements for a wedding in the lodge this summer."

Matthew, stunned, looked at her in silence for several seconds. Then, letting out a whoop, he grabbed her and gave her a big bear hug. "Laura, that's *wonderful* news!" He looked every bit as pleased as he sounded. "Why haven't you told me this before? In fact, why hasn't that oversized oaf said anything?"

He tried to feign a hurt look at the slight.

As Paul approached, minus Amy, who was busy picking out CDs to liven up the party, he took one look at both Laura's and Matthew's faces and immediately suspected that Laura had leaked the news to his friend. Any doubts were quickly dismissed when Matt, wild-eyed and grinning ear to ear, abruptly tackled him and proceeded to wrestle him to the ground, all the while yelling, "You dirty dog! Why didn't you tell me?"

Laughing, grunting, rolling around on the oriental rug, the two friends, softly, good naturedly pummeled each other, mindless of the expensive suits they wore and the valuable French provincial furniture around which they rolled. It was a fitting way for two old friends, whose first good-natured wrestling matches had taken place more than twenty-five years earlier, to celebrate Paul's good news.

And a great way to liven up the party. When Amy walked in and discovered the source of the commotion, she emitted a loud, enthusiastic "All right!" Then, before things could die down, she put on an old Rolling Stones album, cranked up the volume, and borrowed Shawn from his wife for some serious bumping and grinding on their makeshift dance floor.

The rest of the evening could only be described as joyous. Well, maybe raucous fit, too. For everyone present, all sentimentality, all sadness, was temporarily shelved, as months of hard work and bottled up pressure were unleashed in pure, unadulterated celebration.

By the time they were ready to leave, the entire cast and crew were aware of Laura and Paul's engagement. The evening had become as much a celebration of that news as it was a celebration of the end of shooting on *After the Dance*. The love and good wishes expressed upon hearing their news touched both Laura and Paul.

As they stood in the foyer of the suite, getting ready to leave, Paul turned Laura to him and pulled her into his arms. The kiss they exchanged began sweetly but quickly escalated to a fiery, tongue prob-ing feast, which led to Paul reaching under Laura's dress while Laura, putting up no resistance, moaned softly in anticipation.

It was Laura who first became aware of him standing there—a bellboy, just leaving the suite with a tray of dirty dishes in hand. The young, awkward teenager looked absolutely amazed.

Laura was so self-conscious and embarrassed that his actions failed to register as odd. While she pulled at her skirt to straighten it, and ran a hand over her disheveled hair, he simply looked from Paul to her. Then back to Paul.

Finally, he said, "Damn!"

That was it. Just the one word—"damn" Then, a friendly smile broke over his face.

"Hi there, Mr. Brooks!"

Sometimes Paul Brooks felt like he was snake bit.

*   *   *

Sunlight drifted slowly through her bedroom win-dow the next morning, rousing her gently from a deep sleep. Laura thought at first she was dreaming. Not willing to let the dream end, she instinctively did what she'd done countless times as a child when awakened in the middle of an especially good adventure—she willed herself to fall back into a deep slumber and resume things where they'd left off. In this dream, she lay snuggled, spoon style, in the curve of Paul's body.

After the loneliness of her empty bed the past two years, it wasn't surprising that she didn't want it to end—that she wanted to be able to experience the warmth, the safety, of his body pressed into hers just a bit longer. But what happened next was even better than being able to resume a dream where it left off. For in the next moment she realized that she wasn't dreaming after all! He was actually there beside her. It was a beautiful morning, following an especially beautiful night (she now recollected), and as the sun shone through her bedroom's bay windows, she lay there in the arms of Paul Brooks! No dream could be this incredible. She felt his soft, steady breathing on the back of her neck. His long, powerful arms encased her; his strong thighs pressed against hers. She lay there contentedly and tried to remember when she'd last felt this good, this happy. When she'd last known such comfort, such wholeness. And such passion. Her thoughts turned to the night before.

The kids were spending the weekend up in Bellingham with her parents. Following the party, she and Paul had hurried back to her place. After an evening of restraint, necessitated in part by the demands of hosting the celebration, both of them could hardly wait to be alone, to get their hands on each other. She thought of how incredibly handsome Paul had looked the night before. He always looked wonderful to her. Whether he was wearing sports clothes, jeans or sweats, Laura never failed to be struck by his good looks. His grace and power. But last night, dressed in his tan Armani suit, he'd taken her breath away. As good a time as she'd had, as wonderful as everyone had been when they'd heard of their engagement, it had been difficult to share him with anyone when he looked like that. She'd been surprised and a little embarrassed to find her eyes following him all too frequently, feeling like a young girl with an enormous crush on him, yet she was helpless to stop. It wasn't just his enormously good looks. It was just *Paul*, just the way he was. The way he looked directly into the eyes of whomever he talked to. The tilt of his head that indicated he was listening intently. The ease of his laugh. The confidence in his walk and posture. Watching him, she was struck more than ever by the ease with which he combined his extraordinary physical strength and an equally extraordinary sensitivity, with neither quality compromising the other. This morning, lying there contentedly, listening to his steady breathing, she remembered that observations like that had once caused her pain—the pain of knowing just how incredible a man he was, but believing he would never be hers. Truly hers. But as she'd slowly realized the depth of *his* love for *her*, the depth of his commitment, she finally reached a place where observing these qualities in Paul gave her unbelievable pleasure. Throughout the night she realized that he'd looked for her as well, needing to see her, establish contact, even if only in the form of that look of his— the one that both melted and stirred her. A couple hours of that—of watching him from across a room— and she was ready to go stark raving mad. Finally, as they'd prepared to leave, neither one of them had been able to restrain themselves anymore. Laura smiled at the thought of how far they might have gone, right there in the hallway, had that bellboy not stumbled upon them.

Her lips curved up in just the trace of a smile as she thought back to the rest of the night. With the kids gone, it had been their first chance to spend a night together; but, knowing they had the entire night

ahead of them had not diminished the urgency with
which they'd made love. At least not the first time.
Her smile widened at the thought of how many times
they'd made love in that seven or eight-hour span. She
nestled deeper into Paul's curvature, pressing her bottom into him, causing him to stir, but not awaken.
But as exciting, as satisfying, as their initial uninhibited lovemaking had been, and as gently and tenderly
as they'd made love later in the night, what had been
even more special to Laura had been the chance to lie
together quietly, holding each other, and finally, drift
off to sleep. The comfort of having Paul at her side,
his hand reaching for hers in the darkness. Yes,
definitely, these things had meant the most to her. The
incredible joy, incredible sense of well-being and safety
that having him next to her, in the still of the night,
gave her. And now, the comfort of waking to him.

A morning person, Laura had never been one to
linger in bed for long. She considered the morning
hours the best of the day and was always eager to get
started. Having Paul there tempted her to stay in bed
forever, but the sunshine filtering through the sheer
curtains was its own temptation. And she knew Spencer would be standing statue-still in the sun, letting it
warm his back, eye keenly trained on the path leading
from the house, waiting for her. And breakfast. She
could already hear the dogs sniffing at the closed
bedroom door, eager to be let outside. So, wrapping
herself in a soft terry bathrobe, she tiptoed out of the
bedroom and, after silently greeting each dog with a
big hug, she headed for the kitchen, where she opened
the doors to let her panting companions out, then
started a pot of home-ground Irish Cream coffee.
With the sound of the coffee dripping and its aroma
starting to fill the kitchen, she stuffed some treats for

the dogs into the pocket of her robe and headed out the back door toward the barn.

Both dogs, tails wagging, wet noses sniffing at everything in sight, including Laura's bare legs, followed along behind her. Laughing, she reached into her pockets and tossed each one a small biscuit. "Now stop tickling me," she scolded good naturedly, wiping the wet traces of their noses off her calf.

She smiled at the sight of Spencer waiting for her, and the sound of his throaty greeting. On cold, wet mornings, she would hurry into the shelter of the barn, pour some oats into his bucket, put some hay in his feeder, then stand, usually with coffee cup in hand and watch the big horse as he ate. But this morning, the sun was already invitingly warm, and she wanted to stay outside for a minute, so she stopped and let herself into the corral with him. The big gelding knickered upon seeing her hand disappear into her pocket, knowing it contained either a carrot stick or slices of apple. She handed him the apple she'd cut in quarters, then, arm resting on his neck, stood alongside him as he chewed it. For the past couple of years, as much as she'd enjoyed mornings like these, they still brought a sadness to her. But this morning, there was no sadness. It occurred to Laura at that moment, she had everything she needed to be unreservedly happy in life. Two children she absolutely adored. A comfortable home for them. Her beloved animals. A career that, though not all-important to her, did challenge and stimulate her. And Paul. Paul was the missing link—the one without whom she'd ached with loneliness. The one she never expected to again find. And at that very moment, he lay, still sleeping, in her bed. She felt unbelievably blessed.

But Paul, who'd awakened minutes earlier to the

aroma of freshly brewed coffee, no longer lay in bed. He stood watching her from the bedroom window. He knew what she was feeling. Not just because he could tell by the contented look on her face, the joyful way that she hugged her horse as he shifted his weight into her—though those were obvious indications of her happy thoughts. Most of all, he knew just what she was feeling by his own sense of happiness, his own feelings of immense well-being. Somehow, even though he'd never experienced anything quite like it before, he intuitively knew that these feelings, by their very nature, *had* to be shared. One person, alone, did not, *could* not feel this way, he realized as he stood watching Laura lead Spencer into the barn. What he was feeling, for the first time in his life, was that he was no longer alone. He had Laura now. And last night, the first night that they'd been able to sleep together, to wake at four A.M. and make slow, sensual love to each other, then drift back to sleep, was just the beginning of a lifetime together.

He wasn't a particularly religious man, but he was fast becoming a spiritual man, fast realizing that a whole new life lay ahead. A life where it was matters of the heart, not of the material world, which would provide the greatest rewards. A sudden awareness of his morning hardness caused him to grin and to modify his reflections somewhat. Well, maybe this new life wasn't *entirely* spiritual, he mused. After all, it did have its physical aspects, too. It did have its physical rewards.

Laura returned to the bedroom several minutes later, carrying a tray with coffee, juice, wheat toast and granola. A thick newspaper was tucked under her arm.

She kissed him on the nose, arranged the tray in

front of him, extracted the sports page and handed it to him, then climbed in bed next to him. Then, as if they'd been doing it for years, they sat there, ate breakfast and read the Sunday paper. They talked about the Seattle SuperSonics victory the night before. Laura read their horoscopes. Paul fed the dogs his leftover toast.

For Laura, it was a return to normalcy. A return to the beauty and comfort of a shared life. A life she'd never again expected to find.

For Paul, it was a morning unlike any he'd ever had. So comforting, so homey and real. Yet so simple. He felt unbelievably moved by it. Unbelievable happy. And unbelievably excited about marrying this woman and spending the rest of his Sunday mornings in bed beside her.

18

Lenny Coleman had an uneasy feeling about this deposition. He'd not been able to shake a gnawing suspicion about Mackenzie Montana. Sliding behind the wheel of his rented Cadillac Seville, he was thinking that maybe if he'd been able to meet with her in person instead of doing all the preparation for this deposition by phone, he wouldn't feel this way. But she'd refused to return to L.A. in time to actually meet with him, which meant they'd spent hours on the telephone going over every question Coleman anticipated she'd be asked today.

At least they'd arranged to meet for breakfast, so they'd have an hour together before the ten A.M. deposition was scheduled to begin.

He pulled out of the underground parking garage at the Sheraton and headed north down Union, went one block and then turned west to double-back toward the Four Seasons, where Mackenzie was staying. He observed that Seattle, the city about which he'd read so much recently, the so called "perfect" place to live, seemed to have at least one major drawback—if this were any indication, Seattle's traffic was every bit as obnoxious as Los Angeles'. He glanced at his watch, but saw that he had plenty of time.

He pulled into the circular drive of the Four Seasons, left his car with the valet and headed into the hotel. Scanning the elegant lobby, he realized that he and Mackenzie hadn't specified where they'd meet, so he walked over to a house phone to call her room. As he stood listening to the phone ring, something out of the corner of his eye caught his attention and he turned toward the bank of elevators. That's when he first saw her. She'd just gotten off the elevator and was heading toward the cafe. As cool a customer as Lenny Coleman was—a man reknowned for the poker face he maintained during negotiations—he could still feel his jaw drop at the sight of her.

Mackenzie Montana, head held high, moved gracefully across the lobby. Her hair, untamed and glorious as ever, was swept to one side and loosely knotted. At first, Lenny was merely surprised by the style of the suit she wore. But then in a split second, the realization had struck him. With her long legs very much on display and the loose, flowing shape of her trapeze-style jacket, she had almost been able to pull it off. But as she walked, the giant, rounded protrusion of her stomach could not be camouflaged. Mackenzie Montana was pregnant!

Lenny didn't call out to her, but instead let her go on into the restaurant, unaware that he'd seen her. He needed a minute to let this sink in. Pregnant! Now it all made sense, why she'd been so elusive, why she resisted his attempts to schedule a deposition, to the point that he had to threaten again to drop the case if she didn't appear this time, why she'd been pleased to hear the actual trial was months, maybe a year, off. Why hadn't he trusted his instincts? He'd known something was not right. Why hadn't he pursued the matter further? He knew the answer. It was a combination of his having had an unusually heavy caseload recently, one that made it difficult to undertake any task that wasn't absolutely essential, and his ego. That had been the other reason he'd not heeded his instincts. His attraction to her. And the prospect of adding her name to his forever-lengthening list of entertainment heavies he represented. All the wrong reasons.

He was angry with himself. Angry with her. But, being the inveterate professional that he was, he knew he needed to bury that anger. At least for the time being. He'd taken on this case, and now he had to represent her as best he could. At least today, at this deposition. Later would be another story. But today, Mackenzie Montana was still his client, and as such, she was entitled to his best effort. With that mindset firmly in place, he entered the restaurant.

She didn't rise when he approached the table, but instead, shot him a dazzling smile and extended her arm. "Lenny, you look wonderful!" she gushed. "How was your flight up last night?"

"Uneventful," he answered dryly. "Which does not appear to be an adjective I'll be able to use for today." The message was clear, but Mackenzie chose to play dumb.

"Now don't tell me you're nervous about this deposition thing," she batted her lashes at him. "I have total confidence in you, Lenny."

"I may be good, but I'm not a magician," he answered gruffly. At Mackenzie's puzzled expression, he continued. "Even *I* can't make that belly of yours disappear." It was unusually rude, unusually crass for him, but he couldn't resist saying at least that much.

337

For once, Mackenzie Montana was speechless. Her face reddening, she finally spoke, in a nervous, high-pitched voice that was barely audible, "I didn't think you'd notice."

At that, he laughed heartily and shook his head. Before he could respond, she continued.

"Even if *you* noticed, they may not. I've only gained seventeen pounds, and I think this suit hides that pretty well. Besides, what if they *do* notice? What the hell business of theirs is it if I'm having a baby?" Her voice was growing stronger, more emphatic.

"Mackenzie..." he started with a disgusted tone, poised to launch into a lecture about the lawyer-client relationship. About her duty to tell him anything as significant as the fact that she was pregnant. About the position she'd now put him in—giving him no warning, no time to prepare for this new development, to analyze its implications in their lawsuit. The position she'd now put *both* of them in. But then he looked at her and decided not to bother. Decided that he couldn't afford wasting precious time lecturing to her. They had some serious thinking to do. He glanced at his watch. The deposition started in 45 minutes. "Holy shit," he said under his breath.

Then, turning down the waitress's offer to take their order, Lenny Coleman saw to it that he and his client stopped the idle chatter and got down to business.

*   *   *

The deposition was being held in a conference room at Winnifred and Barry's offices. The law firm had extended an open invitation to be of help whenever they could. Laura hadn't wanted to take the

338

deposition at the Brooks building for a number of reasons, primary of which was the effect that a chance encounter between Paul and Mackenzie might have on the deposition and on both her and Mackenzie. In addition, if the case were to go to trial, she'd already decided to associate Winnifred and Barry on it. Laura knew her limitations. She wasn't too proud to admit that a trial of this nature might be too big for her to handle alone.

She arrived at nine and immediately got to work in the conference room they'd reserved, going over her notes. The firm's offices were on the 39th floor of the Washington Mutual building. The offices reeked of elegance, the decor clean, sparse, and unquestionably pricey, with marble columns in the reception areas, marble corridor floors, and an abundance of glass everywhere one looked, designed to maximize the view of Elliott Bay, some 39 stories and several blocks away. As was typical of downtown law offices, rooms experiencing heavy client use, as well as the offices of the senior partners, lined the floor's western wall, the one with the view.

Laura had been pleased to be given one of the most desirable conference rooms, and as she sat thinking, gazing out at the Olympic mountains, which were barely visible on this partly cloudy day, she reassured herself that things would go smoothly this morning. She wouldn't let the sight of Mackenzie Montana rattle her. After the magic of the past few weeks with Paul, she felt confident that she could do it. She would be able to remain detached and professional.

Still, her heart jumped into her throat at the sound of the door being opened. But it was only the court reporter, a young woman whom Laura had specifically requested. Someone she'd worked with a number of times when she was with Emery, Johnson.

"Susan!" she smiled at the lovely woman who entered the room. "I'm so pleased you were available today."

Susan Carlson was pleased to see Laura, too, and as she went about setting up her equipment, the two brought each other up to date on what they'd each been doing the past couple of years. The conversation was superficial, but pleasant. It helped Laura keep her mind off Mackenzie Montana.

At precisely ten o'clock, the door opened. In walked Lenny, followed closely behind by Mackenzie. She wore a loose fitting trench coat over her mint-colored suit.

Laura stood and extended her hand politely, first to Lenny and then to Mackenzie. The women's eyes met briefly, but did not linger. Laura then introduced each of them to Susan. She offered to take Mackenzie's coat, but Mackenzie responded that she was getting over a bad cold and would prefer to keep it with her.

Finally, the group settled into their respective places. Laura sat at the head of the table with Susan on her right. On her immediate left was Mackenzie Montana. Lenny Coleman sat on Mackenzie's left.

Laura looked over at Susan to see if she was ready. At Susan's nod, she began speaking for the record. "This is the deposition of Mackenzie Montana, plaintiff in the case of Montana vs. Brooks Productions Company. This deposition is being taken pursuant to notice and in accordance with the Washington Code of Civil Procedure, Washington Supreme Court rules and all local applicable rules." At this point she turned to Mackenzie and explained, "Ms. Montana, I'm going to be asking you a series of questions. You must respond to these questions verbally and not with any gestures, such as a nod, which, of course, cannot be recorded by Ms. Carlson. If you don't understand a question, you may ask me to repeat it." Then, turning to Susan she asked, "Ms. Carlson, will you please swear the witness?"

After Susan Carlson swore in Mackenzie Montana, Laura turned to Mackenzie and began asking questions. As was customary, the initial questions focused on obtaining basic information. Name, address, age. Then the questions turned to Mackenzie's career, to the films she'd done. Laura focused particularly on her last one, *Busting Out*.

"*Busting Out* did a lot to advance your career, didn't it?" she asked Mackenzie, who, suspicious of what Laura was getting at, responded with a simple, "Yes."

"What was your compensation for that film?" Laura continued.

"One and a half," answered Mackenzie.

"One and a half *what*?" asked Laura patiently. "Million? Points?"

"Million," answered the star.

"And is it not true that, with the tremendous commercial success of that film you became very much in demand in the industry?"

"You could say that," answered Mackenzie.

"In other words, at this point in your career, you do not need to worry about being out of work, do you?"

Before Mackenzie could answer, Lenny spoke up. "I object to that question, Ms. Kennedy. It calls for my client to make conclusions that are purely speculative and entirely too subjective."

Coleman knew that Laura was trying to establish the fact that, even if a contract was found to exist,

Mackenzie had not been damaged financially as she could at any time find another film to star in. Undoubtedly one that would provide a more lucrative compensation for her services.

"Let me rephrase that, then," answered Laura. "Ms. Montana, if *After the Dance* had not come up, if you'd never discussed or even entertained the idea of starring in it, what would you have done? Professionally speaking, that is."

Mackenzie thought long and hard before answering. She, too, knew where Laura's questions were heading. "There would have been other films for me to star in," she began. Lenny flinched a little. "But *After the Dance* was more than work to me. It wasn't about money. You know that," she said to Laura, her look growing hostile. "I was willing to do this one strictly for the points. This was about my entire career. About my range as an actress. It was the first role I'd been offered that had any real substance. That was not a blonde, or red-headed, bimbo role. It was my first chance to show everyone what I'm capable of. *That*, to me, is worth *more* than the one and a half million I got for *Busting Out*."

Laura had to admit that the answer was a good one.

Lenny Coleman was impressed. Maybe he could relax—just a little bit.

After about 30 minutes of this line of questioning, Laura suggested that they take a short break. She was about to get into the details of the negotiations between Paul and Mackenzie. They could all use a breather before tackling that. Plus, throughout the deposition, she'd been puzzled about something. Mackenzie had still not removed her coat, which struck her as more than a little odd, especially since the room was growing stuffy. Used to always seeing the flamboyant star with a minimum of clothes, this trench coat thing just did not sit right with Laura. She had expected Lenny to instruct his client to tone her dress down for the trial, but this was overkill. It was just a deposition—to her knowledge, she thought sarcastically, the transcript wouldn't reflect the star's attire. She couldn't for the life of her figure out what, if anything, was going on, and if something were, how it might relate to their case. But intuitively she sensed there was a connection.

Before heading for the coffee room, which was separated from the conference room by a small kitchen, Laura told Mackenzie where she could find the ladies room. Then, excusing herself, she left. But she did not go far. In the kitchen, which was empty and dark, she turned to look back. Then, realizing she could not be seen by them, she stopped to observe Lenny and Mackenzie. It was not a habit of hers—to spy on opposing parties and their counsel—and from where she stood she was not able to hear their conversation, but something made her stop and study Mackenzie.

After Laura left the room, Mackenzie started to get up to go to the bathroom, but Lenny Coleman reached for her arm and stopped her. "You're not going anywhere," he said rather forcefully. Though he'd hidden it well with Laura in the room, she could tell he was furious with her.

"You've got to be kidding!" Mackenzie exclaimed, incredulous. "My bladder's about to burst."

"I don't want you strutting around here." Coleman's tone was firm. "She hasn't picked up on it yet, but if you start parading around, I guarantee you, she will."

"But I thought you said you wouldn't help me hide it," Mackenzie answered testily, sounding like a snotty child pointing out a contradiction in her parents' behavior.

"I'm *not*. And like I told you, you must be completely honest with Ms. Kennedy if she *asks* you point blank if you're pregnant. But while I'm not willing to hide your pregnancy from her, I do not have an obligation to alert her to its existence." He clearly looked troubled by the position she'd put him in. "So let's just not advertise your condition. Okay? Now you sit here while I use the restroom." He got up to leave, then turned and looked at her again. "Don't move. Do you hear?"

After seeing Lenny Coleman leave, Laura was about to abandon her position in the kitchen and head to the restroom herself. But then she saw Mackenzie look around stealthily, stand, and remove her trench coat. Lying the coat on the back of her chair, Mackenzie walked over to the side table to pour herself a drink from a carafe of ice water.

It wasn't until she turned, giving Laura a side shot of her that Laura saw her bulging middle. Laura gasped out loud at the sight. Mackenzie Montana *pregnant* was about as foreign a concept, about as unlikely a sight, as she'd ever seen. Immediately after the initial shock, the significance of this discovery to their case began sinking in. If the star was pregnant, she could hardly be successful in a suit for damages! In her research, Laura had come across a case that held that a pregnancy that wasn't disclosed to the studio at the time of casting and that would necessitate either a rewrite of the script or extraordinary shooting measures to hide its existence was grounds for the studio to dismiss the actress. At the time, Laura had breezed through the court's opinion, looking for other rulings that might have some relevance to their case—

never imagining how applicable the pregnancy ruling would be to their own situation. They *had* her! Laura knew that she should be overjoyed at this revelation. But there was something else there, in the back of her mind, something so dark she dare not even think about it. Especially right now. Right now, she had to act, and act fast.

Her legal sixth sense told her to expose this pregnancy now, before the deposition was over. Make it of record. It might well put an end to this case. Once and for all. With that thought in mind, she headed back into the conference room, startling Mackenzie with her sudden appearance.

Upon seeing her, Mackenzie hurried back to her chair, muttered something about how chilly the room was, and, before Lenny had a chance to return and see what she'd done, put her coat back on. And when Lenny and Susan returned just seconds later, Laura resumed the deposition without a hint of the discovery she'd made moments earlier showing on her face.

Because of this, this mask of ignorance that Laura wore, her opening question blew Lenny Coleman away.

"For the record, Ms. Montana," she asked nonchalantly, "when is your baby due?"

The room grew absolutely still. Even the steady click click of Susan's rapidly moving fingers fell silent. At first Mackenzie looked stunned. But seeing immediately that Laura intended to play hard ball, she decided to get maximum mileage, maximum satisfaction, from the situation. "Let's see," she said. Holding up first one finger, then another, she started counting, "September 25th to October 25th to November 25th to..." making a great show of it. Finally, reaching her ninth finger, she concluded, "June *25th* must be when I'm due!" a phoney, wide-eyed look of innocence on her face.

Laura could feel her stomach knotting, the adrenalin coursing through her, causing her heart to pump wildly. September 25th. She didn't have time to think about it now, but instinctively she knew that there was a purpose to the show Mackenzie Montana had just put on. But she couldn't dwell on that now. She had to maintain her calm. Proceed with the deposition. Problem was, her mind was spinning, whirling around and around by the growing emotional response that was overcoming her. She had trouble remembering just where her line of questioning was supposed to go. She hadn't expected this turn of events, so she hadn't prepared for it. She was flying by the seat of her pants, which she was most capable of doing under ordinary circumstances, but right now it was becoming increasingly difficult as the seconds passed.

With a great effort to concentrate on the legal issues at hand, she finally continued, "Ms. Montana, shooting on *After the Dance* was only completed this past week. In light of your pregnancy, how did you expect to be able to play the part of Ashley Cowles, when by my calculations you would have been seven months pregnant before the film was completed?"

Mackenzie looked at Laura. For the first time she noticed that Laura no longer wore the wedding ring she'd seen on her hand that day they'd first met in Paul's office. Then she flashed back to that afternoon that she'd waited outside the Brooks building, hoping to catch Paul as he left work. To try to talk to him. Make peace with him. She'd waited until the lot had pretty much cleared—until there was only Paul's car and one other car left in the lot. And then she'd seen them in Paul's office, what they were doing in there.

Watched as Laura climbed on top of Paul and screwed him, right there in his office. At the recollection of that sight, her eyes grew suddenly hard. Everyone present could see the transformation, though the thoughts that gave rise to it would never be known to them. Lenny had this uncanny feeling that he should stop his client, but stop her from doing *what*, he did not know.

All eyes were on her, waiting for an answer to Laura's last question. Finally she shook the image of Laura and Paul from her head and answered, "I assumed Paul would work around the fact that I was pregnant. Either write it into the script, or shoot me in a way that hid the fact."

"And just *why* would Mr. Brooks be willing to do such a thing?" Laura quizzed her, with a fury growing within her. She was amazed and angered by the audacity of this woman.

Knowing full well what the impact of her next words would be—in fact *savoring* that very thought—Mackenzie Montana looked Laura Kennedy right in the eye.

"Why do you think he'd be willing to?" she said, the ends of her beautiful mouth turned up in a most wicked smile.

Laura could not answer. Her mind was a dead space, blackened by a terror that gripped her.

"Because the baby I'm carrying is his." Placing her hands lovingly, seductively on her stomach and arching her back to enable her to further torment Laura with the sight, Mackenzie Montana dug the knife in deeper. Then twisted it.

"Paul Brooks is my baby's father."

* * *

It had been the worst four days of his life.

Laura had disappeared on him. Literally disappeared. He hadn't seen or talked to her since Sunday, the day after they'd spent their first night together. They'd had the most wonderful week-end together. They were excited about their upcoming trip to Montana. They were planning to leave in just a few days. But first she had to do the deposition.

The deposition. Paul was certain now, as he sat waiting for the transcript to be delivered, that something had happened there. Something between Laura and Mackenzie Montana. Something that caused Laura to run away. He'd suspected as much from the very start, but those first hours, that first day, he still couldn't rid his mind of other explanations for her disappearance. Explanations that were too horrible to acknowledge—that something, something terrible, had happened to her. So, after the absolute terror of those first 18 hours—before the police officer called—the realization that this had to do with Mackenzie Montana had actually been a relief to him.

He'd been a basket case all day on Monday, knowing that the deposition was taking place. Starting at noon, he must have called Laura's house a half-dozen times, even though she'd assured him it would be late in the afternoon before she arrived back home. When he still got no answer at five p.m., he drove out there. Even if Laura weren't home, he fully expected to see Christopher and Hailey. But no one. The place was strangely empty and silent. The dogs didn't even seem to be there.

He sat in his car in Laura's driveway for two hours. Every once in a while, when he thought he would go nuts, stark raving nuts, just sitting there, he'd get out and shoot a couple baskets—Christopher, uncharacteristically, had left his basketball on the front steps—but even that didn't help relieve the tension. Didn't stop his mind from torturing him with what might have gone on at the deposition. He tried to imagine the worst scenario, just what might have happened between the two women. Laura may have found out about his night with Mackenzie Montana. He wouldn't put it past Mackenzie to tell her, even in the setting of a deposition. Yes, *that's* what had happened. Laura knew now. She knew about him and Mackenzie.

She hadn't *wanted* to know. He thought back to that first night they'd made love. He'd tried to tell her that night, but she stopped him. She said she didn't want to hear it. If only he'd told her, instead of letting her hear it from Mackenzie Montana. He felt ill. And angry. With Mackenzie Montana, but most of all, with himself. How could he have let it happen? And now this, this wondering where Laura was, what she knew, what she was thinking. It was sheer torture. Which is just what I deserve, he told himself. The only thing to do now is deal with it. Explain to Laura. Tell her it hadn't meant anything to him—that he'd all but given up on her at that point. That he had had nothing but regrets ever since. He'd ask her to forgive him. Beg her to.

Finally, worried that she might be trying to reach him at his house—maybe she was sitting there in his driveway at this very moment—he decided to head home.

But when he reached his house there was nothing. No Laura, no messages. He tried to remain calm, but by midnight, when she still didn't answer the phone, he was ready to explode. That's when he'd begun imagining terrible things. What if it had nothing at all to do with the deposition?

He remembered the accident—the car whose horn had caused Spencer to mow Laura down—and the strange phone calls Laura had received months earlier. With those thoughts he climbed back into his car and sped back to her house. Literally sped—up to 97 mph, to be exact. He knew, because that's what the cop clocked him at. Just before he pulled him over on I-405.

Considering the speed, and the fact that he hadn't pulled right over upon seeing the flashing lights behind him—for one crazy moment, he'd refused to stop, refused to let some cop delay him from finding Laura—Paul thought that Officer Williams had actually been a remarkably good sport about it all. Once he'd explained why he'd been driving so fast, what his concerns were, the young police officer had offered to accompany him to Laura's house. Of course, he'd have to issue the ticket, but that could wait. Paul left his car on the side of the freeway and hurriedly climbed into Williams' police car.

They pulled into Laura's driveway minutes later. Her car was not there. They checked the garage. Nothing. The place looked empty. But the light over the front door was on, as was the one just outside the barn, which she always left on at night. A knock at the front door brought no response. Not even barking. The only sign of life was Spencer. Paul went to check on him and found him standing quietly in his darkened stall.

They circled the house, peering in windows, looking for any signs of foul play. Nothing. Everything looked completely normal. Still, Paul had wanted to break in. To get a better look at the entire house. But Officer Williams refused. There was nothing to warrant it, he said. Aware that Paul was less than appeased by what they'd seen, he promised to come back in the morning, as soon as it got light, and do a more thorough examination. Maybe then he'd force entry. Paul finally agreed and the young officer drove him back to his car. He urged Paul not to worry and promised to contact him the next morning. Then he wrote him a ticket.

It was just after nine A.M. the next morning when Officer Williams called. He told Paul that when he'd returned to Laura's house about 7:30 A.M., he'd run into a neighbor kid who was there feeding the horse. According to the teenager, Laura had gone out of town unexpectedly and had asked him to feed the horse twice a day and turn lights on and off. The boy couldn't tell the officer where Mrs. Kennedy was, only that she expected to be gone at least a week. She'd given him the number of a friend of hers, someone named Corinne, to call in case of an emergency. Williams had taken the number down. The boy didn't know anything else.

Paul thanked Williams profusely for the information, and for the trouble he'd gone to. Think nothing of it, Williams told him. Then he confessed that he'd been a fan back in Paul's U.W. days, and it was a pleasure to get to meet him. Even under these circumstances. He wished Paul well and told him he'd be happy to help out anytime he could.

After this call, after he knew that Laura had left of her own free will, knew she was undoubtedly safe, Paul could finally begin thinking clearly again. Now he was without doubt as to what had happened at the deposition. Somehow, Mackenzie Montana had let it be known that they'd slept together. And Laura, unable to face him—whether out of hurt or anger he did not know—had taken the kids and gone away. Probably to think. To figure out how to cope with what she learned. That would be just like her, Paul thought. Laura was not one to strike out in anger. To force an unpleasant confrontation with him, face to face. No, it was much more like her to go off and deal with it alone. Plus it wasn't really all that surprising a decision for her to make. At least, that's what he told himself. After all, they'd been planning a trip anyway. The kids' spring break was starting this week. She'd undoutedly decided to just go ahead with the plan. Yes, that was undoutedly what she'd done, he assured himself. She'd decided to take the trip they'd planned without him. That conclusion brought him comfort.

At first, he wanted to follow her. To Montana. But then he called and found out that she hadn't checked into the Aspen Lodge after all. He called all the other hotels and resorts he knew of in Whitefish. None of them had a Laura Kennedy registered. Not wanting to leave and miss her should she call or return, he finally decided to stay put. Just give her this time, he counseled himself. Then, once she returned, he'd be able to explain. Be able to win her forgiveness. It may not be easy, and it may take some time, but eventually he would get her to forgive him. He was confident of that. After all, it had happened just once, in a moment of extreme weakness. And over the past few days, he'd frequently reminded himself of how easy-going and undemanding Laura was. If any woman could understand, even forgive, such a transgression, it was Laura. They were too much in love with each other, too happy together, for this to jeopardize their future. He told himself that over and over. No, he could work this out with her. He just had to be patient. Wait for her to return and give him a chance to explain things.

But even as he reassured himself, another voice whispered unsettling things to him. Things like, "But this is *Mackenzie Montana* we're dealing with." Nothing more, just that—a reminder that this wasn't just anyone he'd had a fling with. It was Mackenzie Montana. As if that fact overshadowed all the others, all the logic he'd been using to stay calm. He tried to imagine what might have been said at the deposition, just how Mackenzie might have blurted it out. What Laura might have been put through, when she was just trying to do her job. The thought sickened him.

Finally, it dawned on him that everything she'd said had been recorded! There had to have been a court reporter there. Of course! Why hadn't he thought of it sooner? He buzzed Candy and instructed her to get ahold of the court reporter and tell her to send the transcript of the deposition over immediately. When, minutes later, Candy stood at his desk and told him the transcript wouldn't be available for another week, he'd grabbed the piece of paper on which was written Susan Carlson's telephone number and picked up the phone himself.

The impatient, demanding tone he'd started off with with Susan wasn't a good idea. Paul immediately regretted it. Susan Carlson had been polite and professional, but unbending, in her prediction that the transcript would not be completed for another week. Laura knew that, she told him—knew how long it took to get the transcript from a deposition. Hearing the familiarity in Susan Carlson's voice when she called her "Laura" softened his own voice. The strain he was feeling was audible to Susan. He told her that Laura wasn't just his company's attorney, but that she was also his fiancee and that she had left town immediately after the deposition. Without a word. He knew something had happened at the deposition and he had to find out what so he could do something about it. Before he went crazy.

He wasn't used to pouring his heart out like that to anyone, much less a complete stranger. But he couldn't help himself. And this approach was far more effective than the threatening one he'd started off with.

Susan Carlson was silent for a long time. She was touched by the desperation in his voice. Suddenly, it all made sense—the look on Laura's face that day, her trembling hands, the suddenness with which she'd ended the deposition... And though Susan's heart had gone out to Laura that day—which made a part of her want to tell this guy what a big jerk he was and slam down the phone on him—something in his voice made her heart go out to *him* as well. Before she hung up, she promised she'd start working on the deposition and he'd have it the next day.

When he arrived for work this morning, Candy told him Susan Carlson had called and said she was messengering the transcript of the deposition over this morning. It should arrive by eleven o'clock.

And that is how it came to be that at 11:43 A.M. on that fateful Friday morning, as he finally reached the last page of a document entitled, "Transcript of the Deposition of Plaintiff, Mackenzie Montana, In Re: Montana vs. Brooks Production," Paul Brooks' world—the one that had been so beautifully full of promise and happiness just five short days ago—blew sky high.

*   *   *

Corinne wasn't sure she was doing the right thing.

She'd never met him, but that hadn't stopped her from feeling incredibly angry with him this past week. It had broken her heart to see Laura on Monday and just when she'd been toying with the idea of calling Paul Brooks and giving him a piece of her mind, he called her instead. When he did, he sounded much different than she expected. His voice was soft and desperate sounding. She fought her reaction, wanting to remain angry with him, to strike out at him, but instead, she found herself feeling just a bit sympathetic toward him. He asked to see her, to talk to her about Laura. She hesitated, trying to sort through her ambivalent feelings. "Please," he said. Just that. "Please." And she agreed. But now she wasn't feeling very good about the decision. *Maybe*, she told herself—and this was the key to her keeping her word to see him—maybe by meeting him, she could help Laura in some way.

She'd been upset all week—ever since Laura called late Monday morning and asked her to come right out. She rushed over to Laura's house and listened as Laura told her everything that had happened. Told her about her and Paul's engagement. About how incredibly happy she'd been. And how that morning's deposition of Mackenzie Montana had shattered all her dreams.

She'd never seen Laura like that. Not even in those months after Michael died. It alarmed her to see her friend so dispirited. There were no tears. No hysterics. What she saw on Laura's face was worse than that. Far worse. It was... a word for it was hard to come by. *Blank.* That's it, thought Corinne. Her friend's face looked blank. Empty. There wasn't even the grief that she'd seen in her eyes after Michael's death. It frightened Corinne to look into eyes that were usually so full of emotion, to see instead a flatness that had never been there before.

Laura was already packing when Corinne arrived. At first Corinne tried to dissuade her from going away. But Laura was adamant about it. She had to get out of there. Now. She needed to put as much distance as possible between her and Paul, as quickly as possible. Corinne could understand her friend's reaction, her need to flee, but it frightened her to think of Laura going off in that frame of mind. Still, she knew better than to argue with her. And so, rather reluctantly, she helped by packing for Christopher and Hailey.

They were going to Carmel. Corinne didn't comment on Laura's choice of destinations. She knew that Laura and Michael had honeymooned there. Over the years, Laura had talked about Carmel frequently, and always with great fondness. Years earlier she told Corinne about her and Michael's dream to retire there. On the ocean. But she hadn't mentioned the little beach town since Michael's death. Until Monday.

When Corinne asked her how long they'd be gone, Laura said she wasn't sure. The kids' spring break was coming up next week, so they could stay two weeks and still only miss the four days of school remaining this week. That blank look on her face. Corinne shuddered—she suddenly had the feeling Laura might leave and never come back. But then she'd seen her with the dogs. Huddled down in a crouch on the kitchen floor, with an arm around one dog on either side of her. Tails wagging, tongues lapping at her face, they were alert, happy to have her attention. She stroked each one and explained that she had to leave them for a while. It was the only time Corinnne had seen just a hint of tears in her friend's eyes. The only time Laura allowed some emotion to surface. From the dogs' happy reaction, Corinne thought Laura might just as well be telling them that she was going to the store to bring them back the world's biggest, juiciest bone. But without Laura, she knew those two would soon be lost. Still, the scene had relieved her, assured her that Laura would indeed be back. Laura Kennedy wasn't about to abandon those dogs.

Corinne promised Laura she'd take care of things at the house. She'd make sure the neighbor's boy fed Spencer. And she would drive the dogs up to Bellingham that very afternoon. Laura knew they'd be safe and well cared for at her parents' house. By the time the kids got home from school, the car was packed and ready to go.

That afternoon, Corinne stood there in the driveway waving goodbye, with a lump in her throat and an aching heart, and watched as the family that meant so very much to her went off to heal. Again.

And so, with that memory in mind, the sound of Paul Brooks' voice on the phone that morning had not exactly been a welcome one. Maybe she could help Laura, she reminded herself as she pulled into the parking lot at Brooks Productions. But in her heart she did not hold much hope.

Sitting in the reception area, waiting for the sharp-tongued blonde who sat at the desk to finish her telephone conversation—this must be Candy, she thought, remembering Laura's description of her—thoughts of the only other time she'd been in the Brooks building returned to her. She smiled at the memory of her and Laura's race to the sauna that night they'd gone back there, after dinner at Cucina, Cucina. It had been, what? Six months ago? Laura had been in such a good mood. To Corinne, it had been a significant night—the first time since Michael's death that Corinne had seen the fun, carefree side of her friend re-emerging. A side she'd always loved. She knew then that Paul Brooks was in large part responsible for Laura's long-awaited recovery, her long-due return to life after the loss of her husband. Corinne had been so relieved to see it, so sure it was the right thing. How many times had she encouraged her friend to go for it? To take the job? To take a chance with Paul? She encouraged her—probably even pressured her—even though Laura had told her repeatedly of her fears. Her fear of being hurt by Paul. And that's just what had happened.

Great advice, Corinne, she now chided herself. Why didn't I stay out of it? Maybe none of this would have happened if I hadn't interfered. Hell, I was even the one to tell her about the job opening here at Brooks Productions! Good friend *I've* turned out to be. As she sat waiting for Candy to hang up the phone and let Paul know she was waiting to see him, she began feeling so angry at herself—and at Paul Brooks—for allowing Laura, and undoutedly, *sadly*, the kids as well, to get hurt, so full of regret, that she talked herself right out of her meeting with Paul. To hell with that asshole, she told herself, standing to leave. Laura would be better off without him. Why would I even consider talking to someone who'd hurt her so?

As yet, Candy hadn't so much as acknowledged her, so it would be easy to just sneak out...

But just as she started to do so, the door to Paul's office opened. They'd never met. Thinking that even if it were Paul at the door, he wouldn't know who she was, Corinne picked up the pace as she headed for the stairs. She did have the urge to take a look at him. After all, she'd heard so much about him. But she didn't dare.

Paul resolved *that*. She heard a deep, rich voice call to her, "Are you Corinne?"

Giving just the briefest thought to ignoring him, she hesitated just a moment before turning, but then she stopped and turned. Knowing intuitively *who* she was and what she was doing, Paul hurried down the hall after her. He'd almost caught up to her. He was only three feet away when she turned to face him.

Corinne hadn't been prepared for him to be quite so good looking. And big. Instinctively, immediately, her attitude toward him softened. What really influenced her was the pained look in those beautiful green eyes of his. He looked tired, terribly anxious. Sad beyond words. She recognized it as the same look she'd seen four days earlier. In Laura's eyes.

He ushered her back to his office, shooting at Candy, who was still lost in her personal telephone conversation, a dirty look—in recognition of the fact that if it weren't for his timing, Corinne would have been long gone before Candy even noticed her. And her visit was so important to him. She was the only one he knew who'd had contact with Laura, who could tell him what was going on with her. He'd heard Laura speak of her frequently and knew how close they were. And, as the boy who was feeding Spencer informed him that morning when he'd driven out to Laura's house, Corinne knew where Laura was. Yes, he was incredibly anxious to talk to Corinne.

He thanked her for coming, his expression making it clear just how much this visit meant to him. Corinne felt an involuntary outpouring of sympathy for him. Seeing him in person had radically altered her conclusions about Paul Brooks these past few days. Corinne was a good judge of character, and it was just that—character—which now jumped out at her as she sat observing him. Character plus dizzyingly good looks. She sighed. What a combination. Why is it I never find guys like this, she wondered. But at least Laura had. And that's what this is all about, she reminded herself. Laura and Paul. She felt renewed determination to do something to help the two of them work this out.

But determination and optimism were, in this case, two radically different things. In reality, knowing Laura as she did, she suspected there was little reason to be hopeful. But maybe she was wrong. The least she could do now was help Paul, even if it were only by letting him know Laura was all right. At least physically. As geniune as his concern for her was—his love for her was plainly written all over his face—he probably deserved at least that.

After they settled into chairs in his office, Paul turned to Corinne and asked, "Just how much do you know?" Paul always preferred a direct approach, and right now he didn't have it in him to be anything but blunt.

"Everything," answered Corinne truthfully.

"Where is she?" he asked intently.

Corinne looked equally determined. "I can't tell you that."

Paul could see this would not be easy, but he'd decided he was not going to let this woman leave his office without telling him where he could find Laura.

"*How* is she?"

"I haven't talked to her since Monday."

"And how was she Monday?" his voice sounded strained as he began to think he'd have to drag each and every word out of Corinne's mouth. He was growing impatient. He realized that she was only trying to protect Laura. In light of what happened, he couldn't blame her. He knew what Corinne must be feeling toward him. He remembered how hostile she sounded at first when he called her earlier that day. But he also sensed a kindness in her. And he was grateful to her for coming there. He was happy to know Laura had such a friend. But right now, what he needed were answers.

"She was broken hearted," Corinne replied huskily.

Paul flinched. He'd been haunted by the thought of how he'd hurt Laura. The woman he loved so completely, passionately. A woman so full of gentleness and grace. He felt ashamed to know what she must be going through. How betrayed she must feel.

His own voice choking with emotion, he looked into Corinne's eyes and said pleadingly, "I have to see her."

Corinne could see that Paul was suffering. She was feeling diametrically opposed emotions sitting there. One side of her was still furious with him, wanting to punish him for hurting her friend. The other could barely stand to see this man, who obviously cherished Laura, in so much pain. The latter emotions were taking over.

"Paul, I just can't tell you that. I'm sorry. But, obviously Laura feels she needs to be alone right now, and I have to respect that."

"Corinne," Paul responded in an emotional voice, "I realize just how horrible what I've done to Laura is. I would do *anything* to undo it. But I *can't* undo it. What I *can* do is go to her and apologize. Ask for her forgiveness. Try to convince her that my life does not seem worth living without her, and that I'd gladly spend the rest of it, each and every day, making up for what I've done. And then," he finished sadly, "it's up to Laura." He paused. "Please, at least give me the opportunity to do that much. For Laura's sake as much as mine."

Corinne, despite her tough exterior, her strength and independence, was an undying romantic. And Paul Brooks had struck this chord in her. She was so moved by the depth of his love for her friend and by the obvious panic he felt at the thought of losing her. It's no wonder Laura fell so deeply in love with this man, she thought, as she sat silently struggling with how to respond.

Finally, quietly, she spoke. "She's in Carmel." Paul listened intently, willing her to go on. "She's staying at a place called the Lamplighter Inn. I have the telephone number of the office, but the rooms don't have phones in them."

"All I need is an address," Paul answered.

She stayed for another ten minutes. Paul had wanted to hop right up and be on his way to the airport, but he felt such gratitude to Corinne that he didn't want to appear rude by rushing her.

Finally, Corinne stood. She told Paul she was happy to have met him. She meant it.

Before she left, she turned to him and offered these words, "I know Laura appears to be fragile. Maybe that's because she's such an open, emotional person. And I know that she's been hurt, twice now, so deeply that she *could* just withdraw into her shell. Permanently. Into her own little safe world, with Hailey and Christopher and her animals." Paul realized that this woman understood Laura exceptionally well. Perhaps even better than he did. He too had fears of what had happened causing her to withdraw and to give up on any life outside of that she'd created on her little farm in the country. That was his greatest fear—that he might have forever scarred her, and that he would be left without her.

Corinne continued, "But underneath it all, that girl has tremendous strength. And passion. I've seen it. Now, whether or not it's great enough to see you two through this, I don't know. I doubt that *she* even knows. But I suspect that it might be."

Her hand was on the door knob now, but before she twisted it open, she added, "And for what it's worth," her smile was kind, "I hope it is."

Paul smiled back and watched as she left.

Minutes later, he too hurried out of his office. Stopping at Candy's desk, he announced, "I'm leaving town. I don't know when I'll be back. Just put everything on hold until you hear from me."

Candy looked perturbed. Paul hadn't talked to anyone all week. Literally, hadn't talked—unless gruff, one-word answers could be considered talking. She knew it had something to do with Laura, who had disappeared. Now this. Who was that woman who'd just left Paul's office? She'd never seen her before. But apparently she'd managed to snap Paul out of the funk he'd been in. None of it sat well with Candy, who still wished she could have Paul Brooks to herself.

"Where are you going?" she called out, as his head disappeared down the stairwell.

"To find Laura," his disembodied voice responded. Seconds later she heard the heavy front door one floor below slam shut.

"Shit!" Candy threw her appointment book down, hard, on the desk. Then, picking it back up, with all her strength, she gunned it through Paul's doorway, as if he were standing there. Yep, she threw that thing right at him.

Right at Paul Brooks where he was most vulnerable.

Right at his heart.

*   *   *

They hadn't stayed at the Lamplighter on their honeymoon, but each day that she and Michael walked to Carmel Beach, they passed it. And each time, Laura had exclaimed in delight at the cluster of little cottages that looked like something straight out of a story book. Their last day in Carmel, she stopped and picked up a brochure, which she'd carried in her briefcase ever since, transferring it over the years from one worn-out attache to the next. So finally finding herself there after all these years didn't really surprise her—she'd always known that one day she'd return to Carmel and stay at the Lamplighter. It was the circumstances under which she found herself there that she could never have expected. And the fact that she'd be there without Michael.

When they arrived on Tuesday, the only thing available was the Early Bird Room. It was small but delightful. Glass louvered windows, and cafe curtains with a Dutch door led to the overflowing flower garden. She would have been content to stay there, even though there was just the one bed that she and Hailey shared, with a couch for Christopher. But once Hailey laid eyes on the Hansel and Gretel Cottage, Laura could tell her little girl would be satisfied with little else. And the next day, when the owner informed her that the larger cottage was available, Laura booked it for two weeks.

The Hansel and Gretel Cottage was as comfortable

as it was charming. With an old English cobblestone walk leading to its front door, its high-pitched, flagstone shingled roof, brightly colored doors and trim, and flower boxes spilling over with blossoms, it looked like a cottage that should be nestled deep in the woods. One inhabited by elves. Or a princess. Laura didn't blame Hailey for her enthusiasm. She'd reacted much the same when she'd first seen it years ago. With Michael.

She hadn't been sure whether it was wise to return to a place so full of memories of Michael, whether it would soothe or enhance the pain she was feeling. But after one or two days in which she was little more than a robot going through the motions, trying to convince the children that they were there to vacation, to have fun, trying to minimize the worry she saw in their eyes every time they caught her gazing off; after two days of *living hell*, she'd actually found herself feeling a little better. Just *feeling*—that alone was significant. She actually believed that she might be beginning to heal. Not that she'd ever get over what had happened, but the panic that had engulfed her those first days, when she wondered whether she had it in her to go on, was lessening. She was beginning to believe that she could, at least, go on. She hadn't gotten beyond that yet, but that in itself was a relief. And that's how she knew that she'd made the right decision in coming to Carmel.

It was a good place to heal. A great place for the kids. They were three short blocks from the ocean and beach. Every morning, after going out to breakfast and browsing through the countless shops that line Carmel's charming streets, they'd head down to the beach. It was already spring break for Carmel schools, so the beach was full of kids. It hadn't taken long for both Hailey and Christopher to make friends. While Hailey and her little friend built sandcastles and examined the interesting seaweeds that washed up, especially the ones with huge seeds that popped loudly when stepped on, Christopher learned a new sport, one that he quickly excelled at, and one that actually brought him in contact with girls. Beach volleyball. As with basketball, his athletic skills soon made him a standout. And a welcome addition to the group of locals.

While the kids played, Laura either sat back and watched, letting the sun's warmth and the rhythmic crashing of the waves soothe her, or she walked barefoot just along the waterline. Later, when they'd tired of playing and she had Christopher and Hailey situated back at the motel, she'd return and walk for miles. Sometimes just back and forth along the beach, but oftentimes winding her way beyond the beach, and up along the streets lined with million-dollar homes. She found the walks therapeutic. The fresh air, beauty, peace, friendly faces along the way—it all reminded her that life goes on. She'd had a life before she met Paul Brooks. A good life. Maybe it had been lonely, but still, she was blessed to have as much as she did. And she would have a life again. A life after Paul Brooks. She told herself that over and over. She didn't yet believe it, and she wasn't sure she ever would, but it became a recurrent theme in her thoughts and in the pep talks she gave herself whenever she saw a couple strolling along the beach hand in hand.

If nothing else, the trip had done one very important thing for her. By distancing her from Paul, by giving her that perspective that often comes with getting away, she realized how important it was to keep trying. Not to give up. For her sake, as well as the kids. She would not retreat back into her world of isolation. She couldn't afford to do that. To do so now might mean she'd spend the rest of her days hiding out there with her kids, her beloved dogs and her horse. The temptation to do so was enormous, but she knew that she had to fight it. She had to go on with her life, even if it seemed hollow. She had to go through the motions, and maybe, just maybe, some day it would feel a little less empty to her.

She knew she would never love again. She would never *let* herself love again. No, that was out of the question. But neither would she let herself drop out again. Like she'd done after Michael's death. No, this time it would be different.

The first thing she was going to do upon returning to Seattle was contact Emery, Johnson. They'd always made it clear that her position with them was there for the asking. Well, she was ready to ask. Yes, she would concentrate on her career now. The kids and her career. She would throw herself into her work. Maybe she'd get serious about riding again, too. Maybe it was time to get that second horse, so that Chris or Hailey could ride with her.

So, as the days went by and Laura felt the numbness receding, she resolved to fight. Maybe because she knew that the moment she stopped fighting, she'd be lost. Maybe because she knew the only chance she stood was to keep going, to stay busy. Because the moment she stopped, the moment she allowed her mind to wander, she saw him. Paul. Talking to Matt and Amy at the cast party. Propped up next to her in her bed. Playing basketball in her driveway with Christopher. Staring lovingly across his desk at her.

And the moment that happened, the very moment

that his image appeared, her chest felt a pain so sharp and so wrenching, her eyes became so blinded by the tears over which she had absolutely no control, that she was totally incapacitated. Reduced to a state of helplessness and despair that threatened to just swallow her up.

But she wouldn't *let* that happen. She would not do that to Christopher and Hailey. She would not subject them to that. Again. Ever.

And with that in mind, she walked. On and on. Sometimes with fists clenched. Sometimes totally oblivious to people, cars that passed by her. Intent. Determined. Planning a future for her and her kids. A future that did not include Paul Brooks.

*   *   *

It was a cool, overcast day, a not unpleasant change from the idyllic weather they'd had since arriving. They started the morning off like every other—walking down to breakfast at Kara's Kitchen, then roaming the streets of shops, drifting into each one that caught their eye.

The day before, Christopher had found a sports shop in the plaza and, after waiting patiently for Laura and Hailey to thoroughly peruse I. Magnin, he'd succeeded in getting them to accompany him to "look" at the basketball jerseys and T-shirts that the store had stocked for March madness—the NCAA year-end tournament that had recently ended. Laura knew that when Christopher asked her to "look" at anything, what he really had in mind was her buying it. Not wanting to put pressure on her or make her feel guilty for refusing, he resisted asking for it outright. This had been especially true since Michael's death. Even though she'd never given them any indication that finances were a concern, both children—but especially Christopher—had become more practical, less apt to ask for needless expenditures. Still, she could tell how much he wanted the T-shirt with the North Carolina logo emblazoned across it in bold letters. It gave her as much pleasure as it did him to give him the go-ahead sign. She chuckled as her skinny 13 year old, who was fast approaching eye level with her, chose a man's size large in both the T-shirt and shorts. She'd grown used to seeing him swim in his loose-fitting athletic garb, his skinny legs extending down from his baggy shorts and monstrous black Nike Air's encasing his unusually large feet—shoes that indicated he had a lot of growing to do. The look was always finished off with a baseball cap, which rarely had the name of a baseball team on it. Today he wore a black Seattle SuperSonics cap. Backwards. And, as they headed back to their cottage, a big smile.

Due to the weather, the kids weren't much in the mood to go to the beach that day. A day in their cottage, with Hailey's coloring books and Barbies, and Christopher's Gameboy, sounded good to them, so Laura headed off alone for her daily walk.

She'd only been gone half an hour when they heard a knock at the door. Christopher was the first to reach it, with Hailey just steps behind. When he opened it, there stood Paul. Christopher let out a whoop of delight. Once Hailey saw what it was all about, she threw her arms around Paul, who hugged them both happily, but as he did so, scanned the room, expecting to see Laura.

"Hey, Guy," Paul responded, still looking around uneasily for Laura, but terribly pleased to see them, pleased to see their reaction to his unexpected visit. He ruffled Hailey's hair affectionately, then turned to

369

Christopher. "Great shirt," he said acknowledging the North Carolina T-shirt Chris had already changed into. "Where'd you find that?"

Excitedly, Christopher answered, "At the little mall in town. It's just a couple of blocks from here. There's a cool sports shop. Want to go there with me?"

Paul had to laugh at Christopher's unbridled enthusiasm. "Maybe later we can. Right now, I'd like to talk to your mother. Where is she?" By now he'd concluded Laura was not in the tiny cottage.

"She's down on the beach," Hailey answered cheerfully. "Want me to show you?"

"Thanks, Peanut," Paul smiled at her. "But I think I should see her alone first." Then, seeing a cloud pass over the little girl's face at his answer, he added, "You understand, don't you?"

"Yep," Hailey said. Suddenly both kids looked markedly less excited than they had just minutes earlier when he'd arrived.

"Okay, you two," Paul could not ignore the change in their demeanor. "What is it?"

Hailey and Christopher looked at each other. They were remarkably close, especially in light of the seven year age difference. They'd always been that way, but their father's death had brought them even closer. When Paul's gaze came to rest on Hailey, she looked at Christopher, counting on him to handle whatever it was that seemed to be on both of their minds.

Christopher, looking quite somber, was clearly uncomfortable being the spokesman, but his need for reassurance—and more importantly *Hailey's* need for it—outweighed the natural reluctance of a 13 year old to delve into adult matters. "Paul..." Christopher began, but his voice just sort of drifted off and his struggle to find the right words became painfully obvious to Paul.

As anxious as he was to find Laura, and as much anguish as there already was in Paul's heart, the sight of these two children, whom he held so dear, looking so troubled, nearly destroyed him. He took each child by the hand and led them to the couch. He seated himself there next to Christopher, then pulled Hailey onto his lap.

"Okay, let's talk," he said gently. "What is it that's bothering you two?" He didn't know what Laura had told them, but he felt certain it was the situation between them that had suddenly drained the joy from their faces.

Christopher took a deep breath, then, looking anywhere but into Paul's face, asked in what could be mistaken as a casual tone had Paul not known better, "Are you and Mom breaking up?"

"Is that what she told you?" Paul searched both children's faces for an answer.

"She just said that she doesn't want to talk about you anymore," answered Hailey truthfully. Christopher poked his little sister angrily.

"Shut up, Hay," he said.

"Well, she did!" answered Hailey, hitting him back.

Paul grabbed both of their arms gently, but firmly. He suspected that their fight was more an expression of fear at what was going on between Laura and him than anything else. Holding onto them tightly—actually feeling that he never wanted to let them go—he spoke to them softly.

"I love your mother more than you'll ever know," he said, emotion welling up inside him. "And I will do anything to stay with her. With you." Their eyes looked at him hopefully. "But that—whether or not we stay together—is something we have to work out." He thought about what he was saying, trying to decide what to tell them—hoping that he'd be seeing them again and again, but fearful that this could be one of their last times together.

"But whatever happens, I want you to promise me something. Promise that you'll be especially good to your mother, that you'll give her lots of love and support." They both nodded their heads in silent agreement, eyes big and somber. "And promise to remember that no matter what happens," he could feel himself choking up, but he had to say it, "no matter what happens, I love you all. All three of you. And I always will. Will you remember that?" His hands tightened even further on their arms. He couldn't stand to see the sadness in their eyes. It was in such stark contrast to the joy he'd seen in them just minutes ago. They both nodded again. A terrible sadness settled over all of them.

Paul finally stood and walked to the door. They each gave him a big hug—both holding onto him a little longer than usual.

As he stepped outside, he turned to them and smiled. "Wish me luck!"

Hailey and Christopher stood in the doorway, hand in hand, and in unison cried out, "Good luck!"

It was the last he saw of them.

* * *

The beach was empty, save for an older man strolling along the water line, seemingly impervious to the increasing intensity of the rain, with two well-heeled Golden Retrievers at his side.

Paul had driven the three blocks from the Lamplighter Inn to the water, and now sat in his rented Pathfinder, scanning the beach and beyond for sight of Laura. He'd debated about whether he should walk or drive in the direction the kids had pointed him. Since the weather had worsened in the few minutes he'd spent in the cabin with Christopher and Hailey, he quickly decided to take the car, instinctively wanting to offer its shelter to Laura. But she was nowhere in sight now, and he was beginning to wonder if she might not have abandoned her walk on the beach for the more welcoming atmosphere of some of the local shops. Just as he was about to head back toward town, he saw her.

She was coming around the furthest point of the sandy beach, heading in the direction of his car, which sat in a parking lot at the entrance to the public area. She walked steadily, eyes cast downward as if looking to see what the waves had washed up, arms wrapped around herself as if she were cold. Her lovely hair was rainsoaked—her hood, which would have offered protection, hung down her back from the oversized black sweatshirt she wore. Her gait looked athletic and strong, but her posture, the way she hugged herself, and her slender, bare legs made her appear frail and vulnerable at the same time. Paul's heart ached at the sight of her.

When she was within ten yards of his car, he stepped out. The sound of his car door slamming shut brought her eyes up. At first, expecting to see a stranger, her look was disinterested, almost vacant. But within just a few of Paul's very rapid heartbeats, her eyes met his in recognition.

She looked at though she'd seen a ghost. She stopped dead in her tracks, eyes wide, mouth half-opened in a look of...of what, Paul wondered. Fear? Pain? Intuitively he knew it was both.

As nervous as he was to be face to face with her for the first time since they'd learned that Mackenzie Montana was carrying his child, his overriding emotion was utter joy at seeing her. The fear, *panic* really, of the past week, his intense need for her—for her touch, her soothing voice, for the simple sight of her—suddenly overwhelmed him. He rushed forward to her, ready to grab her, to pull her into his arms and envelope her. But when he neared her, neither of them still having spoken, she stepped back. It was a spontaneous movement on her part, one without thought, not meant to be cruel or hostile, but nonetheless, which stopped him in midstride.

She was the first to speak.

"Paul?" was all she said. She said it like it was a question. Her voice sounded childlike.

Still wanting to hold her, Paul restrained himself and stood facing her. He settled for reaching out and placing his hands on her shoulders. She didn't resist his touch, but neither did she seem affected by it, as was he by the familiar feel of her small-boned frame. Her eyes looked into his. They were as direct and open as he'd come to expect them to be. Somehow that reassured him.

"I've been worried sick about you," he said hoarsely. "I didn't know what to think. Where you'd gone..." his voice trailed off. More words weren't necessary, as his eyes reflected the extent of the fear he'd experienced the past few days.

Seeing the pain in them, Laura had to look away. It was her only hope of maintaining her composure. She was so shaken by his sudden appearance, so overcome merely by his physical presence. She could not afford to feel *sympathy* for him. Yet her every instinct made her want to comfort him, to take away the hurt she saw in him, to pretend none of it had happened and that nothing had changed between them.

But it *had* happened. And nothing would ever be the same.

"I didn't mean to worry you," she finally responded. "How did you find me?"

"Corinne told me you'd come here. She didn't want to tell me. I more or less forced her to. Then, once I got here, the kids told me where I could find you."

She turned back to him at his mention of Christopher and Hailey. "You've seen the kids?" She asked weakly.

He nodded.

"What did you tell them?"

"I told them that I love them, and that I love you more than anything in the world. And I told them that we had some things to work out." His hand dropped from her shoulder and reached for her hand. "Did I say the right things?"

She pulled her hand out of reach and turned away from him. "There *is* no one right thing to say," she answered, her voice shaking. "I just don't want them to be hurt. Not anymore than they've already been."

"Laura, look at me," Paul commanded.

When she turned to face him again, he cupped her chin in his hand and spoke.

"I don't want to hurt the kids. You know that. I'd do anything to avoid hurting them. I love them more than I could ever have dreamed possible." He saw a rush of emotion in her eyes at his words. She tried to pull back, to escape his touch. The intimacy of his words and eyes were too much for her. But he would not loosen his hold on her. He was going to force her to face him, to look into his eyes while he said what he had to say.

"And I love *you*, Laura Kennedy," he said with heart-wrenching emotion. "I love you more than you will ever know. More than life itself." His face was streaked with rain. Tears welled up in his eyes. "And I will not lose you. I cannot. Whatever it takes, I will get us though this. I will make it all up to you." He paused, searching her face for reassurance. "You *have* to let me do that. For the kids' sake as well as ours. You have to let me make it up."

Finally, tears now blending with the rain on his cheeks and chin, he dropped his hand from her chin, as if giving her permission to retreat.

But this time she did not turn away. She stood facing him, her own tear-streaked face turned up to his, and spoke softly.

"It's too late, Paul. It's too late. The damage has already been done. And it's not something that can be undone." Now it was her turn to reach out for him. She grasped his wet arm, like a child trying to get his parents' full attention, and went on. "There's a child involved. A baby. *Your* baby. And that is not going to go away. That's not something that *can* be undone."

Paul stood, frozen, listening to her. Knowing what she was going to say, knowing that she was right. Wishing he could undo it all.

"We'll deal with that," he said. "Together. We can do it Laura, I know we can."

"I can't. I won't." She answered tearfully.

"I cannot deal with it, Paul. With her having your baby." Her words came out between soft sobs. "I cannot stand the thought of it," she whispered, "much

376

less the sight of a baby of yours and that woman's."

"Then you won't have to," Paul offered quickly. "I won't ask you to do anything you don't want to. If that's how you feel, Laura, then the baby won't be a part of our life together."

"But it *will* be a part of your life." He did not challenge her statement. "And you can't live two lives, Paul. I won't let you. I wouldn't do that to you. And I wouldn't do that to your baby."

Paul's face was clouded with grief. "What are you saying? he asked her.

"I'm saying that you should be there. For your baby. When it's born. When it's growing up. Every day. And I know that you will have to be—that you couldn't have it any other way." She took a deep breath and wondered if she could make it through the next few minutes.

"And I'm saying that I can't be a part of that. I don't *want* to be a part of that." Not unkindly, but with characteristic directness, she finally said the word's he knew would come. "I'm saying that it's over, Paul. It's over."

He felt like a two-ton weight had suddenly been anchored to his heart. He turned numbly to head back to his car. Before he climbed into it, he stopped and turned back to her.

She'd sunk down to the ground and was seated, head buried in her hands, on a big rock.

"Will you be okay?" he asked.

She lifted her face from her hands and turned to look at him one last time. I shouldn't have done that, she realized immediately. I shouldn't have let myself see him leave.

Her own heart literally breaking into pieces as she sat there, she summoned one last smile for him. "I'll be fine," she said gently. "I'll be fine."

19

Matthew stood in the doorway to his friend's office. He'd run into Paul in the hallway just a few minutes ago, but now he was nowhere to be seen. A pair of Gucci loafers on the floor and pile of clothing on the couch gave him a clue as to where his troubled friend had gone.

He walked back out of the room to Candy's desk and asked, "Is he out running again?"

She nodded, with an exasperated and somewhat concerned look on her face. Paul was worrying all of them these days.

"You'd think he was training to run a marathon," was all she said before resuming her wordprocessing.

Matthew quickly changed, left the building and headed across Elliott. If Paul had taken his ordinary route, he would have started off north along the waterfront, would turn around at the Magnolia Bridge and head back this way. He should be able to catch him there. If he hadn't already gone by.

He settled down on the grass in the shade of a tree and enjoyed the early June morning. It was unusually warm for June in Seattle, which meant girl

watching was at its best. He was so distracted by a
couple of thirtyish woman speedwalking by in their
lycra bike shorts that he almost missed the sight of
Paul streaking past them. He had to sprint to catch up
with him.

Paul barely turned his head upon hearing the
footsteps join his.

"What's up?" was all he said. His face was as
expressionless as it had been for the past six weeks. It
gave Matthew the chills to see.

"I thought I was your running buddy," he started.
"How come you didn't tell me you were going running when we saw each other a while ago?"

Paul looked over. His expression altered somewhat. He realized he'd been neglecting their friendship
and did not want to hurt Matthew's feelings. But he
hadn't wanted company. These days he rarely did.

"Sorry, Matt," he said genuinely, "I'm not real
good company right now."

"Good enough for me," his friend answered.

Paul smiled slightly and wiped the sweat off his
brow. It actually was nice to have Matt running
alongside him again. Maybe he'd been wrong to shut
him out since he and Laura split. He knew he'd been
wallowing in his misery, which was something he'd
always detested in others. But he couldn't help himself. Or maybe he just *wanted* to feel miserable.

They ran in silence to the piers. Summer tourists
were already much in evidence. It soon became necessary for them to dodge bodies on the sidewalk. As
they approached the aquarium, which already sported
a line, they turned to each other simultaneously and
said, "Let's get out of here."

They crossed the busy street, and had hesitated
just a minute, debating about which direction to head,

when they noticed the trolley approaching. "What do you think?" asked Matthew, nodding to the big red car that ran back and forth, parallel to the waterway.

Paul flashed him the first real smile Matt had seen in some time and said, "Let's do it."

Matthew reached into the hidden pocket of his Nike running shorts and dropped a handful of coins in the box as they climbed on board. Several blocks later, just north of the Kingdome, they disembarked and soon found themselves running freely in the industrial area sandwiched between downtown Seattle and West Seattle. The views now were considerably less aesthetic, but the running was better. And conversation was again possible.

After a few minutes of silence Matthew could sense that Paul was loosening up.

"So, do you feel like talking about it?" he asked. "Have you talked to her? Or seen her?"

"Talked to her? No," Paul responded. "I've seen her. Twice now. But not in the way you mean."

At Matthew's quizzical look, Paul explained. "She goes for a walk every day. With her dogs. I found this spot on a hill that overlooks the railroad tracks where she takes them. Once in a while I see her there."

Matthew looked dumbstruck. "You mean you just go there and wait? Just *in case* she shows up? And if she does, you don't even talk to her?"

Paul nodded. "I just need to see her. To know she's okay."

Matthew was wordless for a minute, letting the significance of what he heard settle in.

"And what about Mackenzie Montana?" he asked after a while. "When's the baby due?"

"Any day now," answered Paul.

"And when it's born?" Matthew pressed.

"I'm going to be there, if I can. Actually, I'm heading down there day after tomorrow so I can be close by when Mackenzie goes into labor."

"And what about you and Mackenzie?"

"There *is* no 'me and Mackenzie'," Paul stated gruffly. "There never has been. And there never will be."

"Does *she* know that?"

"She's starting to get it," Paul answered. "I think she still harbors some delusions that once I see the baby I'll change my mind, and the three of us will live happily ever after. But that's not going to happen. I'm going to be a father to the baby. A good father. But I will never be any more than that to her. Never more than the father of her child. The sooner she realizes that, the better."

"And Laura?" Matthew asked tentatively, fearful he was pushing his friend's limits with this inquiry, but needing to know the answer.

Paul stopped running, as if it were impossible to think about Laura, impossible to talk about her, and coordinate his strong, graceful strides at the same time. His big frame dripped with sweat, and his shoulders, usually so erect, momentarily slumped.

He looked off in the distance, not able to make eye contact. "I'll never give up on Laura," he said softly. "But right now, I know that I have to leave her alone. I can't put her through any more. I've hurt her enough already, and I'm not going to take the chance of hurting her even more."

Matthew reached over and rested his arm on his friend's shoulder. "Maybe things will work out, Paul."

Paul turned his head and looked at Matt. He was such a good friend. So loyal and so genuinely concerned about Paul's happiness. He wanted to say something to him to express his appreciation, to let him know what their friendship meant to him.

Matthew, who was feeling similar emotions and could practically read his buddy's mind, smiled fleetingly before dropping his hand from Paul's shoulder and dropping into a racing position. "Beat you back to the tracks," he challenged.

Paul laughed, then dropped his large frame into a similar posture.

"You're on, Asshole!"

And the next second, the two friends—side by side, as they'd been for a quarter of a century now—went racing down the street.

*   *   *

"Shit!" she yelled, already in motion.

Corinne jumped out of bed so suddenly that Mark didn't know what to think. They'd been lying there, reading the morning paper after a short session of lovemaking. Until now, it had been one of their typical Saturday mornings. He always told his wife he had to go into the office, but instead, he'd head over to Corinne's condo. They'd make love. Then he'd fetch the newspaper from the front stoop and climb back under the covers with her.

As he watched her reach for the phone, newspaper still in hand, he asked, "What's going on?"

Corinne didn't answer, but within seconds he heard her greet someone, "Christopher? Hi, it's me, Corinne. Where's your mom?"

She was silent for just a moment, then said, "No, no don't get her. Not yet anyway. Listen, Chris, I want you to do something for me. It's important.

Have you guys gotten the paper yet today?"

"No? Good." She look relieved. "Now listen. When you do, I want you to take Section E out of it. That's the 'Living' section. Throw it out. Get rid of it. Don't let your mom see it. Do you understand?"

"Yes, it does have something to do with Paul." She continued, "It's something that would upset her. And I just don't want to take the chance of upsetting her." She was silent as she listened to Christopher's response.

"I know, Honey. I know you don't want anything to upset her either. You're a good kid. The best. You know that, don't you?"

She laughed at Christopher's response. What a kid, she thought. Wise beyond his years. Thank God she got him before they'd gotten the paper. "Listen, I think I'll head out there for a little visit. How does that sound?"

"Thanks. I can't wait to see you, too. Tell your mom I'm on my way. Oh, and Chris. I don't want *you* to read that section either. Okay?"

After hanging up, she turned back to Mark, an apologetic look on her face.

"Laura?" he asked.

Corinne nodded. "Take a look at this," she said, handing him the section she'd been reading peacefully just a few minutes earlier.

It was at the bottom of the page, in the "Seen and Heard" column, the one full of celebrity gossip and innuendo.

The first item was a short paragraph on Fergie, the Duchess of York. Seems Fergie was photographed poolside, topless, with her "financial adviser." The palace thus far had not commented.

It was the next two paragraphs that had sent

Corinne flying out of bed.

> Unwedded bliss. Mackenzie Montana and an
> as-yet unidentified head of an up-and-coming
> production company became parents yesterday
> afternoon in Beverly Hills. Our sources tell us
> the baby, an adorable eight-pound boy, looks
> a lot like daddy. According to these sources,
> Ms. Montana has been hinting that the sound
> of wedding bells may soon be making beauti-
> ful music with the sound of the baby's coos.
> Stay tuned...

The next paragraph read:

> On a completely different topic (or is it?),
> *After the Dance*, the Brooks Productions movie
> released just two weeks ago to rave reviews,
> continues to be moviegoer's first choice this
> week. Paul Brooks (head of his own up-and-
> coming production company) continues to de-
> cline interviews. Strange publicity stance for a
> studio head to take. Do you suppose there's
> something Mr. Brooks doesn't want to talk
> about? We'll keep on this one for you. Stay
> tuned...

Corinne waited for Mark to look up after finishing
the last paragraph.

"Can you believe it?" she asked angrily. "Those
assholes. Do you know what this will do to Laura if
she sees it?"

"Corinne," answered Mark using his voice of
wisdom (as Corinne called it), "you know you can't
shield Laura from this, don't you? Even if you keep
this article from her, do you really believe she won't

read about this somewhere else?"

Corinne grew stiff. She hated that tone of his. And she hated what he was saying. Especially because she knew he was probably right. But that wasn't going to stop her from doing everything in her power to protect her friend. Mark wouldn't understand. He was too damned pragmatic. Too fucking practical to understand. At times like these, she was glad he was just her lover and not her husband.

She was still buttoning her blouse as she left the bedroom. She could hear him calling her, heard him cursing her "foolishness" as she hurried out the front door.

As she shifted her little car into reverse and backed out of the garage, she thought she saw movement in the bedroom window. She was pretty sure Mark was standing there, trying to get her attention, but she made a point of not looking. Because, at that moment, she really didn't care much about Mark and what he thought. In fact, she really didn't care at all.

But she did care about Laura. And the kids. And, foolish or not, she would see to it that they were shielded from this kind of talk. She had a couple things going for her. It was summer, so the kids were out of school. That meant they were less exposed to other kids and their talk. And Laura had started back at Emery, Johnson. Corinne could make sure she wasn't exposed to any of this there. No one at Emery, Johnson would dare make mention of it—not if it meant risking incurring Corinne's wrath. Of that she was sure.

Mark stood at the window and watched the white BMW disappear down the hill with his headstrong mistress behind the wheel.

She was a maddening woman. Feisty, firey. Pas-

385

sionate. A perfect lover. And, apparently, a damned good friend. More and more he was coming to appreciate her. To wonder what life would be like if they were married.

Naw. Can't be, he told himself. Never. He was already married. To a good woman. A little dull, a little fat, always on his case, but still, they'd been together forever, and to change that was more of an undertaking than he was prepared to take on.

Besides, he finally told himself, before reluctantly climbing back into his clothes, he and Corinne had too much fun together. And marriage wasn't supposed to be fun.

Or was it?

*   *   *

Mackenzie Montana grabbed the button that hung over the side of the bed and pushed it frantically.

Within seconds a smiling face appeared in the doorway. "Yes, Ms. Montana? What can we do for you?"

Over the soft cries emitting from the little bundle laying next to her on the bed, Mackenzie demanded loudly, "Get him out of here."

The attractive red-headed nurse reached for the baby. As soon as he was in her arms his crying stopped. She stood for a moment, gently rocking him, admiring this perfect little being she held. His little eyes closed peacefully.

Before turning to leave, she looked at Mackenzie. "Sure you don't want to keep him a while? I think he's ready to sleep now."

Mackenzie glared at her. "I need to take a shower. My fiance is coming soon." Before the young woman was out of the door, she added, "and bring him back before Paul gets here."

The nurse nodded, and tightened her hold on the baby protectively. This one's really bad news, she thought as she closed the door behind her.

Using the button next to the one she'd just pressed to call the nurse, Mackenzie raised the top half of the bed until she was in a sitting position, then reached for the antique silver mirror on the side table. She held it just six inches from her face and carefully scrutinized what she saw. No make up on yet, but the porcelain skin and luminous green eyes did not need it. Her bushy mane of hair looked equally striking without help.

Satisfied that she still looked gorgeous, she dropped the mirror onto the bed next to her and lifted the cover that hid the rest of her from sight. This would hurt a little more. A *lot* more. Even Mackenzie Montana could not escape the havoc that pregnancy and childbirth wreaked on a woman's body.

Her already large breasts were swollen to their absolute limit. They felt rock hard to the touch. Blue veins, in an ugly patchwork effect, stood out everywhere. They hurt. Especially her nipples. That baby was destroying them, she thought angrily. Just look. They were red and cracked from their numerous, unsuccessful, attempts at breast-feeding. And if she didn't find a way to get rid of all that milk accumulating in them, her breasts felt like they would literally explode.

Looking at them, she made a decision. That was it. Enough of this breast-feeding crap. For four days now she'd been listening to everyone tell her how it just takes time. Some babies are slower than others to grasp it. Well, her baby just ran out of time. No milk from mama's breasts for that one.

But what about Paul? He'd indicated several times now that he was pleased she was planning to breast feed. What would she do about Paul? She thought for a moment, then a smile broke out on her angelic face. She would tell Paul that the doctor had ordered it! That he was concerned about the baby's weight loss. Paul had already shown great concern over the fact that the baby had lost a pound since his birth. He didn't realize that was to be expected. Yes, she thought, pleased with herself, as long as it's couched in terms of the baby's well-being, Paul would not be a problem. Her milk would dry up in no time and before she knew it, she'd have her old, beautiful breasts back again.

The rest of her body might not be so easy to restore. Her stomach looked flat enough as she lay there on her back. But she could pick up the skin on her belly and lift it several inches, like she used to do when she was a little girl with the inches of extra skin on the neck of her friend's pug puppy. And, if she rolled onto her side, she could feel her skin slide down, off her stomach and onto the bed. But she wouldn't look. Couldn't bear to look. Her hips felt wide. Even her thighs, her pride and joy thighs, had suffered. She lifted each leg. At least the rest of her legs were as beautiful as ever.

She made a mental note to call Carlos at Barneys of New York and have him send her over half a dozen outfits in a size 8. She grimaced at the thought. Size 8!! God, if she'd known ahead of time what all this pregnancy would entail, she might have thought twice about it. But at least things seemed to be going well with Paul. True, he wasn't exactly *warm* with her. But he absolutely melted every time he saw their

baby. That's how she knew her plan would work.
And she'd be back in a size 6 in no time.

* * *

When Paul arrived an hour later, the first thing he
did was head over to the huge viewing window at the
nursery to see if Peter was there. He was pleased
when he saw that, for a change, he was not. Usually
he was the only baby in the nursery, as Mackenzie
was the only mother on the floor who chose not to
have her baby room in. He'd held his tongue so far,
trying to avoid getting into it with Mackenzie, but
every time he walked in and saw his little son lying
there looking so alone, he felt sick. Give her time,
he'd told himself. She wasn't exactly the nurturing
type. But she was coming along. At least she'd decided to breast feed. Frankly, that had shocked the
hell out of him. It was a good sign.

As he headed past the nurses' station for Mackenzie's
room, the nurses did their customary twittering and
eyelash batting in his direction.

"Morning, Mr. Brooks," said the friendly redhead
who'd taken such an interest in Peter. He smiled back
at her. He liked her and greatly appreciated the extra
attention she gave his son. "Your fiance is waiting for
you," she continued.

He almost stopped in his tracks at that last re-
mark. "Fiance." But discretion permitted him only a
slight frown as he continued on down the hall.

When he opened the door to Mackenzie's room,
his anger was abated immediately by the sight of her
propped up in bed with a little bundle in her arms.
His little bundle. His son.

Mackenzie beamed up at Paul, the picture of

maternal bliss. "Here comes Daddy," she cooed into the little blanket. She extended her arms—a little too quickly, Paul noted—to offer him his son.

Paul happily accepted the offering and gently pulled the blanketed infant up against his chest.

Something happened to Paul Brooks every time he looked at his newborn son. Every time he held him. Every time he *thought* of him. Something wonderful, and mystical, and moving. Something very, very profound. There were no words to describe it. Words weren't necessary.

Mackenzie Montana could see it. It hurt her, because *she* did not feel it. It, in fact, made her feel abnormal. Left out. But it also gave her great hope. She knew that her role as mother to Paul Brooks' son gave her tremendous power. Sitting there, watching Paul watch their son, she knew that the infant was the key to getting what she wanted. And what she wanted, more than she'd ever wanted anything else, was Paul Brooks. He was the most incredible man she'd ever known. Physically, without doubt, the most attractive, with his size and strong, masculine features. They would be the perfect Hollywood couple. A publicist's dream. Mackenzie Montana and Paul Brooks—Mackenzie Montana-Brooks, she mentally corrected herself. And in addition to his looks, there was his stature in the entertainment world. Before *After the Dance*, Brooks Productions had already established a widely respected image in the industry. But *After the Dance* would make them the studio of the '90s. She may have lost her role as Ashley Cowles, but what really mattered was that, in the long run, she will have gained the opportunity to star in the many films Brooks Productions would be generating in the years to come. Films and roles that would gain her the respect she deserved. It was *perfect*. Too perfect.

"How's the nursing going?" Paul asked her, pulling her abruptly from her daydream.

Her smile turned to a look of great sadness, of great disappointment. "Not well, Paul," she sighed. Here goes, she thought. "I'm afraid I've got bad news. Dr. Abrams thinks little Peter—" She always paused when she used the name, like she had to think hard to remember it. She only used it when Paul was there. He'd chosen the name "—little Peter is not doing well. He's lost more weight. Dr. Abrams thinks it's time for me to give up on nursing him and put the sweet little guy on a bottle. For *his* sake." She tried to work up a little tear, but couldn't. Still, she could see that it had worked. Paul looked concerned.

"The doctor thinks he'd be better off on a bottle?" he asked.

She nodded, as if she didn't dare speak for fear of bursting into tears at the thought of the great sacrifice she was being asked to make.

"Then let's get him on a bottle," he said without hesitation. "Immediately."

Mackenzie nodded obediently. Paul was one man she didn't mind taking orders from. At least for now.

As he always did, Paul stayed for a couple of hours. The baby slept peacefully in his arms the whole time—Mackenzie had given him a bottle just before Paul's visit to ensure he'd be on his best behavior. It was the first good meal the little guy had had. Resting in his father's strong arms, with a full tummy, he was completely content. Occasionally his little blue eyes would open. Whenever they did, Paul spoke to him softly.

"Hello, little man," he said in a whisper. "How's my guy?"

Peter's little fingers grasped onto Paul's thumb and held tight. Then the little eyes closed again. Paul smiled down at the tiny person in his arms, as his eyes filled with tears.

The whole scene was enough to disgust Mackenzie, who had yet to feel any real bond with her baby. But she smiled sweetly and said all the right things. She was good at that. Sometimes Paul even thought it might be sincere.

They didn't speak much. It had already become a pattern. He'd arrive, take over the baby and sit there in silence. She'd try small talk, but Paul wasn't interested. The only thing he wanted to talk about was Peter.

But today, that would work just fine. Today she *wanted* to talk about Peter. It was the perfect way to get things moving in the right direction.

"Paul," she finally said, "Dr. Abrams also told me that Peter and I can go home tomorrow. Isn't that wonderful?"

"Yes. It is," Paul said, but his real thoughts were anything but happy. At the hospital, he knew Peter was being looked after, cared for. What would happen once Mackenzie took him home? He'd been worried about this for days now. So worried that he'd already made plans for a nurse to move in with Mackenzie. But he hadn't told Mackenzie that yet. Before he had a chance to, she was speaking again.

"I've asked Maria to make up the guest room for you," she was saying. "It's a wonderful room. Right next to the nursery, so you'll be close to the baby." She was studying his reaction carefully. "And it adjoins my room. Once I'm feeling better, you can just move in with me," she added nonchalantly.

Paul looked as though a Peterbilt truck had just

run over his foot.

"You WHAT?" he asked, trying to keep his anger in check, not wanting his voice to awaken the baby. "You told Maria WHAT?"

"I told her to get the guest room ready for you," she answered him. "Why would that surprise you?"

"Just what made you think I'd be moving in with you?" he demanded. "What were you thinking?" He looked incredulous.

"I was thinking that you'd want to be with the baby. With Peter. Are you saying you don't want to be with us?" she asked. She thought throwing the "us" in was a good ploy. Time for him to start thinking of her and the baby as a package. A package deal. "Is that what you're saying?"

Paul knew he was being baited. Knew she was setting the trap. He'd been waiting for it.

He stood, Peter still sleeping contentedly in his arms, and walked to the door. He signaled the red-head. Then when she responded, he asked her if she'd please return Peter to the nursery.

He kissed his son's forehead gently and handed him to the nurse. When they'd left, he shut the door and approached Mackenzie's bed.

For the first time since she'd had the baby, Mackenzie felt frightened by Paul. She didn't like the look in his eyes. Maybe she hadn't approached this quite the right way.

"Let's get this clear," he started. Nothing that started with "Let's get this clear" ever turned out to be something you wanted to hear. Mackenzie observed that it was amazing how Paul could transform himself from a gentle giant one moment to a quite menacing figure the next. She tried to look fragile. Vulnerable.

"I've rented an apartment in Century City," he

said. "Just a few minutes from your house. That way I'll be able to spend as much time as possible with Peter. I'll have to split my time between Seattle and Los Angeles, but when I'm down here, I plan to spend every spare minute I have with my son.

"I will *not* move into your house. Not now. Not ever. If that disappoints or hurts you, I'm sorry. I do not want to hurt you in any way. Quite the opposite, in fact. I want to be your friend. I want to give you support. Financial, emotional, whatever you need. But we will never be more than friends, Mackenzie. Friends and Peter's parents. Do you understand?"

Mackenzie remained silent, her face betraying no emotion, as he spoke. She couldn't believe what she was hearing. What he was telling her. That she'd gone through all of this for nothing? He had to be kidding!

He just needed time. More time. It hadn't been a good idea to spring his moving into her house on him. She should have realized that. But soon, when he saw how good the three of them were together; soon, when he realized that she and Peter were a two-for-one deal, he'd come around.

She'd get herself back in shape and he wouldn't be able to resist her. Just like he hadn't that night in Seattle.

And so, instead of threatening him, instead of tears, hysterics, she simply smiled sweetly.

"Whatever you say, Paul," she said. "Whatever you say."

*　　*　　*

Forty years old. God! The dreaded day had finally arrived. Laura rolled over onto her elbow and looked at the clock on the bedside table. Seven A.M.

She settled back into the pillows. Thank God her birthday had fallen on a Saturday. With any luck, she could spend the day alone with Christopher and Hailey. Avoid anyone making a big deal of it. She'd always hated that—surprise birthday parties, people making a fuss over her. But the prospect of it this year would have been unbearable. This was *not* a day to celebrate.

It wasn't the usual worries a woman had turning forty that were weighing so heavily on her. The physical signs of aging. Though she had some of those—the fine lines around the eyes and mouth, the occasional gray hair, more-rounded hips—Laura knew she'd never looked better. Ironically, her looks mattered less to her now than they ever had. In the whole scheme of things, she'd long ago learned that physical appearance was overrated. No, for Laura, turning 40 hurt for another reason. It hurt because she'd always envisioned herself happy and secure by then. It had never even occurred to her that she might be alone. That at age 40 she would have experienced so much pain and disappointment, so much *loss*, that she'd have all but given up on achieving any degree of happiness other than that she derived—gratefully, immeasurably—from being a mother.

She'd never imagined a Paul Brooks in her life. And a Mackenzie Montana. Her greatest dream. And her worst nightmare. And that they would *both* have come true.

She closed her eyes and wished she could fall back to sleep. When would she be able to stop thinking about him? To put him out of her mind? Would the pain be as acute on her fiftieth birthday? Her *eightieth*? Nothing would surprise her. Not when it came to Paul.

It hadn't made matters any easier when the movie became such a big hit when it was released. It seemed that everywhere she looked, in the newspapers, on television, in magazines, she risked seeing Paul's name, or worse, his face. *After the Dance* was a phenomenon.

A very real part of Laura cheered for its success. She felt happiness for Paul and the many friends she'd made—Matthew, Amy Griffin... all the people she'd worked with at Brooks Productions. A part of her still took pride in Paul's accomplishment.

But still, it hurt so much. So damn much.

When she was in Carmel, she fooled herself into thinking she could come home and make a new life. Forget about him. Forget that Paul Brooks even existed. She'd go back to work at Emery, Johnson. Be able to concentrate all her free time on the kids. Take up riding again. Yes, in Carmel it had all seemed simpler.

But then he'd found her. One day, she looked up and there he stood. And she knew right then, in that very instant that their eyes met, she was crazy if she thought she could ever get him out of her system. Crazy to think she could forget.

Everything around her reminded her of him. Restaurants she drove by. Clothes hanging in her closet. Beautiful sunsets. Her children, especially her children. She knew how much they missed him and knew how much they, too, had been hurt. And they'd been so wonderfully sensitive to what she was going through. She could see them censoring themselves, and each other, not wanting to say anything to upset her. Last night after dinner, Hailey had gotten up from the table, and as she walked past Christopher, she'd teasingly twisted the ball cap he was wearing backwards around so that the bill faced forward, and said, "Here's how they wear them in the NBA." It had been a standing joke between Paul and Christopher, a little thing they shared. Paul always teased Christopher about wearing his caps backwards. As soon as the words left her mouth, the two of them shot worried looks at Laura. She smiled reassuringly at them, while inside she died. One more time.

Yes, things had been hard enough for Laura without having to deal with the success of *After the Dance*. The other night she'd turned on *Evening*, Seattle's local nighttime magazine, only to see footage of the premiere leap out at her. She'd jumped up to switch off the TV, but just as she reached for the button, Paul appeared on screen, and something stopped her. As painful as it was to see him—dressed in his tuxedo, looking even more handsome than she remembered—she couldn't turn away. The unbelievable pleasure that she'd derived so often from simply looking at him still held her captive. And while her knees felt weak and her throat ached with tears she knew would come, she could not help be thrilled again by the sight of him.

And there was something else that kept her from turning off the TV. It was something in his eyes. Though he said all the right things in his interview—about being thrilled with the success of *After the Dance*, about the big plans Brooks Productions had for the future—there was no joy, no pleasure, in his eyes. The mischievous glint was nowhere to be seen. Paul Brooks, Laura realized with a start, looked as unhappy as she was.

Strangely, that gave her no satisfaction.

Laura's thoughts were suddenly interrupted by a

sound just outside her door. She quickly wiped the moisture from her eyes and turned, just in time to see Hailey's little round face peek inside. Hailey was always smiling, but the smile she wore right now, a huge one that exposed a large toothless gap along her upper gums, looked like something out of a television commercial—one of those beautifully done film commercials that keep you smiling on into the next ad.

"Mama?" Hailey asked. She still occasionally used that name for Laura, and Laura loved it. "Can we come in?"

It's amazing how much pain in a parent's heart can be erased by a child's smile. At least temporarily. Laura sat up and, patting the bed beside her, said, "Want to climb in?"

With that, the door swung fully open and amidst Hailey's delighted giggles, in walked Christopher, carrying a breakfast tray, with lighted candles topping a stack of pancakes a good four inches tall.

"Happy Birthday!" they shouted at her as they climbed onto the bed on either side of her.

Christopher carefully placed the tray over her lap. "We didn't have enough candles, Mom," he said, then he looked worried, as though maybe he'd insulted her.

"Good!" laughed Laura. Then after the kids sang "Happy Birthday," she blew out all eleven candles.

"Did you make a wish?" asked Hailey with great seriousness. Laura had once told Hailey that all the really important things she'd ever wished for when blowing out her birthday candles had come true. It was true back then, before Michael's death. And ever since she'd told her little girl that, Hailey refused to make light of the wishing ritual.

"Of course, I did!" answered Laura gaily. "I

wished for breakfast in bed, with my two favorite kids, and I got it!"

"But, Mama," answered Hailey wisely, "we're your *only* two kids. And we brought you breakfast *before* you made your wish."

So much for the little white lies, thought Laura.

For the time being, feeling nothing but the tremendous love that they shared, the three of them laughed, talked, exchanged stories and shared Laura's birthday breakfast.

And, as it turned out, thanks to her two adorable—and adoring—children, Laura could not have asked for a more perfect birthday. Even though it was number 40.

* * *

Laura had just returned from a Show Cause hearing when she saw the message sitting on her desk. Matthew O'Connor had called. Slipping off her conservative black blazer—typical attire for days she was to appear in court—she picked up the small rectangular piece of paper that, for some reason, had caught her eye the moment she'd walked into the room.

"10:15 A.M. Matthew O'Connor. Only in town for today. Please call. 285-8500." It was the number at Brooks Productions.

Moments later, she was staring into space, message still in her hand when Corinne walked by her open door. Upon seeing her, Corinne stopped, entered Laura's office and shut the door behind her.

"Everything okay?" she asked. She suspected that whatever was bothering her friend, it had to do with Paul Brooks. By now, she recognized the look—the one that overtook Laura's face everytime something reminded her of Paul. The Paul Brooks look.

Laura held out the message without saying anything.

Corinne glanced at it, then back at Laura. "Gonna' call him back?"

Laura smiled. It was a weak smile, but weak or not, it made Corinne feel better.

"Yes," she said. "I'll call."

"Want to talk a little first?" Corinne offered.

"No," answered Laura, grateful to have a friend like Corinne. "But thanks."

Before leaving, Corinne gave Laura a reassuring smile. "I'll be in my office the rest of the day."

Laura sank back into her white leather chair. Matthew had called. The message was simple enough. Innocuous enough. But her reaction was anything but.

For the past three months, she'd done everything she could to avoid anything that reminded her of Paul. Of course, that was impossible, as just about everything reminded her. A song on the radio. A male voice. A beautiful fall day. Especially one like this one. This morning, crossing the Evergreen Point Bridge, the vivid blue sky mirrored in the waters of Lake Washington and a sea of magnificent fall colors—rich, wonderful oranges, reds and yellows—dotting the shorelines and hills overlooking the lake, she'd been reminded of similar days a year earlier. Mornings when she'd been driving to work, to *Paul Brooks*, so happy, so full of life, so aware of the magic of a beautiful fall day in Seattle. So unbelievably anxious to get to the office. She'd remembered those feelings and suddenly wished for an early winter—thinking, somewhat irrationally, perhaps, that the day's beauty only made it worse. The memories of Paul. But she knew better. Knew that from now on, everything, nothing, could and would bring him to mind. She crumpled the message into a tight ball, and aimed at the wastebasket. She missed.

But her reaction to hearing from Matthew was not *solely* one of pain. At the same time that just seeing his name there on her desk disturbed her, it also made her feel good. Even happy with the knowledge that he hadn't forgotten her. She'd grown so fond of Matt, and then, just like Paul, he was gone. No longer in her life. It had been her choice. She knew that, that he had probably refrained from calling to spare her just the confusion she was now feeling. But still, she missed him. And it felt good to know that he'd called.

She tried to hold that thought when she reached for the phone and dialed, but when Candy's familiar voice answered, Laura's hands were shaking. She wondered if Paul were there, just one room away, sitting in his office. She could picture it all so well. Too well.

To Laura's surprise, Candy greeted her warmly, telling her how much they all missed her and asking her, with what seemed to be genuine interest, how she and the kids were. She even tried to make Laura promise to stop by Brooks Productions some time but then, at Laura's silence, backtracked immediately and suggested they meet for lunch somewhere instead.

Candy put Laura on hold and within seconds, Matthew's melodious voice was on the line. As he'd always been able to do with a simple smile or gesture, in just one word, Matthew managed to envelope Laura with his warmth and affection. "Laura!" he exclaimed joyously.

This time the smile on her face was big. And genuine. "Hi, Stranger," Laura answered softly.

They made small talk—Laura congratulating Matthew on the success of *After the Dance*, and Matthew inquiring about the kids, and in turn, congratulating Laura on her return to Emery, Johnson. At the mention of her job, something struck her.

"Matt," she asked, her tone clearly puzzled, "how did you know where to find me?" It hadn't occurred to her until just then to wonder how it was that Matthew knew to call her there. After all, she hadn't seen or spoken to anyone at Brooks Productions since she left so abruptly. How would anyone there know that she'd gone back to her old job?

Matthew hesitated just an instant before answering. "Paul told me," he confessed.

His response took her breath away. Paul! How would Paul know that she'd returned to Emery, Johnson? Both Laura and Matt knew that now they were on shaky ground. It was just what she'd been afraid of. The feeling, the sick, sick feeling that overcame her at the mention of his name. Hoping to avoid further conversation about Paul, she let it drop.

Even though one of the reasons he'd called was to talk to Laura about Paul, Matthew knew better than to say another word about him. Instead he suggested meeting for a drink after work. And when Laura resisted, her composure having been badly shaken by the knowledge that Paul knew what she was doing, Matthew resorted to trickery. Well, maybe it fell short of trickery, as it *was* the truth, but nevertheless he used his news, to manipulate her. To force her to agree to meet with him.

"Laura," he pleaded. "You *have* to. Please. I need your advice. It's about Amy."

Laura, still hesitant, couldn't help but be curious. "Matthew, what is it?"

Matthew knew he had her. He could tell by the

tone of her voice, the concern in it, that she cared enough about him to risk subjecting herself to painful memories of Paul by meeting with him.

"I'm planning to ask her to marry me," he answered proudly. "And I need your advice."

"Matthew, that's wonderful!" she cried, and without another moment's hesitation added, "Of course I'll meet with you."

*   *   *

Several hours later, they sat facing each other at a window table at Cutter's, both wearing similar expressions of undisguised pleasure at being reunited.

"You look gorgeous," Matt observed admiringly. Despite the distinct sadness that frequently shadowed Laura's face, she did look more beautiful than ever. Matthew wished Paul could see her right now—that it was his friend sitting opposite Laura Kennedy on this beautiful September afternoon instead of he.

"You're as handsome as ever, too," Laura answered affectionately. "Being in love obviously suits you."

Matthew beamed at the reference to Amy.

"How is she?" Laura asked. "Is she here, in Seattle? I'd love to see her." She was surprised by her own words. Surprised by the truth in them. She *would* love to see Amy. She missed her, just as she'd missed Matthew. And sitting there with him now, she realized that she didn't want to let their friendship die. It might bring back painful reminders to remain close to Matt and Amy, but she would deal with that. They were important to her and she was not going to lose them, too.

"No," answered Matthew. "She's still down in

Los Angeles. I just came up to check on the houseboat and pick up some things. I'll be heading back there tomorrow."

"Were you serious about the two of you getting married?" Laura asked, her pleasure at the mere thought written all over her face.

"You *bet* I am," he answered, a wry, half-smile twisting his lips. "Think she'll have me?"

"She'd be a fool not to," Laura answered warmly. "And Amy Griffin's nobody's fool." She smiled at him. "Now tell me about your plans. Where will you live? I hope it's here in Seattle. After all, Amy loves your houseboat!"

Matthew chuckled, "If it weren't for that houseboat, I may not have gotten to first base with Amy. She fell in love with it first, then decided maybe she liked having me around, too. But, seriously, while we're planning to keep the houseboat and spend as much time up here as we can, for the next few years we'll be pretty entrenched in a project we're working on in Los Angeles."

Laura looked surprised and pleased. "You mean another movie! Leave it to Amy to already have found another role, so soon after *After the Dance*!"

"It's not a movie, Laura," Matt said, suddenly sounding somber. "Amy's giving up acting. At least for now. She's found something that's more important to her than her career." His look was intense. "Actually, we *both* have."

"Matthew, tell me! What are you talking about?"

Matthew leaned forward onto his elbows, bringing his face within inches of Laura's. When he spoke again, his eyes revealed a great passion, the intensity of his emotions.

"You know, Laura," he started, "when I met

Amy, my whole life changed. I don't just mean because I fell in love with her and had someone to share my life with again. That was certainly a big part of it. But there's so much more."

Laura was silent. She listened intently as Matthew tried to explain the transformation that Amy Griffin had inspired in him.

"After my sister died, I really didn't know if I could go on. I didn't know if I even *wanted* to. I'd lost so much faith." He shook his head slowly, remembering. "All I knew was that I had to find some way to get over it, to deal with it, if I were to have any hope at all of even functioning again."

Laura wondered if Matthew knew just how close to home his words were hitting. She suspected he did.

"I thought that writing my book would do that for me," he went on. "That it would help me get over Colleen's death, enable me to resume my old life. And to some extent, it did. It certainly was therapeutic for me to express what I'd gone through, what she meant to my parents and me. What losing her did to us. I guess what it did was make the loss bearable— and, believe me, that was no small feat. But I still felt empty. And before I met Amy, I'd pretty much come to the conclusion that the emptiness, that huge void, was never going to go away."

Laura felt as if he'd stepped inside her skin, her heart, and was describing, with great insight and accuracy, her feelings—her life the past few years, the way she'd felt after Michael's death. And now the way she felt without Paul.

Matthew could see how his words were affecting her. He hated hurting her, but he wanted her to know what he had learned. What he was still learning. He wanted to give her hope.

"But then I met Amy," his pained expression vanished, instantly replaced by a look of joy. "And before I knew it, I was looking forward to getting out of bed in the morning again. I was wanting the phone to ring. I was appreciating it all, appreciating just being alive again. It was a miracle, Laura." His eyes filled with emotion. "A miracle."

As he was speaking, Laura's mind wandered back to her first weeks at Brooks Productions, when she and Paul were just getting to know each other. Just falling in love. Then the Christmas they'd spent together, and the happiness she'd felt just recently, after they'd gotten engaged. She knew what Matthew was talking about. Only too well. Falling in love with Paul had erased all the pain. It had made everything right.

But both she and Matthew knew that things hadn't turned out so well for her and Paul. Had they? There was no Mackenzie Montana in Matthew's story. Still, she was happy for Matt and Amy. And she wouldn't let her pain diminish that. It was reassuring to know that *someone*—someone who mattered to her very much and who deserved it very much—was going to have a happy ending.

Matthew was still talking, but his tone had grown more excited. "Yes, falling in love with Amy changed my life—practically overnight," he was saying. "And now that we have each other we've both realized that we've been given a gift. And we've decided it's time for us to give something back."

Laura could tell by the gleam in his eyes that Matthew was about to divulge something tremendously important to him. And, apparently, to Amy as well.

"Matthew, what is it?" she asked. "What are you talking about?"

"Laura, have you heard of Seattle's Bailey Boushay House?" he asked.

"Isn't that an AIDS hospital?" Laura asked.

"It's actually a home, not a hospital," Matthew explained excitedly. "It's one of the most innovative facilities in the nation for AIDS patients. The whole concept is centered around helping patients remain independent and not institutionalized. At least, for as long as that's possible. The care teams at Bailey Boushay House visit patients living at home—provide medical and nursing attention, as well as counseling and nutritional assessment. And, when it's no longer feasible for a patient to remain at home, Bailey Boushay has beds and resident treatment available. Instead of spending their last days in a hospital patients die with dignity, in a caring environment, with knowledgeable, specialized professionals there to do everything they can for them." His tremendous enthusiasm lit up his face. "It's a wonderful place, Laura. Amy and I have spent hours and hours there. The people are just incredible. They care. They really care. And that makes a difference—a tremendous difference—to the patients. It's someplace where they are totally accepted and understood. Where no judgments are made. And where everything humanly possible is being done to help them." He suddenly grew grim. "I just wish Colleen had had a place like that," he said softly.

"Is that what you're trying to tell me," Laura finally spoke. "That you and Amy are going to work at the Bailey Boushay House? But I thought you just said—"

"—No, we won't be working *there*," Matthew smiled proudly, looking like a child who is holding a present behind his back, just waiting to surprise its recipient. "What I'm trying to tell you is that Amy and I are going to start our *own* version of the Bailey Boushay House! In Los Angeles."

"Matthew," cried Laura. "That's wonderful!" Suddenly she was overcome with emotion—admiration and pride and gratitude. In this crazy world, there were still people like Matthew O'Connor and Amy Griffin. She reached across the table and took Matthew's hand in both of hers. "You're really something. Do you know that?" she asked. Matthew smiled shyly. "It's just like you to turn your personal tragedy into others' good fortune."

"No," Matthew corrected her, "please don't think of it that way. I'm nothing special. This is something I'm doing for *myself*. For Amy and me. *I'm* the lucky one. To have the opportunity to make a difference. To have Amy by my side, as committed—no, even *more* committed—than I am. And to have the financial backing to be able to undertake something this big. No, this is no sacrifice on my part. Because what I'm going to get back from this will exceed—many times over—everything I put into it."

"And Amy wants this as much as you do?" Laura asked. "Enough to give up her acting, especially now, right after she's gotten such rave reviews for *After the Dance*?"

"She wants it even more than I do," answered Matt. "If that's possible. Whose idea do you think this was, anyway? *I'm* certainly not smart enough to come up with it," he grinned. Matthew's pride in Amy's commitment was obvious. "She's even donated all her earnings from the movie. We both have."

"Matthew, how generous of both of you!" Laura exclaimed. "But you'll need even more that that to get started, won't you?"

Matthew shook his head in disbelief. "You're not

kidding. You wouldn't believe how expensive just building the home will be, exclusive of operating expenses. And we're starting out modestly—we'll only have 20 beds to start with. Then, through fundraising and, hopefully, grant money, we'll expand. As rapidly as possible. We're talking many millions of dollars before we even accept our first patient. But we're already close to that. Thanks to one major benefactor."

"Must be someone pretty special," Laura offered, and then, with a quick look into Matthew's eyes, she knew. It was Paul.

"He is," answered Matthew, his gaze unwavering. "Very special. Paul has pledged fifty percent of the net from the movie."

He could see what his words were doing to Laura, but couldn't stop himself. "As I'm sure you've heard, *After the Dance* has become one of the biggest hits of the year—it's already brought in over thirty seven million dollars! It's just phenomenal. Actually, Paul wanted to donate seventy-five percent, but Amy and I refused to let him."

In that one moment Laura knew she'd made a mistake in coming. She still wasn't ready for this. Damn you, she thought. Damn you for reminding me of how outrageously special a man Paul Brooks is.

"I'm very happy for you and Amy," Laura said abruptly, reaching for her purse. "And I wish you the best of luck..."

Matthew grabbed her wrist as she stood to leave. "Laura, please, don't go like this."

She stood facing him, all the emotion drained from her face, looking suddenly very tired. "Matthew, I know what you're trying to do. I can't say I blame you. And I don't mean to be rude. But I do not want to hear about him. I can't..."

"He's miserable without you, Laura." Matthew couldn't stop himself. He had to say it. He had to let her know.

Laura's eyes flickered with pain, then grew empty again. She sat back down and spoke softly, measuredly, "That's not what I want. I don't *want* him to be miserable. No more than I want to feel as miserable as I've felt these past months."

"Then why not try?" Matthew pleaded. "Why can't you two just try to work it out?"

Don't you know, Laura wondered. Do you really not understand?

"Paul has a new life," she finally answered. "He's a father now. There *is* no 'us' anymore. There can't be. And I have to *accept* that and go on with my life." She was silent for a moment, then she said resolutely. "I *have* accepted it."

But then her voice suddenly grew weak, her eyes misted over and she said in a voice that was barely a whisper, "He's never even called." Matthew leaned closer, barely able to make out her words. "Not once, in all this time. If he really wanted to work things out, wouldn't he have at least called?"

Matthew opened his mouth, about to blurt out what he knew about Paul, but something stopped him. Suddenly Paul's words came back to him. He remembered his friend telling him that, above all else, he wanted to spare Laura any more pain—that was why he'd said that until things were resolved, if they *could* be resolved, he had to let her go. It was Laura Paul had been thinking about, Laura's welfare. And here Matthew had blithely thought he could intervene. Who was he to meddle in their lives? Perhaps it would never work out for them. Was he doing Laura any favors in stirring up old feelings? The answer to that question could be found across the table from him. It was on her face. And so, instead of telling her that his friend actually parked his car where he might catch a glimpse of her on her walks, that he was so depressed he wasn't even showing up at the gym for their Thursday night league games anymore, he remained silent.

And in his silence, in Matthew's failure to reveal what he knew, any hopes that Laura Kennedy had subconsciously harbored about her and Paul Brooks—and she *did* harbor them, at that very moment she realized that she did—any such hopes simply died.

20

Paul didn't bother knocking. He knew, by the absence of Mackenzie's Jaguar out front, that she wasn't home. And Diane was used to his letting himself in.

He walked down the hall that led from the entryway to the kitchen, passing the formal living room on his left and the room Mackenzie referred to as her "English Pub" on his right. It was just after noon—usually Diane and Peter could be found in the sunny country kitchen at this hour. As he entered the pine paneled room, he immediately saw that it was empty, but the smell of freshly baked bread drew him to the marbled topped cutting board which was located under the window overlooking one of Mackenzie's several gardens. He was helping himself to a slice of Diane's whole-wheat sourdough bread, still warm to the touch, when he heard the Scottish nurse's hearty laughter outside.

He looked up to see Diane, Peter nestled securely in the crook of her arm, swinging gaily in a huge hammock suspended between two trees. As it inevitably did, the sight of Diane and Peter together brought a smile not only to his lips, but even to the eyes that rarely smiled anymore. A ceramic bowl on the counter contained some of Diane's homemade butter. Paul smoothed a knifeful of it onto his slice of bread and stood watching the two of them as he savored the luxury of some good home cooking. When he'd hired Diane to take care of the baby, he hadn't asked her about her skills in the kitchen. The discovery that she was a first-rate cook had therefore been an unexpected treat, especially since he was growing increasingly tired of restaurant fare. Back in Seattle, he'd always enjoyed cooking for himself, but he never felt like cooking down here in Los Angeles. His apartment was adequate—comfortable, though sparsely decorated— but it wasn't home to him, not like his place in Seattle. Of course, nothing down here was like Seattle. He was growing more aware of that by the day. But Peter was here, so for the time being at least, he was willing to put up with it in order to be able to spend time with Peter. But he *did* miss home. Mostly, he knew he missed Laura.

He was still staring out the window, lost in thoughts of Laura when Mackenzie's voice startled him back to the present.

"Well, well," she said icily, "look who's here. Daddy."

Mackenzie and Paul's relationship had been going rapidly downhill—deteriorating at about the same rate as her confidence in her plan to trap Paul into marriage. As she grew less sure of her chances of success, she grew increasingly bitter. But what bothered Paul much more than her unpleasant attitude toward *him* was the fact that she was also growing increasingly disinterested in Peter. He'd vowed to confront her today about her attitude toward their baby, an attitude that he felt amounted to out and out neglect. He'd hoped to be able to be civil about it, to have a calm, reasonable discussion, to suggest that maybe they'd all be better off if *he* were to have custody of Peter, but the tone of her voice told him a reasonable discussion was unlikely right now.

"Been working out at the club again?" he asked, noting her attire of a low-cut, thong backed leotard and tights. In Seattle, Mackenzie Montana would have stopped traffic in what she was now wearing. But down here, it was so commonplace that woman like Mackenzie even did their grocery shopping on the way home from a workout. Why bother to change clothes first? The bottle of Evian and bakery bag full of bagels indicated Mackenzie had stopped by Marie's Bakery on her way home from the club.

"Don't tell me you actually noticed," she chided, strolling past him to the kitchen sink. Peter was only three and a half months old, but Mackenzie was already back in form. And she knew it. She stood with her back end—which, with just a thin strap of material running down the center over sheer tights was well exposed—to Paul, taking much longer to wash her hands than was necessary.

"Mackenzie, I want to talk to you about Peter," Paul started.

"Peter. Our son," Mackenzie mocked, turning to face him. "Just what is it that you want to discuss?"

"Well, to start with, I've been wondering just when you plan to move into the house you bought on Lake Washington."

Paul had vowed not to pressure Mackenzie into moving into her Seattle home. At first he'd been appalled when she told him, just days before Peter's birth, that she'd bought the house and was just waiting for it to be decorated. But as the weeks, then months, wore on and he became increasingly disenchanted with Los Angeles and increasingly disturbed by his long absence at Brooks Productions, he realized that the house was a Godsend. They'd agreed long ago that Mackenzie would move as soon as she was back on her feet. He wasn't happy about the prospect of her living in Seattle, but if it meant he could be near Peter and stay in Seattle at the same time, he'd finally decided he was all for it. Especially because it would mean that he could keep a close eye on her and the baby.

Recognizing immediately how important it was to him that she move up to Seattle, Mackenzie responded instinctively—she lied. "I've put the house back on the market."

"You WHAT?" Paul asked incredulously. "You're never even set foot in it since you've owned it!"

"I've decided I'll be staying here. On a full-time basis," Mackenzie answered. "Or I should say WE will be staying here on a full-time basis. Don't want to forget little Petey, do I?"

The truth was that until just this minute, she hadn't really given the matter much thought. In fact, she'd been thinking of taking a trip to Seattle soon to check the new house out. But as it was becoming increasingly clear that Paul had no intentions whatsoever of getting involved with her again, much less marrying her, why would she want to exile herself to Seattle? No, it didn't make any sense at all. Especially when she could see how badly he wanted her to do just that.

Paul was dumbstruck. He knew that he'd made a mistake in revealing that he wanted her to move. He knew he'd just given her another means of getting even with him. He grew silent, trying to plot his strategy. He still wanted to talk to her about Peter. This had not been a good start. When would he learn, once and for all, that angering Mackenzie Montana accomplished nothing?

"What's the matter, Paul," Mackenzie taunted, "are you getting homesick?"

Her face softened then, and she approached him seductively, not stopping until her chest pressed against his. Paul did not move. Not one muscle.

"Maybe I can help you out," she purred, moving closer still. He could feel her pelvis against his thighs, feel her hips grinding against him slowly, sensually. "We were so good together, weren't we?" she whispered. Paul still did not resist.

She reached up and placed a hand on the back of Paul's neck, pulling his mouth closer to hers. Her entire being was suddenly on fire with desire for him. It had been over a year now since he'd made love to her. Over a year that she'd dreamt of his touch, of his strong, demanding body. Of his force. She wanted him right then, right there. In the kitchen. On the countertop. And, miraculously, it was about to happen! She could feel his arms raising. She shivered with anticipation, remembering their night together—he'd been the perfect lover. She closed her eyes, waiting for the feel of his strong hands on her heaving breasts.

Then suddenly she felt them. His hands. But *not* on her breasts, as she'd expected. Not on her rear end, as she'd wanted. No, they were on her shoulders. They were pushing her away! Gently, firmly, they were pushing her off him!

She opened her eyes and glared at him. "What's wrong? Aren't I good enough for you any more? Is

416

it *her*?" she hissed at him. "Is it Laura?" she demanded to know. "*Say* it, Goddamn it. *Say* it!"

"Yes," Paul answered calmly. "It *is* Laura. I'm still in love with Laura."

Mackenzie gave him one last withering look, then turned and started to leave.

"I should have run her down myself," she said as she was halfway out the door to the front hall.

Paul froze for a moment, the impact of her words settling in. Then he bolted after her.

He caught up with her at the front door. Her back was to him as she reached for the door knob. She didn't realize he'd followed her, and when he grabbed her roughly by the shoulders, she gasped in surprise.

He turned her, forcefully, to face him. She struggled to get loose, but his hands clamped down on her shoulders so hard that she winced. "Let me go," she cried. "You're hurting me!" At the sight of the rage on his face, her anger turned to fear.

"It was *you*!" he cried. "It was *you* in that red sports car. The one that honked and caused Laura's horse to run her down. That was you, wasn't it? And those phone calls. To Laura's house. The hang ups. That was you, too!"

Mackenzie froze, numb with fear.

He shook her then. "Tell me! Tell me!" he shouted at her ashen face. "It was you, wasn't it?"

"Yes," she finally said, knowing that she had no choice but to tell the truth. "Yes. It was me." Her voice quivered.

His eyes blazed with fury. But then, as abruptly as he'd grabbed her, he let her go. He could hear Diane and Peter in the kitchen now. Undoubtedly, they'd heard him, too. He knew he should go to them, he should explain to Diane what his outburst was all about.

But the violence he'd been feeling, the *rage* that he'd been consumed with just by looking at Mackenzie, just *thinking* about Laura's accident that day, of her lying in the hospital bed, frightened not only Mackenzie Montana. It had frightened Paul, too.

He didn't dare say one more word. He didn't dare stay.

Instead he opened the front door, walked out to his rented car and climbed in.

By the time he reached the corner, his hands were shaking so badly that he had to pull the car over and sit. Sit and wait for the anger to subside.

*   *   *

It was a routine conference. Laura had requested it. She'd recently taken on a new client—a young woman who had purchased a copy/printing franchise, the type that every strip mall has. The woman had paid well over the true worth of the business, in large part because she'd been misled as to the relative value of already existing franchises. When, after two dismal years of trying to make a go of it, she'd discovered that other franchise owners had paid far less than she for their businesses, she'd come to Laura to see what recourse, if any, she had. Laura believed the seller had violated the Washington State Franchise Investment Protection Act by failing to provide adequate disclosure to the young woman prior to the sale. She was planning to advise her client of such and to inform her that the act provided that she could sue the seller for rescission, but before doing so, she'd called a meeting with the litigation team who would be handling the case if the matter actually ended up in court.

The team consisted of Robert Caldwell and Tom Richardson. Robert Caldwell was one of Emery, Johnson's top litigators. Laura couldn't stand him. His sexual innuendos and subtle put downs had long ago caused her to steer clear of him. But, in addition to being an excellent litigator, he was the firm's resident expert on the franchise law, and it would have been a disservice to her client not to consult with him before advising her on a course of action.

Tom was one of Laura's favorite associates—an easy-going, soft-spoken man in private, but a competent attorney who was proving to be an especially effective litigator. Robert and Tom frequently teamed up on commercial litigation cases. It was for that reason, as much as her disdain for being alone with Robert, that Laura had asked Tom to attend the meeting today, too.

Robert and Laura had a bit of a history. Robert had at one time been very attracted to Laura, but after she'd made it clear that she didn't reciprocate his feelings, he'd taken it as a personal affront. Robert Caldwell wasn't used to being rejected by women. In a twisted sort of way, he'd been pleased to have Laura return to Emery, Johnson. He'd gotten no small amount of pleasure from the rumors about her and Paul Brooks—too bad their breakup hadn't seemed to thaw Laura's icy demeanor, thought Robert, noting that Laura seemed as abrupt and businesslike with him today as she had the first time she worked for the firm. He glanced in his briefcase as the meeting got started, wanting to make sure he hadn't forgotten to bring along his little surprise.

Laura started out by apprising her colleagues of the facts on the case. She'd also spent some time in the firm's library and now produced several cases that were relevant to some of the major issues, as she saw them.

"And so you see," Laura concluded after her presentation, "I believe that my client's case is strong enough to bring suit for a violation of the act. But before I meet with her again, I want to make sure I haven't overlooked anything." She looked first to Tom and then to Robert. "And, of course, there are never any guarantees when it comes to litigation. I want to make sure my client is fully apprised of what to expect, in terms of legal fees and a time frame, if she *does* decide to pursue this. That's why I asked for this meeting. Your input would be much appreciated."

As usual, Robert was impressed with Laura's preparation, but also as usual, he refrained from saying so. In fact, his first instinct was to try to find a hole in her case—which was just what Laura wanted from him. If she was going to recommend that her client proceed with costly litigation, she wanted to make sure that she'd first foreseen every conceivable weakness in their position.

"What about laches?" Robert asked in his vintage "I can't believe you didn't already think about this" voice. "You say she'd operated this business for almost two years now. If I'm the seller, I'm going to scream laches loud and clear. And I think the court will listen."

"Not if she just recently discovered the price that other franchisees paid for their businesses," countered Tom. "Until she learned that, she had no reason to think that they'd mispresented the value of the business. Besides," he added, "there's authority that says laches cannot be raised as a defense to FIPA."

"Thanks, Tom," Laura offered. She turned to

Robert. "I was concerned about laches, too, but as Tom says, there's strong case law that says a person can't be accused of an inexcusable delay in the exercise of his rights if he's not even aware that they've been violated. I feel confident that we can defeat any laches defense they raise. Is there anything else that bothers you about our position?"

Both Robert and Tom raised several more issues, but after 45 minutes discussing them, it was the consensus that Laura's client did, indeed, have a strong case. It was agreed that Laura would handle the case until trial was unavoidable. Not only was it her client, but of the three of them, she was probably the strongest negotiator. Laura always felt that women, with an inborn need to harmonize and find common ground, were by their nature more suited to negotiation; while men were the natural litigators. Robert and Tom would take over for trial.

Laura noticed Robert reaching into his briefcase just as the meeting was ending. She stood to thank both men for their time, when Robert turned to Tom and asked, quite rudely as Laura had barely gotten her words out before his interruption, "Tom, have you seen today's *USA Today*?"

Tom looked puzzled and embarrassed by Robert's behavior. However, not wanting to embarrass Laura by taking Robert to task in front of her, he simply shook his head.

Handing him the entertainment section, as though Laura weren't even there, Robert gloated, "Looks like pretty boy Paul Brooks is having himself a hard time."

Laura froze.

"Yep," continued Robert, "Mackenzie Montana had to get a restraining order. To keep him away from her and their baby. Seems Brooks was a little jealous over the fact that she was seeing a little too much of her personal trainer, and he got a little rough with her."

Before Tom—who wanted the newspaper he was being offered as much as he wanted the plague—could take it from Robert, Laura exploded. "Give me that!" she demanded, snatching it from Robert's extended hand.

"Well, well," Robert observed. "A little touchy about Mr. Brooks, aren't we? I didn't realize you had a thing for the macho type. Maybe *that's* where I went wrong." He laughed cruelly. "Maybe Paul Brooks isn't quite the man you thought he was, eh?"

With that, Tom, too, erupted. "That's enough, Robert! What the hell are you trying to accomplish?"

"Me?" he asked sarcastically. "I didn't do a damned thing. All I did was read today's paper. I'm not the one who was beating up on his girlfriend."

Laura was scrambling to get all her papers back into her briefcase, desperate to get out of the conference room before she did something she'd regret. But it was too late.

"You will never be *half* the man that Paul Brooks is," she said to Robert in a voice that was strong and sure of itself and of what it said.

Robert's smirk faltered momentarily at her words, but he recovered quickly and was just opening his mouth to respond when Tom grabbed him.

"One more word," said Robert's easy-going partner, "and you'll have my fist for lunch."

And with that, their meeting ended.

21

The wedding invitation was in Saturday's mail. Laura was surprised to see it. After all, it had only been a few weeks since she'd seen Matthew. He hadn't indicated that the wedding would be so soon. In fact, when they'd met at Cutters he hadn't even asked Amy to marry him yet. Guess she said yes, thought Laura with a wry smile.

The invitation was elegant and simple, announcing a three p.m. ceremony in two weeks. It would be at St. Matthew's, a little Episcopal chapel located just one block away from Seattle Center. There would be a small party afterward at the houseboat. In a script that she recognized as Matthews, a note was scrawled, "Decided not to waste precious time! Please share our happy day with us. Love, M."

Laura dropped onto the stool next to the kitchen sink. What was she going to do now? If the wedding were in Los Angeles, she could get out of going rather easily. But with it right there, how could she possibly not attend? Matthew knew what he was asking her, yet he'd still sent the invitation. Not only *that*, obviously in anticipation of her response, he'd written that note, making it crystal clear how important it was to him that she be there.

He was really putting her on the spot. She half-resented him for it. But the other half of her wanted to be there, to see her two dear friends united in marriage. She wanted to see, first hand, that dreams still do come true. At least for some people. Yes, a part of her really did want to be there. Paul Brooks or not.

Maybe, just *maybe*, she told herself, Paul wouldn't even be there. After all, he seemed to have his hands full right now. She let out a weak, bitter laugh at the understatement of that thought, then tried unsuccessfully, to shut out memories of the article she'd read about the restraining order—the one that asshole Robert had stuck in her face. Yes, Paul definitely had his hands full. A new baby, one who he could not even see at the moment, and a tempestuous relationship with Mackenzie Montana.

It's funny, Laura thought, throughout all of this, I never really believed Paul had any feelings for Mackenzie. In her mind that was never really a factor in her ending their relationship. Certainly the fact that he'd slept with Mackenzie hurt her very much, but she could have gotten over that. It might have been difficult, but she knew that they could overcome it. But the baby was a different story. The baby changed everything. She knew that Paul would be a devoted father to the baby. It wouldn't have surprised her for Paul to have married Mackenzie just for the baby's sake. But it never occurred to her that he would actually fall in love with Mackenzie Montana. Until she read the article, that is. Apparently Mackenzie Montana had finally succeeded in working her magic on him. So well, in fact, that he'd become overwhelmed with jealously over her sexy lover. What other explanation for Paul's behavior could there be?

When she'd first read about it she hadn't believed it. The Paul Brooks she knew did not have it in him to frighten a woman. But she'd read two accounts now of what had happened. In one, the Scottish nurse who cared for their baby, a woman who struck Laura as inherently decent, corroborated Mackenzie Montana's allegations—that Paul had grabbed Mackenzie by the shoulders and shook her violently. Something about the woman's words had rung true. As difficult as it had been for Laura to believe, something told her the story was, indeed, true. And the only thing she could imagine, the only thing that could possibly have had such a transforming influence on the Paul Brooks *she* knew was jealousy. Apparently even Paul Brooks was not immune to it. Yes, the story *must* be true, she'd finally concluded. And for the thousandth time, she died a little bit more.

Her thoughts returned to the wedding invitation sitting on the counter. She just didn't know if she had it in her to go. And she hated herself for it. For being so weak. For the fact that she still was walking around like a wounded animal. She didn't know how she could face it alone. Face Paul alone.

But she *had* to. Really, there was no question about it. She would go. After all, she couldn't possibly hurt anymore than she already did. Could she?

She'd just made up her mind to attend the wedding when Christopher bounded into the kitchen with Jake at his heels. A gooey looking tennis ball peeked out from either side of the dog's mouth.

"Hey Mom," Christopher said enthusiastically, "you have to see this new trick Jake can do!"

He stood in front of the drooling yellow lab and

motioned for the dog to sit. Jake obediently dropped his rear end to the floor. Then Chris bent down, eye to eye with Jake, and said enthusiastically, "Jake, let's play catch!"

Jake, ball in mouth, raised his head back, then quickly dropped his nose down, letting go of the ball as he did so. It took one bounce, then landed in Christopher's waiting hands. Christopher looked at Laura, a huge smile erupting. Then, he turned back to Jake and lobbed the ball to within inches of the ten-foot ceiling. Jake leaped gracefully and caught the ball in mid-air with effortless athleticism.

They repeated this ritual two more times. Each time Christopher commanded Jake to throw the ball, the intelligent, eager animal did so with amazing precision. Laura was duly impressed. She shook her head, laughing, and reached out to pat a proud Jake on the head. "Good boy, Jake," she said affectionately. Jake's tail thumped the ground. He looked from Christopher to Laura, delighted to be the center of attention. Laura reached into the cookie jar—the "dog" cookie jar, the one right next to the jar the kids had labeled the "people cookie jar"—and extracted a biscuit for Jake. He accepted it politely, then padded off to enjoy it in privacy.

Laura and Chris laughed and watched him go. Then Christopher went to the refrigerator, grabbed a Pepsi and a piece of last night's pizza, and headed up the stairs to his room.

"Chris?" Laura called out, as his head disappeared up the stairwell.

Christopher stopped, retraced his steps and leaned over the railing. "Yeh?"

"How would you like to be my date at Matthew O'Connor and Amy Griffin's wedding in two weeks?"

she asked tentatively.

Now, Christopher was like any other 13-year-old boy when it came to weddings. But something in his Mother's tone, something in her eyes, made him think twice before responding with the "You've got to be kidding?" that was on the tip of his tongue.

"Are they the people from the movie?" he asked, as his mind quickly processed what was going on.

Laura nodded.

Christopher stood suddenly, bumping his head against the overhang above the railing as he did so. "Ouch!"

Laura jumped up. "Are you all right?" He was growing so fast these days that the poor kid didn't seem to able to judge distance too well.

He held out his hand to stop her from coming over and making a big deal of his injury. Used to be he loved her attentions, but these days it wasn't cool to have Mom making a big fuss over it every time he hurt himself.

Rubbing his head, a goofy smile on his face, he finally answered, "That'd be fun, Mom," he said. They both knew it was a lie, but it was one that made him feel good the moment it left his lips.

"You mean you'll go?" Laura answered, not even attempting to hide her surprise.

"Sure," he said, disappearing once more up the stairs. "I'll go."

She sat quietly, staring at the invitation. Feeling touched by Christopher's selflessness, his kindness. I can do it, she told herself. I can do it. How bad can it be? Christopher will be with me. We'll just sneak into the wedding—maybe even arrive a couple minutes late to avoid any chance of running into Paul before the ceremony. I'll make sure Matt and Amy see me, then we'll leave. Right after the ceremony. She knew Matt and Amy wanted her at the reception afterwards, too, but *that* was out of the question. She was willing to show up for the wedding, as a gesture of her friendship. But that was her limit. A party, one with Paul there, was definitely out of the question. Matthew would just have to understand.

I can do it, she repeated, before starting to unload the dishes from the dishwasher. I can do it.

And like that, like the little train saying "I think I can, I think I can" Laura began preparing herself for Matthew and Amy's big day.

*　　*　　*

On the day of the wedding, Laura was a mess. She hadn't slept more than an hour or two at a time the entire night before. Once when she *had* succeeded in falling asleep, she'd dreamt that she ran into Paul and Mackenzie Montana at a movie theatre. In the dream, they were seated two rows ahead of her. The movie had already started so the theatre was quite dark. She hadn't recognized them at first. Her attention had simply been drawn to a couple sitting in front of her because of the way they sat cuddled together—closely, very closely, with her arm draped around his shoulders. A couple obviously very much in love, a sight that Laura was somehow always drawn to. *That* had caused her to study them. The movie's first scenes took place inside a shadowy apartment, leaving the theatre shrouded in its own dark shadows, but the scene shifted to a sunny day on the beach and suddenly, as she watched this couple's heads silhouetted against the screen, the theatre brightened dramatically. And just at that instant, just as the brightly lit screen threw its light into the audience, the woman had turned and whispered seductively into the man's ear. At that instant, Laura saw that it was Mackenzie Montana and Paul that she'd been observing! In her dream, Laura had let out a loud gasp, which, of course, caused both Mackenzie and Paul—and about 20 other heads—to turn in her direction. The worse part had been the look on Mackenzie's and Paul's faces when they recognized her. Paul smiled, a friendly smile. The kind you use when you run into a favorite former neighbor or an old classmate. A smile like he was just pleased as punch to see her again. A "Hi, Laura, what a wonderful surprise! Would you like to share a tub of popcorn with my lover and me?" kind of smile.

Mackenzie Montana had smiled, too. But her smile was anything but friendly. Her turned-up lips and gleaming, cruel eyes had "Look, Bitch, look who has him *now*" written all over them.

Laura awakened in a cold sweat, her heart pounding. She sighed with relief when she realized it was just a dream. But the relief was short-lived, because seconds later she remembered that Matthew and Amy's wedding was tomorrow.

*   *   *

By the time she and Chris climbed into the car the next afternoon—after Christopher had waited patiently as Laura changed from one outfit into another—they had just 25 minutes to make it into Seattle, find parking, and get seated for the three o'clock ceremony.

"You look great, Mom," said Christopher, glancing at her anxiously as she backed down their driveway. She'd finally settled upon a simple black sheath of a dress, with a rounded neckline and above-the-knee length. She accented it with a strand of pearls. With her hair worn long around her shoulders, the look was subtle and elegant. No match for the flashy Mackenzie Montana, she thought as she took a final look in the mirror, but *it's who I am. It's me.*

Laura smiled at Christopher, reached for his hand and gave it a little squeeze. "Thanks, Honey. You look pretty good yourself." She meant it. Chris had taken great care to look the part of his mom's companion, wearing a moss-green silk shirt she'd bought him (never really expecting to see it on him) and nicely tailored chocolate colored slacks. He'd even managed to get a little lift in his short sandy hair. The sides, which were always closely shaved, offered little opportunity for creativity, but by blowing-dry the top and generously spraying it with styling spray, he'd succeeded in adding a good half-inch to his height. Laura wasn't sure whether it was the hair spray or some cheap cologne she smelled sitting there next to him, but she was touched by the effort he'd put into his appearance.

Traffic was unusually light. As they crossed the Evergreen Point Bridge and passed by Husky Stadium she realized why. It was the Huskies' last football game of the season. Half of Seattle could be found seated in the massive stadium, an imposing structure that, from the bridge and water (which is how many a fan travels to games, by boat) looked like two giant cobras squaring off—two mirror-image "Z's" ready to spit at each other. The other half of Seattle could be found at home watching the game, which, Laura thought, *is just what Christopher would be doing if I weren't dragging him to this wedding.* Once again she was touched by her boy's selflessness. He hadn't even mentioned the fact that he'd be missing one of his beloved Husky games. It renewed her determination to make the best of the situation.

There was considerably more traffic around Seattle Center. Then Laura had trouble finding the chapel. When she first received the invitation, she remembered driving by the Queen Anne church before, so when she left the house, she didn't bother to bring the directions that had been written on the invitation. But once she got in the vicinity, her mind, in its state of near panic, went blank on her. They'd driven round and round, passing by the same houses and businesses several times when Christopher suddenly shouted, "There's Paul's car!"

The sleek white Porsche Targa was parked on a side street they'd just passed. She backed her car up and turned down the street. The church was a half a block ahead. As they approached, a car pulled away from the curb, giving them a parking spot practically at the chapel's front door.

Laura's heart had dropped to her stomach at the sight of Paul's car. She knew that if Christopher weren't with her, she would have driven right on by the church and on home. But how could she let him see his mother running away like that? The answer was simple. She couldn't. And so she parked the car, and as the two of them climbed the steps to the church, she linked her arm with the arm Chris offered her.

They entered the vestibule. It was empty. The heavy wooden doors leading to the chapel were closed. They opened them and snuck quietly into the back of the church. The ceremony had already begun. Laura was relieved to see the chapel was only two-thirds full. She started toward one of the empty pews at the back, subconsciously preparing for her quick get-away—which would be easy if they were seated in the last row—but before she and Christopher reached it, she felt a hand on her elbow. She almost jumped out of her skin, afraid it belonged to Paul. But to her relief, she turned to see another friendly face—that of Mike Boyd, who looked especially handsome in the black tuxedo garb of an usher. Laura smiled back at Mike and, feeling utterly helpless, offered no resistance as he proceeded to steer her and Christopher all the way up the aisle to the second row! They were on the right side, the groom's side. The quiet entrance she'd hoped to make had turned out to be anything but, as friendly faces all around smiled a welcome at her and Christopher.

So far she hadn't seen Paul, but then, as they were settling into the pew, she caught sight of Christopher's big grin. Her eyes automatically followed his and soon met with Paul's. He was standing at the front of the church, in the wedding party. Matthew, Amy and a woman whom Laura did not recognize all stood with their backs to the congregation, facing a silver-haired priest who was reading from a prayer book in his hands. On Matthew's right stood Paul, half turned to watch Laura and Christopher's entrance. He wore a black tuxedo. He looked sensational. The smile he'd directed at Christopher faltered somewhat as his eyes briefly locked with Laura's. Then he quickly turned back to the altar. Laura sank into the pew, her knees feeling like she'd just finished running a marathon on mountainous trails.

Most of the ceremony was a blur to her. Even though she was seated at the front of the little chapel, she barely heard the priest's words. She didn't know *which* was racing faster: her *mind*, tormented with fears—What would she say to Paul? Had he and Mackenzie reconciled? Was Mackenzie sitting there somewhere behind her? How could she make her getaway now that she was seated there?—or her *heart*, which she could feel pounding frantically against her rib cage. She even looked down at her chest, certain the thumping would actually be visible. It wasn't.

She barely even noticed how lovely Amy looked. Or how happy and proud Matthew looked. She certainly never noticed that Paul's legs were as unsteady as hers. In fact, she did everything within her power to avoid looking at him.

At least, until Amy and Matthew turned to each other and said their vows.

But when they did, when the two of them stood facing each other, and voiced the words they'd each written to the other, words so full of love, so full of hope, so joyous; when she saw the wonder on their faces, the sheer bliss that this day brought, Laura Kennedy was as rapt as every other person in that chapel that day. And in that moment, that moment that she let down her guard, instinctively, she looked at Paul.

He was standing next to Matthew, his back to Laura. She couldn't see his face, but something in his posture, in the downward tilt of his head, told her that he, too, was moved by the words they were both hearing. As Laura sat staring at Paul's back—suddenly not caring whether Mackenzie Montana was there, whether she, or anyone else for that matter, could see that Laura was staring at Paul—tears sprang to her eyes. For a moment she let herself imagine that it was her and Paul up there, gazing into each other's eyes, promising each other a lifetime of the incredible love they'd shared. And for one moment, just one brief moment, she halfway believed, she almost sensed actually, that Paul was lost in the same dream.

But the next moment, the terror was back. The organist began to play, and before Laura knew it, Amy and Matthew were floating down the aisle. They were followed by two very happy older couples—obviously Matthew and Amy's parents.

It was over so fast. Before she had a plan formulated for her escape, Paul was standing in the aisle, at the mouth of their pew. Smiling at them. Not his beautiful, mischievous smile, the one she always visualized. It was a tentative smile, almost shy.

And before she knew it, Christopher had literally jumped over her and rushed to Paul's side. By the time she'd reached them, Paul had enveloped her son in a big bear hug. Now both Christopher and Paul wore big, unadulteratedly happy grins.

She stood face to face with Paul, Christopher sandwiched between them, and could not speak. She literally did not have a voice.

Paul seemed satisfied to simply look at her. The truth was, he could have stood there like that—arms around Christopher and finally face to face with his beloved Laura again—forever.

But Nancy Carson, a production assistant at Brooks Productions, put an end to any such possibility by rushing up and hugging Laura.

"Is it really you?" she asked dramatically. "I've missed you! We all have."

Laura hugged her back, grateful for the interruption. As she tried to carry on an intelligent conversation with Nancy, she watched Paul pull Christopher away, toward the crowd gathering at the back of the church. Watched as the two of them, their happiness at being together again unmistakable, stood in line to greet the newlyweds. She watched as Christopher's mouth never stopped moving, as he excitedly brought Paul up to date on his life, and Paul, never losing his smile, listened attentively.

Laura and Nancy brought up the rear of the receiving line. Luckily Nancy was a talker. She chatted on animatedly, giving Laura a chance to think about whether she should tell Matthew and Amy that she would not be going to the reception. She decided not to say anything now. She and Christopher would make their exit and head home, and she would call Matthew later to explain.

But things didn't exactly go as she planned. By the time they reached the newlyweds, Paul and Chris stood waiting for her. She could feel Paul's eyes on her, could feel herself blushing under his gaze. She kissed both Amy and Matthew and told them how very happy she was for them. Amy squeezed her hand and thanked her for coming, in a way that told Laura she understood how difficult the whole thing had been for her. Matthew grabbed her for another big hug and whispered in her ear, "Thanks." Then as she turned toward Christopher and Paul, he asked, "You're coming back to the house, aren't you?"

Laura looked startled. She was preparing to blurt out some lame excuse when Christopher asked excitedly, "Can we Mom? Please? Paul asked me to ride with him. Is that okay?"

All eyes were on her. Somehow she managed to smile graciously and say, "Sure, Honey, that's fine. You go ahead and I'll meet you there."

She glanced at Paul, who mouthed a silent, "Thanks."

Laura nodded dumbly, wondering just how things

could have gone so wrong. She was dying to get out to her car.

A couple minutes later, she climbed into her car, waved goodbye and pulled away. She was able to hold back the tears for exactly two blocks. But then she was stopped by a traffic light. She watched as a little old couple hobbled across the street together, trying to hurry before the light changed, holding onto each other protectively. They looked like they had been together for the better part of a century. Just as they reached the curb closest to her, they turned and smiled triumphantly, lovingly, at each other.

And that's when the tears finally came.

*   *   *

It took Laura at least half an hour to work up the courage to head toward Matt's houseboat for the reception. Feeling numbed by the scene at the wedding, she pulled into a parking lot and sat, watching the foot traffic—mainly young families—heading across the street to Seattle Center. There was always something going on there, and on weekends it was a favorite destination for families with young children. She and Michael had brought the kids down many times over the years.

The reminder of Michael and their many happy years together comforted her. More and more these days, that was true. For the first couple of years after his death, the memories were incredibly painful, but recently—was it ever since she'd met Paul?—she was deriving more comfort than anything else from thoughts of Michael. She sat and thought about that a while. Maybe *that's* how she would eventually come to feel about Paul, she thought. But as quickly as that thought entered her mind, she dismissed it. There were certainly many similarities between Michael and Paul. Both were unusually kind men. Both were athletic and good looking. Both were wonderful with the kids. But somehow she knew that thoughts of Paul Brooks would never bring her the peace that those of her former husband now brought. For as short as her years with Michael now seemed, as cheated as she'd felt for having him taken from her already, they had still lived and loved fully—never doubting one another, always there for each other. They'd known, for many years, the peace that comes with unquestionable love and commitment. And with Paul, there were just too many regrets—too many "could have beens". Too much left unsaid. A whole life together, a life they both knew would have exceeded their greatest expectations, that would never be. No, thoughts like that could *never* bring her comfort.

It was dark by the time she reached Lake Union and found the pier for Matthew's houseboat. She'd never been there before, but as she walked down the dock, all she had to do was follow the sounds of music and voices that greeted her in the cool night air. As was true of most of the docks, there were half a dozen residences on each side. Matthew's was second to the last, on the south side of the long dock. In order to take advantage of the wonderful view of Seattle's skyline, the living room was situated at the far end of the structure. Entry was through what would typically be thought of as the "back" of the house—through an enclosed porch that was located just behind the kitchen. A wrap-around deck, with an abundance of neatly chopped stacks of wood, encircled the entire house.

As she stepped onto the ramp leading to the

houseboat, Laura could see into the well-lit house. The tiny residence was packed with people. In the living room, she could see bodies bouncing and swaying to the rhythm of Bobby Brown's "Get Away." Several people stood talking in the kitchen. Suddenly, to her horror, she saw that Paul was standing alone in the back porch. It looked like he was smoking a cigarette. Her instinctive response was to high-tail it back to her car, but when she turned to go, she could see the outline of a couple heading down the dock in her direction. She was trapped. Then it occurred to her that the deck might lead to another entrance to the house. She disappeared around the corner behind the porch just before the approaching couple reached the ramp.

Her plan might have worked, as the deck *did* run all the way around to the sliding glass doors off the living room, but the two-foot high stacks of wood that ringed the perimeter of the house were just a forerunner to the obstacle that Laura now encountered. The deck, which was only three feet wide, was completely obstructed by a massive pile of uncut firewood. If she hadn't felt so panicked, Laura knew she would find the whole thing hilariously funny. As she viewed the huge chopping block with three axes embedded in its top surface, she couldn't help but conclude that Matthew must be a little obsessive about this firewood thing. But right then the humor of it escaped her, as she stood there in the dark, wondering what to do.

Through an open window behind her, she could hear Paul greet the couple as they entered the porch. Then there was silence. She felt ridiculous standing there, shivering. From several minutes of silence she finally concluded that Paul must have returned to the party, but no sooner had she started for the porch door than she heard Matthew's voice.

"Here you are!" she heard him say, obviously to Paul. "I've been looking for you."

"I stepped out here to have a cigarette," Paul's familiar voice answered.

"That bad, huh?" asked Matt. He hadn't seen Paul with a cigarette in years.

She heard Paul make a short, throaty laughing noise. A kind of acknowledgment or admission. But his tone was pleasant. "Listen, I couldn't be happier for the two of you. Today's been something. Really special."

"What about seeing Laura?" Matthew asked.

Laura's heart stopped.

Paul was silent for a moment. "She's really something, isn't she?" he asked quietly.

Laura couldn't see Matthew as he nodded in response.

"And Christopher," Paul continued, his voice sounding noticeably happier at just the thought of him, "God, it's good to see him! What a great kid. And it's not just because he's Laura's son. Even if I'd never fallen in love with Laura, I'd love that kid."

For the first time that day, Laura smiled.

"What about *your* son?" Matthew continued. "What about little Peter? Has anything changed there?"

At these words, Laura's whole body tensed with a tremendous sense of dread at the thought of having to hear Paul discuss his baby. The baby he'd had with Mackenzie Montana. She couldn't believe this had happened. Of all the situations she'd envisioned when she'd thought about this day, *this* was far worse than anything she could have imagined. She wished that someone would turn up the volume to the music she felt vibrating through the walls of the houseboat, so that she would not have to hear Paul's answer.

Paul's voice lost all of its enthusiasm. "Nothing's changed. I still can't see him." The pain that not being able to see his baby caused him was audible. "I've got an attorney trying to fight it, but he's not terribly encouraging. After all, I've admitted it. I *did* get too rough with her. I grabbed her by the shoulders and shook her. And I shouldn't have done it. I know that. But I couldn't help it, Matt. I honestly couldn't help it."

Matthew's voice sounded incredulous. "She actually made you that jealous?"

Paul half snorted, half laughed. "I forgot that we've never had a chance to discuss this." He paused. "Jealous? No," he said bitterly. "Angry... *furious*, yes. I've never been so fucking angry in my entire life."

"What was it? What did she do?"

"Remember when Laura was hurt last winter?" Paul started. "Do you remember my telling you about that car? The one that honked—just when Laura was about to get ahold of her horse? That was the reason Spencer bolted like he did. The reason he trampled Laura." Paul paused for a moment, trying to get his mounting anger back in check.

"Are you telling me that Mackenzie Montana had something to do with that?" Matthew's voice sounded even more incredulous.

"That's right," Paul answered. "When I was at her house that day, she blurted it out. She admitted it. That it was *her* in that car. Since then, I've realized that it had to be her who let the horse out that day, too. And when she admitted it that day, I just lost it. That's when I grabbed her and shook her. I shouldn't have done it," he said again. "But I just couldn't help

myself. I'm lucky I had enough control to leave when
I did."

Matthew sounded stunned by Paul's revelation.
"And then she had the nerve to make up the story
about you being jealous? To get a fucking *restraining
order* to keep you away from your own baby?" His
voice was strained with his own growing anger. "She
did that to you?"

Paul was quick to respond. "Listen, Buddy, this
isn't the time for us to be discussing this. It's your
wedding day. I shouldn't have told you this today. I'm
really sorry, Matthew."

"Sorry!" Matthew responded. "Sorry? You don't
have a damn thing to be sorry about! It makes me
sick to think that she's done this to you. That you
can't even see your own son. Have you explained why
you did it? Did you tell your attorney that?"

"I explained it to *him*," Paul answered. "But I
told him I didn't want him to use the information."

"Why the hell not?" Mat asked. "Surely it would
make a difference if they knew the real reason why
you'd gotten so angry with her."

"Because I don't want Laura dragged into this."
Paul sounded resolute. "This baby has already caused
her enough pain. There has to be some other way to
get this thing resolved. Without having to involve
Laura."

Before Matthew had a chance to respond, Laura
heard the door from the kitchen open. A female voice,
displaying more than a hint of intoxication, gushed,
"Hey you two! Why would the two best looking men
here be hanging out back in the porch? You come
back in right now and join the party. Do you hear?"

Laura could hear Paul and Matthew chuckle good
naturedly. To her relief, they let the unidentified

woman coax them back inside.

She stood there in the dark, stunned by what she'd just overheard. It was almost too much to process. All she wanted was to get Christopher and get out of there. But there was no way she could walk into the party and risk facing Paul right now.

Peeking around the corner first to make sure no one was around, she hurried back down the dock to her car. She only had to drive one block to find a 7-11 with a pay phone out front. She breathed a sigh of relief when directory assistance answered that they did indeed have a listing for a Matthew O'Connor. She dialed the number, then held her breath as she waited for someone to pick up the phone.

She got her first lucky break of the day when Nancy Carson answered. Without pressing her for explanations, Nancy obligingly went to find Christopher.

When Chris came to the phone, Laura asked him to meet her at the foot of the dock. And, just five minutes later, Laura and Christopher Kennedy were finally on their way home.

*   *   *

What she'd learned standing out there on Matthew's deck, shivering in the frigid night air, haunted Laura.

It had been exactly one week since she'd heard Paul explain to Matthew why he'd lost his cool with Mackenzie Montana. A week since she'd found out that it had been over *her*, and not over some wildly jealous feelings he had for Mackenzie. A week since she'd seen him. Seen his wonderful, smiling eyes. His unnerving good looks. His incredibly sweet and gentle way with Christopher.

And a week since she'd heard the pain in his voice.

She'd been able to think of little else. The pain had been so real, so *audible* when he spoke of not being able to see his young son, that it had taken all of her restraint to keep from running to him—taking him into her arms like she'd grown so used to doing and holding him. He'd told her once that she made all the pain go away when she held him. And that's just what she wanted to do now. Go to him. Hold him. Make all his pain go away.

But something stopped her. She was starting to realize that something would *always* stop her. Her heart said to go to him, but there was another voice, a much stronger voice that reminded her of the pain caused by Paul Brooks. Reminded her that he still hadn't called her, and that he'd now chosen a life with Mackenzie Montana. With their baby. No, calling him would just make matters worse. It would just slow the healing process that much more.

Seeing him had been bad enough.

But seeing him had also been the greatest joy of her past few months. No man had ever affected her like Paul Brooks. No man ever would again.

"Can I help, Mama?" The sound of the barn door closing and Hailey's little voice abruptly yanked Laura back into the present. All week it had been like that at work. She'd sink into thoughts of Paul, only to be snapped back to reality by some half-worried, half-annoyed voice asking, "Laura? Are you okay? Did you hear what I just said..." She'd felt like telling them, no, I'm not okay, all I want is to be left alone, but had prudently decided against it each time. But this time, when it was her beloved little girl's voice, the interruption was a welcome one.

"Hi, Sweetie," Laura smiled, laying the pitch fork she was using to clean Spencer's stall against the wall and walking over to the half door that led to the rest of the barn. When she saw Hailey's attire, she had to stifle a laugh. Hailey loved to play the part of the equestrienne. She had on jodhpurs, which made her sturdy little thighs look twice their size, one of Christopher's old jean jackets, and a pair of Laura's old riding boots that she'd handed down to Hailey, expecting them to fit her when she was in her teens. They came up to mid thigh and caused her to take short little steps, dragging her feet along the ground to keep from slipping out of the big boots.

Laura bent over the half door of Spencer's stall and gave Hailey's button nose a kiss. "I'd love some help!" she said. "Why don't you get the brushes and help me groom Spencer."

"Okay!" Hailey answered enthusiastically, as she shuffled over to the bench to grab the tools and grooming caddy. "Can I help you clean his feet too?" She especially loved the ritual of going around the big horse, tapping him gently on the front of the fetlock, and watching as the intelligent and accommodating animal lifted his hoof for inspection.

"Better grab the pick, too," Laura added.

They worked side by side, Laura taking the top half of Spencer and Hailey brushing as high as her short little arms could reach. Hailey never stopped talking. One long string of questions—"Is Spencer ticklish?" "Does he get stomach aches?" "What if his tail never stopped growing?"

It was just the medicine Laura needed.

But the very realization of *that*, of the comfort she would always find in her two children, of the utter joy that spending time with them brought, reminded her

444

again of Paul, of the fact that, in a rather convoluted way, she was partially responsible for his not being able to see his baby. She had Christopher and Hailey. Paul should have his son.

It had always been Laura's nature to right wrongs. Her parents had always teased her about the number of strays—animals *and* children—she'd brought home over the years. As a child, she believed she could make everything right, if she just came up with a plan, if she thought about it hard enough. But as an adult, she was finding that all too often, she felt helpless. People were homeless and starving. They were dying of AIDS. She wanted to help. To make a difference. And she knew that, in theory at least, one person *can* make a difference. She did some of the little things—donating money, voting for the politicians who took a compassionate stand on human issues. But all too often, she felt overwhelmed and helpless. And *guilty*, going to her comfortable home in the suburbs each night. Turning off the TV when it became too painful to watch. But the desire to make a difference was still there. The need to right the wrongs was as strong as ever.

And that day, as Laura Kennedy drank in the presence of her precious little girl, as her somber mood lightened and she found herself humming along to country songs and laughing at Hailey's antics, a plan began to formulate in her mind.

It was *not* a plan to get Paul back. No, Laura no longer dared to even think of that possibility. It would be far too painful to think about that, knowing it could never be. But maybe there was *something* she could do. Maybe, if her plan worked, she would at least be able to right one wrong. And maybe, just maybe, she'd get some sense of satisfaction from being able to do that.

If her plan worked.

* * *

Neil Roberts wasn't surprised to find Mackenzie Montana still dressed in lingerie when he arrived for their 11 A.M. meeting. Many a time they'd sat conducting business with her dressed in next to nothing In the summer they invariably sat by the pool, so that Mackenzie did not have to waste precious sunning time in meetings. Her thong bikinis left nothing to the imagination. In a way, he found what she had on this morning far sexier—a cream-colored penoire set, just diaphanous enough to allow him to see the outline of her body when she stood and went to the door to yell for Maria. No, nothing about Mackenzie Montana surprised him anymore. Especially the sight of her sumptuous body. It was one of the little perks of his job.

After watching Mackenzie chastise Maria for the time it took to bring them their Evian and a plate of fruit, Neil sat quietly, waiting for the right moment to announce the purpose of his visit. He wanted to be sure he had her full attention when he told her. He didn't have to wait long.

"So, Neil, tell me," his sultry client demanded as she reached for a plump strawberry, "just *what* was so important that it couldn't wait until I get back from my trip to Palm Springs?"

Mackenzie was planning to leave for the desert that afternoon and hadn't been pleased when Neil insisted she see him before she left. She'd had enough of Los Angeles' gloomy winter skies. And she needed a break from the baby. Late yesterday afternoon she'd called Thomas Biscayne, ex-head of Paramount, who of late was rumored to be next CEO at Warner Brothers, and finagled an invitation to his Palm Springs estate. It hadn't actually taken much finagling, as on numerous occasions Biscayne had made it clear that Mackenzie Montana would be a welcome guest anytime, anywhere. She'd always blown him off in the past, but then, yesterday morning, she'd picked up the latest issue of *Architectural Digest*, which happened to feature a six-page spread on his "little desert getaway." Once she saw his incredible oasis, with its lavish guest house, swimming pool and tennis courts, she reconsidered the indifference she'd always shown to him. It only took one brief phone call to obtain the desired invitation. Now she had lots of shopping and packing to do in order to leave this afternoon and she hadn't been pleased with Neil's interference.

Neil was hoping for a warmer reception than this one, but knew that his news would not disappoint Mackenzie. She'd been complaining bitterly ever since losing the part in *After the Dance*. The fact that the movie had then turned out be such a hit only made matters worse. It had been almost two years now since *Busting Out*. In this business, it was suicide to go too long between projects. He'd known that his job was on the line. The call from Scott Marius had come just in time.

Mackenzie looked pissed off. You ungrateful little bitch, he thought before opening his mouth to speak.

"I have good news," he finally announced. "Scott Marius called yesterday. They'd like to talk to you about playing the lead in *Friendly Fire*."

Mackenzie looked stunned. It took a full fifteen seconds for her to respond with a squeal of delight. "*Friendly Fire*! My God, Neil, that's incredible!" She jumped up and crossed the Oriental rug that separated them to give Neil an enthusiastic hug. And an unobstructed view down the front of her chemise.

Neil Roberts felt a brief, unfamiliar surge of satisfaction and pleasure at her reaction.

"Tell me more," Mackenzie urged him excitedly. "How did you manage to get them to consider me?"

It was, after all, an unlikely role for Mackenzie Montana. *Friendly Fire* was the true story of a married couple who served together in Desert Storm. Sergeant Robert Cooper, the husband, was killed by what turned out to be friendly fire during the initial skirmishes of the war. Despite being granted an immediate discharge of duty to return to the States, his wife, Patricia Cooper insisted on remaining on duty and went on to serve heroically until the end of the war. When many Americans expressed outrage at the fact that American soldiers were killed by the bullets of their fellow soldiers, Patricia Cooper's defense of the military's conduct and her own heroic action made her an instant celebrity. Several of the major studios had vied for Cooper's cooperation in making the movie of her story, but it had been Scott Marius of Five Star who finally succeeded. When months earlier Mackenzie had expressed to Neil an interest in playing Cooper, Neil had responded with a diplomatic, "You must be out of your mind." But despite his misgivings, he'd proceeded to quietly court Marius, using Mackenzie's new motherhood as a means of persuading Marius that Mackenzie's image was changing, that the public was ready to accept Mackenzie in a serious role. Her days as a sexpot were behind her. At first Marius was unwilling to buy into it. But as precious time passed, none of the actresses Marius originally imagined in the role felt right to him. And then another factor came into play—the length of time it took to get Patricia Cooper's cooperation. Desert Storm had become old news. A bankable star like Mackenzie Montana might now be necessary to renew America's interest in what happened during the short war. For these reasons, Marius finally agreed to at least talk to Mackenzie Montana about the role.

"Now don't get too excited," Neil cautioned Mackenzie. "It's way too early for that. Marius has made it clear that he has serious reservations about you playing the role. It's just that he's warming up to the idea and he wants to sit down with you before things go further."

"What are his reservations?" Mackenzie asked, then added, "As if I didn't know." She had a sudden recollection of sitting in a room with Paul Brooks, Matthew O'Connor and Neil, and addressing the very same question. Only *that* time it was about her playing the role of Ashley Cowles in *After the Dance*. The same old thing. Would she ever be able to get beyond it?

"He's not sure the public will be able to accept you in the role of Patricia Cooper," said Neil, knowing his answer was unnecessary. "But I've been halfway successful in convincing him that you've changed. Your image has changed. Ever since the baby was born. I've really played that up. Told him it's the reason you've been so low profile the past year. That you've been turning work down to be here with Peter. That *everything's* changed now."

"And he bought it?" Mackenzie asked skeptically.

"Not one hundred percent. But I can tell he's giving it serious thought. He *wants* it to be true. He knows he needs some star power to make this movie work. People don't care about Desert Storm anymore.

It's a great story, but now they've lost interest. He needs someone who can sell tickets," Neil continued. "*You* sell tickets."

"So what's next?" Mackenzie wanted to know.

"What's next is you meet with him in two weeks. When he gets back from France. And until this thing's decided, until you've got the part—no, until you've *finished shooting* the part—you keep your nose clean." Neil realized that he liked the feeling he was getting, telling Mackenzie Montana what to do. And she was actually listening. "Do you understand?"

"I understand," answered the young star unequivocally. "I'll be a good girl. I promise."

* * *

Laura stepped out of the taxi and handed the driver thirty dollars. She carried her briefcase in one hand and a small overnight bag in the other. She hesitated for a moment at the curbside check-in, then quickly decided to carry both bags on the plane with her. With any luck, she would be back in Seattle that very night. Why risk losing her luggage on such a short trip?

She entered the airport terminal. It was 8:45 A.M. The line at the Alaska ticket counter was a long one. She glanced at the TV monitors to check on the status of her flight. It's departure had been delayed fifteen minutes, to 9:30. Glancing one more time at the long line, she decided she had time to call Corinne at her office.

Corinne seemed surprised to hear from her. "Where are you?" she asked as soon as her voice came on the line. "You didn't change your mind about going, did you?"

"No," answered Laura. "I'm at SeaTac now. My plane's running a little late so I thought I'd call."

"Are you nervous?" asked Corinne. "I still wish I were going with you."

"I'm fine," Laura answered. "And I meant it when I said it wasn't necessary for you to come with. Really, Corinne. I appreciate your helping me get ready for this, but I can handle it from here."

"Good," answered her friend. "Do you have everything? The affidavits? And a copy of the rental agreement? How about the..."

She was cut off by Laura's laughter. "I have *everything*. Don't worry. You're a regular mother hen! I think this detective work suits you. Maybe when I get back we should think about starting our own agency—'Stone and Kennedy—P.I.s for hire'. What do you think?" Corinne's rich laughter blended in with Laura's. "The only thing that worries me is the possibility that I'll go all the way down there and she won't show up."

"But wasn't she supposed to be returning from Palm Springs yesterday?"

"Yes, but it would be just like her to not show. She was really difficult to pin down. Here I thought she'd love the chance to have a show-down with me. Especially on her turf. But I practically had to threaten her to get her to agree to see me." Laura was quiet for a moment, reflecting on the conversation she'd had with Mackenzie. "You should have heard her voice, Corinne, when she realized it was me on the line. She practically started hissing. I don't know which one of us loathes the other more. I think the only reason she finally agreed to see me was purely out of curiosity."

"You didn't give her any idea of why you're coming, did you?" Corinne asked.

"No, absolutely not. I wasn't about to lessen the impact by warning her. I want to take her completely off guard. I'm sure she thinks it has to do with her suit against Brooks Productions. That's what I *let* her think it was about."

"Good," Corinne responded. "I just wish I could be there to see her face."

"Don't worry, I'll describe it all to you in great detail when I get back." Laura glanced over at the shortening line. "Looks like I'd better get going now. Listen, Corinne, thanks so much for everything you've done. I hope you know how much I appreciate it."

"Don't mention it," answered Corinne. "That's what friends are for. And Laura..."

"Yes?"

"Good luck!"

*   *   *

Mackenzie Montana was sitting at the oversized desk in her office, phone cradled between her shoulder and her ear while she applied a final coat of fire-red polish to her nails, when Maria announced Laura Kennedy's arrival.

"Have her wait until I'm ready," Mackenzie ordered, then she waved her housekeeper out of the room.

Neil Roberts, who had a sixth sense when it came to Mackenzie Montana, was on the other end of line. He hadn't heard all of Maria's words, but he knew instinctively that something was up.

"*Who* is there?" he demanded to know.

"Laura Kennedy," Mackenzie announced matter of factly, after just the briefest of pauses. The truth was that she was feeling anything but matter of fact about this visit, but she wasn't about to let that show.

"Laura Kennedy! What the hell is that all about?" Neil had a way of overreacting to things, but with Mackenzie Montana he always had this feeling that the other shoe was about to drop. Something told him that Laura Kennedy was the other shoe.

"How do I know?" the feisty star answered, fighting to keep her own anxiety in check. "She called and said she needed to talk to me. I assume it has something to do with the lawsuit."

Neil was silent for a moment. "That's something else I've been meaning to talk to you about. The lawsuit."

"What about it?"

"You're going to have to drop it."

"What?!!" Mackenzie could hardly believe her ears. "Screw you! I'm not dropping that fucking lawsuit! No way, Neil."

"Marius asked about it the other day. I told him you'd dropped it."

"Just where do you come off telling him *that*?" the volatile star fumed.

Neil felt exasperated, but he knew he had to get through to his pig-headed client before Laura Kennedy stepped into her office. "Mackenzie, listen to me. Listen good. Do you want this part in *Friendly Fire*?"

"That's a stupid question. Of course, I do," Mackenzie answered angrily. It was all she'd thought about since hearing she was being considered to play the role of Patricia Cooper. She hadn't told Neil, but at the time he'd brought up the role, she'd actually been reading a screenplay called *Down and Dirty*. It had been so long since she'd worked and she was getting so bored with staying home and listening to Diane fuss over the baby, that she'd decided she might just accept the part of the ex-stripper trying to make it in the business world, even though she knew full well that to do so would practically seal her fate, in terms of being forever typecast as a bimbo. No, Neil didn't have to remind her of how important the role in *Friendly Fire* could be. No one appreciated that fact more than Mackenzie.

"Well, I'm telling you, no one is going to touch you with a ten-foot pole if you go around suing studios for breach of contract. Do you understand? This man still has serious reservations about you. I've got my work cut out for me convincing him that you've changed enough for this to work." Neil was getting worked up now. "Don't screw this one up, Mackenzie. Do you hear? Don't you dare screw this up."

Mackenzie had already decided that Neil was becoming a real pain in the ass. She might have to consider getting rid of him. But not before she had the part in *Friendly Fire* all sewn up. No, she couldn't afford to do it just yet. That part meant too much to her.

"Stop being so paranoid. I won't fuck things up," she responded. Then, before Neil had a chance to say more, she hung up and, being careful not to smudge her fresh nail polish, pressed the intercom button.

"Maria, I'm ready."

She stood for a moment to catch sight of herself in the elegantly framed mirror which hung over a French console table on the opposite wall. She was pleased with what she saw. She looked tanned and refreshed after her week in Palm Springs.

She slowly surveyed the richly furnished room, her eyes coming to rest on the floor-to-ceiling, paned windows that showcased her sparkling swimming pool and beautifully maintained gardens beyond. Pretty impressive, she thought smugly. Laura Kennedy, eat your heart out.

Suddenly she had a wonderful idea. There was just one more thing that was needed to complete the whole effect. She pressed her intercom button again and this time, punched the number to the nursery.

"Diane?" she called impatiently, worried that the door to her office would open at any moment. "Bring the baby down." Then, as an after thought, she added, "And make sure he looks cute. Put him in something special—something new."

Just as she placed the phone back in its receiver, Maria entered with Laura Kennedy.

"Ms. Montana," Maria started to say, "this is..." but she was cut off mid-sentence by her boss.

"I know who this is. Now leave us alone," Mackenzie ordered. Then, suddenly wanting to appear civilized, she added, "Please."

Maria looked startled at that last word. Was she hearing things? She disappeared quietly, shutting the double doors behind her.

Mackenzie got up from behind her desk and walked over to her guest, until she and Laura Kennedy stood face to face. Neither woman spoke. With mock graciousness, Mackenzie gestured toward the two hand-embroidered wing-backed chairs that flanked the fireplace.

When they were both seated, it was Mackenzie who finally broke the silence.

"So, do you want to tell me what this is all about?"

Her tone was neutral, but the cat-like eyes could not hide her contempt for the beautiful, poised woman sitting opposite her. The truth was that even in her magnificent home, Mackenzie Montana felt outclassed by Laura Kennedy. And that infuriated her.

Thinking of this very moment had been making a nervous wreck out of Laura the past few days, but now that the time had actually arrived, she felt absolutely calm. And determined.

"I'd be happy to. It's about Paul." Laura looked Mackenzie straight in the eye when she delivered her next words. "And his son."

Mackenzie was taken off guard. She'd known that whether he were openly discussed or not, Paul would have a lot to do with the purpose of Laura's surprise visit, but she hadn't expected Laura to be so direct. And what was this about Peter?

"Do you mean *our* son?" she practically hissed, furious at Laura's reference to Peter as *Paul's* son.

Laura did not flinch. "Yes, your son. Peter."

Mackenzie was about to go off. Hearing the familiarity with which Laura spoke her son's name was too much for her. How did she even *know* his name? She must be seeing Paul again. She was sleeping with him! She *had* to be. How else would she have the nerve to come down here and meet with her face to face? This was the last straw.

"You conniving little bitch!" Mackenzie practically spat her words into Laura's face. "How dare you bring my son up? Just because you're fucking his father doesn't give you the right to even speak his name!" Her newly polished fingernails dug into the arms of the chair. She looked ready to spring.

For a brief second, Laura debated about letting Mackenzie believe she was still involved with Paul. Then she spoke. "I am *not* sleeping with Paul. I no longer work for him. In fact, other than seeing him very briefly at Matthew and Amy's wedding, I haven't seen him or talked to him in six months."

"Then why are you here?" Mackenzie asked warily. This was making no sense at all. If Laura was no longer Brooks Productions' attorney and she wasn't seeing Paul, what the hell was she doing in Mackenzie's house?

"I want you to let Paul see his son. That's why I came down here. To get you to agree to drop the restraining order."

First, Mackenzie Montana looked stunned, but within seconds, her face lit with a grin. The grin gave way to a wicked laugh.

"You *what*?" she blurted out through her laughter. "You want me to do what??" Mackenzie hadn't expected anything quite so entertaining as this. She was actually beginning to think she might just enjoy Laura Kennedy's visit.

"I want you to call your attorney and direct him or her to file a motion to dismiss the restraining order that is keeping Paul from seeing his son."

Something about the confidence with which Laura spoke wiped the grin off Mackenzie's face.

"And what makes you think I would do *anything* that you asked of me?" she asked, her eyes narrowing.

Laura reached for the slim briefcase she'd set on the floor next to the chair. She balanced it on her lap, unlatched the top and extracted several sheets of paper from inside. Then she rifled quickly through the papers, looking for two in particular. When she'd found them, she handed them to Mackenzie.

"What's this?" the actress demanded to know.

She could see immediately that the one on top was some type of legal document.

"That's an affidavit," answered Laura without expression. "Actually, you might want to look at the other one first. It's a police report. It was taken the day my horse, Spencer, got out of his corral—actually, the day he was *let* out of his corral."

Mackenzie's eyes narrowed even further as she shifted papers to look at the document entitled "Accident Report." She was silent.

Laura continued her explanation. "As you can see, the report states that I was injured when a sports car—a red sports car—honked and frightened Spencer just as I was trying to get a hold of him." Laura studied Mackenzie's face, which was still fairly non-committal.

"The next document," Laura went on, "is an affidavit. If you'd like to read it now, please be my guest. But I can save you the trouble by telling you what it says. It's the sworn statement of a witness to the accident that day. He states that the red sports car, the one that honked and caused my horse to bolt, was a 1993 customized Ferrari. You see, this guy just happened to be a car nut. Apparently he'd noticed the car even before it honked. He even describes the detailing on the car—a special racing stripe. And the wheels. They were customized, too. Go ahead, read it," Laura urged.

Mackenzie wasn't about to accommodate her. She dropped both papers to the floor and looked at Laura defiantly. "What the hell does any of this have to do with me?"

Laura smiled calmly at Mackenzie. Then she reached into her briefcase for one last paper and, holding it in front of her, she started to read:

"Rental agreement. On this second day of February, 1993, the undersigned (hereinafter "Lessee") leased from Luxury Cars To Go (hereinafter "Lessor") the following vehicle: 1993 Ferrari..."

"Give me that!" Mackenzie Montana hissed, snatching the document from Laura's hands. Sure enough, it was the lease agreement for the car she'd rented while she was in Seattle. Her signature was at the bottom, in a big, dramatic scrawl.

"According to that lease agreement, you were supposed to keep the car for two weeks, until the 16th," Laura went on. "But the agent there—by the way, he remembers you very well; he's a big fan of yours—told me that you returned the car early. On the evening of 8th. Said you told him you were leaving town unexpectedly. He even showed me the car. Nice car. Very flashy. Red, with pinstripes down both sides. And customized wheels." Laura continued to study Mackenzie Montana's reaction. "The accident occurred on the afternoon of the 8th. Some coincidence, huh?"

Mackenzie Montana knew she was in trouble. But no one, especially Laura Kennedy, was going to get away with threatening *her*.

"Just what do you think you've got here?" she jeered. "So I rented a red car. What if I did happen to be driving by that day? You actually want me to believe you can prove anything? What, are they gonna' come and get me, lock me up, for honking my horn? Ha!" she laughed. But it was a laugh that did not ring with any measure of confidence.

"I'll tell you what I have here," said Laura, leaning toward Mackenzie, with a look on her face so intense that Mackenzie shrunk back involuntarily. "What I have here is enough to go to the district attorney, who I happen to know quite well, and ask that charges be pressed against you. For assault and battery. I *may* also be able to convince him that it was *you* who let

459

Spencer out that day, in which case he'd add trespass and larceny to the charges. And I am fully prepared to bring a civil suit against you as well. And, I will tell you, that even if I cannot prove my case, even if I don't win, the media will absolutely eat this up. Mackenzie Montana. Horse thief. Common criminal. Yes, they'll have a lot of fun with this."

"You wouldn't dare," said Mackenzie. But she knew that Laura *would* dare. Suddenly Neil's words came back to her: Stay out of trouble. Keep your nose clean. Scott Marius is still nervous about your image. How the fuck could the timing on all this be so unbelievably bad?

"Try me," Laura responded, with a look that signaled she meant business.

A soft, gurgling sound caused both Mackenzie and Laura to turn suddenly toward the door. Unbeknownst to both of them, Diane had been standing there, with Peter in her arms, for several minutes. Fascinated by what she was hearing, she'd remained silent. But Peter, growing bored, had now given their presence away.

At first, Mackenzie was relieved to see them. At that moment, she wanted nothing more than to rub Laura Kennedy's nose in the fact of Paul's betrayal. She strode purposefully over to where Diane stood and reached her arms out for her son. But Peter, who at six months already knew what he did and did not like, buried his head in Diane's ample bosom and clung tight.

"Give him to me," Mackenzie snapped at the Scottish nurse.

Laura watched in amazement as Mackenzie awkwardly took her son in her arms. The one thing Laura had most feared was having to see this child—the offspring of Paul and Mackenzie Montana. But watching him now, his adorable little face all pursed and ready to cry as he held his arms out to Diane, hoping to be rescued, her heart went out to him.

He was a beautiful child. Round faced, with perfect features and silky blonde hair. He had Paul's beautiful eyes and his mother's peachy complexion. His big eyes flitted from Diane to Laura, and when Mackenzie dismissed Diane, and she turned to leave, he began to cry.

Laura watched as Mackenzie tried to quiet him. It was clear she didn't have a clue as to what worked. His initial whimpers had now turned into big racking sobs, with Peter trying to catch his breath in between. Finally, not able to stand by idly for a moment longer, Laura reached her arms out for him.

"May I?" she asked, her eyes glued to the sad little face which now looked hopefully at her outstretched arms.

Mackenzie Montana froze. Peter, sensing the eruption that was about to take place, grew silent.

This was the final straw. There was just so much Mackenzie Montana could take.

"Get out!" she screamed hatefully in Laura's face. "Get out of my house!"

Laura hesitated, reluctant to leave Peter with Mackenzie in her near hysterical condition. But just then Diane, who had never left the other side of the door, reappeared.

As Laura retraced her steps to the front door, she could hear Mackenzie Montana's furious voice, lashing out at Diane for bringing Peter down to the office when he was obviously not feeling well.

Laura felt sorry for Diane. How on Earth did she put up with that? But her sympathy for Diane was vastly overshadowed by her concern for little Peter. Her heart went out to the little guy. She found it difficult to leave without first making sure that he was all right. But she knew that her staying would only aggravate the situation. And it had been clear to her that Diane dearly loved her little charge. Diane would see to it that he was okay.

At least he has Diane, Laura reassured herself as she climbed into her rented Acura. And soon, he should have his daddy back, too.

*   *   *

There were only two things in his life that really mattered to Paul anymore. His son and Laura. All the other stuff—the success of *After the Dance*, his growing financial security, a pleasant lifestyle—none of it really mattered to him if things weren't good with Laura and Peter. Which is why the last month had been the worst of his life.

It had been bad enough to lose Laura. He used to scoff at the notion of a broken heart. Not anymore. Maybe if he'd known what it felt like to have your heart truly broken he'd have been more sympathetic those few times when *he'd* been accused of breaking one. Not that he had ever been unkind; but more than once, at the end of a relationship, he'd silently endured tears and recriminations, all the while wondering just why it was that women had to be so damn dramatic about such things. Well, he may not have broken down over his and Laura' split, but the pain he felt went well beyond tears. It was as acute and excruciating as any basketball injury he'd ever suffered. But the pain of a dislocated knee or torn hamstring eventually went away. And from what he could tell so far, the pain of a broken heart never did.

The only thing that had gotten him through the past few months without Laura had been spending time with little Peter. And then, with her twisted mind and a restraining order, Mackenzie Montana had managed to take that away from him, too. For a man who'd always prided himself in his strength and self-sufficiency, he'd felt so disconsolate for a while there that he was actually frightened by his despair.

The only bright spot had been Matthew's wedding, being able to see Laura again and spend some time with Christopher. Seeing her had at least temporarily lifted his spirits. It had also given him a renewed sense of purpose: he *had* to make things work out. He and Laura *had* to be together again. But there was one problem. A rather significant problem. Laura would hardly even look at him at the church. And she'd never even shown up at the party afterward. In the days after the wedding, for the first time, it occurred to him that maybe Laura no longer loved him. That he'd somehow managed to do so much damage that a reconciliation was now out of the question.

And those thoughts had really sent his emotions on a downward spiral.

The call from his attorney had come just in time. Just when he felt on the verge of losing what little faith he had left.

Standing at the kitchen phone, Paul couldn't believe what he was hearing. That Mackenzie Montana had suddenly, inexplicably, reversed her position on his being able to see Peter. The restraining order had been lifted! When would he like to see his son?

He was out the door so fast he left the water for his macaroni and cheese boiling on top of the stove.

Mackenzie was just pulling out of the drive when

he pulled in. As they passed each other, she looked right through him, as if he didn't exist. Paul didn't care. At least she hadn't tried to stop him.

Diane, who'd seen his car pull in, was standing at the opened front door. She wore a huge, happy smile. When Paul reached the two steps leading to the house, she opened her arms to him. The two of them hugged in unabashed joy.

"Welcome back!" she cried exuberantly.

Paul gave her a big kiss on the cheek. "Where is he?" he asked anxiously, unable to wait a moment longer to see his little boy again.

Diane led him to the nursery, where Peter lay sleeping in his crib. She stood back against the wall as Paul approached it reverently and leaned over to look at the child he hadn't seen for almost four weeks. All that Diane could see from where she stood was Paul's back, but when he turned to look at her, she wasn't surprised to see his eyes reddened.

"He's grown," Paul whispered emotionally, a big grin on his face.

"He's crawling now," Diane announced proudly. "He's into *everything*."

Paul laughed and turned back to stare into the crib. Diane quietly stepped out of the room.

Ten minutes later, Paul found her in the kitchen. She was kneading dough. She smiled at him.

"Still out?" she asked.

"Like a light," Paul responded. Then the two of them fell into silence. Paul watched her strong fingers expertly weave the dough into a braid.

"Mr. Brooks," Diane finally said, "there's something I want to say. Something I need to apologize for."

Paul knew what was on Diane's mind. "It's not

necessary, Diane. You just told the truth. You had to do that."

Diane felt a rush of relief at his words, but she had to make sure he really understood what had happened. Why she had corroborated Mackenzie Montana's story.

"They wouldn't listen to me. They only listened to the part about what I'd seen that day. I *did* tell them that you shook Ms. Montana by the shoulders. That's what I saw, and that's what I told the police. But no one would listen when I told them what kind of a man you are. That she had to have done something terrible to make you that upset. When I told them what a wonderful father you are. And that Peter needs you. I felt so bad...so guilty for what I'd said. For being partly responsible for keeping you away." It looked like she might break down and cry, but Diane was from good, strong Scottish stock and she regained her composure immediately.

"It's been horrible," she went on. "So horrible. Little Peter has missed you so much. She's been so awful. Never paying any attention to him. I've just prayed that you'd be able to come back."

"What happened?" Paul asked. "What made her change her mind?"

Diane looked at him in amazement. "You mean you don't know?"

Paul looked puzzled. "Know what?"

"It's that attorney. That woman attorney. She's the one who got her to remove the restraining order."

"Woman attorney?" Paul asked. "My attorney's a *man*. And he didn't seem to know anything about why Mackenzie had this change of heart."

"No," Diane explained, "not your attorney down here. This was a woman attorney from Seattle. She flew down here two days ago. Mackenzie told me to bring Peter in to the office while she was here..."

"You don't mean Laura, do you?!!" Paul asked in amazement.

"Yes, Laura, *that* was her name!" answered Diane. "As I said, I was just supposed to be bringing the baby in. It seemed really odd to me. I think Ms. Montana just wanted to show him off, cause she never wants him around during her business meetings. But this time she called and told me to bring him down. And they didn't know I was standing there. They didn't know I heard the whole thing..."

"What? *What* did you hear?" Paul could hardly believe his ears. Laura had actually been way down in Los Angeles to see Mackenzie! What on Earth had *that* been about?

He was absolutely rapt as Diane described the scene she'd witnessed.

"You should have seen her, Mr. Brooks," she said excitedly. "You should have seen her. She was really something. Your lady friend. I've never seen Ms. Montana lose her cool like that, but that lady friend of yours, she really got to her!"

"Diane, please," Paul pleaded, "start from the beginning. Just what was Laura doing here?"

"She came to get Ms. Montana to lift that restraining order."

"What?!" Paul was dumbstruck.

"She wanted her to let you see Peter again. She told her that. And she told her that if she didn't, she'd make sure Ms. Montana got in big trouble. Something about a car she'd rented and an accident she caused. It had something to do with a horse. That friend of yours—Laura, isn't it?—she had all kinds of legal documents. I didn't get a look at them, but I could tell that they made a pretty good case against Ms. Montana. You should have seen her face when your friend handed them to her." Diane tried halfheartedly to stifle her smile. "I've never seen anything like it. That lady friend of yours, she said she'd take them to the police if Ms. Montana didn't back off on this thing with Peter...Mr. Brooks?"

Paul had dropped his face into his hands.

"Mr. Brooks? Are you okay?" Diane sounded alarmed. "Mr. Brooks!!"

Paul lifted his head. His lips were drawn back in a smile of utter astonishment and joy. He simply could not find words to express what he was feeling at that moment.

But Diane found just the right ones.

"She's some lady, that friend of yours. That Laura," she said admiringly. "She's some lady."

Paul could only nod in agreement.

22

"Hailey," Laura called down the stairs, "do you know where Christopher is?" She'd just looked in his bedroom and found it empty.

"He went over to Joe's to play basketball," Hailey called back from the living room. She was nestled deep inside her Barbie sleeping bag, which she'd parked in front of the television. It was Saturday morning—the best day of the week for cartoons.

"Without even telling me?" Laura said in a voice that was not loud enough for her daughter to hear. "That's strange." Christopher was usually so good about telling Laura what he was up to.

She went into Christopher's room, straightened his half-made bed, then, in keeping with his recent request, shut the door as she left. More and more Chris was guarding his privacy. Laura could see the teenager thing that she'd heard so much about from friends emerging more strongly with each passing day. His voice was changing. Girls were calling. Christopher needed his space now, and she would respect that. Still, she was feeling sad to see her son growing up so quickly. Taking off without telling her his plans was definitely something new. Something that they would have to discuss. After all, he was still only thirteen years old.

She descended the stairs to the living room and smiled at the sight of Hailey, all but hidden in her sleeping bag. At least Hailey was a long ways from being a teenager. Hailey was still her little girl.

"How about taking a walk with Jake, Cheyenne and me?" Laura asked.

"But, Mom," Hailey answered anxiously. "It's Saturday. All the good cartoons are on. Do I have to?"

Laura shook her head and smiled. "No, you don't *have* to," she answered. "I just thought it might be fun."

Hailey had already turned back to *Scooby Doo*. But as Laura left the room she looked up and called out after her, "Love you, Mama."

"Love you, too," answered Laura as she headed for the kitchen, with both dogs at her heels.

"Looks like it's just the three of us," she said, reaching down and patting each on the head. "As soon as Chris gets home to watch Hailey we'll go."

"Who are you talking to, Mom?"

Christopher's voice made her jump. He'd just returned home and on his way through the kitchen he'd stopped to rummage through the cupboards for a snack.

"Chris!" Laura exclaimed. "You scared me!"

Then, remembering his question, she laughed. "I was just talking to the dogs." Suddenly looking very concerned, she asked, "Do you think *everyone* talks to their dogs?"

Christopher walked over to his mother and put his arm around her. "Sure they do, Mom."

Laura looked at her son with affection, and then, with some effort, tried to adopt a stern expression.

"Christopher, I'd like an explanation for your leaving this morning without even telling me where you were going."

Christopher tightened the arm around her. "I'm sorry, Mom," he said. "You were taking a bath when Joe called, and I thought I'd only be gone a few minutes. He just wanted to show me how he can get rim now."

"Getting rim," Laura had learned several weeks ago—when Christopher had exploded into the house to announce he'd reached this milestone—meant being able to jump up and touch the basketball rim.

"Well, in the future, please don't leave without telling me first, okay?"

Chris pecked her on the cheek and nodded agreeably.

"When are you taking the dogs out?" he asked nonchalantly.

"Before too long. You can stay with your sister for an hour or so, can't you?"

"Sure, but I think you ought to go soon. It's really nice out there now."

"Maybe I should just run into town for a few groceries first," Laura wondered out loud. "We're out of almost everything."

This idea seemed to disturb Christopher. "Mom, don't worry about groceries. You should go on your walk first."

Laura looked amused. "Is this actually my son, the-human-garbage-can, speaking? The one who panics when we run out of snacks?"

"I just think you should go while it's sunny. They're saying it's supposed to rain again this afternoon."

Laura had never known Christopher to pay any attention to weather reports before, but she kept that observation to herself.

"Okay, I suppose it *would* make sense to walk while it's so nice out."

As she went to her room to grab a sweatshirt, she could hear the phone ring. Seconds later, Hailey's little voice called out, "Mom, Corinne's on the phone!"

She reached for the phone next to her bed.

"Corinne!" she exclaimed happily. "Just in time. I was just heading out the door for a walk. How about if I wait for you to come join me?"

"No can do," Corinne answered cheerfully. "Got a hot date in one hour."

Laura settled down on the bed.

"You and Mark doing something special today?" she asked. She tried to feign interest, even a little *enthusiasm*, but she'd long since lost her enthusiasm about Corinne and Mark. She'd come to the conclusion that Mark spelled nothing but heartbreak for her friend—which is why Corinne's next words almost knocked her over.

"Mark and I are history," Corinne announced proudly.

"What?!"

"Yep, I finally did it, Laura," Corinne explained. "I finally told him to go fuck himself." She giggled at the recollection of the conversation she'd had with him just the night before. "I finally saw the light, finally realized what a dead-end street Mark was. I know *you* saw it long ago, but you never said anything. And I love you for that. You knew me well enough to know you couldn't change my mind about it, so you just kept you mouth shut. But I always

471

knew how you really felt."

"I just didn't want to see you get hurt," Laura explained. "I just want you to be happy."

"I know you do. And, with any luck, that just might happen."

"Corinne, tell me!" Laura pleaded. "Just what happened to make you change your mind? And what about this hot date you have today?" Then she realized the connection. Laura couldn't wait to hear her friend's news.

"*John* is what happened," Corinne chuckled. "John Carroll is what happened. I met him the other day. In court. He represented the husband in that case I've been working on so frantically the past couple weeks. You know, that nasty divorce. The one where they're fighting over everything. Who gets the Jag, who gets the condo in Palm Springs, who gets the fucking dog... er, sorry, Laura, I didn't mean it that way. The dog actually sounds like a pretty sweet dog, but..."

Laura laughed heartily. "Don't worry about it, Corinne. I get the picture. But tell me more. About John. About how you met."

Corinne took a deep breath. "Well, I was great. I mean, I was *on*. Really on. The first day of the trial, I went strutting in there. I looked great, I felt great. And then I look over and see the most gorgeous creature I've ever seen sitting at the defendant's table. It was like something out of a movie, Laura. And the incredible thing was that I knew he was thinking the same thing. I could see it in his eyes." Corinne paused, savoring the memory of that first meeting. "Anyway, I could tell it was as hard for him as it was for me to concentrate on the trial. We both couldn't wait for it to get over so we could start talking civilly to each other. And, to give us both credit, we both were doing a damn good job for our clients that first day."

"How did it end up?" Laura asked, her professional curiosity momentarily overshadowing everything else.

Corinne laughed. "You wouldn't believe it, Laura. The second day of trial, and we'd expected this trial to last seven or eight days—there was just a *ton* of money and property involved—anyway, the second morning I walk in there and my client asks to speak to me in private. She then proceeds to tell me that she and her asshole husband had reunited the night before! They wanted to call it off!"

"After all the preparation you put into it?" Laura asked indignantly.

"Hey, don't worry about it," Corinne assured her friend. "Any other time, I would have been pissed. But I couldn't have been happier about it. All I wanted was for the trial to end so that me and Pretty Boy could hook up."

Laura sat back and thoroughly enjoyed Corinne's colorful description of what happened next, of the next few days in which she and John Carroll got to know each other. She hadn't heard Corinne sound so happy in years.

"I just have a good feeling about this," Corinne was saying. "And it's not just because the sex is so great. Or because he's so damn pretty. It's a lot deeper than that. He's decent, Laura. He's really a decent human being. And as gorgeous as he is, as hard as it was to believe, it actually seems that he's been as lonely as I've been all these years. And we really connected. I could tell he was as moved by what was going on between us as I was. Yup," she finally finished, "I just have a good feeling about it.

A real good feeling."

Laura suddenly realized that she was crying. She wasn't sure whether it was out of joy for her dear friend's newfound happiness, or out of sadness at the recognition of the passion in Corinne's voice. The reminder of the incredible power that such passion has to heal and bring joy. The reminder of how painful it is to have such passion, and then lose it.

"I'm so happy for you, Corinne," she said, wiping her cheek and making an effort to sound cheerful. "When do I get to meet him?" She managed to sound genuinely enthused.

"Do you really want to?" Corinne answered. "I'd love to bring him out there to meet you and the kids. I've already told him all about you. Would that be okay?"

"Of course it would be!" Laura answered. "I'll tell you what. Why don't the two of you come out tomorrow night for dinner? Does he ride? If it's a nice day, you could even come early, and I'll saddle Spencer up."

Corinne giggled again. "He's a city boy, Laura. I don't think we could get him on a horse. But I know he'd love to come to dinner. I'll just check with him, then get back to you later today, okay?"

By the time she and Corinne finished their conversation, Laura realized that both kids were standing at her door, staring at her.

"What is it?" Laura asked curiously as she hung up the phone.

Hailey and Christopher looked quickly at each other. Then Chris said, "Still going on your walk?"

"Yes," Laura said with a quizzical look on her face. "Change your mind about going with me?"

"No," both kids answered in unison. Then, without another word, they both hurried off to their respective rooms.

A few minutes later, Laura and the dogs were headed out the door. As she reached the end of the driveway, she turned toward the house. She could have sworn she saw Christopher and Hailey peeking through the slits of the wooden blinds in the den. Was she imagining things, or were both kids acting a little strange this morning? She squinted in the morning sun to get a better look. No, nothing. Must be imagining things.

Christopher had been right. It was a gorgeous day. After a week of solid rains, a high pressure area had moved in overnight. At 31 degrees it was unusually cold for Seattle, but the sky was absolutely cloudless and the mountains, covered with 18 inches of new snow, were more spectacular than ever.

She took her regular route, which started out along the Tolt pipeline. She walked the trail for almost two miles. It was a popular riding trail and, she was passed twice by friendly riders on horseback. There were several hills along the way and she would stop briefly at the top of each one to survey the incredible vistas. At the highest point of her route, she plopped down atop a big rock. It was a good place to reflect.

She sighed. She felt so happy to know that Corinne was in love again. So relieved to learn that she and Mark had called it quits. But she couldn't ignore the sadness that had settled over her upon hearing the magic in Corinne's voice. She'd felt that same magic so very recently and now it was gone. Now all that was left was pain. She looked around at the breathtaking beauty around her. At least it was a beautiful day.

But the truth was that even the beauty of the day

caused her more pain than pleasure. That seemed to be true all the time now—things that you'd expect to bring happiness actually made her feel unbelievably sad.

She tried to hide it. She'd been so terribly sad for so long that she'd become an expert at hiding her grief from the children. But at times likes this, times when she was alone, she had the luxury of letting her feelings surface. Feelings that had everything to do with Paul.

Two days earlier she'd called Ann Trueblood, a friend of hers from law school who now practiced law in Beverly Hills, and asked her to check the court records to see if Mackenzie Montana's restraining order had been lifted. Laura had been relieved when her friend didn't ask questions about why she wanted the information—the last thing she wanted was to discuss her relationship with Paul. But she *had* to know if her plan, her visit to Mackenzie, had worked. She had to know whether Paul had been reunited with his son.

Ann had called back later that same day and reported that the restraining order had, indeed, been lifted. The news lightened Laura's heart just a bit. But the news was bittersweet, too, as Ann felt compelled to pass along the latest industry gossip—according to good sources, Mackenzie Montana had just been cast as the lead in *Friendly Fire*. Hollywood was abuzz with this surprising information. Laura responded to this news with mixed feelings. Anything having to do with Mackenzie Montana upset her, but maybe having a new focus in her life would cause Mackenzie to back off from Paul and the baby.

She'd thought about Paul's baby a lot this past week. Ever since seeing him she couldn't *help* but think of him. Ever since she'd seen his absolute terror at being held by his own mother. It had broken her heart. He was such a beautiful child.

He was Mackenzie Montana's baby, but, more importantly, he was Paul's baby. And she couldn't help but feel a tremendous concern and affection for him because of that simple fact.

More and more she realized just how deeply she loved that baby's father. More and more she missed him. And more and more she wondered why she'd done what she'd done and just how she was going to be able to live without him.

But she no longer seemed to have much choice in the matter. She had long ago decided that if they were to get back together it would be up to Paul to make the first move. Maybe it was because of some false sense of pride. Or maybe it was more a result of her insecurity. She had to know that Paul wanted it—that he wanted it desperately—if she were to be able to overcome her insecurities about him. *Whatever* it could be attributed to, she knew it had to be that way. It had to be at Paul's initiative. And apparently he was not interested in getting back together with her. After overhearing the conversation he and Matthew had on the houseboat, she'd fleetingly had some hope that he was still in love with her. But he'd never even called. He'd never tried to see her. No, she knew she had to give up any hope of reuniting with Paul. She'd known that for some time now.

But knowing it on a subconscious level and learning to accept it were two entirely different things. She did not know if she would *ever* be able to accept it.

Well, she finally thought, standing and stretching before starting off again, moping is not going to get me anywhere.

She turned off the pipeline where she always did and headed for the last stretch of her walk—the railroad tracks that would take her to within half a mile of the house.

She walked with her head down, keeping an eye on the wooden planks, knowing from her years of walking the same tracks that those planks that were still in the shaded area would be slippery with the morning's frost. The dogs had run ahead and were unusually active, their noses frantically sniffing as they raced back and forth, as if they were on the scent of something.

She had just reached an open stretch and had started to pick up stride when something on one of the planks caught her eye.

It was paint. White paint. And she almost thought that she could smell the distinctive odor of fresh paint.

Though this portion of the track had been getting the sun for almost an hour, the track was still slightly damp and the paint seemed to have run, making it difficult to make out what appeared to be a word scrawled in big letters across the eight-foot length of wood.

As she stopped and tried to read it, Laura shook her head. I really must be going crazy, she thought, recalling her suspicions about the kids just a little while earlier. My imagination is going berserk.

She could almost swear that the word painted on the plank was "Laura".

She laughed out loud at the ridiculousness of the whole thing. Get a grip, Laura she told herself.

She walked on. But she'd gone no more than 100 yards when she smelled fresh paint again. This time the word was clear.

"Kennedy."

She stopped and stared at it. No doubt about it. Someone had just painted the word "Kennedy" on the railroad track.

She picked up her pace. The next word was again about 100 yards from the last.

"Will." Just that. "Will."

Laura looked around and could not see a soul. By now, the dogs were frantic. They'd picked up a scent and were running way ahead of her. She called to them to come back, but they ignored her. She began to run after them, calling frantically: "Jake, Cheyenne, come back. Come!"

"You." She didn't even stop at the next word.

"Jake! Cheyenne!" she called. The dogs never even turned to look back as they disappeared around a bend.

The next word stopped her in her tracks.

"Marry."

"Laura... Kennedy... Will... You... Marry..."

She looked up and suddenly she could see them, *all* of them, standing on the hill just ahead. They were watching her.

It was Paul and Christopher and Hailey. As she ran toward them, passing the final word, "Me?" tears streaming down her face, she saw someone else. A *little* someone else. It was Peter, in his father's arms.

As she drew within 50 yards of them, Paul turned to Christopher and handed him the baby. Then, he, too, started running. Toward Laura.

He held his arms out to her and she fell, sobbing into them.

As he lifted her lovely chin toward his own tear-streaked face, she could hear her children laughing. Cheering. She even thought she heard the baby let out a short, happy shriek.

And as their lips met, as she finally held this man in her arms once more—this wonderful man who meant everything in the world to her—the only other thing that she was aware of, the only sound that was louder than her frantically beating heart, was the sound of Christopher's newly husky voice:

"Sweet!"

Don't Miss
These Current
Peanut Butter Bestsellers

The Thirty Hit Season
by D. Michael Tomkins
$5.99

After the Dance
by April Christofferson
$5.99